ALREADY DEAD

ALSO BY JAYE FORD

Beyond Fear

Scared Yet?

Blood Secret

Darkest Place

*All titles available now in Aust/NZ

Coming February, 2022:

Already Gone: A Miranda Jack Novella

For dates and news on the international release of Jaye Ford thrillers, sign up for her newsletter on her website www.jayefordauthor.com

ALREADY DEAD

JAYE FORD

For Christine Stinson and Isolde Martyn, for much more than a place to stay at the other end of the motorway

1

Jax loved a good what-if, especially the kind that offered a bit of safe, imaginary action. Back in the days when she'd worked in a newsroom, carjackings had always started the round-the-office hypotheticals. What would you do if someone got in your car with a gun or a knife or a syringe of blood?

There was never a shortage of escape plans: grab the weapon in a surprise counterattack, leap out of the car when it slowed for a corner, slam a fist on the horn to attract attention. A muscled-up cadet once tried to demonstrate a Hollywood-style headbutt-and-run manoeuvre, as if anyone other than Tom Cruise could pull that off.

It was easy when you were sitting at a desk with a coffee and time to think about it. When it happened to Jax, she wasn't that fast or clever.

She was waiting for traffic lights at the start of rush hour on a Monday afternoon when a man opened her front passenger door, got in and pointed a gun at her chest. Counterattacks didn't cross her mind. Neither did the horn. She just felt the grief and doubt of the previous moment evaporate as she stared at him in silent, stunned incomprehension.

'Drive.'

His first word was little more than a growl but it made her jump as though she'd been zapped by static electricity. She didn't do as he ordered, though. Turning to the windscreen, she saw the light had changed to green and the queue of traffic ahead was pulling away, the first car already into the right-hand turn. It was where she'd wanted to go five seconds earlier.

As though he'd got in the wrong car, she said, 'This is the lane for the motorway.'

His reply was through clenched teeth. 'That's where you're taking me.'

She glanced beyond the edge of the overpass to the six lanes that headed in and out of Sydney. *No. No way.* It was a 110-k zone down there. Hours and hours worth of high-speed driving all the way up the coast to Queensland.

Without a thought to the concept that she was in no position to tell a man with a gun anything, Jax jerked her chin at the bumper-to-bumper traffic barely moving in the lane on their left. 'I'll merge in there and stop past the lights. The tank is full. Take the car. Take everything and just leave me there.' She swung her head, craning for a view over the boxes on the back seat, ignoring the blare of horns from the vehicles stacking up behind them, searching for a gap she could merge into.

'Drive down the fucking ramp.'

The terse order was laced with impatience and, for the first time, a buzz of fear edged into Jax's incomprehension. But still, her brain refused to take note. *It's not a carjacking,* it told her. *Look at him.* He was wearing nice trousers and a business shirt. His cuffs were rolled up and his collar unbuttoned like a politician on the hustings. In the silence of her hesitation, his mouth opened up like a cave and fat veins pulsed in his neck as his voice filled the car.

'Drive!'

That was when it hit and the what-if escape plans crashed through her mind like they were being shouted through a loudhailer. Jump out. Hit the horn. Christ, she didn't know how to headbutt. And now it was too late. Every other bastard was already blaring their impatience and if she leapt from the car it'd be right into the path of the vehicles pushing and shoving to get around her.

Slamming the gearstick into first, Jax found the accelerator and jerked forward . . . almost stalling, trying again, grinding the gears. Then the lights turned amber and her foot went for the brake.

'No. Go. Go!' he bellowed.

She felt the touch of hard, cold gunmetal on her ribs and understood - clearly, terrifyingly - that she was in all sorts of trouble. Lungs seizing, heart thumping, she finally did as she was told and drove, picking up speed in the turn, heading down the ramp to the wide ribbon of motorway.

'What do you want?' She meant to shout but it sounded like a wail.

'Put your fucking foot down!' he yelled.

She was just metres from the merging lane, slowing without realising. She didn't want to be on the highway, stuck in the car with an angry man and a gun. She should've pulled over, should've got the hell out, should've . . . She hit the accelerator, wincing at the surge in speed and the van that swerved around her. Shit, she was going to kill herself before he could.

At least Zoe wasn't in the car. Thank God for that. Thank God Zoe stayed with Tilda last night. That her aunt had rescued Jax all over again.

Or maybe rescue wasn't the right word. 'Are you going to hurt me?'

'Don't ask!' he roared. '*Don't. Fucking. Ask.*'

She ducked from the sound, fingers tight on the wheel, tears welling behind her sunglasses: shock and fear and what-the-fuck-happens-now. New tears joining the ones that had already dried on her lashes, that had been ready to splash down her cheeks in the second before he got in. Crying wasn't going to help. Crying was for grief and loss and the stuff that cut you open and laid you bare. Not this. Crying wasn't going to put her daughter back in her arms.

'Shut up. Shut the *fuck up!*'

Jax thought he meant her, thought she'd sobbed out loud, but then he slammed the radio with a fist. He missed the on-off switch and a woman's voice cranked up to full volume.

'No. No!' he shouted, fingers scrabbling over buttons and dials.

Four o'clock news flicked to three beats of music then static then laughing then . . .

'Make it stop!' This time his roar was aimed at Jax, the gun centimetres from her temple.

Her hand snapped out and the radio fell silent. So did he. And Jax clung to the steering wheel, blood pounding in her ears, her eyes on the road, legs so rigid she could barely work the pedals.

Within minutes, the outskirts of Sydney dropped away and the speed limit climbed to its maximum. Cars flew past. A semitrailer rumbled along beside her. A tourist coach dwarfed her in its shadow. She was in the slow lane, hugging the verge. He'd told her to drive, not take on speeding traffic that might slam right into her if she stopped in a hurry. And she might have to - he had a gun.

Shit, Jax. Don't cry. Just drive. And breathe or you'll pass out.

She registered the stink coming off him then. The rank pong of old sweat underlaid with a sharper tang of fresh perspiration. It wafted over her on the air-conditioning, filling her nostrils and sitting on her skin like humidity.

The cool air also made her wish she'd worn something else today. Leggings and a singlet top were sensible choices for cleaning and packing and lugging boxes in the heat. Now she was aware of her exposed skin, the black straps of her sports bra, the hint of cleavage in her scooped neckline, the shape of her legs in the tight pants. Was he aware of them too?

Since taking off at the lights she'd been too scared to do more than glance fleetingly in his direction. When she had, her eyes had been drawn to the dull silver of the gun - still there, still pointed at her, the fist around it using the centre console for support. Now that the shouting had stopped, now that she was hurtling him down the motorway to God knew where, she wanted to get a better look at who was sitting beside her. And where his focus was aimed.

The passenger seat had been shunted back to keep a box behind it from sliding around. She couldn't see him properly without making a big turn of her head, which might just make him shove the gun in her face again. She could hear him shifting about, though, huffing and grunting and murmuring to himself. Leaning into the padding at her back, she twisted a little and flicked her eyes across the car.

He was sitting almost sideways on the passenger seat, a shoulder pressed into the upholstery, face tense and angled towards the back window. When she snatched another glimpse, he was facing front, attention on the windscreen.

And he was nothing like the carjackers of her what-if's. She'd imagined strung out junkies, bank robbers on the run, arseholes trying to take what other people worked for, maybe even rapists. Hoodies and balaclavas and pissed- off threats. The man in her passenger seat wasn't like any of that. His white shirt was crumpled and sweat-stained but good quality. His trousers were the kind of dark-grey fabric that belonged to a suit. He had a black leather belt and polished shoes. Office clothes minus the jacket and tie. A little younger than her, maybe early thirties. Reasonably neat hair, fit. Not Jack Nicholson in psycho mode but Ben Affleck playing businessman-on-a-bad-day.

It was obviously a *very* bad day - and not just for her. As she glanced between him and the road, his head swung from front to back, chin lifting and dropping as though he was looking over and under. Maybe he was watching the traffic, maybe he was worried someone had seen him hijack her car - she hoped someone had - but it seemed to be more than agitated surveillance. Something else was keeping him in constant movement: shoulders shifting, feet shuffling, hands jerking ... all with the pistol pointed at her.

It made her heart pound and her breath uneven and her eyes wet.

Come on, Jax. Don't cry. Think.

She'd been numb for so long she wasn't sure she knew how to think anymore. Twelve months, one week, three days. Before then, when she was whole, she'd written hundreds of stories for newspapers and magazines, had spent her life asking probing questions of interesting people. Her brain was a collection depot of weird facts and obscure pieces of information - polar bears have tantrums, razor blades are one of the most shoplifted supermarket items. *Come on*, she told herself, there had to be something in there that would help.

Right, hostage stories. She was a hostage, more or less, and she'd interviewed that negotiator guy: FBI, in Sydney for a conference. What had he said? Be observant, establish rapport, remind them you're human - it's harder to kill you when they know you as a person. Shit, she didn't want to think about that but . . . Okay, maybe she could ask the guy a few questions. Maybe he'd calm down if she managed to do it without sounding like she was scared shitless. No more or less about that.

'What do you want?' she asked for a second time. It sounded a little less like wailing, a bit closer to hysteria.

His face swung around, dark eyes narrowing, his expression making her wonder what the odds were the gun wasn't loaded.

'What do I *want*?' Not calm, not at all. It was a rebuke, some kind of are-you-serious? 'You don't want to know what I want. You don't want to know anything I know. *I* don't want to know. I can't get rid of it now though, can I? Once it's there, it's there. And it's right *there*.' He curled a finger and jammed the knuckle to his temple, screwing back and forth like he was trying to grind something out.

Jax held on to the wheel, stared straight ahead. So he was a little unstable. Maybe a lot. Paranoid delusions or schizophrenia or a breakdown or . . . Did it matter what it was called? She wasn't a psychologist, for God's sake. She was a journalist. An out-of-work journalist. She'd only ever asked questions for a living. Maybe not so different from a psychologist - except a psychologist would probably know which questions would get her killed.

But she knew how to establish rapport. She'd been asking stuff since she could point and say, 'What dat?' Getting the best answers was all about rapport.

Not that it had helped in the past year. She'd asked plenty of questions and hadn't got any answers, at least none that gave any sort of closure. She'd wondered more than once if she'd lost the knack of asking or whether it was her new reality she couldn't accept.

Right now, she just hoped she could pull enough of her old, competent self together to find a way to talk to this guy without making him want to shoot her.

She watched him for a couple more seconds as he shuffled and swung his head back and forth. She took a breath, tried for calm and composed.

'My name's Miranda.'

His head stopped mid-swing and he eyed her suspiciously for two drawn-out seconds before resuming the arc that took his gaze out the rear window. No ranting, no waving the gun around. It was a start.

'I was heading to Newcastle,' she said.

He didn't move, didn't speak.

'Where do you want to go?'

Head to the front.

Maybe he didn't know where he wanted to go. Maybe he'd just wanted a car leaving Sydney. 'Newcastle's about an hour and fifteen from here,' she said. At the speed she was going, it'd probably take a week.

No response.

'The Central Coast is forty minutes away.'

Nothing.

'Then there's Wisemans Ferry in between. And Lake Macquarie - it's not far from the motorway.' Plenty of places to hide, if that's what he was after. 'There's an exit for the vineyards, too.'

He didn't say anything but the shuffling stopped. He pressed his shoulder into the seat, held on to his seatbelt with one hand, the gun with the other, and stared at the road ahead.

'Friends call me Jax,' she tried again.

His eyes slid towards her.

They made her nervous so she kept her own on the road and continued talking. 'When I was a kid, sometimes I used to hang out with my dad while he was working. People would say, "She's Eustace Jack's girl." Then it became, "She's Jack's." Then they'd just point and nod and say, "Jack's." I started spelling it with an "x" when I was in high school. J-a-x. Jax. It's better than Mandy. You know, short for Miranda. I'm not a Mandy and, well, Jax sort of followed me around.'

She glanced at him again, wondering if her rambling was achieving anything. He was watching her, the gun still pointed her way, his face tight, the muscles on either side of his jaw beating in and out - but the edgy, agitated shifting was gone.

'What about you?' she asked.

He scrubbed his face with a hand, an exhausted, frustrated gesture, digging at his eyes, massaging his forehead. It seemed a good sign, a kind of loosening up.

'What's your name?' she prompted.

The sound that came from him made the hair on her neck rise. A long, low hum behind pressed lips, something between keening and growling. Her fingers tightened on the wheel as it grew in volume, louder and coarser, until it finally burst from his mouth as a guttural roar. Shrinking away from him, arm pressed to the driver's door, her foot hovered between the brake and accelerator.

'My name is shit!' he finally bellowed. 'My name is totally fucked. It's all fucked. Fucked and gone to hell. Blown up and coming back down in bits of bone and guts. That's going to be me. I'm already dead. That's my name now. That's what they called me. That's me. Nice to meet you. I'm Already Dead.'

2

Jax held tight to the wheel and tried to focus on staying in her lane as the man beside her went crazy. He thumped the dashboard, yanked and shoved at it like he was trying to tear it off. He kicked at the centre console, the glove box, the door. Slammed his elbow backwards into the seat as though it'd jumped on his back and he was trying to heave it off. All the time grunting, hollering, bawling out sounds from deep in his chest.

Then he started with his head. One hard bash against the passenger-side window was followed by another and another. Sideways knocks, skull against glass, a crushing beat. Jax couldn't tell if he was trying to break the window or get rid of what was stuck in his head. And all the time, the gun jerked and juddered in his hand.

She watched him, watched the road, panic mounting. Would he give up on the window eventually and remember the gun? Stupid to sit here and wait for it to happen.

She hit the brake, not sure where to stop but desperate for something, anything that might get her away from him. The shadow of a semi-trailer darkened her rear-view mirror, the blast of its air horn making her cringe. Her foot found the accelerator again as she searched the motorway for a place to pull off, trying to block out the head-banging on the other side of the car.

There. A narrow strip of verge beside a sheer wall of rock, the remnants of the hill that the road had been cut through. So narrow she'd have to wait for a break in the traffic before she could open her door and get out, but fuck it. She tapped the brake pedal a couple of times, flicked the indicator, wanting to give the truck behind her as much warning as she could. As her left-hand tyres slid off the tarmac, gravel sprayed the chassis.

The crazy guy forgot the window. 'No!'

Jax ignored him, tightening her hands, locking her arms, sensing the speed and the loose surface under her tyres and the rock wall coming at them fast.

'No!' he roared again. 'Drive. *Drive!*' Lunging across the car, he shoved the wheel. One hard push and the car was jerked back onto the tarmac, leaping across the outside lane in front of the semi and into the next one. A screech of rubber and Jax's head was thrown sideways as the rear wheels lost traction, swinging the sedan back the other way, fish-tailing as she held on - as the tipping, sliding start of a roll built underneath them.

Don't brake. Don't brake. Shit, don't brake.

Then she was hurled in the other direction, the weight of the chassis thumping down hard - and she was driving again, hands clamped, eyes wide, breath frozen in her lungs.

Horns were blaring. Long, angry blasts as vehicles jockeyed to speed around her. She was taking up two lanes, pissing people off. She thought about waving her arms, trying to get someone's attention, but she couldn't bring herself to take her eyes off the road or her hands off the wheel, so she just steered back into the outside lane in the wake of the semi, sucking on the smell of sweat and fear.

Beside her, the crazy man was knocking his head against the window again, yelling and banging. 'Drive.' Bash. 'Drive.' Bash. 'Drive.' Bash.

'*Stop!*' she yelled. As he backed up for another go, she grabbed a handful of his sleeve. 'For God's sake, stop!' It was enough to make him pause, and she claimed the moment to talk loud and fast. 'Stop, all right. Just stop. You're going to hurt yourself or I'm going to run off the road. So just fucking stop.'

He watched her with narrowed eyes, breathing hard. When he answered, his voice was flat, resigned. 'I'm already dead.'

As he started on another thrust, she hauled on his shirt again. 'Yeah, well, as far as I can see, you're still breathing. And you're freaking me out. I can't drive if you freak me out. I don't know where you want to go but we're not going to get there if you smash your head open and I have a panic attack. So sit still for a goddamn minute and let me calm down.'

Still clutching his sleeve, driving one-handed, she pulled in deep, shaky breaths, surprised he didn't try to pull away, unnerved at what she'd just done and said. Christ, the gun was in the hand of the arm she was gripping, dangling between them like a child's mobile. She'd never held a handgun, but the rifle safety that'd been drummed into her as a kid hadn't included being casual with a trigger. A flick of this guy's wrist and a bump from a pothole and she could have a bullet inside her. Maybe it would go right through and she'd be dead before her car slammed into the semi that was now towering above them in the next lane.

No. That wasn't going to happen. Zoe needed her to get home. Their new home.

'Have you finished?' she asked firmly.

'Yes.' It was little more than sound pushed out between locked teeth.

'You won't throw yourself around if I let go?'

'No.'

She loosened her fingers, testing him, ready to keep hold if he went off again. He didn't. He sat facing forward, his breathing not so much panting as forced, frustrated exhalations.

Hers, on the other hand, was hard and fast, pumped up by fear and adrenaline and an intensifying urge to get away from him. If he was 'already dead', what did that make her? Dead woman driving? If he thought he was going to die anyway, what was to stop him shooting her at the wheel or forcing them into a truck? Not a lot of difference between death by bullet or death by car.

So you have to stop him doing that, she told herself. *Somehow. For Zoe's sake.* Because Zoe couldn't lose her, too.

She fumbled for the window button.

'Hey!' he hollered.

'I need some air,' she snapped, keeping her thumb on the switch until the glass had disappeared and hot January air was blasting in her face. She pulled hungrily at it, sweat cooling on her forehead, the tips of her fingers tingling and trembling.

Okay. Okay. She had to try to keep him calm until she could find a reason and a better place to pull over. And soon, because the fidgeting was starting up again.

The talking had seemed to ease that - right up until he went ballistic.

Had she caused it? She'd only asked him his name. And he'd gone nuts earlier when she'd asked if he was going to hurt her. Maybe it was best not to ask anything. Just talk without questions. Great. It was her life's hobby to ask stuff. It was possible she'd never had a discussion that didn't include questions.

He was looking front and back and murmuring to himself again. Some kind of private debate this time. She couldn't make out words, just the tone: reasoning followed by reprimand. Maybe she should leave him to it. Maybe he wouldn't appreciate being interrupted. And she sure as hell could do without the talking. Every conversation she'd had in the last year had been laden with grief and loss and frustration and, right now, she had no idea what to talk about that wouldn't wrench her heart or get her killed.

'What the fuck is that?' His body had gone rigid, his gun pointed at the dashboard.

She frowned. 'The radio.' He'd tried to kill it. Now he didn't know what it was?

'No. *That.*' The gun aimed lower.

Taking her eyes from the road for a second, she saw the bottom edge of her mobile phone. It was plugged into a car charger, tucked into a recess, and the tip of the gun barrel was touching the lead that stuck out. Glancing at him, wondering how far his mind had slipped, she said, 'It's a phone.'

'What the fuck is it doing *here*?' There was anger in the way he said it. And something else. Confusion, bewilderment.

She hesitated and, for a tiny moment, sci-fi movies and time travel and visiting beings slipped through her mind. *Don't be stupid.* He'd lost his mind, maybe he'd lost his memory, too. 'It's a mobile telephone. You take it with you.'

'No, *no.* How did you get it? How the fuck did you get it?'

How had she bought it? 'Everyone has one.'

'It's bullshit. Fucking bullshit. It shouldn't be here. Not *here.*' He slammed the power lead with the gun on the last word, hard enough to knock it out.

'Careful,' she snapped. Reprimand on reflex and, as soon as it was out, she wished she could take it back.

Eyes glared at her, then he grabbed the phone, held it up, turned it around. And around again, as though he really hadn't seen one before.

She wanted to snatch it away, keep it out of his reach. It might save her. It might be her only lifeline if she crashed. If she was trapped or injured, somewhere isolated and alone. If he ...

She sucked in a breath, glanced his way. 'Is there someone you want to talk to?'

He jabbed the mobile at her. 'Not with *this*.'

'I could get them on the phone for you.'

He didn't answer, just turned it off like he'd done it a hundred times; wrenched open the glove box, stuffed it inside, slammed the door. Sat with his fists clenched, one of them hard and tight around the gun. She locked her own fingers around the steering wheel until they hurt, trying to keep down the panic, telling herself he hadn't smashed the phone or tossed it out the window. She still had that.

'No-o-o!' The word was a growl, stretched out, rolling on as he scoured his forehead with the butt of his gun. Back and forth as though he was rubbing a channel into the skin. 'No. No. No. *No* -'

'I used to love this bridge,' Jax said quickly, urgently, speaking over him. 'When we went to the coast for the holidays, this was the first water we'd see.' She lifted a hand from the wheel and pointed at the wide, blue expanse of the Hawkesbury River. 'It's nowhere near the beach, at least not where we used to go, but we'd all chant, "Water, water," and it felt like we were nearly there.'

She flicked her eyes sideways. He was leaning forward, elbows on his knees, the gun cradled between both hands.

'And, ah, we'd always stop at the old Oak Factory at Peats Ridge. It's not there anymore but everyone who ever came up here remembers it. It was a factory for milk and ice-cream and ... and it had a milk bar where they made these unbelievable milkshakes. Thick and creamy like you just can't get anymore.'

He was sitting back in his seat now, head against the baluster, eyes open and staring at the windscreen.

'We did a tour of the factory one year. We had to wear these paper hats and bootees on our shoes, and they walked us past huge vats of milk. The smell was disgusting and my mum almost threw up before Dad could hustle her out.' God, she hadn't thought of that in years. It shouldn't hurt. Twelve months ago it wouldn't have, but grief had sharpened the edges on everything. Her parents had been gone almost twenty years but in the last one she'd missed their presence more than she had in a long, long time. Still, age gave it some distance, and in her thirty-second pause his twitching and shifting had started up again.

'We used to go to Port Stephens at Christmas,' she went on. 'Rent a caravan at one of the beaches and surf and fish and ride bikes and just laze about. If my Aunt Tilda was in Newcastle, she'd come and see us. Sometimes I'd go to her place and let Mum and Dad have a bit of time on their own. Her house is right near the beach, nearly as much fun as a caravan.' Jax smiled to herself - Tilda's house was almost a mansion - and kept talking when she saw the sharp turn of his head to the back window. 'When I was older, I lived with her in Newcastle for a couple of years, then at uni I'd stay with her on weekends. That's where I was going today. To my aunt's house.' Not just Tilda's anymore. Miranda and Zoe's, too.

It was sanctuary, Jax told herself again. Not defeat. And not a subject she wanted to discuss with him. She closed her window, searching for something else to talk about. But he beat her to it.

'Is your husband going too?'

It was the first time he'd spoken in anything resembling a conversational tone but her spine still stiffened with caution. She didn't know whether it was a sign he was settling down or a prelude to another freak out.

And she didn't want to talk about Nick.

'We went other places too. Port Macquarie, Coffs Harbour...'

'Are you meeting him in Newcastle?' he asked more firmly.

Would he smash his head through the window if she ignored his question? 'No.'

'Why not? Where is he?' Demand, not query.

And it was none of his damn business. 'I'm not married.'

'Don't lie to me.' Anger and agitation in his words now.

'I'm not lying.'

'You're wearing a fucking wedding ring.'

She curled her left hand around the steering wheel, too late to hide the slim, gold band she still wore. 'I'm visiting my aunt. She lives minutes from the city but just up the hill from the beach. You can't buy houses like that in Sydney anymore. Not unless you're a billionaire.'

There was no obvious escalation, no sliding up the volume scale, just a deafening roar. *'Don't lie!'*

It made her duck away from him, taking a quick, precautionary flick to the rear-view mirror as she moved. 'I'm not lying. I'm not married. I -'

'You're *all* liars. All of you. Everyone.' He yelled like it was her fault, squeezed his eyes tight, rubbed the heels of his hands up and down his face as though he couldn't take it anymore - whatever *it* was. 'I thought if I went outside -' He stopped, started again. 'I thought if I found someone outside of it ... I thought someone sitting in a car, just sitting in the traffic ... I thought you'd be ... I just want the truth. Why can't you tell me the truth? *Why?*'

Jax watched the road and the gun, back and forth, too scared to speak - but in that moment, despite her fear and his mood swings, she felt sorry for him. She knew how it felt to have questions going round and round, unanswered, unexplained, unsatisfied. And he was a mess. She knew what that was like, too. She hadn't lost her mind in the last year, at least not like this, but she'd known grief and obsession that were so over-whelming she'd sounded crazy even to herself.

The empathy lasted for about three seconds. Until he turned angry, irrational eyes on her, lifted the pistol and pointed it at her face. 'Tell me the truth! Where is your husband?'

Would he pull the trigger if he didn't like her answer? 'Put the gun down.'

'Tell me.' The gun didn't move.

'Please. Look -'

'Tell me the -'

'Okay, okay. I'll tell you but put the gun down first.'

'I put it down when I get the truth.'

The truth. She wished she could give him the truth. Something that was complete and hopeful. Something that would make him calm down, not remind him he was 'already dead'. But as she opened her mouth, all she could think of was the unedited, unanswered story. 'I'm not married. I'm a widow. My husband's dead. Someone killed him.' Then she braced herself.

Jax expected a bullet, a grab for the wheel, the deafening crush of metal. There was nothing but the hum of the engine and the ringing of her ears in the sudden quiet.

'He was murdered?' the man beside her finally asked. Calm, quiet, almost deflated.

What the hell?

Telling him didn't matter now. Reopening the wound wasn't nearly as scary as the prospect of imminent death. 'Murder. Manslaughter. Someone is responsible.'

'How was he killed?'

'He was hit by a car. The driver didn't stop. The police are treating it as a homicide.' As though giving it a category and assigning specialist detectives was enough to claim they'd achieved something in twelve months.

'On a bike?'

'No, running. There was no footpath and he was on the road.' She'd thought the words would hurt more but his direct, unflinching Q-and-A took the emotion out of it. 'The car came from behind. No skid marks, no apparent attempt to brake. Crash investigators say he hit the grille, went over the top and bounced off either the back window or the trunk before he landed.' The Homicide cops hadn't added anything more.

Jax kept her eyes front, the car ahead blurring briefly as tears came and receded again. He didn't speak for a while, just sat sideways in his seat, his stare fixed on the rear window, the taut agitation replaced with something almost calm.

His face was different when he wasn't freaking out. Softer, gentler. Dark, liquid eyes matched hair that kinked into curls above his ears. He was broad through the shoulders but thin, the kind of sinewy spareness that suggested lean fitness, not malnourishment.

'I knew a guy once who hit a pedestrian.' He spoke without looking at her, his tone matter-of-fact, as though they were swapping hit-and-run tales, not the horrific details of her husband's death. 'He said the noise, the *bump-bump* on the chassis as the bloke hit, kept him awake for months.'

She gritted her teeth as the sound she'd imagined over and over for a year ran through her head again. Then, as it passed, as his meaning sank in, she turned sharply to him. He might have been in the middle of a breakdown and his delivery was gut-wrenchingly tactless but he was on the same thought process she hadn't been able to get off since the day Nick died.

'It's not something you'd miss, right?' she said. 'The driver had to know they'd hit him. If they were texting or turning around to a kid in the back, they might not realise it was a person, but they'd know they'd hit *something*. You'd brake and check the rear-view mirror, wouldn't you? And a grown man lying in the road wearing a fluorescent vest can't be mistaken for something else, can it? Which means they either stopped and saw and left the scene or they meant to do it and kept driving. A cruel, self-serving, insensitive prick or a different kind of cruel, self-serving, insensitive prick.' The injustice of it started heating up inside her again. And relief - at saying out loud what friends and detectives kept telling her she needed to let go of. When she glanced back at him, she thought she saw a little more sanity behind his eyes. Logic maybe, something other than anger and volatility. Then she turned her head all the way around to the cars speeding past in the other lane. What was she doing searching for solidarity from a crazy man?

'Oh my God. That's *it*.' His sudden, urgent exclamation made her search the motorway for whatever he'd seen. 'You're Miranda Jack. The journo. The one who was all over the news after that accident.' He was pointing at her - with his hand this time, not the gun - and grinning like it was a victory. 'Your husband was Nicholas Westing, that investigative reporter. He got compensation for those guys in Afghanistan. He was a fucking hero. I fucking knew your car was the one. I was drawn to it, I could feel it. It's a sign - we're connected. Miranda fucking Jack.' Panic rose in her throat. What kind of sign? Was he counting on better media coverage if she died with him? 'Look, I don't know what you're hoping for but I'm not writing now. I haven't got a job. Not since . . .'

He wasn't listening, at least not to her. He was muttering to himself again, nodding and agreeing with his own train of thought.

She held on to the wheel and thought about friends and colleagues who'd pay to be stuck in this kind of drama - 'Reporter tells: How I survived carjacking at gunpoint'. One or two might even be happy to get shot so long as they could phone in the story before it all turned to shit: news-gatherer to the end. And yeah, Jax hadn't worked for a year but she was the daughter of a newspaperman, a journalist at heart - and despite the terror of the last half an hour, the intro to the story had composed itself in her head without conscious thought: *A gunman forced a 35-year-old woman to drive X-number of hours along the M1 motorway today before shooting/crashing/letting her go.* It was training, automatic, like a cop checking faces or a bank teller sorting notes. She could write the hell out of it if she had to. But she didn't want to *be* the story. Not again.

In the months after Nick's death, she'd been dragged into the coverage by his status in the media and her role as former reporter/grieving wife/provider-of-information. It wasn't her way, though. She was old school. She'd learned her trade at her dad's paper, well before YouTube and the publicity machine made stars out of reporters. Eustace Jack had worked the metropolitan news early in his career then moved out west and bought into a small country rag. He'd prided himself on being able to fill any role: manager, editor, sub, reporter - even cleaner when he had to. *What's the story?* he used to say to her and the multitude of cadets who'd passed through his doors. *Write the story. The reporter's not the story. Ask some damn questions.*

In the last year, she'd desperately wanted to lose herself in the comfort of words and details and other people's experiences but hadn't been able to sit at a keyboard without feeling the crush of losing Nick. Now, for the first time, she wasn't sorry she'd lost her craft. She didn't *want* to write this. She wanted to be somewhere else.

With Zoe. For Nick.

'We've met before, you know,' the crazy guy said.

His matter-of-fact, how-'bout-that tone surprised her as much as his words. Did she know him? Maybe she'd been too scared to recognise him. She took a look across the car, tried to imagine him in another context. At the supermarket, the dentist, the gate at Zoe's school. On a job. Nothing about him was familiar but she'd heard the line before. Interviewees had a better memory for the reporter that talked to them than the journalist taking notes from another person at another story. Should she fake it? Take a guess and spin some generic, *Oh that's right, what story was that?*

She didn't dare try a lie. 'I'm sorry. I don't remember.'

'You wrote a story about my platoon when we flew out to Afghanistan.'

He was military? She thought about weapons training and post-traumatic stress disorder, and felt a new level of fear. *He's calmer now,* she told herself. *Don't stuff it up. Talk, don't ask questions.* She forced a smile. 'That was a few years ago.' It had to be - she hadn't written that kind of piece since she'd gone freelance.

'Five. You came out to the airbase and talked to a bunch of us and our families. We posed for photos and you sent copies to a couple of the wives, which was appreciated by everyone. You quoted me in the article, too, which got me some kudos for a bit.'

If she'd spoken to him, she didn't remember. But she recalled the day. It was one of the first jobs she'd done after coming back from maternity leave - a feature piece on soldiers and their families. No politics, no mention of the arguments for and against the War on Terror. The men and women in uniform had been really clear about why they were going to Afghanistan and candid about how they felt. They'd posed good-humouredly for the photographer, dragging her into some group shots they took on their mobiles. She remembered the kids, too, the babes in arms and toddlers who'd had no idea what it was about - and how she'd sat in the car afterwards and taken a few minutes to sob for them before driving back to the office.

'I remember now,' she said.

'Sorry, I should've said. I'm Brendan Walsh.' He swapped the gun to his left palm and held out his hand. All nice and friendly, as though he hadn't almost killed her, as though he hadn't previously told her his name was Already Dead.

Was it a moment of sanity or was he about to grab the wheel and drive them into a truck? She wanted to squeeze her eyes shut and scream but instead she reached across the steering wheel, closed her fingers around his and followed his lead. 'Nice to meet you, Brendan. I'm Miranda Jack. Call me Jax.'

His hand was hot, dry and strong. It gave hers a quick, firm grip-and-pump. Chummy, no power play in it. No captor-hostage thing, either. Or wheel grabbing. She slipped her hand out of his, resisted the urge to wipe it on her leggings and tried to ignore the bass rhythm of her heart: *what-the-fuck, what-the-fuck, what-the-fuck.*

'Yeah, look, sorry about all this.' He pushed his free hand through his hair, a tad sheepish, as if all he'd done was hold her up in the super-market queue.

She didn't say anything. There was nothing to say to that.

'It's just . . . you know.' He shrugged: an apologetic, you-get-where-I'm-coming-from gesture.

Was that it? *You know?* That was his reason for hijacking her car and holding a gun to her head? Well, no, she *didn't* know. All she knew was that she wanted to get the hell away from him and . . .

And maybe he'd just given her an opening. She tried to arrange her face into some semblance of empathy. 'It doesn't have to be like this.' She checked his response, made sure he wasn't about to launch himself across the car before she went on. He was wordless, expressionless. 'You could let me go. I could pull over and get out and you could go on without me.' His face, when she looked again, seemed set a little harder, so she spoke quickly. 'No-one will know. I won't tell anyone. You take the car and I'll call someone to come get me.'

He shook his head from side-to-side, a slow, worried, it-won't-work. 'I can't let you do that.'

'No, really, it's okay. It won't be a problem.' She could hear the edge of desperation in her voice and wondered if it was that or her words that made the agitation start to filter through his body again, flattening his lips, tightening his shoulders. She checked the rear-view mirror, saw a four-wheel drive hitched to a huge caravan on her tail: grey nomads, probably parents, maybe even grandparents; people with plenty to lose if she slammed on the brakes - and with a couple of tonnes of metal to careen into her. Beside her, Brendan Walsh had the gun back in his right hand, was rubbing his forehead with the grip.

Jax forced her words lower, slower, trying for the voice she'd used before, the storyteller tone that had calmed him. 'I've got a friend, another journalist, who won't ask questions. He did it for my husband. I'll tell him I was working on a story, that my contact had to get out of

Sydney in a hurry, that I had what I needed and didn't want to go any further. He'd probably be a little pleased to hear it, actually. That I was working on something again. Not just . . . *you know*.' She glanced at him, wondered how he liked his own vague words thrown back at him.

He didn't. Or maybe he didn't even hear them because he was swinging his head front to back again. Anxious, breathing hard.

'Brendan, it's okay,' she said.

'No.' Head to the front, voice taut. 'No, no, no. We can't stop. They're out there. I can't see them yet but they're there.'

4

J ax checked the rear-view mirror. The cops? Was he running from the cops?

It made sense. He'd wanted to get onto the motorway fast and she was his getaway car. She eyed the gun in his hand. Had he shot someone? Was she going to be number two? Number three? She hoped the damn cops were setting up a roadblock and preparing a tranquilliser for the terrorised victim.

She scanned the traffic around her. The grey nomads were still in her mirror, blocking the view of anything in the lane behind them. To her right, in the centre track, a van advertising pool renovations drove steadily past; a minibus with bored kids in school uniforms eased up behind it. A hotted-up red thing led the charge in the fast lane, going way over the speed limit but only slightly faster than the P-plater in its wake. Nothing remotely cop-like.

'Oh, don't worry. They're out there,' he said, as if she'd doubted him aloud. 'And we're a target. If we stop, we're easier to pick off.'

Pick off? Did cops pick off? They chased, used sirens, drew firearms and shouted, 'Keep your hands away from your body,' and, 'Drop your weapon.' On occasion they shot people, sometimes in self-defence, sometimes by accident or negligence. The cops Jax had met in the past twelve months had questionable tactics, but they were ineffective and obstructive, not quick triggered. Back in the day when she'd done her stint on police rounds, she'd listened to the talk, asked all sorts of questions and learned that a lot of officers hoped they never had to fire a weapon in the line of duty. Cops, as far as she knew, didn't pick people off.

Feeling suddenly hemmed in by other vehicles, Jax checked the road and her mirror again, wondering if the people around her were more dangerous than the man in her car. 'Who's out there?'

She didn't know if it was the question or the answer that he didn't like, but he reacted like she'd wounded him, groaning as though he was in pain, the muscle at the side of his jaw working hard. 'They won't stop,' he finally ground out. 'Don't you get it? They're trained for it, it's their job. They won't stop until they find me.'

Who? The grey nomads with the caravan held the pace behind her. Jax could see the couple: man at the wheel, woman in the passenger seat, both had short, pale hair and sunglasses. Beside Jax was a woman with a child in a safety harness. A bald man in a sleek black car behind that. Jax shot a look at him over her shoulder. *Him?* Was he one of them?

'We can't hide. I tried,' Brendan said. 'I stayed out there as long as I could, but they're everywhere. Fucking everywhere.' His words got faster, desperate. 'You can't escape them, Jax. They crawl and burrow inside you like spiders. Fucking nano spiders. Laying their eggs in your brain, breeding and spreading in your skull. And once they're there, you can't get them out. They're all over us right now. Both of us. And they're watching, letting us think we've got away, but they're not letting us go, Jax. They won't. We can't see them but they can see us.'

He ducked his head, aimed his gaze up through the windscreen as though he might see them overhead. She looked too, the passion of his paranoia making her wonder if there was a chopper up there. All she saw was the clear, deep blue of a cloudless summer sky.

'I'm sorry it had to be you,' he said. Anxiously sincere, sincerely anxious. 'But you understand, don't you, Jax? It was fate. It had to be you. You get that, right?' He looked at her like he wanted her to understand. Needed her to.

What she understood was that if anyone was looking for him, they weren't going to pick him off but pick him up. They'd have white coats - maybe not while they were driving up the motorway - and they'd want to take him to a hospital or a clinic, somewhere he could get treatment. She also understood it was possible no-one was looking for him, that he was running from something in his mind. That he wasn't even 'missing' yet, that he'd tipped over an edge in his lunch break. That no-one knew he had a gun.

She thought back to the moment he'd appeared at the traffic lights. She hadn't seen him approach because there'd been nothing to attract her attention. He'd simply walked to the car and got in. She hadn't freaked out; she'd turned and looked at him. From the outside, from the perspective of anyone sitting in the traffic around her, it would've looked like she knew him, that she'd said, 'Okay, let's go.' No reason for anyone to be worried about her, either.

She scanned the traffic again. The bald guy had passed them, the grey nomads were sharing a snack. Every driver she saw seemed to be doing what she did when she drove up the coast: concentrating on the road and the speed limit and thinking about where they were going. Not noticing her passenger with the gun in his hand and no hold on reality.

'You understand, don't you?' Brendan said. It was both threat and supplication.

'Yeah, of course. I get it. It's fate.' What else could she say?

He collapsed against his seat. It seemed like relief. 'I knew you would. I knew I had the right car.'

Tears welled in her eyes again. Her situation hadn't changed but the reality of it seemed insurmountable now. He thought there were nano spiders in his skull: there was no reasoning with that.

She wanted to hit the brake, swerve, draw some attention, but last time she'd tried to stop he went nuts - and other drivers had simply swung around her, assuming, like she usually did, that everyone else on the road was an idiot to be avoided. She pressed her lips together, blinked hard and drove. Hands clenched around the wheel, jaw locked, trying to calculate how far she'd have to go before her petrol ran out. She'd filled up just before the turn-off. The Mazda was four years old, serviced about a month ago; it had six cylinders and six gears and newish tyres. Not that any of that information helped - she had no idea how to calculate it, just that she could do a trip to and from Newcastle on half a tank. Which meant she could travel for five hours easily, maybe six or more, before she could claim fuel as a reason to stop. They could be in Coffs Harbour by then. A long, long way from Zoe. From home. From their new house that wasn't a home yet.

She pushed that thought away, got back to the ones that were holding her together, distracting her from the fear that was surging beneath them. Back to petrol . . . Stopping and then what? A dash from the car? Shouts for help? A note passed . . .

'How old is Zoe?'

Jax swung her head. He'd been quiet, still, the previous conversation exhausting or settling him. Zoe's name on his lips scared the hell out of her.

'She's your daughter, right?'

How did he know that? Had he seen her? Jax didn't answer, didn't want him knowing anything about Zoe.

'She's, what, six or seven?'

Fear wrapped cold fingers around her spine. He'd chosen the car at random, hadn't he? He'd been drawn to it, it was fate, he'd said. So when the hell had he seen Zoe?

'My kid gets his letters backwards, too.'

She noticed his face was angled into the back of the car. Not at the window but at the boxes stacked on the seat. She'd taken the last things from the house that morning, cleared it out, cleaned it up and wandered through the empty rooms one last time before handing the keys over to the agent. There were bits and pieces from the kitchen and bathroom, the sheets she'd slept in, the old photo albums she hadn't trusted with the removalists, the box of toys that kept Zoe entertained while the truck was loaded. She couldn't see the carton but remembered the crayons and Zoe's tongue doing the rounds of her lips as she concentrated on copying the words Jax had written: *Zoe's very precious things.*

Brendan hadn't seen Zoe. He'd found evidence and was using logic. It was a better thought process than the nano spiders and eyes-in-the-sky stuff, she guessed, but she didn't want to talk about Zoe, didn't want him growing ideas about going to get her. On the other hand, his voice was calm, almost wistful, and she didn't want to lose that either.

'She's six,' she told him.

'My boy turned seven last week.'

'It's a nice age.'

'How many have you got?'

She hesitated, wondering how much she should tell, not wanting to be accused of lying. 'One.'

He nodded. 'Me too.' Nodded some more. 'I love my son.' It was a declaration but it had a question mark: a do-you-understand?

'I'm sure you do.'

'He looks just like me at that age.'

'That's nice.'

'I miss him so much.'

She glanced cautiously at him. Did he miss him because he'd been getting treatment, or was he separated from his son's mother? 'It must be hard.'

'I don't want him to get hurt.'

No, neither did she. 'No-one needs to get hurt, Brendan.' And then the angst was back, the pistol hand to his head, scrubbing his brow. 'You could be my wife, you know.'

Oh, no. 'Brendan -'

'She'll be just like you. I'll be dead and she'll be a widow and my kid will have no father.'

Jax kept her eyes on the road, heart beating hard, no words to give him. Did he have a terminal disease? Maybe that was why someone had told him he was already dead. Or maybe he just thought he was dying. He didn't look well, that was for sure.

'What's it like?' he asked.

What was *what* like? Dying? She had no clue. She didn't want to.

'Being a widow,' he prompted. 'What's it like?'

Did he want to know that his wife would be okay or that she'd be a mess without him? 'Brendan, you need to talk to -'

'It'll happen soon. I don't know when but soon. I got the gun, it was easy. I'm ready to use it, you know. I've got no problem with that.' More head rubbing, scrubbing at his scalp like he needed to get inside it.

And she understood then. He might have a disease, but it wasn't going to kill him. He was planning to do that himself. 'Oh, Brendan, no. It's -'

'I've been holding it off for two days,' he wailed. 'I don't know if I can for much longer. Oh, fuck, *fuck*. I want to get there first but I don't know if I'm going to make it that far. It might have to be you, Jax. You might have to tell her.'

5

Jax knew now where he wanted to go but it didn't make it any better. She was delivering a man to his wife and son so he could shoot himself. In front of them.

Except he wasn't sure if he could wait that long - and if he didn't, she was the stand-by audience.

She tried to hold down the images that were going off in her mind but couldn't. She'd seen too many movies and every gory, bloody brain splatter that had ever flashed on a screen in front of her was coming back.

'I need to know, Jax. What's it like?' he asked again.

She opened her mouth, closed it again, felt like throwing up.

'What's it like being a widow?'

Oh no. He was going to kill himself but wanted a few details on what he was going to miss. Was he irrational for real or just playing nasty, spiteful games? With his wife and with her? She didn't answer, couldn't. It didn't seem to matter.

'I tried to warn Kate but she didn't get it. She didn't know what I was telling her. I *tried* to train her. Before *it* got in there, I tried to ... She should've listened to me. If she'd listened, she'd know, and I wouldn't have to go up there and ... Oh, Christ, it's not Katey. I've got the gun. It's my job. But I want them to understand. Before I have to ... before ...'

Brendan stopped but he'd said enough to make Jax realise it was possible it wasn't a death scene she was delivering him to but a murder-suicide. *Shit*. There were lots of reasons now to pull the car over and run like hell. And throw the keys far, far into the bush. She had to say something.

'Brendan, you don't have to ...'

He wasn't listening. Words were falling out of him like they were joined by string that was unravelling from his mouth. 'I left because I love her. I had to. And now everything's fucked up. She doesn't deserve me. I'm wrong. There's something wrong with me and I have to keep it from Katey and Scotty. And now . . .' He thumped his head with a fist. 'Now *it's* in here and ... If I don't make it, can you make sure Katey knows I love her? That I tried to get to her. That I was thinking of her and Scotty. That I didn't stop thinking about them just because I wasn't there.'

'Brendan. Listen to me. There are other ways, people who can help you.' Not her, that was for damn sure. Nano spiders were her line in the sand.

'No. No, it's too late for that. They're out there, they're coming, I can't stop them. I have to protect Katey and Scotty. They need me. I'm already dead but I can get to them first. I have to try.'

Tears threatened to fill her eyes again - not for herself this time but for the broken man beside her. He was stuck in an awful, illogical mental anguish but despite it, despite the paranoia and confusion, he knew he loved his wife and child. He hadn't forgotten that. Jax had no idea what he was planning now. Maybe he didn't know himself. Possibly he thought killing himself would protect Kate and Scotty, possibly he thought killing them would do it better. Whatever he did, it was going to hurt them - whether he did it in front of them or in Jax's car. He needed a professional, probably some serious medication, but all he had was her. Miranda Jack: sad, broke, unemployed, stuck . . . and only good for asking questions.

She didn't know what to say that wouldn't make him wave the gun in her direction or press it to his forehead and fire. Him dead or her. Fucking hell. But she had to say something. He was watching her, waiting for an answer.

'I can hear in your voice that you love Kate and Scotty very much. You can protect them too. If we stop and get help, you can keep them safe.'

'No, it's too late. I need to know if Katey will be okay. Will she be all right after? Tell me, Jax. Tell me what it's like.'

She wanted to stick with trying to talk him into pulling over, but he was insistent and impatient and she'd already seen what happened when he didn't get the answers he wanted. She sifted through words she could give him. She knew plenty about being a widow, was still bathing and plastering the wound that wouldn't stop bleeding. She just wasn't sure what was safe to tell him. If she invented a happy ending, some kind of life-goes-on, he'd know it was a lie. She needed something that wouldn't break his heart or make him crazy. Something that might make him rethink his role in it.

'It's lonely,' she said.

He nodded. A so-that's-it kind of gesture.

It wasn't what she'd hoped for. 'I mean, she'll have Scotty and he'll have her and they won't be alone, but it's not the same. He's a child and she's the parent and she'll be alone in it. She'll be there for your son, she'll try to be everything for him, but she won't have anyone there for *her*. It'll be lonely for Kate. Without you. And for Scotty too, without a father.'

He nodded again, less matter-of-fact, more thoughtful. When he spoke, there wasn't a hint of anxiety, just a calm, mate-to-mate tone. 'Kate's the best thing that ever happened to me.'

Maybe Kate would keep him calm. 'What's she -' Jax stopped, rephrased it. 'I'd like to hear about her.'

'She was there that day we flew out. With Scotty.'

'I remember,' Jax lied. 'But it was a while ago now. Tell me about her.'

There was silence for a long time and Jax felt the start of a cringe at the blast she figured was coming. But when he finally responded, it was a laugh. A small, throaty burble of humour - and Jax's eyebrows rose in surprise and relief.

'My Katey's great. And smart. A lot smarter than me. She's a teacher, well, that's what she trained for except we moved around a lot and it's hard to get teaching jobs when you do that.' His happy memories seemed to drift into the beginnings of recrimination. Maybe he blamed himself that Kate couldn't get work, or maybe she had blamed him.

Jax just wanted him back at his happy thoughts. 'And she's a good mum.'

'Oh, yeah, the best. Scotty could read before he went to school. That was all Katey. She's so good with him. Fun, too. She loves a party. And tough. Tough as nails sometimes. But soft, you know? Tough and soft. What about you, Jax?'

'She sounds great.'

'No, I mean, what are you like?'

She didn't want the focus on her. She wanted to find a nice, smooth transition back to convincing him they needed to stop and call for help. But he was as calm as she'd seen him and she didn't want to risk losing it - not with kilometres of motorway in front of them and nothing but rock face and bush at the verge.

From memory, it'd be a few more kilometres before a safer, wider place appeared - except now she was hoping she could hold out for something better she knew was looming over the horizon. Fifteen, maybe twenty minutes on were twin service stations: big road stops on either side of the six lanes of motorway with petrol, cafes, McDonald's - and lots of motorists taking a break. If she could convince him they needed to pull in there, to get a drink or visit the loo, getting away from him would be easier.

But she had to get there, had to stop him losing his cool and shooting himself first, and maybe talking and sharing, reminding him of what he had, might be all he needed to hold him steady. Checking the traffic over her shoulder, she slid into the middle lane, eased her foot down on the accelerator and pushed the car to the speed limit. Maybe she could get them there a little faster.

'Oh, I'm not tough,' she said. She used to think she was but the last year had told her otherwise. 'I'm not much fun, either.' Not lately. 'Kate sounds terrific.'

'She's beautiful, too. Really beautiful.'

'You're lucky to have her.'

'Yeah. Yeah, I am.' He nodded, more to himself than Jax. She hoped he was thinking it would be better not to lose Kate. 'What about your husband?' he asked. 'What was he like?'

A small pain snagged in her chest. She didn't want to share Nick. 'He was tall. And fit. He ran a lot.'

'He must've been pretty smart to do that job.'

Persistent, dogged and obsessive. An involuntary smile curled one side of her mouth, making her feel a little like Brendan with his soft chuckle. She glanced his way, saw him waiting for more. Why the hell not if it was keeping him calm?

'Not brain surgeon smart but Nick liked to understand things. He'd pull them apart and find how everything was connected. I don't mean cars or vacuum cleaners; he was hopeless at fixing anything around the house. I mean organisations, businesses, groups of people. He could figure out how they operated, where mistakes were made, how something underhanded could be hidden.'

'Like that compensation thing.'

'Yeah, like that.' He'd spent two years on that story, digging and asking questions, carrying around the details in his head like they'd been surgically implanted. He'd worked long hours, taken a lot of trips, mostly around Australia but once to Afghanistan, another time to Iraq - dangerous places to visit if you're a reporter. It'd been the reason she'd resigned from the paper four years ago and started freelance writing: job sharing the parenting doesn't work when one half of the partnership is entrenched in something else, something important. More important than her three days a week. 'He hated to see people wronged and once he knew there was a story in it, that he could do something to change it, he wouldn't let it go. Nick was a crusader.' Hard to live with at times, but he'd done good things for people who needed help.

'Do you miss him?'

'All the time.'

'Has it been hard for you?'

'It still is. I can't seem to get back on track. Any track. I feel like I'm not the me I used to be.'

'I know what that's like.'

She pressed her lips together in a small smile of acknowledgement. He probably understood more than anyone else she knew.

'You're moving to Newcastle, aren't you?' he asked.

'Yes.'

'Is that why?'

'No. Kind of. I couldn't afford to keep the house and my aunt has more room than she needs. She didn't want to sell, she's got a great spot overlooking the beach, so she offered to have us there until, well . . . until I get myself better sorted.'

'Do you want to live there?'

'I don't know what I want. I need to have a home for my daughter and a job to support her but I don't know what I want anymore.'

'I'm sorry.'

'Thanks.' She licked her lips, thought, *Why am I doing having this conversation with him?* Even worse - why was she taking comfort? He'd lost touch with reality and he had a gun in his hand. Had she lost her mind too?

She checked the traffic in the lanes either side, wishing the twin service stations were closer. The grey nomads and their caravan were almost alongside her in the outside lane, creeping up on her left as though she'd been holding them back. On her right, another P-plater: a young girl in a red hatchback, speeding along as though the colour really did make you go faster. Behind Jax was a dark-blue sedan, headlights on despite the daylight, a man in sunglasses behind the wheel. No white coats, no cops in patrol cars, no-one pointing a gun out the window. She took a quick look at the sky. No choppers either. *Just making sure.*

Oh, man, she had to get out of this car. 'I'm not just lonely, Brendan. I'm scared.' She caught his eye for a moment, looked back at the road as she spoke. 'I'm scared about what's happening here. I want to get back to my daughter. She's already lost one parent.'

It was the wrong tactic. Anxiety began oozing out of him again, making his body tense, his jaw tighten, his hands curl into fists. He shifted the gun from its loose hold on the edge of the seat to beside her on the centre console, his hand pushing at the lid as though it wouldn't stay down.

'Tell me more about Scotty,' she said quickly.

Brendan dipped his head, looked up through the windscreen.

'Seven is a lovely age,' she urged.

Maybe it was the topic or maybe the world in his head had just burst into life again, but he twisted abruptly, his whole body jerking around, eyes aimed at the rear window. From the corner of her vision, Jax saw his gun hand snap out. Felt a brief, hard swipe across her shoulder before cold metal brushed her cheek.

She flinched, ducked, cringed. It was a single movement accompanied by a desperate breathy sound that caught in her throat. She swerved. A horn blared. Her right-side tyres were in the next lane, a car too close at her side. Grappling with the steering, pressing herself into the door and away from the weapon, she swung the wheel back again. The sharp, panicky jolt tossed them both sideways - her temple bumped the driver's window, his gun in her face. Close enough to see scratches on the silver around the black eye of its muzzle.

She should look at the road. She should watch where they were going. But all she could see was *gun* - and Zoe's life flashing before her eyes.

6

T he moment hung in the air. Timeless, suspended, locked in place. As though life or fate or God was reluctant to move on to the next scene. The one where Miranda Jack's face was blown apart by a bullet.

Then it was over and whatever made the big decisions had changed its mind and Brendan was shoving away from her, using his gun hand and the console to thrust all the way back into his seat, gawking at her like she was the one who'd gone insane.

'Christ, Jax. Stay in your lane or you'll kill us both.'

'*Me*? You're the one with the fucking gun.'

He took a second to look at it. 'Yeah. We've both got control of lethal weapons.'

Was he kidding? Neither of them had any control.

'You need to calm down, Jax. Just concentrate on the road and keep your cool.' Something different in his voice: wise instructor to nervous beginner. How many personas were inside him? 'You're doing great, Jax.'

She shot him a glare, made no attempt to contain the words that spilled out. 'On what goddamn scale am I doing great, Brendan? The terrified hostage scale or the taxi to a crime scene scale? And how exactly is almost crashing at high speed in any way great?' They were questions, a whole bunch of them that he wouldn't like - but fear and anger and adrenaline had been set loose inside her, and rephrasing or building rapport was way beyond her.

He chuckled. Not some crazy, throaty cackle, like the kind Jax thought might come out from her own mouth. It was straight out amusement. 'You're wrong, you know,' he said. 'You *are* funny. What goddamn scale? That's a good one. And I wasn't bullshitting, you're doing great. Just try to stay in your lane.'

Stay in your lane, he says. Keep your cool, he says. Concentrate on the fucking road while I point this gun at you. Oh, and try not to kill me with your lethal fucking car. A small, involuntary laugh huffed out of her. Not quite a crazy cackle but close.

He raised an eyebrow, nodded: the wise instructor impressed with her powers of recovery. Oh, man, she needed to scream. Needed to shout and swear at him. To throttle the steering wheel. Open the door and bawl at the drivers who were just speeding right past. To get out and run and run. She needed to ... do something.

'My daughter plays a game.' She said it fast, teeth clamped over the fearful, frustrated, incensed swell of stuff inside her. 'We'll be in the car or out shopping or sitting at the beach and she'll say, "Would you prefer to be eaten by a shark or a lion?" Two shit choices. Chased by a crocodile or a dinosaur? Stung by a thousand bees or dropped off a cliff? I should just pick one, you know? I should go eeny-meeny-miny-moe and say quicksand or funnel-web spiders, whatever. I mean, what does it matter? You're never going to get a choice, right?'

They were questions but they were rhetorical and she hoped that didn't piss him off because the talking was helping. Her, not him. Making her focus on finding words, forming whole sentences, making a point, avoiding the shitty options he was giving her.

'But every time she asks, I do this whole mental evaluation of which death would be worse. I imagine the shark and what it'd be like to be torn to pieces underwater, shaken and mauled by a killing machine, your own blood turning the water red around you. And then I pitch that against the image of being stalked by a huge cat, a tiger say, run down and ripped to shreds on the plains of Africa. You know what I mean?'

'Shark,' he said. 'Definitely shark.'

She glanced at him. He was serious. 'Oh yeah?'

'A big one. White pointer. One bite and I'm dead. Quick. That's how I want it.'

She couldn't bring herself to picture it. Or change the subject. 'Snake or spider?'

He cocked his head. 'Spider. I hate snakes.'

'I killed a brown snake once. With a shovel. I'd go for spider too.'

'Plane or chopper?' he chipped in.

This was nuts. 'Plane. Less chance of being thrown from the wreckage and dying slowly.'

'I've seen that. It's a bad way to go.'

In Afghanistan? Had he survived a helicopter crash over there? Did he have PTSD? She wanted to ask but figured gruesome death distractions were better right now. 'Soldier ants or hyenas?'

'Eaten alive? Fuck.'

There was something more sober in his tone - and a warning in the pause that followed. Jax flicked her eyes across the car. His gun hand was open, the weapon on the flat of his palm like a specimen. He spoke without taking his eyes from it. 'Gun or knife?'

Oh no. No, no.

He sucked in a long, dragging breath.

She tightened her hands on the wheel. 'Brendan. No.'

He pulled in another one - a loud, gulping rasp. She wanted to snatch the gun away from him. She wanted to see Zoe again. She clenched her teeth, kept her eyes on the road.

The next sound made her jaw go slack. It wasn't a deafening blast, it wasn't shouting. It was an anguished sob.

When she realised he wasn't going to pull the trigger, when she could drag her eyes from the lane ahead, she saw his head bowed, his body slumped forward as though his chest had caved in, the curve of his spine shuddering. He was crying. Not a men-don't-cry, holding-it-back kind of thing. Not a sniffling, hiccupping wailing, either. It was a heaving, silent, internalised agony.

Jax glanced back and forth a couple of times, indecisive, anxious. Anyone else and she might have put a comforting hand on their sleeve, muttered soothing, empathetic words. But she wasn't sure it wouldn't have the wrong effect, wouldn't make him rage at her or shoot himself. Maybe leaving him alone with his distress was her best option.

Then the sound of it changed and she realised he was talking. Repeating something. She couldn't make it out over the hum of the engine, didn't know if it was to her or to himself but as she listened, as it droned on, she understood - the words, not the meaning behind them.

'I didn't know. I didn't know. I swear I didn't. Christ, I didn't even know.'

Was that what was stuck in his head? The *it* he couldn't get out? Going round and round in his brain until he lost his hold on everything else. Fear and sympathy pounded in her chest as his repetitions got slower, fewer, finally petering out. Then he sat mute, staring through the windscreen. Or at it. Or at something in his mind.

The rapport-building, the talking, the car games had all ended badly; there was no reason to believe desperate crying would be the forerunner to a better outcome. So she didn't disturb his silence, just inched over the speed limit, unnerved by another pendulum swing of his mood but less terrified now he was finally still and quiet and the gun was resting in loosely curled fingers.

The grey nomads were behind her again, still in the outside lane. Sedans, utes, people movers sped past on the right. The driver in the dark-blue sedan with the headlights on was still in her lane but had dropped back a bit. She didn't blame him. She thought of her phone, wished she could reach it, talk to Zoe, hear her voice, tell her she loved her.

She'd spoken to Tilda only moments before Brendan got in the car. It'd taken longer than Jax had expected to finish up at the house - more because of the pausing for memories than the actual packing - and she told her aunt it would be a couple of hours before she got to Newcastle. It might be another after that before Jax was overdue enough for Tilda to check on her - and Brendan had turned the phone off. Would Tilda think the battery was dead? Maybe it'd be three or four hours before her aunt started to worry. If Jax couldn't stop, if she couldn't get away, if she kept driving at 110 k's, she'd be a long way from home by then.

She glanced at the glove box. Could she convince Brendan to turn the phone back on? A suggestion to check Google Maps maybe, for destinations or directions or . . . Would he let her answer it if Tilda rang? What the hell would she say? It wasn't a movie, there was no version of, *I'll be home late, don't wait up*, that Tilda would interpret as, *I'm in trouble, call the police.* Jax had lived with Tilda for two years after her parents died and on weekends for the two semesters she'd spent at Newcastle Uni - and until the last twelve months, their get-togethers had been haphazard and social. Jax's nickname was as close as they got to family code.

The twin service stations must be close now. Jax checked the clock on the radio and felt a jolt of surprise. 5.12. She'd only been on the motorway fifty minutes? It felt like days. She was exhausted. Her top was wet under the arms and down her back, and the coffee she'd bought before she hit the Harbour Bridge was letting her know it would need a release before long. Not desperate yet but another near- miss and it might be an uncomfortable story.

The last exit to the Central Coast came and went. Brendan didn't move. Neither did the gun. Then she saw the sign she'd been waiting for. Big and blue, lots of symbols: petrol, food, coffee, toilets. Two kilometres.

She waited until she could see it in the distance then took a breath, broke the silence. 'There's a service station up ahead. I need to stop.' She figured if he flipped out, she could hit the accelerator, screech into the parking area, throw herself out and hope someone came to her rescue.

'No,' he said.

'I had a coffee before you got in. See?' She tapped the plastic sipping lid on the cup in its holder, flicked the blinker and began to drift into the outside lane. 'I need a bathroom.'

'No.' Firmer.

'The next stop is another forty minutes, at least. I can't wait that long.'

He angled his face to the left-side mirror, tension stiffening his neck. Behind them, the grey nomads were well back, the dark-blue sedan in the space between.

'I can't hold on much longer. We have to stop.'

His breathing sharpened, his fist closed around the gun. The entrance was up ahead. She was taking it, whether he liked it or not.

He didn't try to stop her. Just watched the motorway and the mirror as she slowed on the entry road and bumped over a speed hump, her heart pounding as petrol bowsers came into view. There? Should she pull in there? Only two cars, no drivers pumping fuel or walking about. Up ahead was better. She knew the parking area - six or more rows of slots, cafes along two sides. She'd never seen it anywhere close to empty.

As she passed the petrol station, Brendan did the front- and-back thing. Maybe he'd seen the dark-blue sedan. It had pulled off the motorway behind them and made her wonder briefly if Brendan was right and someone was after him, but the sedan turned towards the pumps.

'Where are you going?' Brendan asked.

'There's a cafe around the back. The toilets are clean and the food's good.' Organic produce for the health-conscious traveller.

'No food. Drive in there.' He pointed to the first lane, maybe wanting to make the decisions again. She didn't mind, it was where she'd planned to go.

Plenty of cars, a man and a woman walking towards the cafe, three bulky, twenty-something men were heading out of it. She wanted to hit the button for the window, shout at the top of her voice. *Not yet,* she told herself. She was strapped into a seatbelt; she had to be able to move fast - and she needed protection, something solid she could throw herself behind.

Choosing a slot between a chunky work truck and a family-size car, she searched for an escape route as she steered slowly in. If she stayed low when she threw herself out and kept below the passenger window while she ran, she might make it even if he fired the gun.

She stopped nose-to-nose with a car in the next lane. Her fingers were on the door handle as she pulled the handbrake. She shifted her other hand to the seatbelt clasp, ready to release and run . . . then something warm and strong closed around her wrist.

'You're in this with me, Jax.' Brendan's grip held her arm in place; his voice made her raise her eyes to his. 'It's fate, remember. Your car was there. We do this together.'

7

W hatever had loosened inside him to make him sob had been
screwed back on tight. There was no trace of tears now.
What Jax saw in his eyes was flat, hard and unnerving.

Her fingers were still on the door handle. She still had a chance.
'Yeah, sure.' She leaned away from him, tugged on the arm he held.

It didn't move. Brendan's grip was a vice, crushing her flesh. He bent
towards her, his face in her space, his voice low and measured. 'We stay
together. Do you understand?'

She swallowed on the fear wedged in her throat. 'Yes.'

'When your belt is released, you climb across the seat and get out my
side.'

'I won't -'

'I need to get home, Jax. We do this together. I can protect you. Okay?'

She needed protection *from* him. 'Okay.'

'Unclip your belt. Leave your handbag.' He kept his hand around her
wrist as she lifted one knee then the other over the gearstick and shuffled
across. 'Wait,' he ordered.

Still holding her arm, the gun at the small of his back hidden from
outside view, he stood, head above the doorframe, body moving as
though he was scanning the car park. Jax did the same from inside,
desperate for a way out, someone to shout to, a place to hide. The three
young guys passed the rear window and kept walking. A woman in the

next lane was helping two young children. At the cafe, the couple disappeared through automatic doors. There were more people in the car park but too far away to be of any use. The twenty-somethings were her best chance. But the kids were close. And Brendan had a gun.

'Now.' Brendan dragged on her arm, pulling as she clambered out beside him. He wasn't as tall as she'd thought. She was a little above average, he was only half a head more.

The sun was blazing in the west, filling the air with humid January heat. It felt sweet and clean after the stifled tension in the car. Jax squinted in the glare, swinging her head to look for the twenty-somethings. They were two cars past hers, opening doors: one on the driver's side, two with their backs to her, all three with their heads down, balancing food as they pulled handles. She looked the other way. The kids were playing statues in the next lane, arms in the air, striking poses in the gap between the vehicles in front of Jax's. A straight line from here to there. She imagined gunshots and small bodies bleeding on the tarmac. She couldn't run that way. And the other direction, towards the young guys, meant getting around Brendan first.

Then it didn't matter which way she went. The pistol was pressed into the curve of her waist and she had no chance at all.

He whispered in her ear, 'Give me the keys.'

She passed them.

'The gun goes in my pocket but it stays in my hand.' He raised his eyebrows at her. She nodded. 'We walk together, like a couple.' His grip on her wrist slid to her hand. It was strong and hot and crushing her fingers. He swung the car door shut, walked ahead of her to the lane, pulled her alongside with stiff-armed force, spoke quietly as they headed towards the cafe. 'I wait for you while you go, then we come straight back out to the car. Okay?'

She nodded again. A lie: it wasn't okay.

The car park had been her best chance and he'd taken it away. Up ahead, a man in a high-vis work shirt walked out through the automatic doors, aimed a ball of rubbish at a bin. Okay, there were people inside. She didn't want anyone to get shot, she had to avoid that, but maybe she could create a diversion, whisper a message: *I'm a hostage, call the police.* And she was going to the bathroom. She'd used it before here - long sink, three or four cubicles, overhead windows. He couldn't stay with her the whole time.

The glass doors slid open and the smell of fresh coffee washed over her. There were tables on the left, most of them empty. Open fridges on the right, a single customer inspecting sandwiches. At the counter in front, the couple from the car park was placing an order. Jax took her sunglasses off and hooked them onto the front of her singlet top. She wanted her face on display, wanted someone to see the terror in her eyes.

Brendan dropped his mouth to her ear. 'Just keep your cool. You're doing great. Great on the scale of no-one-will-pick-it.' He winked.

She wanted to be sick. Wished she could unclench her stomach enough to actually do it. That would cause a diversion.

As Brendan walked her shoulder-to-shoulder through the centre of the cafe, she searched for faces, anyone looking her way. There were none. Every single customer ate or drank or stared at newspapers, phones, the distant horizon. Avoiding eye contact, like she did when she came in for a break from the driving. Brendan steered her past the counter as though he'd been here before too. Maybe he had. Maybe he preferred organic produce when he wasn't thinking about killing himself.

There were no doors to the restrooms, just a gap in the wall and left to the Men's, right to the Ladies'. He turned right, marched her into the women's bathroom, stood in the narrow corridor between the long sink and the cubicles and said, 'Which one?'

They were alone. All four doors were open. She walked to the one furthest from the exit. 'I'll meet you outside.' 'You'll meet me right here. I'm not leaving you alone.'

'It's the women's toilets. You can't stay here.'

'I can stay where I like.'

Yes, he could. The gun gave him permission.

'Don't be long,' he said.

'I'll take as long as I need,' she snapped back. Pulling the door, she turned the latch, looked up at the row of windows above. High and narrow. She'd have to stand on the seat, drag herself up by her fingers. And there was no point: the glass was reinforced with wire mesh. Bad. All bad.

She heard footsteps on the other side of the door - Brendan pacing the corridor, stopping outside her cubicle. She shut her eyes, held squeezed fists in the air and clenched her teeth on a long, internalised scream. There was no escape here. No gaps under the doors she could belly-crawl through. No lipstick in her pocket she could write a note with. No keys to scratch a message. Tears filled her eyes as she sat. She gave in to them this time, her face crumpling, breath jagged, mouth open in a soundless wail.

The crash on the door jerked her out of it.

'Come on!' he hissed. 'We need to ...'

More footsteps: the *click-clack* of high heels.

'Oh.' A woman's voice.

'Yeah, sorry,' Brendan said. 'My wife's sick. I want to make sure she's okay.'

Jax stood, yanked at her underwear. 'No. I'm okay, I'm -'

'Morning sickness,' he said, talking over her. 'Actually, all-day sickness.' He laughed a little.

'Oh, right. No problem. I'll come back.' Footsteps moving away.

No, stay! Jax fumbled the lock, pulled the door, saw Brendan filling the space. Stepped past him in time to see the swirl of a floral skirt disappear around the corner.

'It's all right, she's gone.' He placed a firm, solid hand on her shoulder as he spoke.

Shoving it off, she watched herself in the mirror as she washed trembling hands at the sink. She looked like shit. Pretty much the way she felt. Sweaty and dirty and panicky. She splashed her face with water, wiped mascara from under her eyes, their pea-green dulled and darkened by fear and exhaustion. She tugged the band from a shoulder-length mess of blonde hair and refastened it, pulling herself together, steeling herself for the next bit. Hoping there was a police tactical response team armed and waiting for them in the cafe.

There wasn't. It was just the same crew: eating, drinking, waiting, staring. She thought about shouting - and about the gun. She couldn't duck, Brendan was holding her too tight; she didn't want to get shot and she didn't want to be responsible for a massacre. So she searched faces again, passed customers and staff, food in the fridges, three cappuccinos waiting to be collected. She wanted one. She wanted all three. And a stiff drink followed by a lie down.

At least Zoe wasn't here. She could be grateful for that.

There was a smoker at the single table outside. A semitrailer blowing exhaust. A queue for the McDonald's drive-through. Way down, in the slot where the three twenty-something guys had been, a man was talking on a mobile. As she walked beside Brendan, his arm holding her close to his side, she watched the man. He was between two vehicles, only head and shoulders above it - dark hair, sunglasses, collar and tie, phone to his ear. As they approached, his head turned and he faced them over the roof of a dark-blue sedan.

Her pulse picked up. Was it the guy from the centre lane? The one who'd turned off the motorway behind her? Hope swelled in her chest - and an impulse to wave and shout. But Brendan's hand was clutched firmly around hers and she remembered his words: rambled ones about people looking for them, about being a target.

The guy lifted an arm and rested his elbow on top of the sedan. Jax couldn't be sure where his eyes were behind the sunglasses but she fixed her own on him, willing him to see her desperation, hoping he wasn't there to pick her off. Three cars from her own, another two from his, she watched as he pulled the phone from his ear, tapped the screen and laid it on the roof. He didn't leave, made no move to walk away or open a door. He just turned his head left and right in a brief, casual glance around the car park, then back to her. Or Brendan. Or the lane they were in. Maybe he was waiting for someone in the cafe. Maybe he was waiting for another call.

Definitely watching and waiting.

She checked the parking area. There was no-one else in her lane, no-one in the next, no-one close enough to hear her if she shouted. The guy by the blue sedan was her last chance. Trained people who won't stop, Brendan had said. He also thought he had nano spiders in his head. Was any of it real? Some of it? Which bits?

As she passed the bumper of the car beside hers, the guy turned his face away. Forearm on the roof, phone still there - another person not wanting to make eye contact. Brendan steered her ahead of him between the two vehicles, pressed her back to the passenger door and released her hand to reach into his pocket for the keys. She looked to where the kids had played earlier. It was two car-lengths from here to the next lane. The gun was in his pocket. Could she make it?

'We get in the way we got out.' Brendan's voice was in her ear and something hard pressed into her thigh. Glancing down, she saw he'd taken out the gun, was holding it low and out of sight as he fumbled the keys on her ring.

No running, not with that there. Shit, she was going to end up back in the car with him. She took a brief glance over her shoulder, saw the guy by the blue sedan, his face turned towards them again. There was no mistaking it this time, even with the sunglasses. He wasn't bored with waiting and casting his eyes around. There was no attempt to shift his attention when she saw him. Not anything like every other person she'd seen. He was watching them. Both of them. Taking in the whole scene as though he'd paid tickets to see it.

Jax's heart thumped. *Trained people who won't stop.* He was tall, wide across the shoulders, lean. Mid-to-late thirties. Collar and tie, black-framed sunnies. He seemed cool, composed, alert: bad guy or bystander? Maybe he had a white coat in his back seat.

She jumped as her locks released, scooted sideways as Brendan reached around her for the door handle. He held her in place with the flat of his palm in the centre of her back, opened the car, pressed her forwards. Two seconds and she'd be in the car again driving God knew where, possibly to Brendan's death. Or hers.

As she reached the doorway, she reeled her head around. She figured the man would have looked away again, that she'd have to get his attention, wave or shout and risk getting shot. But she didn't have to. His gaze was already there, as if he'd been waiting for her to turn. He'd lifted the sunglasses and the eyes she hadn't been able to see were light in colour, steely and focused on her. Not Brendan, not both of them. Just her.

She met them with her own, felt a buzz of connection, as though his vision had an energy that had reached out and touched her. And without thinking about who he was or what he wanted, Jax mouthed two words across the space between them: *Help me.*

T hen Jax was in the car, shunting across the passenger seat, lifting her legs over the gearstick with Brendan close behind. She glanced sideways as she pulled her seatbelt on, couldn't see the blue-sedan guy from there, wondered if she'd made things better or worse. Or whether they'd changed at all.

'Come on. Start the car.' Brendan was anxious again. Not the nano spider angst, just in a hurry to get out of the car park.

She backed out, caught sight of the guy. His sunnies were back on and he was talking into the phone again as he watched her vehicle pass. Brendan saw him too, turning his head to stare as the dark sedan disappeared behind them. God, she hoped the guy was talking to the police. Hoped the person on the other end wasn't 'trained' and waiting for Brendan on the motorway.

She paused at the exit, unnerved and ticked off that she was behind the wheel and heading for another suicidal round with traffic. Last time, she'd only had her imagination to scare her. This time, she knew life and death were on board and fighting over the navigation.

'Jax, come on. We can't sit here like this.'

She flicked her eyes at the rear-view mirror, saw the nose of a dark-blue car edging out of the lane she'd just left. It was him - it had to be. He was following? Maybe it *wasn't* safe to sit too long.

Hitting the accelerator, pushing the car to 110, she slipped onto the motorway between a flat-top truck and a bus. There were only two lanes now and Jax merged into the faster one, staying with the pace, wanting to keep ahead of whatever was behind. For ten minutes, she saw nothing but a mishmash of the same fast-moving flow she'd watched for more than an hour. Then, half-a-dozen cars back, the dark-blue sedan moved left between the two lines of traffic. Two minutes later it slid right again. Two cars behind her. Speeding up, getting closer.

He was probably continuing his journey, she told herself. That's what people at service stations did. He'd called the police then got back on the road. He'd stopped for petrol and ... what? Moved his car to the cafe parking to get out and make a few phone calls. Who did that?

Brendan's earlier angst had turned to stillness: gun in his hand, upright in his seat, his attention on the small mirror on the outside of the passenger door. Maybe he'd seen the blue sedan, too.

They passed a turn-off, then another one.

'Change lanes,' Brendan snapped. He waited two beats. 'Now.'

'There's a car beside us.'

'Get ahead of it.'

Speeding up, flicking the blinker, she slid left. As Brendan swung his head to the rear window, she watched the traffic in her mirror. A white ute slipped into the hole she'd made while other cars moved up. About thirty seconds later, the blue sedan merged. Three vehicles behind her.

'Move back again,' Brendan told her.

She didn't want to jockey in and out of the fast lane. Didn't want to argue either - and she wanted to know what the guy from the car park was up to. She tapped the blinker.

'Hit the pedal,' he ordered.

As she pulled ahead, the blue sedan stayed where it was, let four cars pass, then merged right.

'Fuck.' Brendan spun around, ducked his head, checked the sky.

Jax looked too - no clouds, no choppers. What was real and what wasn't?

He swung to the back, to the front, lifted the gun, lowered it to the seat. '*Fuck.*'

Alarm fired inside her. 'What?'

'They found us. They've got us. We're fucked.'

Why was *she* fucked? They were after him, weren't they? 'How do you know?'

'We're being followed. Dark-blue Falcon. Five cars back. See it?'

Jax lifted her chin as though it was the first time she'd checked. 'Yes.'

'It was in the car park. Arsehole driver was watching us when we left. I should've stopped him then. Fuck. *Fuck.* We've got to get off the road.'

'It's the motorway. We can't just *get off*.' Her voice was high with fright, his panic infecting her. Had *she* done this? Was it real? She thought back to the man's gaze on her in the seconds before she was pushed into the car, the buzz as their eyes touched. No smile, no hostility. Possibly a question.

Possibly she'd just been desperate for help.

'We might be able to lose him if we can get off,' Brendan said. 'When's the next exit?'

'I've no idea.'

'Shit.' Head front then back then front again. 'Drive.'

'I am.'

'Well, stand on the fucking pedal!'

His agitation scared her. The thought of it turning violent scared her more. The speedo climbed to 130, 135. She didn't have a lead foot, didn't spend her driving life over the speed limit hoping a camera didn't pick her up. Her hands were clammy, shoulders tight, teeth locked. Two vehicles back, a four-wheel drive opted out of the race and moved into the outside lane. The blue sedan closed the distance.

A sign. To Newcastle, to every major stop between here and Brisbane. No exit coming up.

'Fuck,' Brendan said.

'He's behind us,' Jax said. 'What can he do from back there?'

'There's more than one.' He said it as though she was stupid. 'And I'm not the only one with a weapon. They've got them. They're prepared. Guns and knives and ... I didn't, I swear I ... and ... and fucking missiles.'

Jax pressed her lips together, blinked hard. He was going to lose it while she was twenty k's over the speed limit. She'd been a news reporter once, had seen the wreckage of fatal car crashes, and her memory was throwing up horrific images she'd tried to forget. Of crushed and charred vehicles, of covered bodies on roadways. And images that would never leave her, that the police had shown her: Nick's body, covered and photographed without a vehicle in sight to explain it.

She clenched her teeth, eased her foot off the pedal. The car behind, a silver BMW, almost kissed her bumper before dropping back.

'Yeah. Yeah, you're right. Good thinking. Do it fast with this guy in the way. Catch him off guard,' Brendan said.

Do *what*?

He spoke with his face turned away, twisting to his left. 'Now.' The front end of a semitrailer was lumbering beside them, its load two car-lengths long. What was he thinking? 'Get in front of it and do it, Jax.'

She hit the accelerator, moved in front of the huge engine, scanning the motorway ahead. There was no exit. Did he want her to get off the road here? It ran straight for at least a kilometre and the verge was narrow, bordered by bush and a low metal guardrail. Not a good place to pull over, not with an eighteen-wheeler on her arse.

'Where is he?' Brendan asked.

As she glanced at the rear-view, the blue sedan slipped in behind the semi. 'Just merged. A couple back.'

'Okay.' He faced forward, spine pressed into the seat, slid the pistol chamber back and forth with a *chnk-chnk*, something proficient and practised in the way he did it. 'Listen up. We pull over, let him fly past, give him a head start and get back on the road. Then we take the first exit. Ready?'

'No, wait. I can't pull over here. It's not wide enough.'

'We have to work with what we've got.'

According to what manual? 'We don't have to do it here,' she said, hearing the plural 'we' and wondering when they'd become a team. 'He's behind us. He probably can't even see us around the truck. We can wait until there's somewhere better.' Where her side of the car wouldn't be taken off by the grille of a speeding truck.

'Fuck!' He swung his head to the rear window. 'Did you see that?'

'What?'

'Cop car. Heading south. Lights on, no siren.'

The north- and south-bound streams were separated by a wide strip. For much of the distance up the coast, the space was filled with bush or cut rock, blocking the view of oncoming traffic. Sometimes there was a gap - dirt and rubble or a stretch of tarred surface where emergency vehicles could turn around and highway patrol cops sat with radars. Jax glanced across a clearing at the sparse flow heading south, craned her neck for a view in the mirror, but couldn't see through thick scrub.

'But it was going the other way,' she said.

'They're coming from Newcastle, not Sydney now.'

Who? The police? The cops were trained and wouldn't stop. They had guns ... but missiles? 'You're worried about the police?'

'Cops will fuck it up. That arsehole's back there *now*.' There was a jerking tremor in his gun hand as he wiped it across his upper lip. 'I wanted to see Katey. One more time. Just one *fucking* time.' Jax jumped as he lashed out with a foot, kicking the floor under the dash. 'I'm not going to make it. I'm not going to get there. It's coming. It's coming soon.'

But he was starting to fall apart now.

Jax wiped a clammy hand down her thigh. She'd thought she had it worked out. That Brendan had bad guys in his head. That he wanted to kill himself to stop them, wanted to see his wife and son first, maybe take them with him. Now she had no clue. Perhaps it was pointless trying to make sense of it.

They were approaching another emergency vehicle turning area. On the south-bound side, a big white sedan, similar to the dark-blue one behind them, was gunning it in the fast lane, riding low, flying past other vehicles. Small red lights danced along the bottom edge of the windscreen. Police. She glanced in the rear-view. Had she been slowing without realising it? The semitrailer was in the inside lane now. Only one car between her and the guy from the rest stop.

He sure as hell wasn't a bystander. Had he called the cops and was keeping tabs, hoping to catch it on his phone and upload it to YouTube later? Or had someone else in the cafe seen her distress and called Triple-o, and the driver with the sunnies was the arsehole Brendan was worried about?

And where were the damn police cars? If the ones they'd seen were looking for her, how long would it take to turn around and head back? Maybe she should pull off like Brendan wanted. Take her chances on the verge, let the blue sedan go past, and wait for the police - or just run for her life. Any of that might be safer than staying in the car with Brendan.

The road up ahead disappeared around a bend. She had no idea what lay beyond it - possibly more narrow verge. But this was a motorway, and drivers had to stop sometimes - road workers, emergency services, people with car trouble - and traffic engineers made sure there were safe places to do it. She didn't need a whole damn car park, though. Another metre-width of verge would be fine. It would be fucking fabulous.

'We're on, Jax.' Brendan's voice was a taut mixture of alarm and efficiency. 'It's happening.' He was sideways in his seat again, shoulder pressed to the upholstery, face tucked behind the headrest like a cop hiding around a doorframe.

Her eyes snapped to the mirror and fear grew hot in her gut. The blue sedan was behind them. She could see sunglasses and dark hair, a black and white top. No shirt and tie. Had he taken them off or were there two men?

'Shit. *Shit*.' Brendan crouched forward, eyes angled up.

Jax followed his gaze and panic surged through her veins like fire. A helicopter was hovering above them.

9

S he hoped the buzz inside her was adrenaline pooling, preparing her for flight when she finally pulled over. Because whatever the hell was going on, she wanted to be out of the car and away from Brendan and whatever else turned up.

In the mirror, she watched the man in the blue sedan lift a phone to his ear. She wanted him to be talking to the cops. Wanted him to be sending a mayday to the military to pick up their damaged soldier. But maybe he was calling reinforcements. Maybe she needed to get the hell away from him too.

'There.' Brendan saw it before she did.

They were around the bend and it wasn't an extra metre of verge. It was a stopping zone with an emergency phone. Wide enough to get right off the roadway, long enough to slow down without skidding and sliding into the guardrail. Enough bush behind it to hide. She hoped.

She didn't flick the indicator, just hit the brake and veered off the blacktop, clenching her teeth and holding on tight as the tyres fought for purchase on the dirt. Gravel sprayed the chassis in a deafening clash. Then they were shuddering to a stop, no time to check the rear-view before Brendan was clutching at her wrist, pulling on her arm. 'Same as before,' he yelled, already half out the passenger door.

She grabbed for the handle on her side. 'No.'

'We stay together.' He didn't give her a choice. As he hauled her across the seats she hit her arm on the centre console, bashed a knee into the gearstick, crushed a hip against something solid; his fingers dragging at her skin, the force threatening to tear her arm from its socket.

Outside, the rush of air from the motorway hit like a cyclone. She glanced backwards, saw the dark-blue sedan rocking to a stop on the dirt, a cloud of dust rising from its tyres, red lights flashing on the windscreen. He was a cop? She wanted to scream for help. Wanted to run for her life.

'Move!' Brendan bellowed over the continuous howl of traffic.

'Brendan, let go.'

He jerked her arm, pulling her around the doorframe. *'Come on!'*

'It's the police.' She hauled against him, dug her runners into the dirt, but they were slipping, sliding on the gravel as he dragged her forwards.

'No. They're here. I'm not ready. I've got to get to Kate.' His voice was all but swallowed up by the roar of a truck and the vortex of air that grabbed at her singlet, sandblasting her arms and face with grit.

Twisting, trying to break free, she saw the sedan's door open.

'Come *on*. We can still make it from here,' Brendan shouted.

Make it where? They were kilometres from anywhere. Just bush and tarmac and a wall of traffic. Behind them, a man's head and shoulders rose above the door. His hands rested on the open frame.

No, not resting. Holding a gun, double-fisted. Aiming it at them.

'Nooo!' she shouted. Turned her head, yelled it at Brendan too.

Then Brendan was in her face, grabbing her by the shoulders, pushing her down and making her run bent over like they were dodging bullets. Had the guy fired already? Then she saw where Brendan was heading, where he was taking her. To the edge of the blacktop.

She fought his hold, yanking, shoving, skidding, desperate. 'No, Brendan, no.'

'We can lose him over there. We've just got to get across the road.'

'It's the motorway.' Wind pulled at her as though it was trying to help him.

'Move.'

'No. We won't make it.' A truck's horn blared, a howling noise that mimicked her own cry as it passed. She could see the edge of the tarmac up close now. Tiny pebbles held together by shiny black tar. This close, the airstream was a force, sucking at her, tearing at her face, filling her nose, her ears. She thought of Zoe and a wail poured from her throat, the sound disappearing on the wind.

'I've got to get to Kate and Scotty.' Brendan was ordering, pleading. There was terror in his voice, in his eyes. Panic and irrationality.

Then his attention skipped away from her. Pupils moving fast, taking in what she'd heard behind her. Not just the roar of moving vehicles but tyres slithering to a stop on gravel, a helicopter up above. She couldn't see them, couldn't take her eyes off the man trying to drag her to her death, but she saw the flicker of decision in his and knew desperation when she saw it.

He had her by the forearms. She turned her hands and closed fingers around his wrists, hollered into the wind, 'Don't, Brendan.'

'They need me.'

'You won't make it.'

He paused, the pull on her arms suddenly letting up as his focus settled on the road behind her. She turned her head, saw a minibus in the inside lane, something yellow behind it, and flashing lights further back. Then, like a leap into free air, her arms swung up and Brendan's hands slipped through her fingers.

What followed came in jagged, jarring slow motion. The whoosh of her own breath as she dragged in air. The incremental turning of her head as the minibus and a bright-yellow hatchback hurtled past at double the speed. The billowing white of Brendan's business shirt as he ran. The throat-grazing force of a shriek that produced no sound. The white smoke of burning rubber on blacktop, the sideways slewing of the minibus ... then screeching tyres and clashing metal and her own scream were shredded together in a single, shattering explosion of noise.

Jax wasn't yelling words now. She was just yelling. Mouth open until her lungs were empty, then filling them up and starting again. She couldn't see Brendan anymore. The minibus and yellow hatchback were locked together. He was somewhere in there or on the other side: maybe he'd made it. Maybe he was in the bush and escaping.

She wanted to run over and help, wanted to run away, wanted to be sick, didn't do any of it. Just stood rooted to the ground, swaying one way then the other, like a tree buffeted by indecision and disbelief and horror.

'... randa Jack.'

Her name. Someone shouting. She looked to where Brendan had gone. There was screaming coming from over there now. Frightened faces peering out of the minibus.

'Drop the weapon!'

Male voice. Loud, aggressive. She turned, saw him. The guy by the blue sedan, except he was in front of it now. Pointing his gun at her.

Her body went rigid. Her brain tried to sift through a barrage of information. Cars stopped in the pull-over zone. Flashing lights. A chopper overhead. Brendan's words: *Trained people who won't stop. Guns and knives and fucking missiles. They've got us, we're fucked.*

The man yelled, 'You need to drop your weapon. Now!'

She glanced behind her, expecting to see Brendan with his gun. What she saw was the black ribbon of motorway stretching into the distance without a single car on it. She swayed a little.

'Is your name Miranda Jack?'

She lurched back. The man was closer, a couple of metres away, holding the pistol with two hands, elbows locked straight, the words a slow, deliberate shout, as though she might not understand English. She tried to look at him but all she saw was the gleam of silver off his weapon in the afternoon glare and the black of a bulletproof vest. She wished she had one.

'Yes,' she cried.

'Miranda, you need to put the gun down now.'

It was only then that she felt the hard, flesh-warmed metal of the pistol tucked inside her left palm. She stared at it, trying to figure out how it got there, remembering the lightness in her arms as they'd swung free of Brendan, the knobs of his knuckles as they'd slipped through her fingers. Had he lost his hold on it or given it to her?

'Do you know the man who was in the car with you?' the man called.

She lifted her eyes from Brendan's pistol, her hand firming on the grip, a finger finding the trigger guard. 'Do *you* know him?'

'Miranda -'

'Are *you* what he's afraid of?' It was an accusation, borne on a new fear that was hardening in her chest. 'What are you going to do to *me*?'

'Jax.'

The name made her pause. Her name. The name friends used. How did he know it?

He took a step closer. She refocused on the physique behind the weapon: long legs, narrow waist, wide shoulders under the vest. Tall, fit, fast, strong. She flicked a glimpse at the bush on her right. She was closer. He had a gun.

'Miranda, I think I know what happened. A man was seen in Wahroonga with a pistol.' His voice was still loud but there was less urgency and demand in it. Now it was filled with a message, a warning: *I'm the one in charge, so pay attention.* 'We can sort it out. But nothing's going to happen until you lose the gun.'

Behind him, uniformed cops had spread out in a semicircle, their weapons drawn from holsters, identical double-handed grips like a rehearsed manoeuvre. Patrol cars were blocking the motorway, lights flashing blue and red.

'Jax. Let it go. Just open your hand and let it fall to the dirt.' He took another step. *'Now.'*

10

W hatever else was going on, this guy was a cop, backed up by a lot of other cops. A headline ran through Jax's mind like breaking news: 'Woman draws weapon on police, shot dead on motorway'. She unlocked her fingers and the pistol dropped to the earth with a dull thud.

'Kick it away.'

She found it with the toe of her runner, sent it sideways. Away from both of them.

'Good.' Two steps closer, gun still firm in both of his hands. 'Are you carrying any other weapons?'

If he was asking that, he had no idea what had happened. 'It wasn't my gun. It's his. His name is Brendan Walsh. He made me drive.'

He spoke as though he hadn't heard her, walking while he did, stepping in so close that he needed to bend his elbows so his pistol didn't touch her sternum. 'I'm going to pat you down for weapons. You need to stand still and keep your hands away from your body. Do you understand?'

'Yes.' Except she couldn't stay still. Her body trembled uncontrollably as he released one hand from his weapon and ran it around her waist. Firm, practised, efficient - the gun still trained on her. His shoulder hovered near her chin; her eyes skipped beyond it, flicking from the uniforms to the patrol cars on the roadway to the queue of traffic banking up behind them. Did they think she was the bad guy?

He stepped back and lowered his voice, a little empathy creeping into it. 'It's okay, Miranda. I've been following you for almost an hour. You tried to speak to me in the car park.'

Her eyes snapped back to him as she pulled in a sharp breath. The man in the car park had been casual, calm - this one was bristling with authority and wearing body armour. But she saw now, the black-and-white top she'd watched in her rear-view was the vest over his business shirt, and the pale eyes ... up close were solid blue-grey, and resolute. The swell of fear she'd been holding at bay for hours turned to anger. 'You saw me all the way back *there*, before we even reached the car park? And you just *followed*? I've been stuck in that car with him for hours. For fucking *hours*."

He slid his gun into a holster at his hip. 'You left the car park twenty-four minutes ago. Three more minutes heading north and you would've hit my roadblock.'

Blinking, letting the news sink in, Jax thought of a roadblock and the kind of yelling, wheel-grabbing panic it would have started in Brendan. Neither of them would have survived. 'Oh, God. Brendan.' She put a hand to her mouth, started to turn, to look for him.

The cop held her in place with a hand at her elbow. 'You need to stay here.'

'Where is he? Is he dead?'

'I can't answer that.'

He didn't have to. The way he kept his eyes on her face and the grip on her elbow told her all she needed to know. That she didn't want to see what was across the road. 'Oh, God.'

The sob came from deep inside her, working its way up and out in a tremor that buckled her knees. The hand on her elbow became a vice at her arm, keeping her upright. Then another one, on the other side. Two people walking her forwards as her lungs grappled for air. Past the open passenger door of her car and her keys on the gravel, to the dark-blue sedan she'd watched in her rear-view mirror. She was lowered into the back seat, words being spoken but not to her. Instructions, questions, answers, multiple voices. Then a uniform was standing in the doorway, blocking the glare of the descending sun, and she was on her own in the car, watching as the man who'd held her to the spot with a gun walked around the grille. She wanted to cry, to howl and gasp and let tears pour unchecked down her face, but it wouldn't come. She'd been holding it back for hours, for most of the day, and now that she wanted to let go, her eyes were dry and her brain felt like it was on pause.

Outside, more people had arrived. Almost a crowd: some in uniform, others in jeans, a few in suits. The cop from the sedan was pointing and talking as he walked. Not telling the others what had happened, not some kind of, *I was here and she was there.* He was giving orders and they were nodding and leaving with a mission. He took a brief call on a mobile, five words tops, then tossed the phone for someone to catch. Clearly in charge of whatever was happening here.

Where the hell had they all come from? She heard Brendan in her head: *They found us. They've got us. We're fucked.* Was she?

On the motorway, an ambulance had pulled up in front of the crash site. Brendan was fucked, that was for sure. She put a hand to her chest, felt her heart slamming against her ribs and her lungs dragging at the solid heat in the car, a film of sweat clammy on her forehead. A loud whining filled her ears, her head. Great, she was having a heart attack.

'There'll be a bottle of water here soon.' The sedan guy was sitting beside her now. The taut authority that had bristled from him two minutes earlier had eased up, but only a fraction - and no shaking, no sweating, despite the standoff and the guns and the crashing cars. 'Are you cold?' he asked, his pale eyes taking in the way her arms were locked across her chest.

Jax shook her head. 'Who are you?'

'My name is Detective Senior Sergeant Aiden Hawke. I'll be keeping you here for the moment to answer some questions.'

Name, rank and purpose. Brief and clear. It said he was in charge and they weren't in here taking a breather now that the weapons were put away. He was a cop, Jax told herself as he turned away to speak to someone at the door. He was the good guy, right? But she was sitting in another car with another man and a gun. It was in a holster but it didn't feel right. It felt like she was still stuck in Brendan's nightmare - crazy, implausible events being driven by his fear and delusion. There *were* people coming after him, like he said; he didn't make it to his family, like he said. He was probably already dead. What was next?

The detective tucked a piece of paper inside his vest as he shifted back to her. 'Did you -'

'Do you know him?' she cut in. It was what the cop had asked her but ... *They found us. They've got us.* 'Is that why you were following me?'

There was a flicker of surprise in his face. 'I saw you swerve into another lane. You almost sideswiped another car.'

Yeah, she'd done that several times but there were at least twenty cops out there - overkill for bad driving. 'Brendan thought someone was after him,' she said. Then, wondering again if it was the police he'd been running from, accusation firmed in her tone. 'Was it you?'

A line appeared briefly between his brows. 'Do you know the man who was in your car?'

'His name is Brendan Walsh. He said people were after him, that they were trying to kill him.'

'So you know him?'

She glanced at the ambulance across the motorway. 'He's dead, isn't he?' She blinked at stinging eyes, trying to force tears that wouldn't come. 'He said they were trained and they wouldn't stop.'

The detective didn't answer, just watched her a moment, his expression giving nothing away except the cogs working hard behind his gaze.

A heavy pulse started up in her neck. Brendan had said the cops would fuck it up. Plural *cops*. Not a whole police force - that didn't make sense. But maybe cops who could make things happen. 'Is that what this is about? All of *this*?' She waved a hand at the activity outside the car, heard the anger in her voice. 'Was it *you*?'

His voice was measured and careful. 'Why did he think people were after him?'

She paused, feeling the prickle of Brendan's paranoia on her skin, suddenly wondering how much she should say, whether she'd already said too much.

'Miranda?'

'He said . . .' *There was something in his head he couldn't get out.* 'He said it was their job.' Her eyes flicked involuntarily to the gun in his holster.

The cop took in her glance, her folded arms, the way she leaned away from him. 'Why was he in your car?'

Jax licked her lips. She'd signalled to this guy in the car park. Maybe *she'd* fucked it up.

'Why are you scared, Miranda?'

She clasped her hands between her thighs. 'I don't know. Should I be scared?'

He took his time to respond. When he did, it wasn't to answer the question she'd asked. 'I want to understand what happened and I need you to help me.'

She settled her eyes on his face, a luxury she hadn't had with Brendan. Detective Senior Sergeant Aiden Hawke looked right back: no angst, no fear, no attempt to dodge her assessment. Just a silent, steady directness. The same look she'd seen over the roof of his car in the parking area.

'He said they had guns and ...'

'And what?'

'Missiles.' It sounded ridiculous now. 'He was terrified.'

The guy said nothing for a second. Maybe he was trying not to snigger, although he didn't look the sniggering type. When he spoke, it wasn't with veiled amusement. It was an explanation, a hint of reassurance in it. 'I was in Sydney for work and heading back to Newcastle. I started watching you after you swerved. I thought I saw a gun in his hand and it matched reports of an armed man seen in Wahroonga. I followed you to the service station, got a visual of the weapon, but I couldn't risk shots being fired in a car park. I've been setting up a roadblock and back-up since then. That's why these people are here.' He cocked his head at the window. 'I've got someone checking his name now. If he was running from the police, he probably had a reason to be scared, but I wasn't tailing him. We weren't looking for him. And we don't carry missiles.'

She waited for a mocking lift of an eyebrow but it didn't come. He wasn't making light of it: he was letting her know she was safe. She heard Brendan's voice again, the rambling, irrational way the words had fallen from him - nano spiders and things stuck in his head - and something large and frightened and half-crazed fell away from her.

The tears came then, tipping over her lids and spilling down her cheeks as though the storage tank in her tear ducts had cracked open. No tension-releasing howling, though, just a quiet sense of relief and exhaustion and sadness. Brendan had scared the hell out of her but he'd been a man in pain who'd loved his family - she'd wanted to get help, not wished him dead.

Beside her, the detective uncapped a bottle of water and pressed it into her hands. 'Sorry it's not cold.'

She didn't care. She lifted it to her lips with shaking hands and drank like she was dying of thirst. Liquid trickled out one side of her mouth. She wiped it with the back of a hand and drank some more.

Aiden Hawke didn't speak again until she'd slumped against the seat, rehydrated but still trembling. 'Are you okay?' he asked.

She didn't know the word for what she was right now. Maybe there wasn't a word for how a person felt after being abducted at gunpoint, terrified, confused, accused, grief-stricken and suddenly safe. It was something, though, and 'okay' was definitely not it. So she met the detective's eyes with an expression that tried to cover it all.

He nodded at her bottle of water. 'Sorry it's not stronger.'

'Me too.'

He smiled a little. It was a nice smile. The first she'd seen in a while. Possibly it was nice any time he did it.

'Brendan said a lot of crazy stuff,' she told him. 'I couldn't tell what was real and what wasn't. He talked about his wife and son. I don't think they're in his imagination. Maybe someone *is* after him.'

'We'll look into that.'

And there it was - another detective with answers that didn't tell her anything. Was it part of their training? 'He's dead, isn't he?'

'Yes.'

At least she finally had the truth on that one. She batted away the tear that fell for Brendan.

'How well did you know him?' he asked.

She shook her head. 'I need to call my daughter.'

He pulled a notebook and pen from under the bulletproof vest. 'Give me her details and I'll have someone speak to her.'

'She's six. *I* need to talk to her.'

'Is there anyone with her?' The question was about safety, not who would answer the phone.

'Yes, my aunt.'

'I'll have a detective call your aunt, let her know you're okay.'

'But -'

'Miranda, listen.' It was sharp, an instruction. 'We're not finished here. You need to answer my questions.' His curt tone conveyed the rest of his message: she couldn't call Zoe until she'd explained herself.

'What do you think I've done?'

11

Something tightened the detective's lips. Frustration, irritation, maybe a hint of amusement. 'I think you need to stop asking questions for a while and try to answer a few. Can you do that, Miranda?' The words were delivered with all the professional directness he'd maintained so far, with just a dash of *for-God's-sake*.

After being yelled at and shoved around and threatened with a gun, it felt good to be causing the aggravation - and he wouldn't be the first detective she'd ticked off with her questions. 'I'll try.'

He took a second to eye her off as though deciding how to interpret her, took down the home number Tilda had had for thirty years and passed it to someone outside the car.

'How do you know Brendan Walsh?' he asked.

'I don't. Or at least I didn't before he got in my car at Wahroonga.'

'Have you ever seen him before?'

'I interviewed him about five years ago for a newspaper article.'

'So you'd met him.'

'I don't remember him. He told me about it. There was a group of soldiers leaving for Afghanistan. I remember the day and the article but not him.'

'Had he been in contact with you since the interview?'

'No.'

'But he knew where to find you?'

'No, I don't think so.'

'He just turned up at your car, said, "Remember me, you interviewed me once," and asked for a lift?'

The edge of doubt in his tone made her hesitate - and remember that ten minutes ago she'd been holding a gun and surrounded by cops in bulletproof vests. This one wanted a reason and, so far, hers wasn't making sense.

She held up a hand. 'Can I start again?'

He pulled his brows together. 'You want to try another story?'

She didn't answer right away. Pulling in a breath, she gathered the facts together in her mind like notes she'd taken at a press conference, then told him. The *what, where, when* and *how*: heading to Newcastle, the gun, the shouting, the nano spiders, the trained people wanting to pick them off. She explained about Brendan wanting to kill himself and believing he was going to die anyway, about trying to get to his wife and son before 'they' got him first. She wished there was a why but all she had for that was Brendan's reasoning and she wasn't sure anyone would work that out.

The detective let her talk, eyes fixed on her face as though he was reading the story there as well. She was almost done when there was a knock on the chassis and a woman stuck her head into the open doorway. 'Sarge?'

'Excuse me a minute,' he told Jax and left her. Not quite alone - a uniformed officer stood at each door.

She took a sip of water and felt fatigue settle over her like a thick blanket. Limbs too heavy to lift, head an unbalanced weight on her neck. She wanted to close her eyes and sleep but her heart wouldn't stop hammering and her lids seemed to be fixed in the open position.

Beside the car, out of earshot, Aiden Hawke stood with his legs spread and his arms folded across his chest as his colleague did the speaking beside him, weapon on the belt of her trousers, clipboard and pen in hand. Out on the motorway, traffic was queued up behind patrol cars - bumper-to-bumper and snaking all the way back to the bend, probably a whole lot further out of sight. Above, two helicopters circled slowly. At least one of them was a TV news chopper.

Footsteps on the gravel made Jax glance at the windscreen. Aiden Hawke and the female detective were now standing beside Jax's car. All four doors were open, and someone was in the driver's seat. Aiden bent at the waist and peered into the rear, nodding while the woman pointed with a gloved hand. As he walked back to Jax, she tried to remember what was in there. A few cleaning products that would only hurt the environment. No gun collection to incriminate her.

The blue sedan rocked as Aiden got in. 'What are the boxes on your back seat?'

'I'm moving house.'

He frowned. 'Is that it?'

'No, the rest went up yesterday. I handed over the keys to my old house this afternoon.'

'You're moving to Newcastle?'

'Yes.'

'Where?'

'Merewether. It's my aunt's house.'

'She has two?'

'No. My daughter and I are moving in with her.'

He nodded.

The was no judgement in it but she wanted to clarify. 'My husband died last year. I had to sell the house.'

'I'm sorry. You're Nicholas Westing's wife, aren't you?'

The question caught her off guard, but she realised he must already know the answer and probably had a lot more information than that. He'd known her name when he pulled up and started shouting, and he'd got Jax from somewhere. He'd followed her for an hour or more, calling in troops, setting up a roadblock, probably checking the record of the owner of the car he was following. Possibly he had her email addresses and the balance on her bank account. 'Yes.'

'It's a good town. You'll enjoy being back there.' Maybe he had her residential history, as well.

'It's not a great start.' This whole day felt like a bad omen, made her wonder again if she'd done the right thing.

'No, I imagine it was a terrifying experience. I'm sorry it had to end like this.' He nodded towards the ambulance that stood like a shield beside the crash scene. Maybe it was for the best that she couldn't see what was over there. She'd had too many ugly images in her head over the past year; she didn't need more.

'Okay,' he said, *we're-done-here* in his tone. 'I'd like to get an official statement from you tonight, while the details are still fresh in your mind. But not here. You'll feel better when you can get away from all this. Do you think you can manage that?'

She wanted to hold Zoe, hug Tilda, have a stiff drink. She also wanted this over. 'Yes.'

'You'll have to leave your car here, so an officer will drive you to the station in Newcastle. One of my detectives has spoken with your aunt but you can call her yourself on the way in. I'll see you there in a while.' He shifted on the seat, getting ready to leave, paused a second and looked back. 'What did you say to me in the car park?'

The moment flashed through her memory. Spine- stiffening terror, the risk of trying to catch his attention, the relief when he was waiting for her eyes. 'Help me.'

He nodded once. Followed it with a sudden smile and a quiet huff of a laugh, as though she'd confirmed what he wasn't sure he'd seen. 'I'm sorry I couldn't make it end there - I didn't want to get you shot.' It was an aside, a sentence in parenthesis without the police-business tone. Maybe a message from Aiden Hawke, guy in the wrong place at the right time, instead of the detective who'd done his job.

'Nothing to be sorry about there,' she told him. Nodding again, he banged twice on the chassis as he got out, and was pointing and talking again before he'd left the doorway.

A UNIFORMED OFFICER told Jax her car would be towed to a police compound, fingerprinted and searched. Her handbag, when it was passed in to her, had clearly been through the search process already. The contents looked like they'd been tipped out and stuffed back in, and she wondered if it had happened before or after Aiden Hawke decided she was a victim and not an accomplice. There was no sign of her mobile. She guessed they'd find it in the glove box if they hadn't already, probably fingerprint it too. What would the detective make of Brendan's prints all over it?

Dusk turned the afternoon to early evening while Jax made the journey into the heart of Newcastle from the front of a patrol car - a trip that was as weird and off base as the rest of the day had been. The motorway heading north was deserted. Aside from a single police vehicle at the roadblock site, there wasn't another car to be seen. Just the faint glow of their own headlamps in the lowering light and the constant stream of traffic heading south.

Inside, the air was filled with the hum of the engine and constant chatter from the police radio. All of it was from the crash site, as though keeping Jax and her driver updated: crime scene investigators arrived, then another two ambulances for passengers in the minibus; a contraflow was being set up, sectioning off a lane on the other side of the motorway to start the process of getting the banked-up traffic moving. And the media made its presence felt - a news chopper had touched down on an empty section of motorway, reporters wanted details and an officer requested a spokesperson.

It was a big story. All of it - the gunman, the police operation, the massive traffic jam. Jax knew the news desk at her old paper would be trying to get a journalist and photographer into a chopper so they didn't have to wait at the back end of the traffic. Other reporters would be working the phones and their police contacts. They'd know it was her by now - the *who* travelled as fast as the *what* when there was an angle, and the angle on this was Nicholas Westing's widow involved in a police drama. His death would be rehashed yet again. Maybe it was just as well Jax's mobile was with the cops - she didn't want to take the inevitable calls.

The officer driving lent Jax a mobile and as she dialled Tilda's number, she tried to scrounge up words and a voice that said she was fine, brave, holding it together. 'Tilda, it's -'

'Jax, honey. Are you all right?' Tilda's 61-year-old voice was tremulous with concern.

'I, I'm . . .' She didn't finish, couldn't speak for the sobbing. 'Tilda, sorry. I'm okay, I just. . .'

'No, Jax, don't be sorry. Just so long as you're all right.'

Jax pulled in a loud, hitching breath, unable to answer, grateful just to hear her aunt's voice, reminded of other times, years ago, and the tears and reassurances between them. Newcastle would be okay. Tonight, anyway.

'I haven't told Zoe,' Tilda said. 'And I kept the news off the TV. Russell rang too, he knew it was you.'

'Yeah, I figured he would.' He'd handled the media for her before and she was hoping he'd do it again.

'Where are you now?'

Jax explained about the statement she had to make, said she didn't know how long she'd be, asked would Tilda pick her up from the station when she was done. It could be hours and it meant bringing Zoe out late but she needed to hug both of them.

At the station, she was given coffee, a chocolate bar from a vending machine and a seat in a glassed-in office that looked like a cross between a kitchenette and a meeting room. After the heat on the motorway, the air-conditioning was freezing, so the officer who'd been her driver found a blanket and then hung about like it was her job to keep an eye on Jax. Maybe it was. What would she watch for - signs of shock or criminal intent?

Jax's cheek was resting on the cool of the tabletop when Aiden Hawke walked in, crumpled shirt the only sign of a long day, his dark hair a foil to his pale irises. She followed him with her eyes until he'd pulled out the chair beside her, then she sat up and rubbed her face.

'Detective Hawke,' she said.

'Why don't you call me Aiden?'

'Aiden, then.'

'How are you going?'

'I've no idea. I've got nothing to compare it to.'

He blinked - not the response he'd expected, perhaps.

'I'm too exhausted to move but I can't close my eyes,' she explained. 'It feels really weird, a bit out-of-body, but maybe it's normal. What do you think?' Her mouth felt loose, the words a little slurry.

'It sounds like you're doing okay but you should try to talk to someone in the next day or so, a counsellor or psychologist. If you can't find one, I can give you the number for a victim support group.'

A full-service cop. 'Thanks.' She wondered if he'd be seeing someone too - he'd pointed a gun at a frightened woman, it would have to do something to his head. Not that he seemed perturbed about it now.

'Before we start with your statement, I want to let you know that our preliminary inquiries are indicating the man in your car *was* Brendan Walsh. He was under treatment for mental health issues and had stopped taking prescribed medication.'

No surprise there. 'Was it post-traumatic stress disorder?'

'PTSD has been mentioned, among other things.'

She nodded. He wasn't the only soldier to be injured by the memory of what he'd seen and done. 'What else?'

'Apparently there'd been some issues around,' he held up a finger, took a notepad from his shirt pocket and read: 'Anxiety, paranoia and fear of delusions.'

'Who feared the delusions? Brendan or the doctors?'

He hesitated. 'I can't clarify that as yet.'

Either way, nano spiders said the delusions had arrived. 'Was he frightened about people coming after him?'

'That detail wasn't discussed in the initial phone call but it's possible, likely even, that none of it was real.'

She nodded. It was possible. She could believe that - but she'd also believed Brendan, at least on some of it. 'Does he have a wife and son? Kate and Scotty?'

'He has a wife and child who live in Newcastle. I can't confirm their names for you.'

'He wanted to go to Newcastle.'

'Is that what he told you?'

'He never said where. He just wanted to get to Kate and Scotty.' And she'd imagined driving all the way to Queensland with a gun in her face. 'Did he go to Afghanistan?'

'We're still accessing his military records.'

'But he was in the military, right?' Or had Brendan read her article and imagined he was at the airbase with the other soldiers?

Aiden took a second to answer. 'There's nothing to indicate anyone was after him.'

She pressed her lips together, irritated that he hadn't given her a straight answer yet, recognising the tactic and already resenting it. She'd had twelve months of Homicide cops deciding how much she needed to know, picking and choosing what information they'd share, feeding it out like scraps to a hungry peasant.

'You're safe, Miranda,' he said.

Except for that - she needed to hear *that*. His words cut through her temper and started a fresh rush of tears. She wiped her face with a corner of the blanket, cleared her throat, folded her arms on the table, grateful for his silence while she pulled herself together.

When she was done, he picked up a pen from the pad he'd put on the desk. 'I'd like to get the details down while they're still fresh. Do you think you can manage that?'

The real question was whether she wanted the details to keep running through her head, weighing her down until she came back to the station to let them out. She knew what it was like to have shock and sadness linger inside her, and she wasn't sure she had room for more. She pulled in a breath. 'Yes, let's get it over with.'

It took another hour to go through it. He asked her to start from when she left the house, steered her back on track when she struggled to stay in chronological order, pressed gently for when and how Brendan had shouted or lunged or freaked out. She waxed and waned between being grateful for Aiden's patience and wanting to tell him to give her a damn break, all the time trying not to let the process remind her of the long hours she'd spent with police over Nick's death - crying, being interviewed, begging for information.

Halfway through, the uniformed cop came back with new bottles of water and a couple of takeaway sandwiches, and left to let Tilda know they'd be finished soon. When Aiden finally drew a line under his notes, Jax stretched her neck side-to-side, a ripple of cracks popping down her spine.

'I'd like to talk to you again when we've finished at the scene and completed the witness statements,' he said. 'Can you come in tomorrow afternoon? It'll give you a chance to add anything else you might remember.'

'I was hoping to forget it.'

He nodded - empathetic but insistent. 'I know you must want to put it behind you but we need to wrap it up properly.'

She thought of the past year, wondering how far they'd get with the wrapping up on this one.

The blanket was still around her shoulders as Aiden walked her downstairs and swung open the door to the foyer.

'Mummy!'

Zoe. Freckles and gap-toothed and soft, brown curls. Dragging Tilda across the waiting area, both of them wearing long, bright scarves and strings of Tilda's customary beads.

Jax dropped to her knees and caught her daughter in her arms. Hot tears welled behind her lids and she squeezed her eyes tight, trying to keep them from Zoe. She didn't need to see her mother like this. Not again.

12

I
t was dark and quiet on the streets of Newcastle as Tilda drove a familiar path home, over the headland and past a long stretch of beach.

'And Aunty Tilda said I could wear her scarf and beads,' Zoe told Jax from the back seat, talking non-stop as though one night apart had been a whirlwind holiday. 'She said I looked ... What was that word?'

'Gregarious,' Tilda answered.

'Oh, yeah. Gregarious.'

And Tilda would know, Jax thought, glancing at her aunt across the car. Wealthy, arty, trim and glamorous in a bohemian, owning-her-age kind of way.

Zoe told Jax about the curry she'd helped cook and the painting at the gallery they'd visited and the peppermint tea she was allowed to taste.

Jax tried to enjoy her daughter's chatter, glad Zoe didn't know what had happened, wincing as the volume grated on the headache pulsating inside her skull. She turned her face to the passenger window and watched the fluorescent white crests of surf on the black ocean, remembering another time in Tilda's car, passing this way with nothing but the clothes she'd been wearing.

That night, the stench of smoke had still clung to her hair from the fire that burned her home to the ground and turned her parents to ash.

Her world-travelling, childless aunt had driven out west and picked her up, and Jax had arrived with no money and shattered by tragedy. Now, nineteen years and a lifetime later, she didn't feel a whole lot different - except this time, she'd brought a daughter.

Novocastrians had a theory that people who grew up here and left would eventually want to come back. There was plenty of reason to: Newcastle was a great place to bring up families or retire, where you could afford to live by the beach without spending every waking hour at a job that kept you away from it. Nick had talked about moving up - he'd figured they could both work from home and enjoy a better, freer lifestyle - but Jax had never wanted to return. Not to live. Newcastle was where she'd grieved, hurt and healed. The concept of returning had always felt like a backward step.

And now she was here and feeling like hell - for old and new reasons.

Tilda pulled the car into the garage and the three of them trundled through the internal door to the large, tiled foyer that sat midway between the two levels of the house. The sight of cardboard boxes stacked to one side made Jax's headache grind and a groan slip from her throat.

'Don't even think about it now,' Tilda said. 'Zoe and I made up your bed and found your jim-jams, didn't we?' Zoe looked up at them and nodded, bouncing strands of hair framing her freckles. Tilda gave Jax's shoulder a gentle rub. 'You don't need anything else tonight but dinner and a Scotch, and both are waiting for you upstairs.'

Jax glanced briefly down the half of the staircase that led to the lower level where she and Zoe would be living. The self-contained apartment had been painted two weeks ago and there was still a hint of the chemical smell in the air that wafted up. It was theirs - lovely, roomy, a financial blessing.

And the end of another life.

Trailing Zoe and Tilda up the stairs, Jax lifted her eyes to the expanse of glass at the top. Even exhausted, she found it hard not to be gobsmacked by the view. Tilda's two storeys were on the side of a hill, the top level looking towards the city, the lower facing the vastness of the Pacific Ocean. Tonight, the suburbs that stretched out below the house were a carpet of fairy lights that edged the surf all the way to the darkness of the next headland. Off to the right, navigation lights on the ships queuing for the port hung like lamps suspended in deep, dark space.

Five months ago, when Tilda suggested the living arrangements, it had been four years since Jax had visited. The house was too big for one person, Tilda told her. The downstairs area had been converted to a flat for a nurse back when Archie, her third husband, was dying of cancer. Jax and Zoe could move in, Tilda said. Have their own space while Jax decided what to do with the rest of their lives. And Tilda could use the time - however long it took - to think about moving somewhere smaller.

Jax and Zoe had come up for a trial run: two nights downstairs, visiting schools and supermarkets, cafes and the beach. That was three months ago - and now Jax was here for a second time ... to stay.

Tilda sat her at the table, delivered a bowl of curry and a neat Scotch, and said, 'Eat, drink and let me get Zoe ready for bed.'

When they were gone, Jax let her eyes wander around the room. She was keyed up and numb, her head ached and there was something wobbly inside her - and she wanted to be home. Her own home. The one she'd made with Nick.

Half an hour later, Jax had kissed Zoe goodnight, stood in a steaming shower and scrubbed at the grit from the motorway and the stink of fear. She wanted to sleep but her blood felt like a white-water course charging through her - way too wired to even lie down. Needing company, padding back upstairs, she was rising from the stairwell when Tilda saw her and switched off the television. Jax nodded at the blank TV screen. 'What are they saying?'

'The traffic's banked up for almost ten kilometres,' Tilda told her, avoiding the real story as she held the phone out to her. 'Russell called again while you were downstairs. He's worried about you.'

'Was he at home?'

'I don't know.'

Tilda dropped ice cubes into two cut-glass tumblers as Jax stood by the windows, fiddling with buttons until she found the last number on the call register: the newsroom. 'Hey, it's me.'

'Fuck, Jax. Are you okay?' He'd been Nick's best friend for years, her self-appointed sergeant-at-arms since his death. It felt bloody good to hear his voice.

'Shaken up, freaked out, mostly just happy to be alive to tell someone about it.'

'Have you seen the coverage?'

She took the fresh Scotch from Tilda, smiled her thanks. 'Not yet. Are they still running it?'

'TV had a chopper in the air when the police reports started coming in. It got there just after the cops. They went live during the news and they've been running the vision every half hour since. It's on again now.'

Picking up the remote from the coffee table, Jax hit power and flicked around the channels until she found it. 'Oh my God.'

The picture was grainy and shaky from distance, but it was clear enough - the pull-over zone shot from above, two figures with guns. Aiden Hawke's arms were an arrow pointing straight ahead as he paced slowly towards her. She was loose and swaying, head turning one way then the other. Then her gun was on the ground and Aiden was patting her down, holding her up, half-carrying, half-dragging her to his car with the help of someone in uniform. It'd felt different to that. Slower, stranger. Less American reality cop show, more bad dream. The sight of it made her bones feel too tight.

'What about the crash?' Jax asked. 'Are they showing the crash? He's dead, Russell. The guy from my car is dead. He ran into the traffic right in front of me.'

His voice softened. 'We know that now but it took a while for the information to come through. I don't think even the cops knew what had happened for a while.' He paused. 'Jax, do you want to say something?'

He wasn't waiting for her to go on. She knew what he meant. They'd been news reporters together once. The four of them: Nick, Russell, his wife Deanne and Jax. Russell was now features editor at the paper and Jax hadn't put 'news' or 'reporter' on her business card in a few years but this was a big story, it was why he was still in the office at 9 pm on a Monday. He was the go-to guy for a quote from her - and he knew how hard it'd been having Nick's story rehashed over and over during the past year.

'I can't do an interview tonight. I can't think straight, I can barely string words together. And I'm already on my second Scotch.' She took a gulp, swirled the ice in the glass beside the phone so he'd hear it.

Another pause from him. She knew he wanted the scoop - who wouldn't? - but they'd been here before. She didn't want to *be* the story anymore, and it'd been his advice twelve months ago to let someone handle it for her.

'What about a statement?' he asked.

'Can you do it?'

'Spokesperson for Miranda Jack?'

'No, it sounds like I've walked off the motorway and hired PR. Make it "family friend".'

'What do you want?'

She perched on the edge of the sofa, trying to think. 'Say he got in the car in Wahroonga. He had a gun and wanted me to drive north.' She stood again and walked back to the windows, thinking about Brendan's break with reality, remembering what it was like to have other people discuss Nick. 'Say he seemed frightened and desperate and he wanted to get to his family.'

'What about you?'

She watched the reflection of herself in the glass, remembered the look in her eyes when she'd seen herself in the cafe restroom. 'You can say I was fucking scared.'

'Hard to put in a headline.'

'True. How about I was scared but I'm okay now. Saddened by the tragic outcome and my heart goes out to his family.' Bare bones but all true. 'You can pretty it up.'

'You want to see it before it goes out?'

'No, I want to ...' *Be someone else.* '... sleep.'

'You sure you're okay?'

'I'm too tired to know what I am. Before you go?'

'Yes?'

'Can you dig out a story for me? Brendan, the man in the car ... he thought I'd interviewed him once, but I don't remember. There was a feature about five years ago, April or May I think. Double-page, soldiers leaving for Afghanistan, headline was something about tears and fears and goodbyes.'

'So it *wasn't* random?'

'Yes, it was. He didn't know who I was until I started talking to him.'

'What did you talk about?'

'Just stuff, anything I could think of. I was trying to calm him down. It didn't work very well but he asked about my husband, wanted to know where he was.'

Don't lie!

She squeezed her eyes shut as Brendan's voice charged through her head. 'He wanted to know how my husband died, then figured out it was Nick and that I was, well, me.'

'Can I use that?'

She sipped on the Scotch, stared at the TV: a reporter was doing a stand-up with the crash site in the background. 'You can say I interviewed him before but keep Nick out of it. He's had enough said about him.'

'Sure. And if I find the feature, I'll email it to you.'

'Will you look tonight?'

'Yeah, sure.'

'Thanks. Now get to work so you can go home and tell your wife you love her.' Like Brendan had wanted to.

As she disconnected, Tilda picked up the remote and aimed it at the television.

'Leave it on,' Jax told her. 'It makes it feel real. I've barely got a scratch on me. I just feel like I've had an injection of adrenaline.' She perched on the arm of the sofa again, sipped Scotch as she listened to the sketchy details in the voice-over: gunman confirmed dead after being hit by a vehicle heading north as he tried to escape police; three passengers from the minibus and the driver of the Ford injured in the crash, none listed as serious; no details on where Miranda Jack was heading when the man got in her car; confirmation the carjacker worked in private security, was living in Sydney but had recently relocated from Newcastle.

He was in private security? An armed guard, a bouncer ... or a body-guard? Had he been guarding someone today? Someone who had people after them?

'You look fearless,' Tilda said, nodding at the TV.

'You think?' Jax watched the scene in the pull-over zone again, muscles clenched as she tried to connect the images with her memories.

'Like you got up in the morning ready for action.'

She'd got up this morning to pack the remains of a life she'd loved into boxes that were now in police custody. 'If I'd known I was going to be on national television, I might've chosen something else to wear.'

'Oh, I don't know. Leggings and a singlet are perfect for a carjacking.'

'You think?'

'Sure. It'll be called carjack couture next week.'

Jax huffed a short laugh, lifted her glass in a toast. 'Here's to being a fashion statement.'

Tilda patted the seat of the sofa. 'Why don't you try to relax?'

She glanced at it from her spot on the armrest. She probably should. She'd never sleep if she didn't loosen up, but the thought of relaxing made her tense. Made her want to be ready to bolt if she needed to. 'No, I'm okay. I'm ... I don't know.' She closed her eyes, pushed a hand into her hair. 'What am I doing, Tilda?'

Her aunt shifted along the sofa, curled a comforting hand around Jax's knee. 'You're trying to cope.'

'I thought coming here was the best thing to do, then I almost got killed on the way. What does that mean?'

'It means life is heartless sometimes and sometimes we have to say "fuck you".'

It hadn't helped in the past year. 'I love it when you get eloquent.'

'I rather like it too.'

Chuckling a little, Jax let her eyes shift around the room again. The furniture was updated, the kitchen renovated and Tilda's artworks - her own and her collection - had been renewed since Jax's days here as a teenager. The past was still there, though. Jax could feel it.

'Will you take Zoe if I die?' she asked.

Other issues had to be taken into account before that decision could be made - Nick's parents and brothers at the very least - but Tilda took her hand and said, 'Of course.' Jax was grateful her aunt didn't try to rewrite history and tell her it wouldn't happen. She'd lost her mother and father in the one devastating fire, Zoe was down one parent already and Tilda had buried two husbands. They both knew the different ways life could be heartless - Jax just wondered whether it was satisfied with what it'd achieved so far or whether it was only warming up.

13

When Jax finally closed her eyes in the quiet of her new bedroom, images ran behind her lids like a confusing, drug-induced seventies movie. Brendan Walsh with a gun aimed at her face. Aiden Hawke with a gun aimed at her face. The motorway, the crash. Yelling, screaming. Then it got mixed up with Nick's crime scene - the one she'd visited, with a bloodstain enclosed by blue-and-white police tape, and the one in photos, with his body under a sheet.

A little before 4 am, she woke crying. Tears streaming, breath catching, a name on her lips, although she wasn't sure which one when consciousness finally took hold. Wiping her eyes, she reached a hand automatically over the side of the bed, felt around for a moment before realising the document box that was always there had been stacked with the packing cartons around the walls of her room. She flipped a lamp on and got up, found it among the larger containers, sat cross-legged on the mattress and lifted the lid. Just walking her fingers along the familiar edges of the hanging files was enough to settle the anxious restlessness of her nightmare. Like an addict preparing a fix.

It was two nights since she'd read from one - not that it mattered where she left off, she knew them all word-for-word. She started from the front again, pulling the first manila folder onto her lap and opening the cover. The words blurred and shimmered in the dim light. She pulled the lamp closer, rubbed at her eyes, at the centre of her forehead where her headache had settled, gave it a minute or two then went in search of painkillers.

None in the boxes in her room or the ones in the hallway so she tiptoed upstairs and tried Tilda's kitchen cupboard, the one above the stove - same place she'd always kept them. Jax downed two, was on her way back to the stairs when the lights of the city outside pulled her in a new direction. On the deck, a gentle, balmy breeze tugged at her hair as she rested her elbows on the railing. She breathed it in, told herself this was what she was here for. To let go, to find a way to heal the gaping hole in her life.

For a year, she'd asked questions and searched for answers. The only thing she'd got was an obsession. It took time away from Zoe, made friends keep their distance and filled Jax with endless circling thoughts. This morning's gasping wrench from sleep was the first time in twelve months she hadn't woken with the sweating horror that Nick's death might never be explained. Brendan Walsh had scared the hell out of her but maybe he'd shoved a wedge into the spinning wheels of her frustration.

You don't want to know anything I know. I don't want to know what I know.

Had PTSD done that to Brendan? How awful did a memory have to be to make a person lose touch with reality? Maybe it took more than one terrible event to make the brain struggle under its burden: the first opening a crack and each one that followed pushing it wider. Or was the damage caused by making yourself front up for more? Soldiers going back into battle, police officers to their jobs, emergency workers to another accident scene.

Jax had suffered overwhelming grief twice in her life and the psychological toll each time had felt like an injury. But she hadn't witnessed the fire that took her parents or the incident that killed her husband. Would she have been pushed over the edge if those images were caught in her brain?

Brendan had scrubbed at his scalp like he wanted to break it open and tear out his thoughts. How much of what had been stuck in his brain was memory - and how much was delusion?

Walking back through the darkened lounge room, Jax opened a laptop on a desk in the corner. She had studied for final school exams on the antique walnut unit and her aunt had run the specs of the slimline computer past Nick before buying it. Jax brushed those memories aside as she accessed her email account, skimming over the dozen or so new emails, not interested in replying to reporters yet, stopping at Russell's name.

His note was brief: *Good memory. You were close on headline and date. It was the first weekend in May. Call me if you need anything.*

Pulse picking up, Jax clicked on the article and read the headline: 'The long kiss goodbye: Tears and fears for families and soldiers'. Scrolling quickly through the first paragraphs, recognising her style more than the words of a story written five years ago, she paused at the first photo - a tear-jerker shot, a soldier snuggling into the chubby cheeks of a babe-in-arms. Not Brendan. Skimming and pausing through a few hundred words of copy, Jax stopped again at a group shot. It was a casual line-up of about fifteen soldiers in fatigues, back row standing, the rest sitting or kneeling on the floor. She zoomed in on the caption, searched the names and ranks.

Second-last mention: *Private Brendan Walsh.*

Enlarging the photo, she slid it across the screen, scanned the faces, her eyes stopping at the bottom right-hand corner, second one in. And her lungs caught on a gasp. He was different - younger, beefier, happier, saner - but there was no mistaking him. Brendan Walsh: dark hair little more than stubble, intense eyes gazing straight down the lens of the camera as though he was staring at her. A tingle rippled across her scalp.

'You were there,' she said aloud. 'That was real.'

What about the quote? *Got me some kudos for a bit*, he'd said. She typed in a search for his name, but the only reference that came up was the one she'd already found in the caption.

Focus drifting away from the monitor, she sifted through her memories of the hours she'd spent at the airbase. Not just grabbing a couple of interviews and leaving the photographer to finish up with the pics. She'd wanted to ignore the rhetoric about the war and cliches of soldiers flying to foreign lands, and try to understand what it was like to live that moment, both for the ones in uniform and those being left behind. It takes time to do that, to make people comfortable enough to talk, to trust the person with the pen and paper, to get them past the bluster of meeting a reporter. It was what she liked most about the job, what she did best.

She'd sipped takeaway coffee with wives and husbands, cooing over a newborn and swapping labour ward stories; she'd cursed fluently with the soldiers so that her nice skirt and heels didn't mark her as straight-laced; and she'd stood around with fit, muscular, well-trained people of rank feeling podgy and strangely civilian. Then she'd singled out a few for interviews - a private who'd seemed introspective and articulate, a woman whose accountant husband was barely holding back the emotion, a weathered forty-year-old leaving for his fourth tour, a wife with three children under five. Not Brendan.

She scrolled back to the group photo, recalling the joking and cajoling it'd taken to pull that shot together. As the photographer had snapped, she'd called out lighthearted questions to keep them entertained and in place: What food will you miss the most? What's the worst army meal? What won't you miss? What won't you leave home without?

Jax wound through the story again to the couple of paragraphs she'd written on their answers. No names, just a representation of their answers, things readers could relate to: liquorice all-sorts, vodka shots, cauliflower in cheese sauce, shitty nappies, wedding ring, suncream. She stopped at the last sentence, the one direct quote: *'Pride,' one soldier shouted. 'I want my wife and son to be proud of me.'*

She remembered now. The question: If you could leave only one word with your family, something they could stick on the fridge and see every day, what would it be? Plenty of words had been thrown back: laugh, love, drink, bills, text, Skype. Then a man had called out, 'Pride,' and it had stilled the laughter. Another man had said, 'Yeah, pride.' Others had murmured agreement and a hand from above had patted him on the head ... It was someone over on the right, maybe sitting on the floor.

She squinted at the photo again. Brendan was on the floor, one knee raised, an elbow resting on it.

'Did *you* say it?' she asked him now. 'Or did you just want to?'

'Jax?'

She jumped so hard her chair scraped on the tiles.

'Are you all right?' Tilda said from the kitchen, the single light above the stove turning her chic white hair into a halo.

'I think I just had a heart attack.'

'Sorry. I thought I heard you moving around out here. Can't sleep?'

'Weird dreams.'

Tilda's slippers *scuff-scuffed* on the floor as she shuffled across the darkened room. 'What are you doing?'

'Russell sent me that article.'

'It's four-thirty in the morning.'

'I came up for Panadol and ...' Jax shrugged. 'I just wanted to see it.'

'Of course you did. You can't help yourself, can you?' Tilda patted Jax's shoulder as she looked at the screen.

'Brendan was confused. He said a lot of things and I wanted to know if this,' Jax pointed at the article, 'was real. And it was. He *was* there. That's him.' She touched his face.

Tilda leaned in, squinting without her reading glasses, face illuminated by the glow. She lifted a hand, ran it over Jax's hair. 'It's sad.'

'Yes. It is.'

'Why don't you try to get some rest? Zoe will be up early.'

'Mmm.'

'You must be tired.'

'Mmm.'

Her aunt slipped her fingers under Jax's arm and tugged gently. 'Come on, honey. Don't exhaust yourself with this too.'

Standing, shutting down the article and her email account as she did, Jax let Tilda lead her to the top of the stairs.

'Don't come down. I'm okay.' She kissed Tilda's cheek, feeling her concerned presence hanging at the top of the stairs until she reached the bottom floor and the light above flicked off.

She didn't go to bed though. Arms folded across her chest, she wandered through the gloom of the sitting room, around the boxes and furniture that sat where the removalists left them. The self-contained apartment was smaller than Tilda's floor above and without the impressive artworks that hung on her walls, but two bedrooms, one bathroom and a cosy kitchen/lounge was plenty big enough for a widow and her six-year-old daughter. *And that's all we are now.*

Down the hall, Jax stood in Zoe's doorway for a long time, watching her sleeping face in the dim light that came through the curtains, telling herself she'd done the right thing. Then she went to her own room, sat on the edge of the bed and cried. Not for the reasons she'd cried on other nights. For another man. For the soldier in the photo and the person she'd met in her car. All the versions of him - happy, proud, frightening, sobbing, desperate, crazed.

And questions started to gather inside her. What kind of man got in a car and pointed a gun at a stranger? What happened to him to make him like that - was it something over there or something here? What was real and what wasn't?

How hard would it be to get answers? He was having some sort of medical treatment, he had a wife, a military history. Maybe a lot easier than the answers she'd spent a year searching for.

14

It was seven-thirty when something hit Jax in the shin. Her hands tightened into fists as her eyes flew open, expecting Brendan's gun in her face.

'Morning, Mummy.' Zoe's smile showed off the gaps where baby teeth had fallen out - three and counting.

Jax cleared her throat, didn't quite manage to loosen the spasm of panic in her gut. 'Morning, Zoe.'

'I wasn't scared last night.'

Well, at least that was one of them. 'Good, baby.'

'I was scared a little bit that night you weren't here and Aunty Tilda slept in your bed, but not last night.'

'Uh-huh.'

'So you didn't have to come into my bed.'

'Okay.' It had helped Jax, though. She rolled onto her back, balancing on the edge of the single mattress, telling herself that her own scary dreams weren't a good reason to start climbing into bed with Zoe. It'd taken months to get her daughter to stay in her own room again after Nick's death - and Zoe didn't need to have her mother waking in fright beside her.

'Aunty Tilda says I'll get used to the sound of the beach,' Zoe said. 'She says then I won't be able to sleep when I can't hear it. Is that what it was like when you lived here?'

Jax rubbed at a knot of tension in her neck, too exhausted by the present to make her memory sift that far back. 'Maybe. I can't remember.'

'Can we go to the beach today?'

'We'll see.' She found a smile, hoped it didn't look like a grimace. Watching the TV version of the motorway drama had made it seem like a nightmare. Then she'd had nightmares and now she wasn't sure she wanted to leave the house. Or drive a car.

When she'd decided to take up Tilda's offer to move in, Jax planned to start the first day in their new home the way she wanted to continue: her and Zoe downstairs, Tilda doing her own thing upstairs - sending a gentle message that they all needed to respect each other's boundaries if this arrangement was going to work. Thanks to Brendan Walsh, there was no food and no flat surface that wasn't covered in boxes.

Tilda had seen the state of their apartment and must have made her own decisions about the first day because as soon as Jax and Zoe were up and about, she called down the stairs, told them to ignore the mess and come up for breakfast on the deck.

'Fruit and toast, nothing flash,' she said, as they sat down to bowls of fresh melon and berries and a selection of fancy jams. Wearing a long filmy beach dress over a black, one-piece swimming costume, Tilda looked like she'd ordered the food from the resort kitchen, not thrown it together herself.

'Where's my cereal, Mummy?' Zoe asked, swinging her legs under the chair, already dressed hopefully in purple swimmers and yellow floaties.

'I haven't found it yet, baby,' Jax told her. 'Have some rockmelon, it's yummy.'

'But I like my cereal.' She was a one-breakfast kid - flakes and milk and a glass of juice, 364 days a year. At least for the last two.

'I know, baby. But you like fruit, too. Here, try a strawberry.' Jax forked three bite-sized berries onto her plate, hoping a useless fact from the collection depot in her brain might help. 'In Germany, some farmers hang strawberries on their cows' horns to make the elves happy.'

Zoe held on to the edge of the table, swinging her legs, making no attempt to eat. Jax poured coffee and took a long gulp as the tension in her neck spread tendrils across her shoulders.

'You ate strawberries for breakfast yesterday,' Tilda reminded her.

'That's because Mummy said you don't have children and you don't know little kids like to have cereal.' She looked at Jax to confirm the quote. Oh, yes, word for word.

Tilda flicked a quick, amused glance at Jax. 'Well, that's true. Maybe you can tell me about this cereal while you eat your breakfast.'

As Zoe ate and explained the joys of breakfast from a box, Jax clung to her coffee and read the local paper. The front page carried sequential photos from the pull-over zone stand-off: Miranda Jack and Detective Senior Sergeant Aiden Hawke with pistols drawn, Jack dropping gun, Jack being searched for weapons, Jack collapsing and being dragged to a police vehicle. And a final overhead photo of the kilometres of traffic backed up on the motorway, as though she was responsible. Well, she was, sort of.

The details of the drama were spread across pages four and five, accompanied by more photos, a map of her route along the motorway and a timeline, including her pee stop at the cafe. The 'gunman' was confirmed as Brendan James Walsh, a private security officer and former infantryman in the Australian Army, who'd completed two tours of Afghanistan.

Jax's gaze wandered to the view for a moment. Two tours of Afghanistan. He hadn't sat in a command centre - the infantry were the guys who saw the action. The way he'd handled a gun had already told her that much.

Plane or chopper, she heard him say. They'd been playing Zoe's game. *Plane*, she'd said. *Less chance of being thrown from the wreckage and dying slowly.*

I've seen that, he'd said. *It's a bad way to go.* Had he seen it in Afghanistan?

She skimmed the double-page spread, hoping it might tell her. A comprehensive yet disconcerting job, she thought. Although it would've been better without the sidebar on her and Nick - investigative reporter killed in hit-and-run, wife's pleas for police to continue investigation, wife tells last month's inquest she hasn't been able to work since the accident, coroner hands down open finding.

Jax stood up and paced to the railing. She took a breath of cool morning air, attempting to appreciate the view but went back to the paper as though it was calling her.

The main story quoted a family friend, a.k.a. Russell: *Walsh was one of a group of soldiers Miranda had interviewed, five years ago.* Blah blah. *Miranda attempted to calm her abductor by talking to him.* Blah blah.

Miranda is fine and resting at the home of a family member, grateful to be alive but saddened by the tragic end to her ordeal. She thanked police for their efforts.

Yes, and Jax would personally like to thank Detective Senior Sergeant Aiden Hawke for not shooting her. And her dead husband's friend for his support as her tragic life once again becomes worthy of front-page news. *Shit.*

While Tilda headed off for her 'few easy laps' of the ocean pool at the bottom of the hill, Jax eyed off the laptop on the walnut desk as she cleared the breakfast dishes. There would be more media coverage online. It might have different information about Brendan; maybe it would confirm what was real or wasn't. On her second trip from the deck, Jax switched the laptop on, watching it warm up while she stacked plates into the dishwasher.

'Can we go to the beach now?' Zoe asked just as Jax put fingers to the keyboard.

She'd finally promised over breakfast - when fresh coffee had taken the edge off the apprehension that had been with her since she left the motorway, and after Tilda reminded her she didn't need to get in a car - that she and Zoe could walk from the house. Jax glanced at the screen, tried to sound enthusiastic. 'Give me ten minutes.'

The stand-off with Aiden Hawke and subsequent ten- kilometre traffic jam had made international headlines. No surprise there: the pictures were impressive and it'd taken hours for the vehicles to clear. But details about Brendan were still sketchy and no-one had come forward with a tell-all about the dead carjacker.

As Jax hit Enter for another search, Zoe ran at her from the top of the stairs, pink plastic bucket and spade now accompanying the swimmers and floaties. 'Ready!'

'Yes, you are.' Jax laughed, told herself not to look back at the screen. She'd promised - and she'd promised herself to do better for Zoe here. Her daughter had missed out enough over the last year, with nothing to show for it. Jax closed the laptop, put hands on her hips. 'So where's *my* bucket?'

Downstairs, though, as she rummaged through boxes for beach towels, the apprehension freshened and she gave up the search, running upstairs instead for Tilda's phone.

'Aiden Hawke.'

'It's Miranda,' she told him. 'From last night.' Then she remembered his calm, unruffled composure and figured it was possible he hadn't gone home and collapsed in a heap like she had, that there might be another woman ringing with the same opening line. 'The carjacking?'

The hint of a smile in his voice. 'Yes, I remember. Actually, it's not one I'm likely to forget. How are you this morning?'

Tired, wired, worried. 'I'm okay, thanks. I wanted to take my daughter to the beach and thought I should check first about. . .' She stopped, swallowed.

'What time to come in?'

'No, I was thinking about what Brendan said. About people following him. I don't want to take her out if there are ... if you've found ... any indication of ...' *I'm not the only one with a weapon. They've got them. They're prepared.*

'Someone pursuing him?' he asked. 'We've found nothing to suggest Brendan Walsh was being followed.'

She'd hoped for, *We've found them, they're in custody* - or even, *Brendan's doctor confirmed it was all in his head.* 'Does that mean no-one was or you're still checking?'

'I understand your fears but I don't think there are safety issues around taking your daughter out.'

He was a cop - why had she expected a straightforward answer? 'Okay. I guess I'll have to work with that.'

'It's also worth considering, Miranda, that if there was someone looking for Brendan Walsh, they have no reason to keep looking now.'

Because he was dead. Slipped from her hands and killed in front of her. She squeezed her eyes shut. 'Yes, that's a point.'

'I'll see you at three-thirty to go through your statement.' It sounded like a reminder.

She didn't need another one. 'Yes.'

JAX KICKED off thongs and sank her feet into the cool morning sand. It was still too early for the January throngs to be out in full and she'd found a spot for her and Zoe in a prime position - between the flags and close to the ragged edge left by the retreating tide. While Zoe got started with her bucket and spade, Jax sat on a towel and lifted her face to a huge dome of deep blue sky. A single wisp of cloud hung high above, as though a bridal veil had been swept up to heaven. A breeze moved gently around her, bringing wafts of salt and suncream and the hot chips someone was eating nearby.

Jax wanted to enjoy it, wanted to breathe out and let go - of yesterday, of the past year, of the questions. But the pain was physical today: shoulders, neck, back, thighs, her right big toe. There were bruises on her legs and arms from being dragged around; she couldn't remember what had happened to her foot but the rest must be from two hours of holding herself rigid and waiting for death. Maybe she hadn't quite stopped doing that, because she also felt jittery and on edge, barely able to loosen the arms that were clutched around her knees.

Watching Zoe dig, she wondered how Brendan's wife and son were holding up this morning, remembering how it'd been after Nick died. At five, Zoe had been too young to understand the permanence of his passing or the hole it had torn in their lives, but she'd understood enough to be hushed and frightened by the sombre-faced people arriving at their house, the continual ringing of the phone and her mother's frequent tears.

Those first hours and days had been filled with a foggy, groggy sense of unreality. At seven forty-five one morning, two and a half weeks after Christmas, Jax had watched Nick pull on shorts and a fluoro vest and kissed him goodbye. Four hours later, she was told he was dead. There before breakfast, gone by lunch.

His body was found by a motorist beside a road in a short stretch of bushland, forty minutes' drive from home. His car was 3.1 kilometres away, parked neatly at the kerb in a quiet suburban street, his wallet in the glove box, laptop on the front passenger seat, and a document box in the rear, the kind he'd used for collecting and collating research. Nick was in his running clothes, car key zipped into a pocket, mobile phone in his hand. He'd lived long enough to try to make a call. Not Triple-o. There were four digits on the screen, the start of a mobile number. Not Jax's. Not Russell's. Someone's.

Brendan Walsh had told Jax his wife would be just like her. *I'll be dead and she'll be a widow and my kid will have no father.* Except Brendan's wife would *know* what had happened to her husband. It wasn't a heroic story, not something she could label with 'pride' - but it would be an explanation.

'Can we go for a swim now?' Zoe was covered head to toe in sand, the bucket and spade tossed aside.

Jax blinked away tears as she smiled. 'I think you need to.'

Zoe chased waves in and ran squealing back out as they followed her up the beach. She rolled about in the shallows, getting tussled and tumbled by the wash of a decent surf. Jax stood at the water's edge, remembering when she'd been the fun mum who'd dug holes and splashed about with her daughter. She'd hoped coming to Newcastle might help her find that person again. Maybe it would, in time, but not this morning. Last night Brendan Walsh had been a circuit-breaker; today he was a ghost at her shoulder, like he'd been in her passenger seat, his fear and paranoia hovering like a stranger who stood too close.

'Look, Mummy!' Zoe was lying in the shallows, water rushing around her as she pointed skywards.

A helicopter was sweeping around the headland, tipping a little as it turned towards the beach. Squinting in the glare, apprehension in her stomach, Jax kept her eyes on it as it followed the shoreline all the way to the end of the beach. *They're watching, letting us think we've got away, but they're not letting us go, Jax.*

Goose bumps rose on the back of her neck as though the ghost of Brendan had reached out and touched her. *How much was real, Brendan?*

Jax pulled her hat lower. 'Time to go now, Zoe.'

15

Tilda was on the phone when they spilled through the front door, breathing hard from their walk up the hill. As they discarded thongs and hats, Jax heard concern in the 'mmm's and 'yes-yes's that drifted down the stairs before Zoe ran up.

'Here they are now,' Tilda said into the receiver. Then, to Jax: 'It's Deanne.'

'Take your shells out to the deck,' Jax told Zoe as she took the phone. 'Hey, Deanne.'

'Russell said you sounded exhausted last night and I thought I'd let you sleep, but I figured you'd had enough by now. How are you?'

Jax smiled at the voice of honey and vice in her ear. Blessed with extraordinary vocal cords, Deanne was the only one of the four friends who'd left the print media for electronic news and had suffered the ups and downs of a career in radio. She was currently between jobs and had spent Friday and Saturday with Jax at the house helping with the packing.

'I don't know,' Jax replied. 'A little numb, a tad jumpy. It feels like a bad dream I can't switch off.'

'It was no dream. You knocked Nina Torrence off the front page.'

'Not sure that's any claim to fame.'

'At least you're alive.'

'There's that.'

Nina Torrence was a high-profile solicitor who'd been found stabbed and thrown from a cliff in Sydney on Sunday. They'd both known her years ago - Nina the clever new lawyer at a criminal defence firm, Deanne and Jax trying to make a start in the print media. She'd given them a few leads, they'd put her name in the newspaper, and the three of them had bought one another drinks. Nina's career shot onwards and upwards; theirs took different paths.

Two days ago, when Deanne heard the news, she'd rung the house. Jax had paused among the boxes, shocked and saddened and trying not to think about another promising life cut short by violence. Right now, she wasn't sure if Deanne's point was that there was plenty of reason to feel better than she did - but, well, it was probably a point worth making.

'You should see someone, Jax.'

She pushed the heel of a palm against the ache in her forehead. She'd talked to someone six months ago, decided she couldn't cope with the dredging up of every damn tragedy in her life. 'How about Hugh Jackman?'

'I've got his agent's number. You want me to put in a call?'

Back in the day, the four of them had joked they could reach just about anyone in the country if they'd pooled their contact lists. 'Is he doing trauma counselling now?'

'Oh, yeah. In big demand. It's the smile - hard to feel like shit when you see it up close. No, really. Do you want me to get you a number?'

Deanne would find her a world expert on trauma and grief counselling. It wasn't that Jax didn't appreciate the offer - or the potential expertise - but they wouldn't be in Newcastle and she wasn't getting back on the motorway for a consult in Sydney anytime soon. 'Thanks but no. Apparently there's a victim support group here.'

There was silence for a moment. 'If you're sure.'

'I am.'

'It's only a couple of calls if you change your mind.' She'd been telling Jax that for months.

'Deanne.'

'Okay, okay. But if you feel like talking, you know I'm always good for it. Anytime, Jax.'

Deanne was a good friend and 'anytime' had meant exactly that for both of them. The last time Deanne took up the offer was at 3 am two years ago when she phoned from hospital after her third miscarriage. Jax took advantage of it a week ago, in the wee hours with cold feet about moving, which was a shift in topic from her usual obsessive back and forth about Nick.

Deanne knew what the last shock had done to Jax - she deserved more than thanks-but-no-thanks. 'I've been thinking about his wife and son,' Jax told her.

'Whose?'

'Brendan Walsh's. He told me his wife would be just like me when he was dead.'

'That's a little close for comfort.'

'Yeah, but they must be feeling like Zoe and I did a year ago.'

'Six degrees of separation, I guess. We're all connected in some way.'

'I know. His wife must have questions.'

There was a beat before Deanne spoke. 'Not everyone needs to know it all, Jax.'

'I keep thinking about what she must be going through.'

'Maybe you should see someone. Before it gets on top of you.'

She knew what Deanne meant: before she *couldn't* stop thinking about it. 'It's not like that.' At least, it wasn't yet.

'Do you want me to come up? I could help with the unpacking.'

And try to get Jax's mind off it. 'No, I think I need to do it myself.' Prove to herself she could achieve something.

'Try to rest. It gets worse when you're tired.'

'I'm okay, Deanne.'

'THERE's no point buying food for lunch if you haven't found plates to eat off,' Tilda told Jax. 'How about I throw something together while you try to get a bit more organised down there?'

It felt a little like being told to tidy her room but it made sense - so much for setting boundaries on the first day. So, for two hours, Jax opened boxes and shoved furniture about with Zoe's help, chatting, laughing, trying to be a happier mother.

Russell rang as they were eating upstairs behind sheer blinds that kept the view in sight and the one o'clock heat at bay - and Jax was ready to talk this time. Victims of crime she'd interviewed had told her the process helped, that even talking to a reporter could put the experience into perspective, and she was hoping it might drain away the ready-to-run sensation she couldn't shake.

Leaving Zoe at the table with Tilda, Jax took the phone downstairs, sat on the floor with her packing cartons and watched the ocean as she talked.

Russell asked how she'd felt, what she'd thought, feared - nothing like the recounting of facts with Aiden Hawke. She remembered more details - Brendan telling the radio to *shut the fuck up*; how he'd let her open the window after going ballistic; saying, *Yeah, look, sorry about all this*; that his son wrote his letters backwards. 'Colour' she'd have called it, if she was writing the story.

It didn't help, though. It just reminded her of the hours of loud, frenzied confusion and that, in the end, she hadn't known what was real. Or how to help Brendan. Like Nick, he'd known death was coming for him and he'd tried to reach someone. He hadn't held a phone in his dying hands, but a message in his head. It was the same result, though - cut off halfway there.

'Anything else you want to add?' Russell asked.

'I don't know anything else. Tell me what you know.'

As he ran through the facts collected by reporters working the story, Jax found a pen and scrawled notes on the side of a packing carton. Brendan had lived in a share apartment in Ryde, on the northern reaches of Sydney, and had worked in security for four months at a business called Secure Force, operated from an office in North Sydney, not far from the approach to the Harbour Bridge. The company employed former police officers and military-trained personnel for private investigations, debt collection, personal security and other related work. Management wasn't commenting on Brendan's role. The Department of Defence hadn't released the dates of his Afghanistan tours or any details of conflicts he'd been involved in, but it did point out that he left when his time was up, not because of a stress-related issue.

'Can I get a photographer to you?' Russell asked when he was finished.

Jax ran a hand through messy hair. 'Give me a break, Russ. I've had about four hours' sleep, I'm weeks past needing a haircut, almost everything I own is packed up in boxes and I look like crap. You've got enough pics of me on file. Just choose something nice, not one of those Miranda-Jack-outside- the-inquest ones.'

Silence for a second. 'You all right?'

'Yep, sure.' She tried to sound like she meant it, but he'd sat with her through a lot of bad days in the past year and his silence said he wasn't convinced. 'It's just . . .' She rubbed her forehead with the heel of her hand, but instead of easing the circuit of thoughts, it sparked a fresh memory of Brendan.

'I *can't get rid of it now though, can I? Once it's there, it's there. And it's right* there.'

Yeah, he was right about that. He was in her head and she couldn't get rid of him.

'What is it, Jax?'

'He talked about nano spiders and missiles and they're obviously not real, but he also talked about his family and Afghanistan and the article I wrote - and they *are* real. He thought people were after him, he said they wanted to pick him off, that I was a target because I was with him. I just wish I knew which camp that part of it was in.'

'Do you think someone could be after you?'

'Out on the motorway, at the end of it all, he almost had me convinced ... but no, not really. I mean, he thought they had missiles. It's just ...' She let the sentence trail off, irritated that she couldn't explain it.

'Just what?'

'Well, if some of it was real and some wasn't, then maybe there are parts that are a bit of both. That could happen, couldn't it?'

'Yeah, I suppose. I imagine there aren't hard and fast rules on how people lose touch with reality.'

She wrapped an arm around a knee. 'What if he followed me to Wahroonga then got confused about it or forgot, and when he realised who I was, thought it was fate putting us together?'

'Followed you, as in a stalker?'

'No, not like that. I wondered if he knew Nick, maybe met him when he was in Afghanistan and, I don't know, wanted to talk to me now that he's not around. You know how some of Nick's stories started, people just turning up and giving him information.'

'You think it might have something to do with Nick?'

She pushed out a breath, her jaw tightening with anger. 'No, not really. But I can't check his notes because the Homicide cops still haven't released his stuff.'

'Jax -'

'Yeah, I know what you're going to say. It's just another opportunity to be pissed off about his case and the files I want back.' And the mobile he'd been clutching, and the contents of his car, and the notes and diary they'd claimed from his office.

'Okay, look,' said Russell, 'I know someone who might be able to get the dates of Brendan Walsh's tours in Afghanistan. We can see if they could've crossed paths. Nothing like checking a few facts to make a couple of old reporters feel like they're doing something useful, hey?'

'Thanks.'

'No problem.'

'By the way, only one of us is old,' she said.

'Aren't you turning forty soon?'

She rang off, running her eyes over the notes she'd made. The Department of Defence was claiming no knowledge of PTSD, but that didn't mean it wasn't there when Brendan left the army or that Afghanistan wasn't the cause.

He was working in security, using skills he'd learned for war.

He lived ten minutes from the motorway on-ramp where he got in Jax's car. If he went there from home, he didn't shower or change his clothes first.

16

M ore calls interrupted the unpacking. Friends who got Tilda's number through Deanne or Russell, and Jax's real estate agent, who saw the news and phoned with her condolences, then asked if there was any chance Jax left a spare key behind.

'There was a vandalism spree in your street last night,' the agent told her, talking fast while she walked. It was probably just to get coffee but it sounded as though she was at the scene, managing the public information. 'Some cars were damaged, pickets ripped off a fence, a few windows smashed and the bastards got into your old place.'

Jax pulled in a sharp breath. The new owner ran a design business from home and had planned to set up his computers in the study after Jax left yesterday. 'Did Graeme lose anything?'

'They didn't *take* anything, they just smashed it up. Hard drives, monitors, a filing cabinet, book shelves. Graeme had dropped off some boxes and they were sliced open. There were even a few holes in the walls. Like I said, a spree.'

Jax got a brief, horrible picture of what it might've been like if she'd been there with Zoe. 'Shit.'

'Just as well you left when you did. Well,' she paused. 'You know what I mean. Anyway, Graeme is worried you might've left a key somewhere, under a rock or something, and is wondering if he needs to change the locks.'

'No, there was no spare.' Just violence in store whether she'd stayed or left. If she was after an omen about moving to Newcastle, she wasn't sure what that meant. She hung up as Tilda appeared at the bottom of the stairs. 'And screw you too,' Jax told the phone.

'Who was that?' Tilda asked.

'Life. Being heartless again.' She passed the handset to her aunt. 'The answering machine can pick up the rest.'

Tilda pointed at her watch - its big, funky dial both fashionable and easy to read. 'Don't you have to see that handsome detective soon?'

'*Handsome* detective?'

Tilda made an indignant face. 'I'm sixty-one, not blind.'

Jax was thirty-five and the detective had pointed a gun at her. Handsome wasn't a description she'd thought to apply. 'In about half an hour.'

'Well, Zoe's fine upstairs. Why don't you go have a shower, do your hair and put on something nice?'

Jax glanced down at her dusty shorts and old T-shirt. 'Gee, do I look *that* bad?'

'You look like you need to be kind to yourself. So when you're finished with the police, you should go and treat yourself. Something to mark the end of ... all that, and the start of something better.'

Kneading the tight muscles in her shoulders, Jax told herself it might help. Nothing else had so far. 'What kind of treat?'

'I don't know. A chilled glass of chardonnay in the bar at The Beach House. It's the perfect day for it.'

Jax made a face, not convinced the company of happy drinkers would do anything to relieve the apprehension that was still hanging about. But she thought Tilda might be right about putting on a better face for Aiden Hawke. Her role as distraught widow hadn't done anything to include her in the investigation into Nick's death, and the stonewalling by the cops had only made her more dogged.

If she could make a better start with Aiden, if he could put Brendan's paranoia into perspective, maybe she could put a full stop at the end of that particular mystery. This one didn't need to be an obsession.

A DRESS and blow-dried hair felt better than she'd expected. Like the first shower after a bout of the flu. But as she pulled her aunt's old Jaguar into the street, something clammy crept up her spine. She scanned the street ahead, flicked her eyes at the rear-view, then hit central locking, wondering if she'd ever be able to sit behind a steering wheel without expecting a gunman to climb on board.

In the waiting area at the police station, she eyed the uniformed cops nice and safe behind a glass partition and felt the apprehension in her gut squirm like a stomach bug threatening. She held a hand to her belly, jumping when a door clicked open.

Aiden Hawke watched her across the foyer like he had over the roof of his car and suddenly it wasn't because she wanted perspective that Jax cared what he thought of her. For twelve months she'd been fragile, off balance, angry, obsessed. Last night she'd been confused, suspicious and half-crazed. Right now, she didn't want the cop who'd saved her to find her weak and brittle. She didn't want to be that, too.

She stood and met his eyes with a lift to her chin. There was professional courtesy in his brief smile - something more in his gaze. He kept it on her as she walked across the room: not ogling of the girl in the bold stripes. Maybe reassessing the tear-stained, dishevelled victim on a better day. Maybe that's what you needed to do when you'd saved a stranger's life.

He held out his hand for her to shake. 'You seem better than you did last night.'

Same firm palm that had patted her down for weapons. 'That wouldn't be hard.'

'It was a tough day.'

'Tough is a good word for it.'

'Did you manage to sleep?'

'Off and on between crazy dreams.'

His pale eyes flicked over her face as though he was deciding if that was good or bad. 'We can talk upstairs.' He led her into a large open-plan office, past the kitchenette she'd occupied the night before to a smaller interview room - just a table, four chairs and a row of windows looking out to the work space.

As he closed the door and arranged the seating, she made her own perusal of him on a better day. No spare flesh under his dark-grey business shirt; his legs in black trousers looked long and fast; something alert and well-sprung about him, as though his normal state was ready-for-action. And, well, thank God for that, or she might not be here. The tautness she'd seen in him last night was gone, his movements more fluid, the planes of his face not so firm. Up close, as he sat and placed a folder on the table, she saw tiredness around his eyes and wondered if he'd been working late on the contents of the file, or whether he'd tossed and turned with visions of her and a gun.

'How did *you* sleep?' she asked.

A quick sideways dip of his head. 'I saw a few different scenarios behind closed eyes.'

'Remembering or doing over?'

'Both. It's a normal process, the brain sifting through an incident.' Was that what a psychologist had told him or had he been there before? He slipped a hand under the top cover of the folder, pulled out a piece of paper and slid it across the desk to her. 'That's the number for the victim support group.'

'Do I look like I need it?'

He took a moment for another evaluation. 'I thought it was better to give it to you now. Some people find it hard to ask for help.'

Hedging already, she thought, taking the page and slipping it into her handbag. 'Thanks.'

He reached under the cover again, came back with her mobile phone. 'Thought you might need it before you get your car back. The battery's dead now but you've got a lot of missed calls.'

'You checked it?'

'It was in your car. I needed to know who it belonged to. The techs said it was still getting calls when they were going through it this morning.'

A tonne of people had her mobile number and she guessed most of them had seen the news sometime in the past twenty-four hours. More than a few of them would be chasing her for a quote - she was glad Deanne and Russell had been selective about giving out Tilda's number. 'Thanks.'

'Have you seen the newspapers?' he asked.

'Only the local one.'

'Nice idea to have someone speak for you.'

'I've done the front-page thing before.'

He nodded as though he'd already seen her headline appearances. She wondered if he'd followed the stories or read them today before slipping them into his file.

'How did the papers find out you'd interviewed Brendan Walsh?' he said.

'I asked a friend to pull the story for me.'

'A reporter friend?'

Who else would have a copy? 'Yes.'

'Why did you want it?'

'Because I couldn't remember talking to Brendan.' Because she wanted to know what was real. Because he'd died in front of her.

'Is it research for a story?'

She hesitated. *You're Miranda Jack. The journo.* 'Would you have a problem if it was?'

'It depends on what you're planning to write. If you're unhappy with the outcome yesterday, I'd like a chance to discuss it with you.'

She kept her eyes on him for a second. The gaze that watched her back looked like a challenge. Was he concerned about criticism? It happened. People, the media, politicians - everyone wanted someone to blame. Yesterday's outcome was tragic, no other way to look at it, but she was glad Aiden Hawke had been on the motorway and that she hadn't been part of a body count.

'No,' she said, 'there's no story. I'm just trying to make sense of what happened. I'm . . . Brendan . . .' She stopped, pressed her lips together, something new joining the apprehension in her stomach and forming words she hadn't spoken yet. 'He needed help. He died in front of me because I didn't know how.'

'You did the right thing out there yesterday.'

'A man who was in my car is dead.'

'You didn't make that happen.'

Her hands curled into fists on the table as Brendan's knuckles slipped through them again. 'No, but it doesn't stop me wishing I could've done something to prevent it.'

'You went home to your family. That's a big thing, Miranda. Cars going at high speed are dangerous and you were driving yours with a gun at your head. Don't underestimate what you achieved.'

He was being kind, she was grateful for that. It had started that way with the Homicide detectives in Sydney. 'I hope you're telling yourself the same thing.'

He paused, maybe a little surprised to have the empathy redirected. 'Something like that.'

'Have you heard how his family is?'

'I spoke to his wife again this morning and she's as well as can be expected under the circumstances. So far, the media hasn't bothered her.'

'Is her name Kate?'

'Kate Walsh, yes.'

Jax nodded, thinking again about Kate and her son, about herself and Zoe. About Aiden and what it was like to be him. Rescuing a hostage and trying not to get shot, then finding empathy for a widow a few hours later. She wanted to ask how he weathered the storm of those conflicting emotions, how he didn't feel like he was being buried by them. Decided he might ask the victim support counsellor to come and pick her up if she did. 'How long had they been separated?'

'He moved to Sydney four months ago for work. She stayed here but I'm not sure she considered it a separation.'

'He told me he'd left her.' Real and not real? 'I was the last person to see her husband alive. She might have questions I could answer.'

'I'll let you know if she asks.'

'I'd like to talk to her. Can you give me her number?'

'No, Miranda. I can't do that.'

His refusal was simple, direct - and it made frustration and resentment swell in her throat.

No, Miranda, we won't share that. Your husband's property stays with us. We decide what you can have. This was a different man and a different death but it felt the same. All she wanted was to know why her mind was being strangled with sad, horrible images - and another cop was telling her to sit quietly and do what she was told.

She took a breath, ready to pick up where she'd left off with the last lot of cops. Saw Aiden across the table, pale irises on her face, something sharp-eyed and perceptive in them ... and bit down on her words.

Don't do it, Jax. Don't start that way. This was a different cop: it wasn't too late for a different approach.

17

J ax rolled her lips together, found a neutral face. 'Why?'

'There are processes that have to take place before that can happen.' Aiden pulled her statement from his folder, already moving on. He hadn't closed the door, though, just asked her to wait on the threshold. 'Can you read your statement through?' he said. 'Let me know if there's anything you'd like to add?'

The official version wasn't like anything she'd ever written - no attempt to make sense of the moment or to convey the high emotions. It was just the facts: times, places, actions, and as much of Brendan's rambling as she'd been able to recall. Reading the document made her hands clammy.

'Is this all you need?' she asked when she'd finished.

'I'd like as much as you can remember.'

'Do you need direct quotes?'

He paused, watched her through half a second of thought. 'Do you have more?'

'The entire drama is on a reel in my head.'

'Then I'd like all of it.'

Her heart thumped as she forced the images and sounds into slow-mo, picking out the detail, putting them into words. Half an hour later, she signed the statement with a trembling hand and Aiden explained the rest of the process.

It wasn't a criminal investigation. She'd been cleared of any intent and Brendan wasn't alive to answer charges. It was now a matter for the coroner. Aiden's job was to detail the chain of events that led to Brendan's death; hers was to give evidence at the inquest. Something to look forward to - another tearful and public event.

As he returned the pages to his file, signalling the end of the process, she figured now was the time to try slipping a toe over his threshold. 'Was Brendan at work yesterday? Did something happen that might have upset him?'

He closed the folder. 'No, he had a day off.'

When she'd done shift work and had weekends in the middle of the week, she'd done housework, shopped, met friends in their lunch breaks and skited about days off. She wondered what private security people did - maybe they went to the gym. Did they meet colleagues or avoid them? 'He said he'd been trying not to kill himself for two days. Did something happen two days before, on Saturday?'

He slid his pen into a shirt pocket. 'I can't answer that yet.'

'Do you know what happened to him in Afghanistan? He talked about a helicopter crash. Was he in one?' She waited while Aiden folded his forearms on the table, not sure if he was pausing for dramatic effect or thinking about what to say.

'I'm sorry, Miranda. I haven't got all the information yet. It's going to take time and there'll be some details I won't be able to share with you. My suggestion is to get some rest, spend some time with your daughter, go to the beach, and if you still want to talk about it in a couple of days, give me a call.'

He clearly had no idea what it was like to be left on the outside after being trapped in the middle. She knew sarcasm wouldn't help but it found its own way to her voice. 'Is that what other people do? Have a surf and forget about it?'

'Some of them.'

'What about the rest?'

He held his hands out, no answer for that. Or perhaps he didn't want her to think there was an option.

'Do they call you back?' she pressed.

'Some of them.'

'Do you answer their questions?'

'It depends on the questions.'

And she'd thought a dress and nice hair would work in her favour. 'Do you ever give a clear answer?'

He hesitated. 'Do you ever run out of questions?'

Familiar hackles started to rise on her neck. 'Not usually.'

One side of his mouth turned up the tiniest bit. She clenched her teeth, told herself amusement was better than the response from other detectives.

'I'm not telling you to forget it,' he said. 'I'm just suggesting you give it some time.' He pushed his chair back. 'And if you decide to call, maybe you can email ahead with a list of questions so I can have a few answers for you.' He raised an eyebrow, more cheeky than patronising.

Okay. Take a breath. 'Thank you.'

He picked up the folder as he stood, making it clear he wasn't fielding any more questions now. Not a whole lot put into perspective, but she'd signed the statement. It was closure, of sorts. She could go and buy herself that drink. Sit on her own and tell herself she'd made the right decision selling up and bringing Zoe here. That a shitty start didn't mean the rest of it would turn out that way. That she'd find work, make friends, put her life back together.

That she couldn't let this thing linger on inside her.

Hitching her bag to her shoulder, watching as Aiden turned to leave, she wondered if goodbye was the best way to go. If she could get a foot through Aiden's door, he might tell her when he had the answers, instead of waiting until she rang. And, well, if nothing else, he was the only person she knew in Newcastle who was within twenty-five years of her own age.

'Can I buy you a drink?' she asked.

He looked back at her, surprise in the rise of his brows. 'You don't need to do that.'

Great, Jax. That door was just swinging to the jamb. 'Sorry, I probably should've explained what I meant.' Aiden tucked his folder under his arm as though he was ready for her to make a report. Heat touched her cheeks like two warm hands and she wished it was as easy as she told Zoe: *Hi, my name's Miranda, do you want to play in the sandpit?*

She cleared her throat. 'Nothing attached, no victim-cop thing, not a date. My aunt told me to treat myself to a chilled glass of chardonnay when I'm finished here and if I go home without wine on my breath, she'll be worried about me.' She laughed, like it was funny her aunt was encouraging her to take comfort in alcohol. 'Actually, I could do with the drink, but sitting on my own isn't all that appealing today and I'm new in town, I don't know anyone else. So I figured, if we're done here, we could just, you know, have a drink.'

His expression didn't change; he just glanced briefly through the glass into the room behind him.

Now it was embarrassing. 'Sorry,' she said again. 'I didn't ask if you . . . you've probably got a wife and kids to go home to. It's fine. Don't worry about it.'

'No. No wife or kids.'

'Right.'

Maybe there were regulations about socialising with victims you'd disarmed. Maybe he didn't want to because she was a victim he'd had to disarm. Understandable. But as she waited for the polite rejection, he flicked a look at his watch, ran a hand down his tie and said, 'Yeah, why not? I'll need about ten minutes to finish up here. Why don't I meet you somewhere?'

JAX WAITED on the deck of The Beach House, away from the other drinkers, the surf at her back and her arms folded. Uneasiness had returned to her stomach and she was wishing she'd suggested coffee somewhere quiet when Aiden walked out through the glass doors. She almost didn't recognise him - he'd found his black-framed sunglasses, lost the tie and looked less like the serious detective she'd been talking to twenty minutes ago and more like an FBI G-man on a drinks break. *Yes, Tilda, well within the realm of handsome.*

It was too hot to sit outside so Jax bought the wine and a beer while he went in search of a table in the air-conditioning. The Beach House was an old-style hotel, for years left in disrepair and only recently reno-vated with lots of glass that showed off the original timber work inside and out. Jax figured she could probably see Tilda's house if she wandered out to the southern stretch of the deck. She found Aiden facing east, in front of a huge window that overlooked sand littered with towels and umbrellas and bathers - and a swell beyond it that had brought out enough surfers to fill a small suburb. It was Newcastle, city by the beach.

'Do you surf?' Jax asked as she arranged herself on a stool opposite him.

'Not in years. How about you?'

'I'm a country girl. Never felt comfortable out of my depth.'

'Well,' he lifted his beer, 'welcome to Newcastle.'

'Thanks.' She tapped her wineglass against it and took a sip, hoping she didn't look as uncomfortable as she felt. It was a long time since she'd sat in a bar with a man. A year since she'd sat in a bar without friends whose main game was to cheer her up and avoid the subject of Nick. Across the table, Aiden had pushed his sunglasses onto his head, and if he noticed her discomfort, he didn't show it.

'Can I ask a question?' she said.

'Just one?'

'I can't promise there won't be a follow-up.'

'Wait a sec.' He took a mouthful of beer. 'Right, go.'

Okay, that was a little cute. Maybe he wouldn't be like the other cops. And maybe she shouldn't push it. 'Last night on the motorway, you called me Jax. I figure a cop can get basic information from a person's registration plates, but a nickname? Is it on a police file somewhere?'

'As in Miranda Jack "a.k.a. Jax"?'

'Does it say that?'

'No.' He chuckled as he glanced out the window, something self-conscious about the way he ducked her gaze. 'I knew who you were. I didn't tell you before because you didn't seem to remember me, but now ...' He did a brief sideways nod. 'We were at Newcastle Uni together about a hundred years ago.'

Well, that was a surprise. She searched his face, trying to imagine him fifteen years younger. Probably studious and sensible, not one of the ra-ras. 'Were we in the same course?'

He gave a quick, quiet laugh. It was uni, there'd been partying and drinking and ...

Oh geez, had she forgotten the cop who'd rescued her? 'Did we ...?' She winced instead of finishing.

He chuckled again. 'No. I was second-year Psych when you were there. We were both at Evatt House.'

The university on-campus accommodation. 'God, I haven't thought of that place in ages.' Back when she was there, it was known as the country kids' college. Technically she hadn't been a country kid after living with Tilda for two years but her aunt had encouraged her to try it - moving out but close enough to go home if she needed to.

After her parents' deaths, Jax had buried herself in schoolwork for two years, blitzed her final-year exams, then had a breakdown. She spent the four months of the Christmas summer holidays suffering crying jags that could last for days, feeling numb and fatigued. A psychologist gave her pills and told her, among other things, to get some fresh air, exercise and write a journal - and she'd started to transcribe her way out of the fog. By the time the academic year began, Jax had been accepted for Law degrees at universities in Sydney and Melbourne, but opted to stay in Newcastle, close to the only family and home she had left. She studied Arts for a year, lived at Evatt House on weekdays and went to Tilda's on weekends, sometimes taking friends and making it a house party, other times retreating to the solitude of her room. She had weird memories of that time - highs and lows, laughter and black days. There hadn't been a lot of studying, she'd been marking time until she graduated from something more personal.

'There were what, two hundred kids at Evatt House?' Jax said. 'Did you pinch the student lists for future policing needs?'

'Actually ...' He did a side-to-side with his head, a little sheepish. 'I got you for Murder Week.'

Jax's shot of laughter seemed to bounce off the window. 'Bloody hell, Murder Week!'

Among the many and varied social events at Evatt House was the annual, week-long game of Murder. Residents were given the name of another student to kill - not for real, obviously, but a hand on the shoulder and the words, 'You're dead,' got you a body plus anyone your victim had taken out. The one with the highest body count won.

'Not a good indicator for your career that you didn't kill me.'

'Well ...' He took a sip of beer. It looked like stalling.

'Well what? I finished the week alive and kicking. You didn't get me.'

'I was studying Psych, right? And I knew I wanted to go into the cops, so I staked you out.'

'What? You staked me or *stalked* me?'

'It was surveillance. And only for a week.'

'Uh-huh. So why didn't you just murder me?'

'What would be the fun in that?'

'Uh-huh. Are you seeing someone about that?'

'No, I became a detective instead.'

It was pretty amusing - except for the thought that her chaotic double life had been under surveillance. After two years at school being the new kid with the dead parents and the flamboyant, rich aunt, the virtual anonymity of uni party life had been brilliant - she'd stayed up nights, laughed too loud, drunk a lot, discovered sex and avoided lectures. She'd also taken time out from it all, retreating to quiet corners around the campus to be alone, reading or writing for hours, sometimes sobbing. Had Aiden seen that? Did he assume she was still that girl? There'd been times in the past year when she'd wished she was.

She raised her wineglass. 'And here's to you becoming a detective. My life saved twice by your vigilance.'

He tapped his beer against it, joined her in the toast as though it was all a bit of banter, but as he drank, his serious eyes stayed on her face. Maybe thinking about the surveillance that had saved her yesterday.

'Is it worse when it's someone you know?' she asked.

'The job?'

'Yes.'

'No. I like my job - knowing someone doesn't change that. But it does make it harder when you have a history with a victim. Even a perpetrator.'

'What's harder?'

'The decisions you have to make get complicated.'

'When did you realise you knew me yesterday?'

'After your rego information came back.'

'Did it complicate your decision to follow me?'

He hesitated. 'It made it more important to get it right.'

'What about the gun thing?'

'What about it?'

'Would it have been complicated deciding to shoot me or is that training?'

He didn't answer until her focus had stilled on the blue-grey of his irises. 'I was never going to shoot you, Jax.'

A pulse thumped through her as she remembered the unwavering barrel of his gun. 'It didn't feel like that.'

'It wasn't meant to.'

She wasn't sure whether to be impressed or uneasy about his acting ability. She was grateful, though, that he'd answered her questions without assuming she doubted his capabilities. Not like the other cops. Not yet. She sipped her wine, watched the surf, watched him as his gaze moved around the room.

'Have you been working in Newcastle since you finished uni?' she asked.

Amusement turned up one side of his mouth. 'I've seen a little more of life than that. I did uniform duty down on the south coast first, then out west, started in the detectives in Penrith then moved to Serious Crime in Sydney for a few years before here.'

No surprise he had a raft of experience. She'd seen him in action on the motorway and the officers who'd moved at his command. But he'd left a Sydney crime squad to work in a regional city. He was unmarried, no kids - it had to be a sideways step. Then again, a couple of years in Serious Crime dealing with the uglier, nastier, bloodier side of life, and perhaps he was doing well not to walk away from the job. 'How long have you been back?'

'Two weeks.'

And he'd walked right into her drama. 'Well, damn, I was hoping for some inside knowledge but you're as local as I am.'

'You can learn a lot in two weeks.'

'Such as?'

'Where to get a decent takeaway. Late-night supermarket. Good places to run.'

'Oh, right, all the stuff I need.' She held her glass aloft again. 'Welcome to Newcastle back at you, then.'

Tilda had been right. The wine and the view and a couple of toasts felt okay. Like time out. A lot better than anything the last twenty-four hours had thrown up. Maybe anything she'd managed in the last ... long while.

'Jax.' He said it as though he was trying it out. 'Can I call you Jax?'

'I think you should.' She leaned in, lowered her voice. 'I've got to tell you, only the cops call me Miranda.' His lips tightened and she felt a buzz of victory - she'd made the serious cop try not to laugh.

'Okay, *Jax.*" He paused, centred his glass on his coaster as if waiting for the humour to disperse before he started again. 'I wanted to let you know I spoke to Anita Lyneham at Homicide in Sydney today.'

Oh Christ, there was no humour in that. Jax's heart thumped and heat rushed up the back of her neck. Sadness, anger - familiar emotions made sharper by the edginess and paranoia floating in her bloodstream. And she saw Brendan again - his hand around the gun as he waved it in her face. Had it been about Nick?

18

'I've passed the details of the carjacking on to her,' Aiden said.
     Detail ran quickly, jarringly through Jax's head - Brendan had seen Aiden watching them leave the car park, said he *should've fucking stopped him then.* The aggression hadn't seemed an invention. Neither had the way he held the pistol. He'd had a break with reality but how far was it from his real self? Had he 'stopped' people before?

Jax had felt sorry for him because of his wife and child, as though loving people made you good. But bad people had families too. Had a man with a wife and child had something to do with Nick's death?

She folded her arms as a different kind of uneasiness worked its way down her spine. 'Oh Christ.'

'Jax, I'm just letting you know.'

It was what she'd wanted, a hook into the investigation. *Don't let him think you can't handle it,* she warned herself. 'Yes, of course.'

'I don't know how often you're in contact with Anita but I thought you might appreciate knowing she's aware of what happened yesterday.'

'So you think it's got something to do with Nick's case.'

'It's procedure.' He said it slowly, as though making sure she understood. 'Your name came up in an ongoing investigation and it makes sense to check out all the references. I thought you might be worried you'd have to contact Homicide yourself. Some people find it difficult to touch base again.'

She took a sip of wine. Not a hook, just behind-the-scenes cop talk. He was right, though, it was always stressful ringing Homicide, but it was more than likely Anita Lyneham was the one who'd told him to pass on the message. The lead investigator hadn't ever been amused by Jax's array of questions. Which meant it would be easier to ask Aiden here and now.

'What happens to the information - will it just go in a file somewhere? A "by-the-way, the widow had a run-in with police". Or do you expect her to follow it up?'

He paused, seemed to weigh up the irritation in her tone. 'I imagine she'll run the details across her own files, see if anything rings bells. Names, fingerprints, something he said, that kind of thing.'

'Can I get access to the results?'

'It depends on the results.'

'Will she pass them on to you?' Maybe Jax could go to him for an update.

'Only if it's relevant to my inquiries.'

A tick of frustration made her turn her face away.

'They're separate investigations,' Aiden explained. 'She's Homicide, I'm a detective in Newcastle. There's no point trying to cover each other's cases.'

She nodded, told herself not to press. 'Did Anita warn you about me?'

He dipped his head to one side. 'I was told there was some friction.'

She huffed with cynicism. 'That's diplomatic of you. I'm impressed you joined me for a drink after that conversation.'

'Long, unproductive investigations are frustrating for everyone.'

'That sounds like an excuse for a colleague.'

'Maybe it is, but I've been there. I know what it's like to want to close a case - for everyone's sake. And I prefer to make decisions for myself about who I drink with.'

He'd staked her out a long time ago, read her mind over the roof of a car, held a gun on her - he had plenty to go on. And perhaps she should leave it there. 'Well, thanks. I'm glad you came.' She drained the last of her wine. 'I think it's time I got going.'

The sun was glaringly low and the air sticky with humidity when they stepped outside. She'd parked in a side street a few blocks away, and when he suggested walking with her, she assumed his cop-like earnestness stretched all the way to chivalry - and her reflex was to tell him she was thirty-five and had never needed an escort. But in the encroaching dark and sudden quiet of the beachside suburb, Brendan Walsh's paranoia pricked at Jax's neck, and she had a sudden urge to run to Tilda's Jag, jump in and lock the doors. Aiden's offer was just fine, thanks.

Pulling car keys from her bag as they walked, she held them in an open palm for a moment and wondered if their friendly drink was enough to get a few more answers. 'Did Brendan have a car?' she asked.

'Yes.'

'Where was it?'

'It hasn't been located yet.'

'It wasn't near the motorway on-ramp?'

'No.'

She stopped beside the Jag. 'Did you look where he was living?'

Aiden pulled up next to her, raised an eyebrow.

'Okay, not there either.'

'Nice wheels.' He bent to check out the interior. 'What is it? A 1975?'

'No idea. It's my aunt's. She bought it new - it must've been some time around then.'

'You should be able to pick up yours from the police compound tomorrow, by the way.'

Jax opened the door and eyed the other cars parked in the street. 'I'd assumed Brendan had ditched his so it couldn't be followed. I figured he'd left it somewhere near the motorway entry and, I don't know, jogged down the road, crossed near the lights and got in the first car with a driver he figured he could scare into taking him where he wanted to go. Me. But if it's not there . . .' She focused back on Aiden. 'Where did he come from?'

'We're still following that up.'

'He said he'd been holding it off for two days. I thought he meant he'd been trying not to kill himself but maybe it was something else. Do you know where he was for those two days?'

'That hasn't been established yet.'

'I thought his panic was because he'd just realised someone was following him. But maybe he spent two days thinking he was being followed.'

'Jax.'

'What?'

'The car will turn up. Give it some time.' It sounded like the voice of experience. It still ticked her off.

'Some *time*? Where's your urgency?'

'There's no reason for urgency. Brendan Walsh isn't alive to answer charges. No-one is under threat and there are other cases that need immediate attention. It'll be followed through, just give it a couple of days.'

He'd used the same phrase back at the station. 'A couple of days. Is that your fallback timeframe?'

'Something like that.'

'How long is "a couple of days" exactly?'

'It's police work, Jax. You need patience.'

She squeezed her eyes closed, clenched her teeth. Time hadn't helped with Nick. Time had only made it harder. 'I had some of that once.'

JAX STOPPED at a supermarket to pick up Zoe's cereal, a few basics for the kitchen and something easy for dinner, frustration and agitation brewing like storm clouds as she wound her way around unfamiliar aisles. Aiden hadn't told her to keep out of it, there were just no answers yet. But she'd been here before and a few days had turned into a year with no answers.

It should have helped that Tilda had a meal waiting when Jax got back, but it made guilt join the brew inside her - the third meal in a day, when she'd wanted to set boundaries. She did her best to be part of the family moment, forcing smiles and small talk, irritated she wasn't unpacked, fed up with the wad of anxiety stuck in her gut, angry at ... herself. At the police. At Brendan: for holding a gun to her head, for sitting at her shoulder, for loving his family and making Jax care about them.

She cleared the table, let Zoe watch TV and ground her teeth in silence as she helped Tilda rinse plates.

'I can do that,' her aunt said. 'Why don't you sit down and relax?'

Jax hauled open the dishwasher. 'I don't feel like relaxing. I want to *do* something.' A bowl slipped in her wet fingers and clattered among the other crockery.

'You could try not to break anything,' Tilda said, slotting it into place.

'Sorry.' Jax grabbed a hand towel, realised her hands were shaking and folded her arms.

'Jax, honey, what is it?'

'I just... I can't stop thinking about it.'

'About what in particular?'

She'd been carjacked yesterday, it should have been obvious, but after the last year of obsessive thinking, it was a reasonable question. 'About Brendan. About all of it. It's a bad song stuck in my head.' She screwed a knuckle against her temple, remembered Brendan doing the same and snapped her hand away.

'Why don't you ring that victim support group? There's an after-hours number.'

'I can't bear talking about it again,' Jax said. 'I feel as though I haven't *stopped* talking about it. I've answered everyone else's questions and I just want some of my own answered.'

'Isn't Russell checking the man's military record?'

'*He* is, yes. I'm not. I'm hanging around achieving very little.' Feeling frustrated, agitated, irritated.

Tilda patted Jax's arm as she reached for another plate, it's only been a day. You need to give yourself time.'

'Yeah, I know. A couple of days.'

'Mummy?' Zoe was standing at the kitchen bar. 'Can I have a drink of water?'

'Sure you can.' Jax poured her a glass, walked around the counter and gave her a kiss on the forehead as she handed it over, guilty again that she hadn't been more interested in her chatter at dinner. 'Be careful not to spill.'

'Aunty Tilda said not to worry because she has tiles and spilling won't hurt them.'

Jax guessed there must have already been an accident and glanced an apology at her aunt. They all needed boundaries so they didn't get sick of one another. 'Okay, but it's good practice to be careful anyway,' she told Zoe, watching as she carried the glass across the room and arranged herself in front of the TV. 'I keep thinking about Brendan's wife and son,' Jax said quietly to Tilda. 'It was Zoe and me a year ago.'

'It must be awful for them. It's all over the news too, like you had it.'

Jax thought of the newspaper coverage this morning. Kate Walsh was probably wondering what the hell had happened. Not the *how* - that was clear enough from the news. The media wasn't going to tell her the *why*, though. The reporters and cameras weren't there until it was over, so anything they offered would be police information or speculation. Kate Walsh was probably wondering what Miranda Jack had to do with it.

Why the wife of a dead journalist had been holding a gun while her husband died on the motorway.

Jax would want to know. She'd want to know everything.

'I should talk to her,' Jax said.

'Brendan's wife? Are you sure that's a good idea? It's over now.'

'It's not what you're thinking, Tilda. Talking to her wouldn't make it worse. It'd be climbing out of a hole before it gets too deep. And maybe helping someone else out of theirs.'

Tilda closed the dishwasher, wound fingers through her strand of beads as she watched Jax from across the kitchen, a mixture of sympathy and concern in her face.

'I always thought if I knew what happened to Nick, I could let it go,' Jax explained. 'Maybe it wouldn't matter if no-one was charged, if I just knew what happened. Even some of it. But I don't know why he was running there that morning, why his laptop and files were in the car, who he tried to call. I want to know those things.' She swiped at the tear that tumbled onto her cheek. 'If someone said they knew what Nick was thinking in those last moments, I'd want that too. Anything. Something.'

Tilda moved along the counter, stood close enough for her perfume to enfold them both. 'When the police came and told me Bill had driven off the road, I knew he was drunk even before the results came back. And I knew what he was like - he wouldn't have been thinking anything in his last moment. Not Archie, though. He was conscious right up until the last hour. He'd said everything he wanted to say and I could see what he was thinking. He was ready to go.'

Jax wiped away another tear. 'Brendan Walsh loved his wife and son. The police won't tell her that.'

'No, they won't.'

'He wanted to protect them. He was going about it the wrong way and the reasons why might have been all in his mind but he was trying to get to them. It would make a difference to me if I knew that about Nick.'

Tilda's gold bracelets tinkled softly as she lifted a hand and slid it through Jax's elbow.

'I can tell Kate Walsh those things,' Jax said.

'Yes, you can.'

'I think she should know.'

'Then I think you should tell her.'

'Aiden Hawke wouldn't give me her number.'

'Then you've got some homework to do.'

19

Jax waited until Zoe was in bed before going online and quickly discovered her first problem. The Newcastle most people referred to was a sprawling assortment of suburbs: old mining towns, mostly, that had expanded and melded together over more than a hundred years and were now home to almost half a million Novocastrians. Technically, though, Newcastle was a postal zone, home to the Central Business District, which meant when she typed 'Walsh' and 'Newcastle' into her search engine, all she got was one Walsh whose address, according to Tilda, was just off an inner-city shopping mall.

It was fifteen years since Jax had lived with her aunt; the BHP steelworks had closed, old suburbs had been rejuvenated and others had grown. She didn't know the new names and couldn't remember all the ones that had been here before, so for speed and ease, she went back to paper and ink and pulled out Tilda's old phone directory.

There were two columns of Walshes, a couple of hundred names - not as bad as it might have been if the family lived in Sydney. Jax worked through the list, taking in the B Walshes, K Walshes and C Walshes (in case Kate was short for Catherine) and pulled Tilda into the exercise to decide which addresses were too far afield to be loosely called Newcastle.

'Thirty-one names,' she told Tilda as she tossed her pen on the coffee table.

Tilda pulled the notepad closer. 'That's a lot.'

'It's not too bad.' Jax had worked phone lists before, tracking down people in flooded suburbs, ringing homes near bushfires to ask if they could see smoke - and, one crazy day, trying to find a couple of monkeys that had escaped from a private zoo. She wanted to start calling now but it was too late to be passing on distressing information. 'How early is too early to start making calls? Seven am?'

'Definitely too early. Give them time to have breakfast and coffee. You should too, before you try to explain anything.'

'Yes, you're right.' Jax flexed her hands, trying to ignore the urge to pick up the phone.

'You look tired. Why don't you go to bed?'

It wasn't ten yet but it'd been a stressful, anxious, shitty couple of days and she should probably try. 'I think I will.' She kissed her aunt's cheek, headed for the stairs and started down without turning on the lights - no point flicking on a dozen tread-mounted bulbs when the glow that came through the frosted glass in the front door was enough to see by. Except halfway down, headlights swept past and Brendan Walsh was at her shoulder.

We can't hide, Jax. They're everywhere.

Leaping across the foyer, fumbling for the light switch, she hit the wall with a thud, swore under her breath.

'Are you all right?' Tilda's voice floated down from above, rows of twinkling lights coming to life on the stairs.

'Forgot where the light switch was,' Jax called. 'Can you show me again how to work the alarm?'

Under Tilda's instructions, Jax armed and disarmed the house, checking the movement sensors in the living rooms and hallways.

'Try to get some sleep,' Tilda called as she flicked off the lights.

Jax padded quietly through the lower floor, aching with tiredness now, but checking locks, putting her phone and the mini laptop she carried in her bag on to charge, turning off Zoe's nightlight, picking up clothes and tossing them into the laundry - tension buzzing inside her again. The street outside seemed ominously close now, the shadows filled with Brendan's voice.

I'm not going to get there. It's coming. It's coming soon.

You didn't *get there, Brendan,* she said silently. Did that mean it was still coming?

There was no indication anyone had been after him - the alert and capable Detective Senior Sergeant Aiden Hawke had told her. It was residual fear she was feeling, brain in shock and all that. It was in Brendan's mind, it didn't have to be in hers.

It didn't mean she could sleep.

She went back to the living room, opened the first packing carton she came to. Kitchenware. Perfect - she had a wall of cupboards to fill and she needed something to keep her body from crawling out of its own skin. She filled shelves and thought about Kate and Scotty Walsh trying to sleep tonight. About Brendan and the message he'd wanted Jax to tell.

About Aiden Hawke making hard decisions, then reliving and redoing. His version of a what-if.

What if Jax had bolted when Brendan first opened the car door? What if she'd been able to escape at the cafe? What if she'd crashed the car? She leaned on the kitchen bench and thought about that.

What if she'd aimed the passenger side at a road barrier and braced herself? Could she have survived that? She had airbags. But what if she'd been injured, unable to get out and run? What if Brendan hadn't survived? Maybe then she'd be asking different questions. Like, what would happen to Zoe if her mum was in a wheelchair, and how did it feel to kill another woman's husband?

Yeah, and maybe some questions weren't worth contemplating.

Jax woke to the shuffle-crunch of Zoe crawling over paper. She'd seen her mother's bedtime reading plenty of times, knew it came from the document box, and carefully, almost reverently, scooped up the pages and moved them to the end of the bed. They hadn't soothed Jax's agitation last night, the words swimming in her eyes as her brain flicked between Nick and Brendan. Questions, details, two crime scenes.

'Morning, Mummy,' Zoe sang when she'd wiggled under the sheets.

'Morning, Zoe.'

'What do seagulls eat?'

'I don't know. Fish. Hot chips.'

'Can we go to the beach today?'

Jax eyed the freckles that dotted her daughter's cheeks. 'We'll see.'

They had cereal at the breakfast bar in their new kitchen, ignoring the appliances Jax hadn't found a cupboard for, counting the ships in the queue off the coast, and calling 'Bye!' to Tilda as she left for a power walk.

The morning heat felt like leftovers from the day before, the air that came through the door sticky and stale before the sun had barely climbed above the horizon. Jax poured coffee, watched sun rays floating on the ocean and tried to forget the images from her dreams, feeling restless, tense, vaguely . . . what? Fearful. No, that didn't describe it. Maybe she'd need to read a psychology text to find the right word for it.

What she needed was to stop thinking and *do* something.

Seven-thirty was too early to start making calls. 'Okay.' She picked up the empty cereal bowls. 'Why don't we slap on some suncream and head to the beach? Be there and back before it gets too hot. What do you think?'

Zoe ran for her floaties.

Tilda spotted them as she strode along the walkway above the beach wall, pulled off her shoes and joined them, getting to her knees and telling Zoe they could reach China if they started digging right there.

Jax left them to it, waded into a buffeting surf and plunged under a wave. The water was bracing and the spectacular view along the shore made her feel like she was swimming in a postcard. She told herself to enjoy it, to loosen up and let the salt water clear out the sludge and muck that was festering, but the splashing about felt contrived and impatience niggled and minutes later she was standing on the sand again, drying off.

'Are you going to help, Mummy?' Zoe called from the pit of a knee-deep hole.

Jax tightened the towel around her shoulders, took a quick look at the clock on the clubhouse wall. Had they only been there forty minutes? 'Maybe.'

Tilda took a break from the excavation, squinted up at her. 'Zoe and I have a little way to go. Why don't you head home, get your calls over and done with?'

Was it that obvious? She gazed along the length of beach, wanting to go, telling herself she should stay. She dropped to her haunches beside her aunt and lowered her voice. 'You had Zoe for me yesterday afternoon. I didn't move here so you'd do all the babysitting.'

'I know you didn't, Jax honey,' Tilda matched her volume. 'And you didn't plan to get carjacked. Go and do what you need to do and then maybe you can stop walking around with your arms folded.' She raised her voice again. 'We're having fun, aren't we, Zoe?'

'Yep.' Zoe grinned, looking like she'd been buried and was digging her way out, not down. 'How long will it take to get to China?'

'About half an hour,' Tilda said.

Zoe pulled a face. 'That long? Can we have a swim after that?'

Jax rinsed off under the public shower and ran the steps up the hill, panting so hard when she reached the front door that she had to bend over and gulp at the air. Man, she was out of condition. She hadn't run since ...

She let herself think about it as she sat to dig for keys in her beach bag, preferring this memory to the ones that kept flooding her mind.

Jax had been a runner at school, in the state team three years in a row. She didn't make that last meet - it was two weeks after her parents died - and she didn't run again until she met Nick in her second semester at Sydney Uni. He was training for the City2Surf, told her she shouldn't bother because she'd never keep up with him. She knew it was reverse psychology but she hated being underestimated.

They'd run together a couple of times a week all the years before Zoe was born, then he'd kept at it and she'd preferred a gym with a creche. Most weekends, though, they'd set off together somewhere nice, Zoe with them in a pram at first, then graduating to a little pushbike. Happy family days that had finished abruptly.

And Jax hadn't pulled on joggers since Nick was killed in his.

She felt the questions starting up again, found her phone as she headed for the stairs, relieved to have a task to keep her mind away from them. Grabbing the notebook with her list of potential Kate Walshes, she was dialling before she'd ditched the bag and towel from her shoulder. The 'hello' on the other end froze the hasty words on her tongue.

The voice was female, not young enough to be Kate Walsh, but real and human, and instead of moving Jax past sad memories, it thrust her back to how it felt to be freshly widowed and taking calls. Delivering a sad message while she was still puffing from a trip to the beach was just rude.

When Jax hung up, she took the phone and notebook to the table and waited for her heart to stop racing before she started again. She left messages on answering machines for the third and fifth names. Number nine rang out. The twelfth was disconnected. At sixteen, a cleaner answered and told Jax the 'K' was for Kiefer, as in Kiefer Sutherland, but he was a chiropractor, not an actor. Tilda and Zoe arrived home after call twenty-two, and Jax took a break to make coffee and giggle at Zoe as she squealed under the cold-water shower at the side of the house.

'Not even a relative?' Tilda asked.

'A couple of cousins but not the right family.'

'Maybe she's not listed.'

'Maybe.'

It was 'No' from twenty-three and twenty-four. She was doodling on the notepad when twenty-five answered and she rattled off her spiel.

The man's pleasant tone was replaced with sarcasm. 'You want to know if *a Kate Walsh* lives here.'

'Yes. The wife of Brendan Walsh.'

'This is the third time I've had you media people asking for Kate Walsh. You lot are bloody vultures. Isn't it bad enough that it's all over the telly without you upsetting her more? If I had her phone number, I wouldn't bloody give it to you.'

Jax hung up and tossed the phone on the table, something hot and mortified tingling in her fingers. She wasn't media and she'd tried not to be vulture-like when she was, but the guy's outburst made her uncomfortable about her motivations - and for feeling better in the few hours she'd been working through the list than since Brendan Walsh had laid his hand on her passenger door.

'I've made some lunch. Why don't you take another break?' Tilda called from the stairwell.

Jax rubbed her hands over her face as she stood. Tilda - dressed and blow-dried already - was in front of her when she'd finished. 'Thanks but you don't need to make another meal for us,' Jax told her. 'I've got enough for a couple of sandwiches. You'll get sick of us.'

'It's already done, honey, and I'm enjoying the company. I'll let you know when I've had enough of you.'

She probably would, but Jax didn't want it to get to that. The three of them had to work out how to live together.

Jax went up, though, wondering if the search for Kate Walsh was unfair on Tilda and Zoe. If she needed something to do, she should focus on making a home for her daughter instead of searching for the wife of a man who'd almost killed her. She kept telling herself that as she went downstairs after lunch and ripped the tape off another box. But she heard Brendan's voice, too.

It might have to be you. You might have to tell her.

Fuck it, there were only six more numbers. She grabbed the phone, dialled number twenty-six. The voice was male. He listened to her pitch and said nothing for five long seconds.

'Who's calling?' he finally asked.

And Jax had found Kate Walsh.

20

Jax spoke quickly, success and a sudden urgency to say her piece making the words tumble out. 'My name is Miranda Jack. Kate doesn't know me but I'd like an opportunity to speak with her.'

Another pause. 'You're Miranda Jack?'

His tone made her hesitate, blood warming her face as she thought about what he must be piecing together: the woman on the motorway, the one holding the gun, the one who'd been with Brendan when he died. Jax wanted to explain it to Kate, not the man answering her phone, but she remembered Russell in the days after Nick's accident, trying to decide what she needed to deal with. 'Yes. I'd like to speak to her about Brendan. About ... what happened.'

There was more silence, longer this time. 'Hold on.'

She heard rattling as he shuffled the phone about, muffled voices, his and a woman's - Jax hoped it wasn't a duo making decisions for Kate.

'Can you come to the house?' he asked.

She'd been ready for a few kind words over the phone, hadn't expected a face-to-face, and swallowed uncomfortably on Brendan's description of his wife as *tough as nails*. 'Yes, of course.'

She wrote down the address, said she'd be there that afternoon, then walked to the window, her eyes roaming the uneven sprawl of houses down the hill. Kate Walsh lived in the same suburb. If Jax knew the lay of the streets, she could probably have picked the house from there.

If Brendan had only told her where he wanted to go, she could have dropped him off on the way to Tilda's.

IT MIGHT HAVE BEEN nice if the cops had considered Jax's near-fatal, high-speed, driver's-worst-nightmare experience before towing her car to a compound thirty k's down the motorway and telling her to go get it herself. If she'd had a choice about hitting high-speed traffic again, she would've passed it up - possibly for the next six years. But Tilda was taking Zoe to a choir meeting and they needed transport.

Tilda drove on the way out while Jax gave directions, gripping her seat and gasping whenever the brakes were touched. She was sweating and slightly nauseous when her aunt and daughter waved goodbye, glad she wasn't going to be responsible for their safety on the return journey.

Fingerprint powder on her green car looked like black mould growing from the edges of the doors. Inside, it was as though someone had held a handful of it in front of the dashboard and blown. It took fifteen minutes to wipe off enough to sit in the driver's seat without getting it all over her pale blue trousers.

She'd wanted to use the drive back to compose some words for Kate Walsh, but she clung to the steering wheel like she might get shot if she didn't stay in her lane, barely reaching the speed limit and tumbling out in front of the red-brick bungalow with nothing but echoes of Brendan's urgent, irrational voice in her head.

The afternoon's humidity wrapped around her like a wet blanket as she eyed the line of vehicles on both sides of the street. It reminded her of the stream of visitors after the news about Nick had spread, and she winced at the thought of a house full of anguished family and friends. Possibly family and friends who thought she'd had something to do with the way Brendan finished up under the wheels of a minibus. Would Kate want them to gather around and listen to what the woman from the motorway had to say for herself? Jax considered staying by the car a while longer, nutting out the best way to express herself, but it was too damn hot ... and it was time to move on.

The man who answered the doorbell looked like he'd spent both his entire life and someone else's outdoors. His skin was the texture of a leather handbag she'd once owned. If he'd smiled, his cheeks might have creased into concertina folds. He didn't.

'Miranda Jack?'

'Yes, I'd ...'

'She's through here,' he said and walked off down a hallway.

There were sounds from elsewhere in the house - a clattering of dishes, voices: an adult and the higher pitch of a child - and Jax's mouth went dry. But when she stepped into a lounge room behind the man, there wasn't a crowd. Not even a small gathering. Just one woman who stood up from a sofa, and the sight of her made Jax's feet stop and her breath catch.

Brendan had said his wife would be just like Jax. But it wasn't the prediction that made Jax pause. It was Kate Walsh herself.

She was exactly like Jax.

Not a carbon copy or a long-lost twin. She was a few years younger, shorter with dark hair and a smattering of freckles, but Jax felt as though she was seeing herself a year ago. Bare feet, cotton trousers, T-shirt, hair pulled back into a ponytail, a scrape of make-up to hide the red eyes and pall of strain, and a tense uncertainty to her whole body, as though she was bruised and bracing herself for the next blow.

And Jax was there to deliver it - however she told it.

As she crossed the floor, her urge was to wrap reassuring arms around Kate, tell her the first year would be hard but she'd make it. The things Jax wished she could go back and tell herself. But Kate Walsh held out a hand and Jax realised she didn't know what the police had told her, wasn't sure what Kate knew or assumed, and so she simply took her offered palm. 'I'm Miranda Jack. I'm so sorry about Brendan.'

Kate's fingers were cool to the touch and uncertain, her voice little more than a restrained murmur. 'Thank you.'

It's your meeting, Jax. 'I don't know what you've been told about me, about what happened, but I wanted to . . .' Jump right in and slap her with it? No, not like that. 'Brendan said - well, he said a lot - and ...' She saw his white shirt billowing as he ran into the traffic and tears stung her eyes. *Shit.* 'Would you mind if we sat down?'

She wasn't sure if Kate's abrupt glance away was discomfort at the tears of a stranger or trying to keep her own at bay but Jax took it as an opportunity to get her own under control. There were more noises from the back of the house as she made her way to a sofa. 'Have you got family with you?'

'Neighbours. My family is interstate. My son goes to school with the boy next door and the ones on the other side do some babysitting.'

I love my son ... I miss him so much.

Jax clenched her hands in her lap. 'How's Scotty doing?'

A frown creased Kate's face. 'You know his name?'

'Yes. Brendan talked about him. And you.'

'The police said you didn't know Brendan.'

'I meant in the car. He talked about both of you in the car.'

Kate sat perfectly still for about three seconds before placing her hands together and holding them to her face like an oxygen mask, breathing or thinking or both. Then she dropped them to the sofa and lifted her chin. 'Were you having an affair with my husband?'

'No. God, *no*.' What the hell had Aiden told her? 'I'm so sorry you thought that but no. I didn't know him at all.'

'That's not what the newspapers are saying.'

She'd only read the local one. 'They're saying we were having an affair?'

'They said you knew him, that you met when you interviewed him. People at the traffic lights said you were waiting for him, that he went straight to your car and got in.'

And sometimes the facts of a story were misinterpreted. 'About five years ago, I wrote a story about some soldiers leaving for Afghanistan. I was at the airbase when they left. He said you were too. Maybe you remember?'

'Of course I was there. I don't remember him doing an interview.'

'It wasn't a one-on-one. He was in a group of soldiers who answered some questions.'

Kate's eyes angled slowly away. Maybe she was trying to remember, maybe reshuffling the information she'd heard and read. 'He got in *your* car, though. Yours wasn't the only one at those traffic lights.'

'I don't know why he chose mine but he didn't make the connection until we were on the motorway. I told him my name and he remembered the story.'

Kate Walsh watched her for a long, drawn-out moment, stiff and still except for the fingers in her lap that were fidgeting and weaving like she was crocheting without wool and a hook. When she finally spoke, her voice was soft, a little wary, but firm. 'So who are you?'

'I'm just the woman who was sitting at the traffic lights when Brendan arrived.'

'No,' she said. 'That's not all. I've seen the pictures. You had a gun. Who has a gun in their car?'

'The gun was Brendan's.'

'My husband didn't own a gun.'

'He had one when he got in my car.'

'Was it for you? Did he get it for you?'

What was she thinking? 'No. He pointed it at me and told me to drive.'

Kate blinked a few times. 'Then why did he give it to you?'

'It ... I don't remember how that happened.'

'You didn't take it from him. He was a soldier and you were driving a car. He must have given it to you. *Why?* What have you got to do with it?'

Uneasiness crept like fingertips down Jax's spine. 'Got to do with what, Kate?'

21

Frustration flashed in Kate Walsh's eyes. 'What have you got to do with whatever happened out there? The police said Brendan hijacked your car. But you ended up holding his gun and now he's *dead*.'

Her last word was hard-edged and angry. Jax had used the same tone more than a few times in the past year to make her point. She saw the one Kate was making - and it wasn't that something else was going on. It was that she didn't understand what the hell had happened. Jax knew what that was like; it didn't make it easier to explain. 'He wasn't shot. I didn't shoot him.'

'No. He was running. The TV said he was running away when he got hit by that bus. You had his gun. The police had to take it off you. Was he running from *you*?'

The accusation stung but considering the media coverage, it was a fair assumption. Possibly it would also be a fair response from a terrified carjacking victim who suddenly found herself in possession of the gun she'd been threatened with. The problem was, Jax had come here to tell Brendan's wife the true story, but her message had been derailed by suspicion and she wasn't sure how to get it back on track without shifting the blame to, *He was running to you.*

Jax rolled her lips together, told herself to start somewhere else.

She talked about Brendan - how he'd thought people were after him, how he said a lot that didn't make sense, how he was agitated and confused. She didn't mention the threats, the scary mood swings, the near fatal crashes - no wife needs to hear that when she's still reeling with her husband's death. Jax said instead that he wouldn't get help, that he'd kept the gun on her, that he'd followed her into the cafe with it at her back and that his paranoia eventually infected her.

'When we pulled over, there were police everywhere. He wanted to run, I had hold of his arms and he ... he bolted and . . .' She closed her eyes. 'And then I was holding the gun. I didn't point it at him. I didn't point it at anyone. I tried to stop him. I didn't want him to run. I'm so sorry.'

Kate listened to it all with her gaze on the floor, wiping tears from her cheeks with a balled-up tissue. When Jax finished, the other woman folded her arms, took a few moments to get words through trembling lips. 'Why are you here? To tell me my husband died because he was crazy? So you can feel better about how it turned out?'

Was that how it had sounded? 'No. I wanted to tell you he loved you.'

'Shit.' Kate swung her face away, her lips crushed together before they disappeared from view, the knobs of her spine shuddering inside her T-shirt.

Jax clenched and unclenched her fingers. This was the moment she was here for, to deliver the details she thought Kate Walsh would want to hear, except ... maybe she didn't need details. Maybe it was just Jax who got fixated on them, stuck in place until she could move on with all the facts tucked neatly under an arm. She closed her eyes, told herself she should leave Brendan's wife with her own grief, not someone else's version of it.

'I'm so sorry,' Jax said again and stood, picking up her bag, planning to leave before she upset Kate more. Then a memory took hold like a hand pulling at her elbow.

I wanted to get there first but I don't know if I can make it that far. It might have to be you. You might have to tell her.

Jax hadn't promised and she didn't know what Brendan had wanted her to tell - but she couldn't leave without making an attempt.

'He was trying to reach you. He thought he was going to die. He told me if he didn't make it, I should tell you.' She stopped. It wasn't the message, but ... 'Tell you that he loved you and Scotty. I don't know why he thought he was going to die. I wondered if he wanted to kill himself but his death in the end was by accident. He wanted to protect you, though. I can't tell you what from but he was thinking of you and Scotty.'

A knock at the front door echoed hollowly down the hallway. Kate didn't move, didn't acknowledge the sound or Jax's words, but the shuddering in her spine had stopped. Now she sat with both hands in fists on her lap, face aimed at the blank wall opposite. Footsteps sounded on carpet; the guy with the leather skin passed the doorway. Jax hoisted her bag to her shoulder, deflated, disappointed in herself. She'd wanted to achieve something better.

As the lock on the front door rattled, Jax tried to explain. 'My husband died last year. I desperately wanted someone to tell me what he was thinking in the last moments of his life. I wanted you to have that. I'm sorry if it's not what you wanted to hear.'

Halfway to the door, Jax saw Kate's face swing around as though she'd decided she wanted the last word. 'Brendan had post-traumatic stress disorder. He got it in Afghanistan.' Kate said it as though it was a disease he'd picked up, like malaria or cancer. 'He had nightmares, anxiety, sometimes flashbacks.' There were voices from the front door. 'He worried about threats he couldn't see.' She interlaced her fingers in front of her, held them out to Jax. An offering, a trade of information.

'Kate?' It was the old guy in the doorway. 'It's those detectives.'

Jax turned as Aiden Hawke walked in, followed closely by the female detective who'd spoken with him on the motorway - two sets of white shirts and black trousers, one with a tie, the other with shoulder-length black hair. In tandem, they looked at Kate, widened their view to the second person in the room, and transferred their focus to Jax. It looked like a rehearsed, three-step manoeuvre. They must have been surprised to see her, not that either of them gave much away: the woman did a slow blink, something flashed through Aiden's eyes. Too fast for Jax to catch before he glanced back at Kate, but it definitely wasn't pleasure at seeing her.

Aiden spoke first, stepping towards Kate as he held out his hand. 'Thanks for seeing us again. You remember Detective Constable Suzanne May?' There were murmurs of 'How are you?' and 'Have you been in touch with your family?', then a loaded silence as the detectives turned to Jax.

'Miranda,' Aiden said, as though he was proving he knew her name. Or was he making a point of not calling her Jax.

'Aiden,' she answered.

He glanced at Kate and back. 'Do you two know each other?'

She frowned. He knew they didn't. 'We've just met.'

He watched her a second longer. 'Are you on your way out?'

That had been the plan before Kate started talking about Brendan, but Aiden's time-to-go tone told her she should do just that. 'Yes. I'm going.' She glanced at Kate, wondering if she'd see her again. 'Thank you for hearing me out.'

As she turned for the door, she remembered what was in her bag, tucked in a pocket and unused for twelve months. *Why the hell not?* She pulled a business card out and placed it on the coffee table. 'In case you want to talk,' she told Kate.

Aiden glanced at it, then at his cop partner and said to Jax, 'I'll see you out.' He followed her down the hallway, standing wordlessly at her shoulder as she opened the door. Did he have news, something he didn't want to say in front of Kate Walsh?

He stepped into the searing heat behind Jax and she waited as he pulled the door almost closed. 'Why are you here, Miranda?'

'Not Jax today?' She smiled. He didn't return it. 'To talk to Kate Walsh,' she said.

'I asked you not to do that.' The tone was mild but the words sounded like a reprimand.

She frowned. 'No, you didn't. You told me you couldn't give me her number.'

'You knew what I meant.'

'I thought it meant you *couldn't* give it to me. If you didn't want me to talk to her, you should've said, "Don't talk to her."'

A muscle at the side of his jaw ticked in and out. 'How did you find her?'

'I looked her up in the phone book.'

'There are about a hundred Walshes in the phone book.'

'It's closer to two hundred. I rang twenty-eight of them.' His eyes held hers, not quite a glare but on the same path.

'I've worked a phone before. I used to be a reporter.'

'Is that what this is about?'

'What?'

'Were you trying to get an interview from Kate Walsh?'

Surprise made her eyebrows shoot up. She spoke emphatically. 'I'm not writing a story. I don't even have a job.'

'An inside scoop is a good way to get one.'

Whoa. She straightened up as though he'd shoved her. Figured if he could accuse her of lying, she could accuse him right back. 'You seem pretty worried about me writing stories. Maybe I *should* start digging. Maybe there's more to why you were on the motorway following me.'

He blinked. 'My concern is about Kate Walsh. Her husband died in an incident that started a media party. She's got no family here, just a few neighbours to look in on her and no experience in dealing with reporters.'

'And you think *I'm* a problem? You should be asking me for advice. I'm the expert on being widowed in a media party. That's why I'm here. I knew you'd only give her the bare essentials and I wanted to tell her what happened. At the end.' She pressed her lips together. *Don't cry now.* 'She should know Brendan was trying to get to her and Scotty.' Her voice cracked on her last words, tears welling as she turned her face away.

On the greying timber decking at her feet, she saw Aiden's shadow cock its head, smooth its tie. After his push for answers, his silence made her glance back at him, hoping he understood. But she was way off.

'This isn't about Nick.' His voice was firm: not empathy but an instruction to step away.

And anger flared in her belly at another cop taking that tone with Nick's name on his lips. She kept her voice low so it wouldn't carry inside. 'What, you have a conversation with Detective Anita bloody Lyneham and you think you know where I'm coming from? Let me guess what she told you. That I liked the publicity: *Watch out for her, she'll be looking to milk it with this one.*'

The momentary slackness to his mouth told her she wasn't far off the mark. 'You need to walk away from this, Miranda.'

She let out a brief, scoffing breath. 'You don't know what I need. You got one part right, though. This is not about *my* husband. It's about Kate Walsh's husband. And I'm glad I came because you left her thinking he was having an affair with me and he ran into the traffic because I was aiming a gun at him. Great police work, Detective Senior Sergeant Hawke. Keep the family in the dark so they don't know what to think. Well, the media isn't the only element in this that Kate Walsh doesn't have experience with. I think she needs advice from someone who's already been fucked around by a police investigation.'

He held up a hand, conciliation in his tone. 'Miranda -'

'And I don't give a shit what you think about me being here.'

If he said any more, she didn't hear it over the thump of her shoes on the verandah and the blood pumping in her ears as she stalked to her car.

22

J ax slammed the car door, fought the key into the ignition, then held on to the steering wheel as her heart pounded so hard she could feel it slapping against her ribs. She wanted to tip her head back and gulp at the air but Aiden Hawke was still watching her from Kate Walsh's porch and she could do without him shaking his head and making more assumptions. So she pushed the stick into gear, negotiated the corner, waited until she was out of sight and pulled over again, chest heaving, fingers tingling, a pulse *whump-whumping* in her ears.

The air-conditioner was blowing a gale but she couldn't breathe. Eyes squeezed tight, she fumbled for the controls on the door handle, found the button for the window, heard the glass start to slide - and memory hit like a brick through the windscreen. Brendan was lunging, shouting; tyres were squealing, horns blaring; the car was swerving, tipping; Brendan bashing his head: *Drive! Drive!*

Then the car door was open and she was tangled in her seatbelt, trying to escape. She was in the road, dodging a passing car, hand to her stomach, vision swimming. And sick. Holding on to the hood, heaving into the gutter like a cheap drunk on a girls' night out.

When there was nothing left, she stood in the shade of a kerbside tree, wiped her mouth with the back of her hand, pushed the hair from her face and burst into tears.

Bloody cops. Bloody Brendan Walsh. Bloody fingerprint dust on her trousers. And the removalists and the bank and the bastard who'd run down Nick. And Nick for running on that road, for not telling her why he was there, for not trying to ring *her*. Every ugly, sad moment that'd brought her to Newcastle again.

She pulled in a breath. And another one. Glanced around at the empty street, at the corner she'd come around, grateful she'd managed to get out of Aiden Hawke's sight before she lost it.

She didn't want to get back in the car, didn't want Brendan Walsh shouting at her while she drove, but it was too hot to walk up the hill to Tilda's. And she wasn't sure it was where she wanted to be - not like this, not with her aunt's concern and Zoe's worried eyes. Shaking, her insides cramping, she sat in the doorway with the engine running until the air-conditioner was blowing cold, then steered the car to the beach, working her way along the foreshore to the harbour, turning around and working her way back again, the sight of the ocean smoothing out her breathing and heart rate, something tight and angry steeling her bones against the trembling.

An inside scoop is a good way to get one. Damn Aiden Hawke. And damn Anita Lyneham.

Eight months after Nick died, when Homicide hadn't come up with anything new since the first weeks of the investigation, when the inquest was rushing at them with no evidence, Anita Lyneham had accused Jax of keeping the story alive for the sake of her own ego. The TV interview had had nothing to do with ego and everything to do with trying to push the questions into new ground. She'd talked about Nick, their life together and the tragedy of his unexplained death, in return for a public appeal for information. Nick had been respected by a lot of people and the story created more coverage than Jax had dared hope for. It also intensified the battle of wills with the detective: Anita Lyneham accusing Jax of using Nick's death for attention, and Jax refusing to see why a public appeal for information was undermining the police. Whether it was the blunt talk between them or protocol - or sheer obstinacy - the detective had refused to share the breakdown from the stream of calls that came in after Jax's interview. And now Anita was in Aiden Hawke's ear. *Damn cops.*

Jax pulled her car into a parking area across the road from the beach, found a spot facing the water. There were vehicles either side of hers, a couple of surfers laughing as they dried off, a runner melting in the heat. She had an urge to get out and walk, to let the salt air fill her lungs and clear out the souring panic, but it fought with an opposing pull to stay hidden and safe within the metal around her. In the end, she wound down the windows and let the afternoon nor-easterly cut a swathe through the car. It blew hair across her face, tugged at her shirt, sent the occasional sting of airborne sand, but her anger hung on, stubborn and determined.

This isn't about Nick, Aiden had told her.

She'd seen the way he'd watched her before he said it. He had a Psych degree under his police badge and had staked her out a bazillion years ago, and now he thought he had her all worked out. He'd done all right at the station the other night, realising her questions were about reassurance. Yeah, and how hard was that? She'd just survived a carjacking, who wouldn't need reassurance? Today, at Kate Walsh's house, he was way off base. He thought she was there because of some sick desire to keep Nick's tragedy alive. He had no idea.

Brendan Walsh had changed the wiring in Jax's head. She had a thousand question but they were new ones and Aiden Hawke had no idea how good that felt. This wasn't about Nick. She didn't want to think about Nick, couldn't bear it any longer, was worried that something inside her was close to breaking.

This was about *her* and what *she* needed.

Okay, yes, if she was honest with herself, it was possible Brendan Walsh had broken something. The nightmares were ugly, she had a constant low-level buzz of anxiety, and she'd just thrown up in a gutter. But it wasn't the worn damaged part of her she needed to protect for Zoe's sake. Right now, she needed to focus on the new questions and give the others a chance to rest.

She grabbed her bag, wound the windows up and stepped out of the car. Crossing the road, she bought a bottle of water from the cafe at the top of the beach stairs, kicked off her sandals, went down to the sand, sat in the cool shade of the sandstone beach wall and pulled a notebook and pen from her bag. She drew a line down the page and marked one side 'Real', the other side 'Not Real', and started writing.

It didn't take long; there wasn't much. The Real side had: army, Afghanistan, interview/quote, Kate + Scotty, and a lot of blank lines. Not Real was an empty column.

Kate said Brendan had worried about threats he couldn't see, but that didn't confirm anything he'd said as Not Real. Aiden told Jax there was no evidence someone had followed Brendan - again, not confirmation.

Then there were the nano spiders and missiles. Okay, something for the ledger. She lifted her pen and paused.

Nick had tracked money, lies and liars through mountains of numbers, correspondence, emails and memos. The evidence had been stacked around his office in colour-coordinated and tabbed files. Print-outs of notes, lists, tables and handwritten pages. And he'd never moved anything onto the ledger until it was confirmed. She flipped the page, wrote 'nano spiders' on the top line, 'missiles' on the next, and stared at the waves cresting and crashing to the sand.

She'd ribbed Nick about going overboard on the research, of prolonging the agony of the detail because he couldn't bear the process to end. When their lives were overrun by a story, it was his saving grace that he could joke about it. He'd tell her he made little piles because a large one would topple and bury him, that he'd found a shopping list buried beneath the paper and some guy was going to be in big trouble for forgetting the carrots, that he wasn't sure if he was looking for a needle or the straw that would break his back. And he always told her the only way to understand the detail was to see the whole picture.

So she closed her eyes, looked at her memories of Brendan and wrote a list of everything he'd talked about: something stuck in his head, Already Dead, the confusion over her phone, helicopter crashes, being lied to, the friend who'd hit a pedestrian, holding things off for two days, Scotty learning to read before he went to school, the something Brendan didn't know that made him cry. And the bit she most wanted proved as Not Real: that people had been following him, trained people who wouldn't stop - and that she'd been in their sights too.

It was a long list, two messy pages by the time she added notes and drawn lines between the connections. And it was late. Not close to dark, but the shadows from the flags and the few remaining beach umbrellas stretched long and dark along the sand. She must have been sitting there for more than an hour. Pulling her phone from her bag as she stood, she dialled Tilda's mobile. 'Hey, it's me,' she told the recording. 'Sorry, it took longer than I expected. Be home soon.'

From the top of the beach stairs, Jax could see the parking area was almost empty, just a line of vehicles in the row that faced the water, hers included. She didn't bother pulling her sandals back on, dangling the straps from her fingers as she crossed the road.

A woman in shorts and a bikini top lifted a collapsed stroller into the back of the first vehicle in the row. Two-thirds of the way down, a man had his back to Jax, unlocking a driver's door. He was wearing a business shirt, the end of a tie blown over his shoulder. Maybe he'd stopped to enjoy the view and the breeze before heading home from the office. As she stepped up to the footpath, a second man in shirt and tie appeared, standing up as though he'd been squatting at the bumper of the same car. She watched them as she followed the curve of the path. Her car was somewhere near there. She couldn't remember how far down the row, couldn't see the colours and shapes past a chunky ute that was between her and them.

Glancing around, she wasn't sure what she was checking for, just curious ... no, *cautious* and suddenly itchy with sweat. She went wide on the path, trying to find the green of her car further down the row, reminding herself Aiden Hawke thought she was safe, that there was no-one after her, that she'd had a panic attack this afternoon and her reactions weren't entirely objective at the moment. Nowhere near objective, if the palpitating of her heart was anything to go by.

And then the pounding got louder. Her car wasn't further down the row. It was right there where the two men were standing. One on each side of it. The man facing her said something. Not to Jax, to the other guy. He lifted his head, turned and looked at her. She stopped, three car-lengths away on the lip of the gutter, watched as his eyes took her in before he stepped up to the footpath.

'Hey,' he called. Deep voice, nothing in it but confidence. 'You Miranda Jack?'

She flicked her gaze to the other guy. He looked right back. 'Yes,' she said.

'Can we have a word with you?' the first guy asked.

She stayed where she was, swallowed in a dry mouth, fingers tightening around the straps of her sandals. Police? A pulse tapped in her temple. Had they recognised her car? Did they have something to tell her? That Brendan *was* being followed? Her breath came faster, her heart beat louder. Maybe she was paranoid. Maybe Brendan hadn't broken anything but infected her.

'Do you mind if we talk in the car?' the guy said, pointing at it.

She glanced at her car, at the second guy, at the first one now smiling at her. There was no spark of decision, no planning. Just instinct. She took a giant step off the gutter, grabbing for the bag on her shoulder, casting a look at the people mover heading her way - and leapt in front of it. Running to beat it, reaching the footpath on the opposite side before swinging her head to see if she'd just made a fool of herself.

The people mover had braked in front of Guy Number One. He had his palms flat on its windows, watching her through them, dodging to get around it as the driver stopped and started, not sure whether to stay or go. Possibly the guy was a cop, possibly he was reacting as any cop would. Possibly, but ...

Her legs moved like they belonged to a wind-up toy. On one side of her, the path dropped two metres to the sand; across the road, the car park was behind her and she was passing big, expensive houses. Guy Number One was in the road behind her, tie blowing in the breeze, pelting along in her wake. No shouting, no orders to stop, no identifying himself as a cop. Just gunning for her.

23

Jax flung her sandals away, slung the strap of her bag across her body and pumped both arms. Up ahead, people blocked the path: a woman with a dog, a man overtaking on a bike. They could protect her. Or they could hold her up and let the other guys get to her.

'*Move!*' Jax shouted, keeping to the middle, pulling her elbows in and wincing as her bag smacked the cyclist.

There was a clatter of bike metal behind her and, 'Fuck.' She didn't know if it came from the rider or Guy Number One, whose shoes were still hitting the roadway with firm, steady beats.

Her breath was jumping and jerking, her chest barely filling, her steps short and panicky, bare feet slapping flatly on the concrete. She had no chance if she didn't get it together. *Come on!* She pulled air through her nose, pushed it out through her mouth; dropped her shoulders, softened her hips. And suddenly her pace felt slow, too relaxed, but she knew it wasn't. She hadn't run for a year but she had twenty-five more of track and trail experience, and her body knew what to do. It had hit its rhythm, knees high, stride long, oxygen powering her muscles. A tiny part of her high-fived herself, while the burning that was starting in her thighs and lungs warned her not to get cocky.

Lifting her eyes to the long white line of concrete that looped over the next headland, that went all the way to the harbour, she knew she had to get off. She was a sprinter; she'd run the four-hundred in school and at uni - the longest, hardest sprint in competition. Back in the day and going flat out, she could beat Nick over the distance, but add another two hundred metres to the equation and he'd catch up and wave as he passed her.

There were runners and walkers heading in both directions on the path. She could stop a big, burly one and cry for help but by the time she'd caught her breath and explained her problem, the guys on her tail could have picked her up and carried her away ... or pulled guns and shot her. *Guns and knives and fucking missiles.*

Across the road, houses and apartment buildings lined the streets that angled away from the water, forming the blocks of a suburb where she used to park on trips to the beach. It was a long time ago but what she needed would still be there: hedges and yards to disappear in.

A glimpse over her left shoulder told her Guy Number Two wasn't in the race. Wasn't anywhere she could see in a brief glance. Guy Number One looked like he'd settled into a comfortable, steady pace well behind her, probably figuring there was no reason to kill himself sitting at her shoulder because she'd run out of puff soon. He was right - but he'd given her room to move. She changed direction by forty-five degrees, leapt onto the road and headed for the far-side kerb of the next cross street, wheeling out wide from him, trying to ignore the hot, pebbly bitumen that cut into the soles of her feet.

The two-lane road was short, with maybe a dozen houses both sides before it met a busy street at its other end. It had a right-hand angle halfway down, a kink like the bend in a dog's hind leg, enough to hide the front of the homes on that side of the street. If she was fast, she could be around there before the arsehole behind her made it into the street.

There was no footpath here, just the tarmac, a row of parked cars and a strip of uneven, unmown grass. Jax skipped between a van and a ute, picked up her feet and bolted for the bend. Toes grateful for the cool lawn, thighs screaming, lungs in spasm.

Around the curve, two driveways ahead, a huge waste skip straddled the verge and roadway like a shipping container that had washed ashore. There was no room between it and a sagging timber fence, she'd have to circle around into the centre of the road where she'd be easy to see. She glanced behind, tried to hear beyond the dragging of her own breath - no movement, just a steady *slap-slap- slap* of shoes on bitumen.

Sensing the pool of adrenaline that had got her this far was almost dry, she pushed once more, legs like weights, feet stinging, expecting a shout or a shot as she looped around the container. At its far side, she grabbed at the ribbed metal, stumbling, grimacing with pain as she flattened against it ... mouth dropping open when she saw what was in front of her.

The shell of a massive house sat in the centre of a deserted building site. A portaloo, upended wheelbarrows, pallets of bricks, and the deep, rectangular hole of an unfinished in-ground pool.

The footsteps stopped. Was Guy Number One watching or leaving? She didn't wait to find out. The back end of the container faced a makeshift driveway - hidden, she hoped, from the street. She took off again, headed for the softer dirt around the edges of the construction space, trying to avoid discarded strips of metal and hard blobs of dried concrete. Chest heaving, heart thumping, she flicked her eyes around, searching for a hiding place. The yard was more rubble than soil and stripped of anything shrub-like, the abandoned machinery too small to disappear behind. The house was wide open front and back, probably waiting for panels of glass. She darted between a side wall and the neighbour's fence, eyeing the two storeys as she reached the rear of the block. The second level would offer views of the ocean; below it, a floor was partially laid on bearers and joists, its timbers supported by foundations rising up from the sandy soil.

Jax threw herself forward, dropped to her elbows and knees, and belly-slithered under the floor. A cool, earthy smell filled her nose as deep shadow closed around her. The handbag that had swung at her hip dragged over the dirt beneath her; the bruises on her shins and knees found solid objects; her forearms and the tops of her feet scraped over rough bumps and sharp edges. Pulling her heels under the last rows of laid flooring, she heard a whistle. A single, loud whip of sound, the kind of noise only made by lips pursed around a couple of fingers. It sent a chill scuttling across her scalp, forcing her faster, deeper under the house.

A long way in, finally stopping, knees to chest, huddling into the rigid column of a brick foundation, she listened for noises from the yard. All she heard was the rasp of her breath coming hard and fast, and blood pounding like reverb in her head. Sweat ran into her eyes, pooled in her bra, trickled into her knickers, squelched behind her knees. Whatever skin was exposed was now caked with dirt. Old and new bruises ached. The soles of her feet felt like they'd been ripped off. Maybe they had.

A car engine slowed, idled somewhere close. Moved on.

Twisting her neck, she watched the daylight where she'd crawled in - the only view she had of the yard. She'd assumed the whistle was a signal, but maybe it'd marked the end of the chase.

Then a crunch. On the rubble in the makeshift driveway. She held her breath, listened, waited. Heard the constant low rumble of cars from the main road; a caw of seagulls; the faint, distant thump of the surf. A scratching on the other side of the foundation she was pressed to.

No footsteps, no voices, no movement in the strip of yard she could see.

Cooling sweat tickled her skin, dirt shifted and scratched in uncomfortable places. Her legs were wasted, heart and lungs still working hard as she kept still, watching the daylight and thinking about Brendan. No sudden, unwanted words in her head now, just his certainty and insistence.

Oh, don't worry. They're out there.

There's more than one.

I can't see them, but they're there, I know they are. You can't escape them.

Were they looking for her now?

Was Guy Number One on the other side of the house, standing, listening, waiting for her to show him where to look?

Jax stayed huddled behind the bricks, scared of moving in case she made a sound. The scratching came and went and started up again while the collection depot in her brain threw up unnecessary facts: Cathy Freeman won the four-hundred at the 2000 Olympics in 49.11 seconds; there was a breed of rat that could grow to six kilos. Eyes now adjusted to the darkness, Jax glanced around, saw dried chunks of concrete, twisted strips of discarded wire, hamburger boxes, used takeaway bags, crushed drink cans - a builders' dumping ground. No monster rats, but something busy and tireless was scratching again. She pulled her legs in tighter, hoped whatever it was didn't reach her. Her left calf balled in a cramp, pain shot through her glutes from a rock under her butt. She winced as something dug into a rib - then gave a small, silent gasp. Her handbag.

The flap at the top had ridden up as she crawled and the inside was full of dirt and underfloor crap. She felt her way past a crusted lipstick, gritty keys and mini laptop, before finding her phone embedded with sand. *Please, please work.* Glancing at the daylight, shielding the screen, she switched it on and sent thanks to the gods of technology as a photo of Zoe showed through a smear of scratches.

She hit 'Contacts' and hesitated. Who? Russell was hours away, Tilda was singing somewhere with Zoe - and she didn't want either of them picking around a building site that may or may not have bad guys lurking. It had to be Aiden Hawke. And she'd just bawled him out on Kate Walsh's doorstep.

He answered on the first ring.

Jax cupped a hand around her mouth. 'It's Miranda Jack,' she whispered.

'Yes.' Not committing himself until he heard where she was going with this.

'Two men.' She started, stopped, swallowed at the fear stuck in her throat like a gag. 'Two men,' she hissed again. 'I was at the beach. They came after me and ... and Brendan said ... Did you send someone? Are there cops looking for me? Are they yours?'

A brief pause, then his neutral voice turned calm and measured. 'Slow down. Tell me what happened.'

She clenched her teeth, glanced at the daylight. 'Two men were at my car. They said they wanted to talk to me. I ran, one followed. I'm in a building site. They were here. I don't know if they've left.'

'Are you okay?'

'No. I lost my shoes.'

A pause. 'Where are you?'

'Under the floor.'

Another pause. 'Jax, where did you run to?'

Of course that's what he fucking meant. 'Merewether Beach, heading towards the harbour. I took a left into one of those streets going left.' She shook her head. *Think.* 'There's a house being built, a skip out front.'

'Are you out of sight?'

'Yes.'

'Then stay where you are. I'll find you.' He sounded like he was already moving. 'Turn your phone to silent and keep it on.' Another switch in his voice - from information-gathering to efficient instruction.

'How long will you be?'

There was murmuring on his end of the phone, more directives but to someone else. *Good. Send out troops.* 'Jax,' he said, 'I've got to hang up now. Don't go wandering around.'

'Do you know who they were?'

'Tell you what. You sit tight, make a list of questions, and I'll try to answer them when I find you.'

24

The scratching stopped and started twice more. The rumble of car engines and the thump of the surf continued unabated. No footsteps, no voices. Not for thirteen minutes, then a shush of sound made her body go rigid. It was followed by the soft clomp of shoes on the timber floor above her head. More than one pair. Then the phone in her hand vibrated. Aiden.

'I took a left off Merewether Beach, found a skip. I'm in a building site and there's no-one here.'

Jax ran her eyes across the strip of light again. 'So they're gone?'

'I told you to stay put.'

'I haven't moved.'

His pause was filled with a step and scrape on the timber. 'Where are you?'

'Under the floor you're standing on. Who else's feet are up there?'

'Detective Constable Suzanne May.'

The one from the motorway. 'Can I come out now?'

There was hesitant shoe shuffling. 'How did you get there?'

'Through the backyard.'

'I'll meet you there.' Footfalls moved in two directions, the heavy ones towards the rear of the house. Jax was still on her hands and knees, picking a wary path through the builders' rubbish, when she saw Aiden's feet land side-by-side in the narrowing strip of daylight. She was so relieved she wanted to laugh.

'In here,' she called.

He squatted and peered into the darkness. 'Need a hand?'

She needed a good cry but when she opened her mouth, it was some kind of been-there, survived-worse attitude that answered. 'Got a rat trap?'

He reached to his waistband as though he might actually have one. 'Sorry, no. How about this?' He flicked on a torch, lighting a path to her.

'Nice.' Very nice. She'd had serious doubts about him this afternoon, but she was revising her judgement as he moved across the strip of daylight to her closest exit point, watching her as though he was ready to dive in if she was grabbed by a rat. Man of action. Absolutely the kind of solid, capable presence she wanted around after being chased under a house. Or almost killed on a motorway. It didn't excuse his attitude at Kate Walsh's house but it gave him a few more ticks on the good-guy side of that particular ledger.

He straightened as she stepped into the fading light of the early evening, his eyes moving over her as though he was checking she had all her limbs. On some plane she was still pissed off with him, but right now all she could think was that he'd dropped everything to find her. And, wow, he looked great. As tall and steely eyed as he had been two days ago, except this time he wasn't pointing a gun at her. She could hug him. Then she was. Her arms wrapped around him, hands clutching fistfuls of shirt, face crushed into his shoulder. And for a second, maybe two, the aftershave-laced smell of him filled her up, his body warmed her bones, the fit firmness of him made her feel safe and ... and the part of her that still felt married made her pull away.

She slapped pointlessly at the dirt caked on her arms and trousers, avoiding his eyes as she examined the crust of grit on her palms, lifting them to show him with a wry grin. A mixture of concern and exasperation washed across his face. It made her feel like a recalcitrant child. She didn't care - the adrenaline that had banked up while she was under the house just wanted an outlet. Three spirited paces across the rubble was all she managed before sore feet stopped her. Hobbling to the edge of the flooring, she sat gingerly. 'Everything hurts.'

'Do you need an ambulance?'

'A shower should be enough.' She lifted a foot to examine the tender sole. 'And slippers.'

Perched beside her, Aiden cupped her ankle in one hand and shone his torch on the damage. The skin was red, inflamed, streaked with blood in a couple of places. His fingers were firm, steady, warm. 'How did that happen?'

'When I saw the two guys at the car park, I tossed my shoes and bolted.'

It took him a second. 'You ran barefoot?'

'And you thought I was worried about my shoes.'

He tipped his head to one side. 'I thought you were upset.'

Something caught in her throat and her vision blurred as the gentle empathy in his voice made her bravado catch and swing like a pendulum. She turned her face away. His hand on her ankle softened, thumb sliding across the dirt with a scratchy rub. It was comfort - she was more than grateful - but he was probably deciding she'd had enough, that any more questions would be best handled with avoidance.

Only there *were* more questions now, starting with: Who the hell had chased her? She lifted her chin, faced him again. 'I want to know what that was about.'

He held her gaze. Not with the standard, neutral cop look or the fore-runner to a refusal. It seemed personal. Intimate and searching. Concern and reluctance in it. Something warm, too, as though the heat of his thumb as it passed over the notch of her ankle was being communicated through his eyes.

She should look away, she told herself. He might see something she didn't want him to. She might find something she wasn't ready for.

'Sarge?' It was the detective from the motorway, Suzanne May, her black hair tied back now and her voice low, maybe not wanting to disturb the neighbours. Or her boss.

Aiden's fingers slipped from Jax's ankle before he turned. 'Yeah.'

'We've got the car. It's parked opposite Merewether Beach.' She jerked a finger over her shoulder. 'Just round the corner.'

When he looked at Jax again, his eyes were back to business. 'Were you in your car when you were approached?'

'No, I was walking to it. They were standing either side of it.'

He turned back to the detective. 'Have it taped off and get finger-printing to put in an appearance.' He stood, directing another question at Jax. 'Can you walk that far?'

'Yes.' If hobbling was considered walking.

'Good. You can tell me what happened on the way.'

He spoke quietly to the detective before she left, then led Jax to the corner of the house she'd thrown herself around half an hour earlier. The sky wasn't dark yet but close, so he lit up his torch again. The earth was harder than she remembered, more painful to negotiate the second time around, and she held on to the fence with one hand as she limped ahead of him.

'I could carry you to the road,' Aiden offered.

'A piggy back?'

'I was thinking more of a fireman's hold.'

And have her sandy arse in his face? 'Thanks but I'll pass.'

The thump of the waves was louder out on the road and eerie in the twilight. The temperature had dropped to a more comfortable level and the breeze that met them straight off the ocean was cool and salty and slightly damp.

'When I called,' she said, falling into step beside him, 'I thought you'd assume I was ringing to apologise.'

'Do you want to?'

'No. Do you?' She heard a quiet huff, somewhere between a chuckle and a scoff. *Guess not.*

He switched off the torch, leaving the streetlights to cast soft circles on the bitumen at their feet. 'Tell me what happened.'

There wasn't much to tell but she went through the details trying to keep to the facts, the way he'd directed when she'd given her statement. They rounded the curve in the road as she spoke, the beachfront path at the end of the street coming into view. A jogger ran left to right, passing a walker being dragged by three dogs.

They'd reached the intersection when Jax finished and she stopped and turned to Aiden. 'Were there cops looking for me?'

He faced the orange glow coming off the sodium lights along the path, looking down to the police car now parked where it had all started. 'Why do you think they were cops?'

'That's what I first assumed. And they looked like you.'

He frowned.

'Business shirt, tie, dark trousers, neat, fit,' she said. It sounded like Brendan, too, minus the tie. It sounded like anyone who worked in an office and went to a gym. 'So were there detectives looking for me?'

'Not any of mine.' He put hands on his hips, glanced around. 'Are you sure the guy was chasing you?'

'What do you mean? He wasn't chasing anyone else.'

'He wasn't just running and you mistook it for chasing?'

'Mistook it?' Did he think she was an idiot?

'Brendan Walsh convinced you there were people after him. It's understandable you might feel uneasy. I'm wondering if you might have misinterpreted what happened.'

'I'm a little paranoid, yeah, but I'm not delusional. And that guy followed me all the way to the house.'

'Are you sure?'

'He was behind me in the side street and then I heard him on the rubble in the driveway.'

'Did you see him after you got to the house?'

She hesitated. 'I *heard* him. And a car.'

'It's a street. People use it.'

'No.' She shook her head - firm, adamant. 'I didn't get it wrong. Those two men were standing by my car, one asked if I was Miranda Jack, then he was powering down the road after me. Arms and legs working it. He didn't decide to go for a jog.'

He nodded again. Took another glance around. 'What about media?'

She wanted to say not anyone she knew, wanted to tell him there was nothing in the story worth chasing now, but she hesitated again. Jax wouldn't pursue the subject of a story if they ran - it didn't mean it didn't happen. The media was a cutthroat industry and it wasn't limited to trained journalists working for publishers and broadcasters these days. Anyone could write what they liked on the net and if you had a mobile phone and a social media account, you could upload pictures as soon as you shot them. Jax and her car had already been splashed all over the news and internet. Had someone tried to make a buck off her? An editor somewhere would pay for pictures of a fleeing Miranda Jack. It didn't have to be about money, though - shots of the gun-toting woman from the motorway might score a lot of hits on YouTube. It might even spark debate about whether she had something to hide. 'Maybe,' she admitted, 'but it didn't feel like that.'

'It's a fair distance from your car to the house,' Aiden said.

She nodded. 'My guess is four hundred metres on the button to the skip.'

'You had bare feet.'

'Yes.'

'Two fit-looking men, presumably with shoes -'

'Only one ran. I didn't see where the other went. But yeah, he had shoes.'

'And you stayed ahead of him. In bare feet.'

She heard the doubt in his voice. It was fair enough. 'A car held him up.'

'You sure you weren't further away when you started running?'

Did he think she'd got the facts out of order? 'No. I used to run. The four-hundred was my event. I've covered that distance so many times I could do it in my sleep. Any further and I wouldn't have made it.' She held an arm out, tracing the curving course she'd taken, remembering her alarm but feeling a hyped-up sense of elation that was better than any first place she'd ever won. 'The corner is tighter than a track and I had to take it wide and cut in fast but the guy had slowed. I think he figured I'd die about here. I almost did but muscle memory and a shitload of adrenaline count for a lot.'

He said nothing for a good ten seconds, something amused working its way onto his lips.

She put her hands on her hips. 'Don't you believe me?'

'Yeah, actually, I do.'

There was something else. 'And?'

'And ...' He raised an eyebrow. 'The four-hundred. That's relatively cool.' He turned, started walking, spoke over his shoulder. 'Come on, Cathy Freeman. Let's look for your shoes.'

She hobbled after him, wanting to raise her arms in a silent cheer. She hadn't got closer than tickets in the stalls to an Olympics, but thirty-five years old, covered in dirt, widowed, worn-out and shaken up - and she could still be relatively cool. It earned him another tick on the right side of her ledger.

'Over there.' She pointed across the road to the hand-railing that kept pedestrians from the two-metre drop to the sand.

'You were on that side of the street when you lost your shoes?'

'I didn't lose them. I threw them. There's one.' A sandal had landed upright beside a lamppost as though she'd simply stepped out of it.

Aiden walked ahead, picked it up and stood for a moment looking down the street to the parking area, as though measuring the distance. About fifty metres, she wanted to tell him. A slow, uncontrolled fifty that was only salvaged because of the people mover that had held up Guy Number One. Then she spotted her other sandal. 'The left one is down there.' She aimed a finger over the railing to the dark beach below.

He turned but looked at her, not the sand. 'Why did you run?'

'I don't know. It, they seemed ... off.'

'That's it? They were off?'

'Yeah.' She shrugged. 'They didn't say who they were and there was something about the way they were looking into the car.' And maybe it was the anxious, unnerved thing living inside her.

He watched her for a beat or two. 'There's nothing else you want to tell me?'

She took a breath, about to say, *Paranoid, remember?* Saw his flat cop eyes and changed her mind. 'No, that's it.'

Another pause. Then he handed her the sandal. 'I'll get the uniform to fetch the other one up.'

She grabbed at his sleeve as he made to walk on. 'It has to be about Brendan, don't you think?'

He took a second to answer. 'It's one of the options.'

In the car park, her Mazda was cordoned off in a rectangle of blue-and-white police tape. Aiden had another quiet conference with another cop, heads together, then pointing at the railing above her sandal. As the uniformed officer trotted across the road, Aiden tapped a message on his phone before joining her again. 'Your car will have to be towed for fingerprinting.'

'Again? I only picked it up a few hours ago.'

'I'll make sure you get it back tomorrow.'

She glanced around the now empty beachfront road, feeling the energy high start to drop, taking her mood with it. 'Right. Well. I'll call a cab.'

'No. Suzanne is bringing the car around. I'll drive you home.'

Ten minutes later, Jax had both sandals and was sitting in the front seat of an unmarked police car giving directions to Tilda's house, the last drops of her adrenaline draining away as though they were being sucked from the bottom of a glass through a straw. She was cold, dirty and exhausted. She wanted a hot shower and a soft bed but would have to hold it together a while longer - the sight of her would be enough to make her aunt and daughter gasp, and she didn't want to make it worse by asking for help to get down the stairs.

Aiden stopped across the driveway and pulled the handbrake. It was almost fully dark outside and his face was in shadow but when he turned towards her, she could see intention in the line of his mouth. He had something to say and she hoped listening wouldn't require too much concentration.

'I like you, Jax. I liked you fifteen years ago at uni.'

Oh no, she didn't want to hear any more. Not now, when fatigue might put the wrong response into her head. When she wasn't sure what the right response was, the one she'd give on a normal day, without the dusky intimacy of the car between them; when she had a chance to think beyond his impressive arrival tonight. She began to raise a hand, but he continued before she had a chance to stop him.

'I know you've had a difficult time in the last year,' he said, 'and I know it's not the first difficult time you've had to deal with. You've got some tough-arsed survivor thing going on and I respect that. I've seen some of the alternatives and believe me, yours is a lot better. You need closure, I understand that. And I want to help you get it.'

'Aiden -'

'This is a police investigation, Jax. There are serious consequences that I won't be able to protect you from if details are omitted. You need to start talking to me. And it needs to happen soon.'

25

J ax opened her mouth and closed it again, her brain trying to catch the meaning of his words, wondering if she was too exhausted to connect the dots. Serious consequences? For her? And she'd been stupid enough to think he was making a pass.

Aiden watched her as though her silence was subtext. 'I know you've had issues with Homicide,' he went on, 'but I don't answer to Anita Lyneham. I run my own investigation and it doesn't have to be like that here. You can trust me on that.'

Jax didn't understand what he wanted or was offering, she just remembered his attitude outside Kate Walsh's house. 'After what you said to me at Kate's, why should I believe that?'

His eyes slid back and forth between hers. Whatever he read, it made his voice almost tender. 'I was there, Jax. I saw what happened. I wrote up your statement. You had Brendan Walsh in your head for almost two hours. I get that.'

She glanced away, an unexpected wetness on her lashes, the gentleness of his tone making her want to talk – about Brendan, the questions, the constant buzz of anxiety. Was that what he wanted? To provide the kind of emotional support that Anita Lyneham didn't consider part of her job? Jax licked her lips, thought about telling him Brendan was standing behind her, whispering in her ear, breathing on her neck.

What would Aiden see then? Twenty minutes ago, he called her relatively cool. It had felt good, possibly in a way she wasn't ready to think about, but right now she wanted him to stay with 'relatively cool'. More to the point, she wanted to be kept in the loop - and explaining just exactly how she was losing her mind wouldn't get her that. She looked back at him. 'I'll think about it.'

Aiden's gaze was unwavering but there was a shift behind his eyes. 'Okay,' he said, voice firmer, 'but I need to inform you that the focus of the investigation will change now. You were chased tonight and it's my job to work out why. You need to know, Jax, that I'm good at my job. I will work it out and it'll be better for you if you talk to me before then.'

She leaned against the door, trying to compute the change in attitude. It was advice, official advice, not emotional support. 'What are you thinking?'

'You have my mobile number. It's on 24/7.'

'That's not an answer.'

A glow lit up the night behind her. He nodded towards the house. 'Your aunt,' he said, and reached for the door.

Jax snapped a hand out, curling fingers around his arm. 'Aiden?'

'Mummy!' Zoe's muffled voice on the other side of the passenger window was accompanied by a tug on the handle. 'Mummy, I can't get in!'

Aiden pushed open his door, turned back before he stepped out. 'Don't take too long, Jax.'

Both Tilda and Zoe were on the driveway. Curiosity must have drawn them out - Jax had been gone a long time and she was returning in someone else's car - but it wasn't what was on their faces when they saw her. Tilda let out a small gasp and Zoe's mouth hung open. 'What did you do, Mummy?'

Good question, Jax thought, glancing at Aiden as he came around the car. 'Silly me, I fell down a hole and the police had to come get me.' She took a step, failing to hide a wince as the swollen putty of her feet hit the hard driveway.

'A *hole*?' Zoe exclaimed, her eyes travelling a circuit from her mother's clothes down to her bare feet and up to the man in the driveway. She hadn't met Aiden after the carjacking, he'd left Jax to hug her daughter in private, but Zoe was connecting her own dots. 'Are you the police?' she asked.

Aiden nodded. 'Yes.'

'You don't have a uniform.'

'That's because I'm a detective. Detective Hawke, like the bird. I've got big wings and sharp claws.'

Zoe giggled but Jax wondered if it was another veiled message for her.

Tilda drew her niece closer, as though the detective had brought whatever happened home in his talons. She glanced warily from Aiden to Jax. 'Are you hurt?'

'Sore feet, is all. And I need a shower.'

'Yes. Yes, of course you do. Come inside. Both of you.'

Jax took a few painful steps, felt Aiden's hand at her elbow and let him help her down the steep drive, not caring now how it made her look. He'd already come to a conclusion without her knowing how he got there.

'We're having ice-cream,' Zoe said as she skipped into the foyer. 'Ice-cream will make your feet better. It always makes me better.'

As she started a complicated hop-jump combination up the stairs, Tilda moved ahead to turn on the lights over the downward staircase. 'Can I make you a drink, Detective?'

'No thanks. I can't stay.' He stopped Jax at the threshold, lowered his head to hers, his words barely more than a whisper. 'Whatever it is, it's not safe to keep it to yourself now.'

She wasn't sure if the closeness was to keep his voice from Zoe and Tilda or to make sure his words hit home, but when he moved away she was left with the warmth of his breath on her cheek and an anxious twist in her gut. He was out in the driveway when she turned, looking back at her, thumb and pinkie to his head like a phone. 'Anytime, Jax.'

She resisted the urge to watch him all the way to the car. What for? To see if he took one last glance before he left. She wasn't sure she wanted him to or that she'd have any idea what it meant. She'd clearly misunderstood his other cues and somehow 'relatively cool' had become deceptive and possibly unlawful. Thirty-five, dirty, beaten down and just plain stupid.

As she closed the door, she saw Tilda watching from across the foyer, a crease of concern on her face. 'What happened, Jax?'

'Mummy, are you coming?' Zoe called from above.

'I'll sit with her. You need to get cleaned up,' Tilda said quietly, taking Jax by the arm and guiding her to the staircase. 'A shower downstairs or the bath upstairs?'

Jax flicked her eyes to the darkness at the bottom of the steps and knew she wasn't ready to be alone yet. 'Upstairs.' She raised her voice. 'Coming, baby.'

Redirecting her to the first step, Tilda said, 'I'll get the bath running.'

So Jax could soak in there all on her own. 'No, it's okay. I think I'll sit with you guys for a while.'

'But you're covered in . . .' Her aunt frowned at her face, her clothes.

'Dirt. Probably some cement dust.'

Reaching up to Jax's hair, Tilda pulled off something sticky.

'Spider web. Yuck. I'm sorry, I'll try not to spread it around. I just need to ...' *Be still, be safe, be home.* 'Sit for a while.'

One step from the top, Tilda asked again: 'Jax, what happened?'

Jax could see Zoe from there, at the table and poking at her ice-cream - and felt the heat of tears behind her eyelids. 'I can't, Tilda. Not yet. I'll tell you later, okay?' Swallowing hard, placing her sore feet carefully, she forced a smile for Zoe. 'Ice-cream and chocolate soup, yum. Maybe I will have some.'

Tilda fussed over her in silence, bringing her a wet cloth to clean her face and hands, then a bowl of vanilla ice-cream with chocolate topping, then a large Scotch on ice. Actually, Tilda brought two of those to the table and started on the second one herself as Jax spun a brief tale about falling into a hole at the beach to satisfy Zoe's questions. Then Jax hobbled down the stairs to put her daughter to bed, breathing in the bubble-bath smell of Zoe's hair as she kissed her goodnight, glad now she hadn't established boundaries and that Tilda had stepped in to help.

Her aunt was running water into a plastic basin when Jax flicked off the light in the hallway. Tilda tipped in a dollop of disinfectant, carried the tub to the floor in front of the sofa and said, 'Put your feet in this.'

As Jax pulled faces at the sting of skin meeting antiseptic, Tilda sat beside her and handed over the rest of her Scotch, waiting until she'd taken a sip before asking again, 'How did you get like this?'

Jax thought about the running and the dirt and the dark and couldn't bring herself to leap right into it. So she started with everything that had come before. Meeting Kate Walsh, arguing with Aiden, throwing up in the gutter, making the list. The longer she talked without getting to the point, the more the uneasiness in her aunt's face deepened. But Tilda didn't interrupt. Maybe she understood Jax needed to talk it out, that in the old days it'd taken time and words for her to find her way to the heart of it.

When Jax got to the part about the two men at her car, Tilda picked up her niece's hand and held it, tightening her grip as Jax described the sprint to the building site and the scrabble under the floorboards.

At the end, Tilda didn't attempt to sum up or tell her she was safe or offer sympathy. Just touched her hair and whispered, 'Jax, honey.'

And Jax burst into tears, sobbing like she hadn't for months. She felt lighter by the time it eased up, although it didn't seem to help Tilda. She rubbed Jax's back, inspected her feet, insisted on applying a lotion to the abrasions.

'I don't know what to make of Aiden,' Jax said, as Tilda dabbed at her toes.

'It can be like that with handsome men.'

A *ha* of amusement jumped from Jax's throat. 'I wasn't talking about his looks.'

'Nevertheless, sex appeal can be very confusing.'

It seemed a ridiculous subject to be discussing right then, but maybe that was why Tilda had changed directions. Besides, her aunt had spent three years studying art in Paris after her first husband died, and another five managing an artists' retreat near Barcelona. She probably knew a lot about handsome men and sex appeal.

'I'm not confused about sex appeal,' Jax said. 'I still feel married.'

'From my experience, that's the confusing part.'

Jax remembered the heat and hardness of Aiden's body against hers, and her face grew hot. 'Aiden thinks I'm hiding something.'

'About what?'

She thought about his words as they'd sat in the car and before that, the way he'd questioned her about the chase. 'About tonight, I think. Maybe about Brendan, too. Or Kate Walsh. I'm not sure.'

'Are you hiding something?'

'I've no reason to.'

Tilda screwed the lid back on the lotion, took up both of Jax's hands. 'I think you should let the police do their job. You've been through enough. You *and* Zoe. That man, Brendan ... you didn't even know him. And he's gone, there's nothing you can do to help him now.'

'It's possible the people who chased me tonight were the same ones after him.'

'Then it's a matter for the police.'

Jax ran a hand through the grit in her hair. 'He wanted me to tell his wife something.'

'Maybe she doesn't want to know.'

And Jax didn't know what his message was. 'It's just. . . there are so many questions.'

'There will always be questions, Jax. As long as you live, you'll have questions. But you have to think of yourself. You're so tense and there's the crying and not sleeping. I know it's only been a couple of days but you're still dealing with Nick and you've been there before. You don't want to go down that road again, honey. You've got Zoe to think about this time.'

It isn't like that, Jax wanted to tell her. It was worse - and better. She'd been scared shitless twice in two days but she felt ... alive. Blood was pumping in her veins, which was better than it lying stagnant inside her as it had for the past year. As it had after her parents' deaths. But she didn't tell Tilda that. She wasn't sure if euphoria was a symptom of some other problem. The kind that went hand-in-hand with imagining dead people at her shoulder. So she just nodded.

Tilda patted her hand like she was a good girl. 'It's not giving up, honey. It's moving on.'

Which was why she was here, in the bottom storey of Tilda's house, Jax reminded herself. She'd come to end an obsession, not start another one. 'Yeah, you're right. Moving on. For Zoe.'

Letting go, stepping back, taking a back seat, not asking questions. All the stuff she was good at.

26

The clock read three fifty-six when Jax woke, her heart pounding, her mouth dry and scary images playing behind her eyelids. She visited the bathroom, drank a glass of water, hobbled around the apartment on sore feet - checking windows and locks, peering into the courtyard, skittish and uneasy.

There was a remedy for this, one she'd discovered in other restless, agitated early hours. Her pacifier, her obsession.

Limping back to her bedroom, Jax lifted the document box onto the mattress, pulled a folder from the front, flicked through it. Shoved it back, tried another. Statements from residents who lived near the road Nick was found on and along the kerb where his car was parked. The list of items from his car and the ones police had removed from his office. The clothes he was wearing, the contents of his stomach, the length of the skid marks his body left in the gravel. And more, much more. She pulled pages from the front, the middle, the rear: random, haphazard selections in a search for a file or a record that would hold her attention. There was always one - but not this morning. And she wondered if the new house, the new bedroom, had finally informed her brain there was nothing more to learn, nothing she'd missed, no two-and-two's she hadn't put together. Or whether there were too many new questions chasing her down. Ones she might have a better chance of answering.

Except she'd told Tilda she wouldn't ask.

She understood her aunt's concern - Tilda had mopped up the pieces after Jax's breakdown fifteen years ago. But with Brendan Walsh at her shoulder and a bunch of scary memories churning, moving on, letting go - whatever it was - felt like falling.

For Jax, surviving shocking, life-altering loss was like running on a treadmill ten metres off the ground. You were fine so long as you kept up with the mat moving under your feet, so long as you kept lifting your knees, pumping your arms and pulling in air. But if you slowed, if you lost momentum, you fell and hit the ground. Hard.

Fifteen years ago, she had.

For the last twelve months, she'd been trying to hold that off.

This week, even before Brendan got in her car - packing up the house, saying the final goodbye to a life she'd loved - the fall had felt close.

Tilda was right. Jax had Zoe to think about now - and her daughter was every reason to keep running.

Jax got up, found her handbag - now free of dirt - took the notebook out, sat on the bed again and flipped to the Real/Not Real ledger.

The man who'd chased her had used her name but anyone who'd watched the TV or read a newspaper in the past two days would. He'd chased her, though, with intent - and if she was right about the whistle and the noise on the rubble, he'd searched for her, too. Quietly, covertly. She wanted to write 'people after Brendan' in the Real column but knew Nick would have said, *Not yet, Jax.*

Turning to a new page, she recalled what Brendan had told her about the pursuers he feared, and wrote:

More than one. Working together. Prepared.

She made more lists after that, reorganising what she had, including who might have answers to what. She ran on the treadmill for an hour before firing up the big laptop on her desk.

There was another email from Russell: *If Walsh ever met Nick, it wasn't in Afghanistan. Tours dates below.*

Jax ran her eyes over the two time periods Brendan had spent in Afghanistan - a total of eighteen months in the desert. Both he and Nick were there in 2009, but Brendan left for the final time five months before Nick's brief visit.

Then she Googled PTSD, the war in Afghanistan, returned soldiers, contract security work and Secure Force, the company that had employed Brendan ... keeping up the momentum, feeling in control, assertive, calmer. She told herself it wasn't about the questions and answers this time. That it was enough to get her thoughts in order, to make some sense of the information she had. That she wasn't letting anyone down if she didn't find the answers.

STRIDENT MUSIC JERKED her from sleep. She bashed the laptop as she fumbled around the sheets for her mobile, swiped the screen, squinted through one eye - seven-sixteen - and croaked, 'Yep.'

'Is that Miranda Jack?' The voice was female, tremulous and vaguely familiar.

Apprehension made her sit up, clear her throat. 'Yes?'

'It's Kate Walsh.' She said nothing more, her words thick with emotion. Crying or trying not to.

Was it grief or something else? 'Are you okay?'

'Can you come back?'

Now? Did she mean now? Did she need the police there too? 'Yes. Yes, of course. Has something happened?'

'I want to know. I want you to tell me all of it.'

JAX SQUATTED in front of Zoe outside Kate Walsh's gate. 'Remember, Zoe, the people in the house are sad today. You know what that's like, don't you?'

Zoe nodded sagely.

'So try to be ... I don't know ...'

'Nice?' Zoe said.

'Yes, baby. Nice is perfect.'

Jax had thought about asking Tilda to keep Zoe with her again. Then remembered Tilda taught an all-day art class on Thursdays and that paint, nude models and six- year-olds just didn't belong together. And Kate had insisted Jax bring Zoe.

Without a car, they'd walked the steps down the hill hand-in-hand, Jax's feet too sore to fit into anything but thongs, her calves and thighs feeling like they'd been pummelled. The memory of the chase made her glance up and down the street again before opening the gate.

The leathery man was at the front door. Eyes peered out of wrinkled folds at Jax and then down at Zoe, who gave him a toothy smile. He didn't return it.

'She's in the kitchen,' he said, and stood aside to let them into the hallway.

Zoe's little fingers crawled inside Jax's palm as they followed him to the end of the corridor this time, into a sunny room the width of the house. The kitchen took up one side, a family area the other, and big windows and glass sliding doors looked out to a neat, square garden.

Kate Walsh was on the kitchen side of a breakfast bar. The small upturn of her lips as they walked in seemed to communicate sadness, exhaustion, appreciation. 'Thanks for coming,' she said.

Jax nodded, understanding the concoction of emotions. 'This is my daughter, Zoe.'

Kate's face softened with the kind of expression that came from finding something sweet in the midst of sorrow. 'Hey, Zoe. I'm making a banana milkshake for Scotty. Would you like one?'

'Yes, please.' Zoe tried out her toothy grin again. Kate smiled back and Jax wondered if her daughter might provide more comfort than she was about to.

'Mummy, there's a swing.' Zoe pointed to the windows.

A play set sat in a back corner of the yard. Closer to the house, a couple of big yellow toy trucks were idle on a mound of sand where a small boy had his head down, digging a hole with a spade.

'You can have a go, if you like,' Kate said. 'That's Scotty out there. I'm sure he'll give you a push.'

Jax gave her daughter a gentle nudge. 'Go and meet Scotty and have a nice time.'

Zoe made big eyes, her kid's version of got-it. As the leathery man slid open the back door for her, Scotty lifted his head and Brendan Walsh whispered in Jax's ear.

He looks just like me at that age.

He looked plenty like his father had three days ago. Not the craziness but the dark hair and eyes, and something about the way the boy cast a sideways glance at the door sent both a chill and a great wave of sorrow through Jax.

Kate must have seen her reaction. 'He looks like Brendan, doesn't he?'

'Yes.'

'Does Zoe look like her father?'

The unexpected reminder of Nick made Jax stiffen.

'Sorry,' Kate said. 'I just wondered if the physical reminder was going to be a comfort or a source of pain.'

'It's okay. Zoe looks like her dad but she's more like me. I guess the reminder is both painful and a comfort. That probably doesn't help much.'

Kate flicked a glance at the leathery man, who was standing by the door watching the children, and lowered her voice. 'Actually, it's good to have someone who'll talk about it.' She lifted a coffee plunger. 'I need more caffeine. Join me?'

'Yes, thanks.'

'Jock?' Kate called across the room. Leathery Man turned his head. 'I'm okay here. I think you should go to bowls with Marilyn.'

He cast suspicious eyes at Jax. 'If you're sure.'

'I am. Thanks, Jock. And Hugh Talbotson is on his way back from Sydney. He'll be here in a little while. You guys need some time off.' Kate waited until Jock had dithered and grumbled for a couple of moments before disappearing out the back door and around the house.

'He's my neighbour,' Kate explained. 'He and his wife Marilyn have been great. They've hardly been home since … since it happened. This morning, he didn't want to leave until someone was here with me. I don't know what he thinks is going to happen. He's a tough old bugger, but it's nice.' She cocked her head. 'Nice to have some time off from them, too.'

Kate talked as she made coffee and blended milkshakes, her voice tight but not the broken, tear-filled one from the phone, giving Jax a brisk update as though she'd asked to be filled in. Kate's parents were in Europe on holiday and wouldn't be back for another couple of days. She had a sister in Queensland who would come down for the funeral. There was no date yet because there had to be an autopsy and the police hadn't confirmed when the body would be released. She hoped the service was held before she had to be back at her teaching job, and she was glad Scotty was on school holidays and the other kids wouldn't be asking about his dad.

Jax 'mmm'd' and nodded through it, wondering if Kate was avoiding the elephant in the room until she could sit down with coffee in hand, or whether she needed to get all the small stuff off her mind before she could concentrate. When she finally fell silent, the children were drinking their milkshakes in the shade outside, and Kate and Jax were sitting in matching sofas. Brendan's wife held a steaming mug between her palms, her eyes focused on the liquid inside, lips a tight line.

Jax mirrored her pose, in no hurry to tell the story again knowing it would hurt someone this time. Her thoughts wandered to the lists in the notebook that was in her handbag and the questions they were prompting. She hadn't come to ask them, had just wanted to help staunch Kate Walsh's bleeding wound, but now Jax was here, she hoped there might be an opening.

'You've got bruises on your legs,' Kate said softly. 'Did Brendan do that?'

Jax glanced at the splotches of colour below the hemline of her three-quarter trousers. 'Not intentionally. He made me get out of the car through the passenger door. I hit the gearstick a few times as he ... helped me across.'

'God.' Kate squeezed her eyes shut, took a gulp of coffee before opening them. 'Tell me. Just tell me.'

If Kate was having a hard time with bruises, Jax thought, she might need a doctor by the time she heard the rest. 'It's not great. He scared me, threatened to kill me and did a lot of crazy talking. How much do you want to know?'

'Sorry. It must be difficult for you to talk about.'

'No, it's okay. I can tell you but I don't want to upset you.'

On the other side of the coffee table, Kate put her mug down and lifted her chin - pride or courage, possibly both. 'For years, I wanted to understand what was going on with Brendan. He tried to explain it to me. We went to the counselling. I watched him suffer through awful nightmares.' She stopped, pressed her lips together, started again. 'I thought he was getting better. *He* thought he was getting better. And then ... *this.*' The word was said through clenched teeth, infused with anger and frustration and powerlessness. 'He had problems but I loved him. I want to know why this happened, why my husband is dead. The police won't tell me the details so I'm asking you. I'm already upset, Miranda. I just want to understand. Does that make sense?'

As far as Jax was concerned, her logic was perfect. 'Yes.'

'Then help me. Please.'

27

J ax told the story again, this time focusing on Brendan's reactions, his moods, what pre-empted the anger and tears, trying to summarise the rambling into something more coherent. As she talked, she watched Kate for a reaction - shock, recognition, surprise, anything that might reveal something of his reality. But Kate didn't speak and barely moved, sitting with her hands clasped tightly in her lap, eyes lowered, braced for the worst.

Jax imagined herself in the same place, hearing ugly truths about Nick three days after he was run down. She would've interrupted with questions and demands and denials. Now, though, after everything, maybe she'd be exactly like Kate Walsh, ready to hear anything as long as it was an explanation.

When she was done, Jax waited for Kate to speak. She didn't. She didn't move at all. 'Kate?'

There were tears brimming in her eyes when she lifted her head.

Jax tried to make her voice gentle. 'You don't seem shocked by any of that.'

Twin droplets tumbled over Kate's lashes. 'I don't know what I feel. Numb. Sick. I was hoping it would be better but I thought it could have been worse.'

'You thought it might come to that?'

'For a long time I was worried he might try to kill himself, but never like this. And not for months. When I spoke to him on Saturday afternoon, he was tired, he'd just finished a long job. But he seemed ...' She stopped, closed her eyes, held them shut for a long moment. 'I was mad at him. I wanted him to come home for what was left of the weekend. He wanted to take an extra shift.'

Jax felt a stab of empathy. An awful last conversation to remember. 'Was he angry?'

'No. Apologetic. He wanted me to understand.'

'Understand what?'

'That earning some good money made him feel better about ... everything.'

'Everything?'

'About the PTSD, about not working, about Afghanistan. Everything that made him feel less of a man.'

Brendan had apologised to Jax, too. *Yeah, look, sorry about all this.* Then he'd gone crazy over people wanting to pick him off. Maybe that was what he'd been like. Apologetic one moment, angry the next. Maybe he'd lost his temper after Kate hung up. 'Was Brendan erratic? Aggressive?'

The shake of her head was sad, cynical, weary. 'Not when I met him. Not before Afghanistan. Back then he was this cool, fun guy wandering through life, having a good time - everyone's mate, you know?' Kate picked up her mug again, just nursed it in her hands. 'His older sister drowned in a boating accident when he was fifteen. He'd decided it was his job to have a good time for her as well. He was an electrician and basically working and partying. He used to joke that I nagged him into the army but it wasn't like that. He'd always wanted to do it, used to talk about it and never did anything. So finally I told him I didn't want to be with someone who didn't follow through, and he went out the next day and got the paperwork.' Kate turned her face to the window, eyes angled to where Scotty and Zoe were sitting in the sandpit, waving their hands around and singing. Jax watched too, trying to align this younger, fun version of Brendan with the one who'd got in her car.

'He loved the army,' Kate said. 'He loved the guys and the training and the whole doing-something-for-his-country thing. It made him feel like a better person, fed his sense of duty.' She turned to Jax, grief and anger filling her eyes and her voice. 'And Afghanistan ruined him. He used to tell people I was the best thing that happened to him but I ruined him, too. I wish I could take back my words and tell him that not following through was fine, perfect, the best thing for both of us.' She pressed a hand to her face, then pulled it away, clenching it into a fist. 'That fucking war was responsible for what happened to him. For what's happening to Scotty and me.' She pointed at the bruises on Jax's shins. 'For what happened to you.'

Jax felt as though the Afghan desert had risen up and thrown sand in her face. She'd only been touched by the war briefly and from a distance. When Nick was researching his big story, she'd read some of his notes, transcribed interviews, run her eyes over the outline of the book he'd started before he died. He'd spent a week over there talking to soldiers and was kept well away from the action, but the photos she'd seen of him in a helmet and bulletproof vest had made her stomach churn. She imagined it was nothing to what Kate and others felt for loved ones who were over there to face the firepower. Even working in the media, Jax had avoided more than a fleeting professional connection. By the time the war had started, she was a features writer - her speciality was human interest, not politics, and her single story on the soldiers leaving amounted to the only words she'd penned about Afghanistan or Iraq. She'd had her own opinion, had argued the case at dinner parties when the troops began heading out, had felt shock and sadness and fury at the fatalities. Now she felt tarnished by it.

And sitting on Brendan's sofa, she wanted to be more than his story-teller. She wanted to rail with Kate, console her, give her someone to cry with. She also wanted to pull the notebook from her bag and launch a thousand questions.

After a career built on drawing people out and a year struggling with sadness and frustration, she knew sitting in a chair didn't get the same results as having something to do while you talked about the hard stuff. 'How about more coffee?'

She suggested they make it together and asked for directions around the kitchen. While she filled the kettle and found coffee grounds, she started on questions that might give Kate's heartache a rest - and possibly fill in a few gaps on the Real/Not Real ledger. 'Brendan said you're a teacher. What do you teach?'

Kate pulled fresh mugs from a cupboard. 'Primary. I've got my own class for the first time this term. Year Three.'

'So you haven't been teaching for long?'

'Ten years on and off, but I've only ever had casual placements. You can't get anything else when you're being posted around with the army, then it took us a while to decide where we wanted to stay. We've been in Newcastle almost three years and it's taken that long to get this position.'

Jax poured boiling water. 'Does Scotty go to your school?'

'Yes, which makes mornings and afternoons easier. I put in a big effort to get a place there for that reason. Made a real nuisance of myself until they started giving me casual classes. Although Scotty'll probably hate it eventually. It's not much fun having your mum around when you're trying to be cool.'

'Brendan said Scotty was pretty smart. That he could read before he started school.'

Kate smiled a little. 'Brendan used to think it was going to make him a Rhodes Scholar or something. Scotty always loved books and we spent so much time together when Brendan was away, and with the PTSD, and ... well, I'm a teacher and I suppose I didn't have anyone else to teach.'

Jax understood that - she asked questions whether she had a job or not. 'What was Brendan like when he got back from Afghanistan?'

Kate kept her attention on the fruit she was slicing for such a long, silent moment that Jax wondered if she was deciding she didn't want to talk about bad days.

'When he came home the first time,' she finally said, 'he slept on the floor. He'd go to bed with me and I'd wake up alone and he'd be on the floor by the door.'

Jax rested a hip against the counter. 'Was he guarding the room?'

'He said he got used to it and found it more comfortable, but I mean, it wasn't next to the bed, it was by the door. And there were nightmares. He'd wake up shouting and on his feet, ready to take off somewhere.'

'Dreaming about what happened over there?'

'He said he couldn't remember. He tried to pretend there was nothing wrong but he spent days just sitting around as though he didn't have the energy to move. Then other times, he'd be anxious and restless, keyed up and short tempered. It was really hard for Scotty to understand.'

'For you too, I imagine.'

Kate put the knife down, lifted the plate, didn't get any further. 'Yeah.' Her voice was quiet, almost a whisper, and her eyes drifted to the window. Eventually, she pulled in a long, unsteady breath. 'Let's sit outside.'

Jax followed her through the back door into the late-morning heat, her interest piqued but discomfort prickling the back of her neck. She liked Kate. Yes, a psychologist would probably tell her there were myriad reasons why she'd want to find a connection with Kate Walsh: Brendan, Nick, death by vehicle, undelivered messages, unanswered questions, and so on. But Jax thought there was more to it. Kate was smart and determined. She worked for what she wanted, tried to look beneath the surface of her life for its truth, and she bought good coffee. Jax liked all of that, told herself she was there to help heal Kate's wound, not probe it with a sharp instrument.

Kate put the plate on a table in the shade and, like heat-seeking missiles, Scotty and Zoe were next to her five seconds later, eyeing off the food.

'Do you like strawberries?' Zoe asked him.

'Uh-huh. Do you?'

'They're my favourite, aren't they, Mummy?'

Not yesterday. 'Sure are.'

'Can we have some, Mum?' Scotty asked, dropping a couple of bright-yellow metal chunks on the table - bits of toy truck from the sandpit.

'You can have a couple each but stay out of the sand while you eat.' Kate moved the truck parts further down the table, saying to Jax, 'He does have whole toys but he takes everything apart. Brendan always said Scotty was going to be either an engineer or a spare parts specialist.' She smiled at the happier memory and Jax reminded herself Kate had already confirmed facts for the ledger: a few ticks for the Real side, zero for Not Real. So as Jax slid a mug of coffee across the table, she thought about other conversations - schools, cafes, sports clubs, the kind of things new neighbours discussed.

But Kate spoke first. 'He was a mess the second time he came back.'

Jax wanted to grab a pen and start writing, but instead she reached across the table, put a hand on Kate's wrist. 'You don't have to tell me.'

'I think I need to,' Kate said, 'and I feel like I can talk to you. You haven't once told me not to think about it.' Her lips flattened in a brief smile. 'I know you've been through a lot. Do you mind listening?'

Something close to a craving pulsed in Jax's veins. 'Please. I know what it's like.'

Kate's eyes slid from Jax to the garden. 'He wouldn't talk about it the second time he came back. Any of it. What happened over there, what was happening with him here. He said there was nothing to talk about, but he was having nightmares, waking up lathered in sweat, yelling and crying, then embarrassed about it. And he was so ... removed. He'd be in the room with us but not *with* us. I used to shout at him just to get a reaction, to try to make him notice me. I just missed his company.'

She stopped, dug around in a pocket for a tissue, wiped her face and drank more coffee before starting again. There were mood swings and alcohol binges, Kate said. He had trouble sleeping and an explosive temper. He couldn't watch the news, he put extra locks on the doors and windows, he was suspicious of everyone. He'd decided to get out of the military and felt guilty about deserting mates who were going back to the war. Kate begged him to get some help, but it didn't come until he was rushed to hospital with chest pains. He thought it was heart failure. It turned out to be a panic attack, a psychiatrist got involved and diagnosed PTSD, and they started down a long road of drug therapy and counselling and dealing with Veterans' Affairs.

'I always believed he'd get better,' Kate said. 'That one day he'd be free of it all and would let Scotty and me in again. I thought we were getting closer, I thought we were going to make it.' She tossed the cold dregs of her coffee onto the grass. 'How the hell do I explain it to Scotty?'

28

J ax wished she had some advice to offer Kate about Scotty, but she'd failed her own child there. She'd never found any reasons to give Zoe for why her father was gone, had only come to the conclusion that if she could follow the trail, she might eventually get there.

Kate's story, on the other hand, was appalling and revealing, but it was history - not an answer, nothing in it to mark up as either Real or Not Real. Jax leaned forward, her forearms on the table. 'Did you know Brendan had stopped taking the drugs?'

Kate nodded. 'He did that six months ago. He thought they'd done enough and wanted to see how he coped without them. At the time, his doctor thought it was a good idea. He might not say that now.'

'How was Brendan afterwards?'

'Good. Better than either of us expected. The best he'd been since he got back from Afghanistan that second time. He said his head felt clearer but I think some of that was just the fact he hadn't fallen apart.'

'Did something happen to set the PTSD off again?'

'I didn't think so but it's such an insidious bloody thing and he got good at hiding it. He had some flashbacks a while ago after a reunion with some of the Afghanistan crew. He'd kept his distance after leaving the army, I thought it was because he was ashamed or embarrassed, but maybe he was worried about what he'd remember. Anyway, the job in

Sydney came out of it and he talked to me about the flashbacks. I thought it was a good sign that he could.' Her hands tightened on her mug. 'Maybe he thought the talking would shut me up.' She closed her eyes, dragged in a breath.

Jax wondered if she was blaming herself for not doing enough or for pushing him too hard. And how much had Brendan been hiding when he started the job?

'Why did he move to Sydney without you?' Jax asked.

'He got the job and travelling up and down for every shift was going to be difficult.'

'But you stayed here?'

Her nod was laced with regret. 'He wasn't sure how long it'd last and he didn't want to move us again.'

'Was he on a contract?'

'No, he was trying to be realistic. He hadn't worked since he left the army and he wasn't sure how he'd handle it.'

'How did you feel about it?'

'I thought it was good for him to be working but I didn't want him to go into security, or to Sydney. I was worried it might make the work we'd put in as a family go backwards.'

Backwards was an understatement. Jax pushed a thumbnail into a scrape on the table, remembering something she'd only summarised for Kate earlier. 'He told me he left because he loved you.'

Kate dropped her head, nodded slowly.

'He said there was something wrong with him and he had to keep it away from you and Scotty.'

She lifted her face. 'He said that?'

'Yes.'

A frown tightened. 'We argued about him going. He felt guilty that I'd had to be the sole breadwinner and for making us move so many times. He said I didn't deserve to be packed up again when he might fuck it up. His words, not mine. He never said anything about having to keep away from us.' She paused, pressed fingers to her lips. 'Oh, God, is that what he thought?'

Kate asked it as though Jax had been his confessor, not his hostage. And Jax had paraphrased without a clue to what he was thinking.

'I don't know,' she answered quickly. 'He was rambling when he said that. I thought he wanted to kill himself but I don't know. He said he loved you, though, and he wanted you to know.' More paraphrasing, but it seemed like the right message this time.

Kate's face crumpled as a sob escaped her lips. She cried silently for a moment, then swiped the tears from her cheeks, clasped her hands tightly on the table. 'Sorry.'

'There's nothing to be sorry for.'

'You're wrong. I'm sorry for a lot of things. I'm sorry I couldn't make him better, that I let him go to Sydney and didn't see it coming. I'm sorry you were caught up in it.'

Jax reached across the table, held tight to Kate's bundle of fingers. 'Oh, that's way too many things to be sorry for. How about you try to trim them down?'

'You think that'd make it better?'

'I think it's like multi-tasking. There are only so many things you can feel guilty about at one time and still do it well.'

Kate wiped an eye. 'I'd hate not to do it well.'

'I'm with you there. I mean, what's the point of feeling guilty if you're only going to be half-hearted about it?'

Kate's eyes met Jax's, guilt and gratitude and a tiny speck of amusement in them. 'He never threatened me, you know. I've seen him worked up, agitated and confused. He even threw things a couple of times, but not *at* me. I was never frightened of him. I wouldn't have stayed if I was.'

'But he could be irrational?'

'It took a while for him to come down from the nightmares some days, and he'd get confused about what was memory or dream. For a long time, he thought he was teaching me something on the computer, but he didn't. I wondered if it was something he'd planned to do but never got around to, or whether it was a recurring dream. I never figured that one out.'

'Did you figure any of it out?'

'Some of it.'

'Like what?'

'He was suspicious of people. He'd question me about the parents of Scotty's friends, write down car rego numbers, remember snippets of conversation and take them out of context. It was embarrassing at times. He didn't always keep it between us. Then, in counselling, he talked about a green-on-blue incident at one of the patrol bases he was stationed at. An Afghan soldier shot two Australians. Our guys were training him, he was living on the base, and it turned out he was a Taliban infiltrator. It happened at a lot of bases but I guess when it's suddenly in your face like that, you'd be suspicious of everyone.' She twisted at the wedding band on her finger. 'It took him a long time to work out how to turn that off.'

Jax remembered the checking back and forth, looking for the helicopter. *If we stop, we're easier to pick off.* 'Did he turn it off?'

'Not entirely, but it improved.'

Had the recent flashbacks brought back some of his symptoms? Or had something caused another flashback after he spoke to Kate on Saturday afternoon? One that made him more than edgy? 'Did he ever think people were following him?'

'No.'

'Did he ever accuse you of lying?'

'No.'

'Did he have a problem with mobile phones?'

Kate looked at her for a long moment, a crease slowly forming between her brows - and Jax realised what she'd been doing. Not listening patiently and talking kindly, but leaning forward and throwing questions like she was reeling them off a checklist. She straightened, eased back, reproof hot on her skin.

Kate shifted slightly, putting a little more space between them. 'Why are you asking these questions?'

'I'm . . .' What? Mining Kate's pain to satisfy her own curiosity. 'I'm looking for answers too. I want to understand why this happened to me.'

Kate folded her arms across her chest. 'Are you . . . planning to sue? Because if you're looking for someone to blame, you'll have to talk to Veterans' Affairs.'

'What? No.'

'Look, I understand it must have been bad for you, but I don't have any money.'

'Kate, no, that's not what I meant. It's just that Brendan . . . well, I'm not exactly sure anymore. It's . . . I feel infected by his paranoia. It's not even that. There was something he wanted me to understand and I want to figure it out.'

Wariness filtered into Kate's gaze, maybe deciding Jax had a different motive for coming here. That maybe she'd shared too much. A sound from the house made her glance away. Jax turned too, saw a man in the doorway.

'Hugh,' Kate said. Not an explanation, more a statement of relief.

As Kate stood, Jax sensed the closing up of whatever had opened between them. She covered Kate's hand before it left the table. 'It's for myself, Kate. I want to understand why I almost died. Why my daughter almost lost both her parents.'

Kate glanced briefly at her, eyes guarded, a little hurt. Then she walked quickly away, across the yard to the house, and embraced the man in the doorway. She seemed to cling to him, a cheek pressed to his chest. Not a lovers' clinch but the kind of desperate holding on Jax remembered sharing with Russell in those early days. Had she given Kate need for rescue? So much for healing wounds.

'Uncle Hugh!' Scotty cried as he ran to join them, the man ruffling the boy's hair when he got there.

Beside Jax, Zoe wriggled onto the bench seat. 'Is that Scotty's real uncle or fake uncle like Uncle Russell?'

'I don't know, honey, but I think it's time we were leaving.'

She held Zoe's hand as they walked towards the house, uncomfortable about interrupting the moment. Nauseated at the thought of herself.

Kate wiped more tears from her face as Jax approached. 'Miranda, this is Hugh Talbotson, a friend of Brendan's. He got him the job in security. He's come all the way from Sydney for us.' It was a message: he was looking after them, they had all they needed. 'Hugh, this is Miranda Jack.'

Jax's name was delivered as though inflection was explanation enough. Miranda Jack - italics followed by drumroll. Hugh obviously got it. His eyes settled on her for a good, solid look. Size, clothes, hair, face, the daughter at her side - a silent, *So that's the woman from the motorway.* Or was it more than that? What had Kate whispered in his ear while she hugged him? Jax felt heat crawling up the flesh on her throat as she waited for him to finish his perusal, taking in his jeans and T-shirt, the barrel chest and huge biceps. He held out his hand. Jax shook it, forced a smile.

'The funeral director will be here in about five minutes,' he told her. 'Kate needs to talk to him.' Time for you to leave, in other words.

'Sure.'

'I'll walk you out,' he said.

And make sure I do it now, Jax thought, although she wasn't entirely unhappy he was there and directing traffic. Kate's family was missing in action, she needed a sergeant-at-arms - and she seemed more appreciative of Hugh than of her crusty neighbour.

Jax looked at Kate one more time, wanting to say something worth-while before she walked out of her life. 'Be kind to yourself,' she offered, borrowing Tilda's philosophy. 'None of this is your fault. I live just up the hill, if you ever decide you want to talk again.' She reached out, clutched Kate's arm briefly, hoping to convey some of the warmth she felt for her. Kate gave a single nod. Acknowledgement, nothing more.

With Zoe in hand, Jax followed Hugh back up the hallway, eyeing his broad shoulders, his muscled legs. He was built like Arnold Schwarzenegger, deflated by about a third. His short-cropped hair showed flecks of small scars on his scalp, as though his head had taken the brunt of a hard life. The slightly reddened line of a scratch behind one ear suggested he was still living it. Jax hoped it wasn't all brawn, that he had the kind of strength Kate and Scotty needed behind them for a while.

As he pulled open the door, Jax reminded herself she'd done what she came for and had learned more from Kate than she hoped - she should leave it at that.

But as she squinted into the sunlight outside, she couldn't make herself keep walking. Not without one last shot.

29

'I'm sorry for your loss,' Jax said.

Hugh Talbotson nodded.

'Were you and Brendan in the army together?' The guy walked like he was ready to salute.

'Yes.'

'Afghanistan?'

He hesitated, watched her for a beat or two. 'We did two tours together.'

'How many did you do?'

'Four with the ADF, eighteen months in private security.'

She tried to look impressed, wondering if he was a glutton for punishment or a soldier of fortune. Why some went back when others couldn't bring themselves to think about it. And how many of the scars on his scalp he'd got over there. 'Brendan must have had a hard time in Afghanistan.'

'Hard place.'

His answer was curt but it didn't seem to be evasion. More like a tough guy's shorthand and, after an hour and a half with Kate's grief, Jax needed to find another gear if she was going to engage him.

'Did you see the chopper crash?' It was a long shot. She didn't know if Brendan had witnessed one but it was the only thing from his rambling she could think to use before she was shunted out the door.

'I saw two go down.'

'Was Brendan with you one of those times?'

His eyes flicked away briefly. 'Yeah, I was there. Three Australians killed, one American, an Afghan interpreter.' Just the facts.

'That would've been a hard day.'

He didn't answer and she wondered if talking about *how* hard was territory he didn't step into.

'It seemed to be hard on Brendan,' she said.

Maybe she hit the right mark because something about the way Hugh held himself seemed to loosen, as though he'd exhaled some of the starch that kept his military bearing in place. 'Kate told me he talked to you in the car. Is that what it was about? The chopper crash?'

'That and other things.'

He nodded. 'I think Kate's heard enough. You've explained yourself, now you need to leave her alone.'

It must have been what Kate told him when he arrived, but his spin on it made Jax defensive. 'She called me this morning. She wanted to talk.'

'She's barely slept since it happened. I doubt she knows what she wants.'

Now Jax wanted to defend Kate. But she didn't. She thought of Russell instead, remembering he'd also suggested to well-meaning colleagues - the kind who didn't know how to let a good story drop - that rehashing the events wasn't in Jax's best interests. 'I'm trying to make sense of it too,' she told Hugh.

'Brendan had PTSD,' he said, as though that covered everything.

'Did you spend much time with him?'

'We kept in touch.'

It could be bloke-talk for sending the odd email, but Kate had gone to him like a friend and Scotty called him uncle. And Hugh had helped Brendan into his job. 'I want to understand what happened to him. Would you talk to me? Tell me about him?'

For five or six long seconds, they eyed each other off across the hall-way. Hugh's irises were hazel, a dull mix of green and brown, but what they lacked in vibrancy they made up for in his direct, fixed gaze. Jax wondered what he was weighing up: was he deciding whether he wanted to know about his friend's last hours, or was Brendan's break with reality a sign of weakness Hugh didn't want to explore? Or maybe Hugh was just waiting to see who'd blink first. She was determined not to, trying to send the message that she was strong and resolute, that she wouldn't turn into a blubbering mess - the kind of thing she figured a guy like Hugh would want to avoid.

'Mummy?' With one word, Zoe popped the thought bubble in the hallway.

'We'll go in a second, baby,' Jax said, as much to her daughter as to Hugh.

He glanced down at Zoe, caught her bored sigh, and the hint of a sad smile softened his mouth, making Jax think she had a chance.

'I don't mean now,' she told him. 'Or here. I could meet you somewhere. Without Kate. Buy you a coffee. Or a beer. Maybe we can both understand what went wrong for Brendan.'

It was at least ten degrees hotter outside when they left Kate's house and, not wanting to look like she was lingering, Jax called a cab as she and Zoe walked the block and a half to the main road. Hugh had agreed to think about meeting her later in the afternoon. She'd written a time and the name of a cafe - the only one she knew in Newcastle - on the back of a business card and told him she'd be waiting there if he didn't call.

It was Zoe's first time in a taxi and she asked questions without pause: how long would it take, how many cabs had Jax been in, where do cabs go at night, how much does it cost to buy one. 'Can you get purple ones?' They were dropped off at the top of the driveway and Zoe ran ahead, ready to draw a picture of the taxi for Aunty Tilda.

'Can I go upstairs and get my colouring things?' Zoe asked, skipping in and waiting at the turn in the stairs for permission.

Jax had told her she wasn't to go upstairs whenever she felt like it, that downstairs and upstairs were two separate houses, even though they didn't have front doors. She was reluctant to let her six-year-old wander around without Tilda, but Zoe had been patient and 'nice' all morning. 'Where are they?' Jax asked.

'On the kitchen bench.'

'Okay. But come straight back down, all right?'

'All right,' she sang, starting on another complicated hop-skip up the steps. If she did it again on the way down, it could take her half an hour.

The heat and the cab and an hour and a half with Kate Walsh's grief had dulled the memory of last night's chase, and Jax was halfway down the stairs, juggling a handbag, two hats and a wad of mail, before the hairs on the back of her neck came to life.

She froze, not sure why. All she could see was the white tube of the stairwell and one of Tilda's pastels on canvas on the wall at the bottom, lit from the right by light spilling in from the sitting room. So she listened. The ocean. A dull clomp from Zoe upstairs. A shush of sound from ...

Thump. Something hard against soft. Footfall on carpet or body into wall. It shuddered through her bones; adrenaline fired like an electrical current. Then her hands were empty and her back was pressed to the plaster, head twisting right and left. The noise had come from deep in the house. Up or down?

Then shoes were moving fast across tiles. Downstairs. A chair clattering. And Jax was bounding - two steps and a leap to the bottom, her shoulder slamming the wall, swinging into her living room as the sliding door rocked in its track and a figure moved fast through the courtyard.

"Hey!" The word tore from her mouth of its own accord. The same force carried her outside and into the heat and glare and the empty square of yard before fear and logic pulled up her fight instinct. She whirled around, the dull clomp from upstairs replaying in her mind. 'Oh, no. Zoe.'

She yelled as she hit the stairs. 'Zoe!' Tried to listen for sounds of her daughter as she thundered upwards, hearing only her own feet and high-pitched panic ringing in her ears. She didn't register the turn in the stairs or reaching the top, just the frenzied swinging of her head as she stood in the centre of the room trying to find her. Colouring pencils spilled from a case on the counter, a pair of sandals were discarded on the floor. Jax was vaguely aware of a need for caution, of trying to sound calm for Zoe's sake. But it was too late to hold her fear in check. 'Zoe!'

'I'm here, Mummy.'

Zoe was on the floor. Beside the TV. Pointing the remote at it.

'What are you *doing*? I told you to come straight back downstairs.' The words tumbled out fast and cross as she lurched across the room, fell to her knees and locked her arms around her daughter's small body.

'Sorry, Mummy.' Zoe's voice was muffled against Jax's chest.

'No, baby. You're a good girl. The best girl.' Her voice was firm with conviction, choked with tenderness.

'My movie won't come out of the player.'

Still holding her daughter tight, Jax lifted her eyes, saw why Zoe couldn't get the disc out. She was pointing the remote at the equipment on the stand under the flat-screen TV - an old CD stacker and video recorder. The DVD player was gone.

Jax glanced around the room. It was barely disturbed, just a few books scattered on the floor by the old walnut desk, a painting knocked askew. And Tilda's laptop was missing. Jax wanted to run downstairs, see what was left, but thirty seconds ago she'd thought someone was still in the house with Zoe. No reason to dismiss that assumption.

Jax slipped her arms from around Zoe's back, pulled her close to her side.

'Mummy?'

Pressing a finger to her lips, Jax made the *shhhh* shape without the noise. Zoe got it, and more. Her eyes widened, mouth closed, and she burrowed into her mother's side - and Jax felt something grow large and hard inside her, something she hadn't felt on the motorway with Brendan. Anger, a protective instinct, a mother's ferocity.

She stood, lifted Zoe off the ground and to her hip. It had been a few years since she'd carried her daughter that way. Zoe had grown, filled out; Jax thought her strained muscles might not manage it. But her daughter was no weight at all. Jax could have carried her across the country.

Eyeing the hallway to Tilda's bedrooms, Jax saw three doors open, one closed - and she wasn't heading down there to check out the damage. Moving quickly, quietly to the steps, she held tight to Zoe as she started down, checked the lower stairwell, crept across the foyer, opened the door just enough to ease them both through, and ran to the top of the driveway.

30

Jax's fingers were trembling as she tapped the screen of her mobile, thankful she'd shoved it in her back pocket when she'd rung the cab.

'I'm glad you decided to call.' It was Aiden, with a hint of it's-about-time in his tone.

'It's not what you think. Someone broke into the house. I'm not sure they've gone.'

A pause. 'Is everyone okay?'

'Yes. I grabbed Zoe and left. Tilda isn't home.'

Zoe had either run out of questions or was tired of her mother's I-don't-know's and was now huddled against Jax as they sat on the kerb under the shade of a tree.

'Where are you?' Aiden asked.

She'd run to a neighbour's house with Zoe in her arms, got no answer to her knock, then stomped about in indecision for about thirty seconds. 'In the street, outside the house.'

'Have you called Triple-o?'

That idea had caused the indecision. 'No. I thought it might take them forever to get here for just a break-in, and it might be too difficult to explain the rest. I thought you'd get here faster.'

Another pause. She hoped Aiden was on the move, not rolling his eyes. 'I'm forty-five minutes away,' he said. 'I'll send some uniforms to you and get there when I can.'

She squinted at the house, at the road, at the midday sun, and hoped they got there soon. 'Thanks.'

'Stay where you are, Jax.'

Where did he think she'd go? 'I left with a mobile phone and my daughter and your guys have my car. I'm not going anywhere.'

It was hot. Zoe was thirsty and hungry. Brendan hovered in Jax's thoughts as she watched the house from the top of the driveway. The figure she'd seen running through the courtyard wasn't a kid. He was male and adult, wearing jeans and something dark on top. Not a shirt and tie, but that didn't stop her thinking about the two men she'd seen at her car last night. The man in her house hadn't been carrying anything, at least nothing big enough that it needed to be hefted under an arm, and yet Tilda's DVD player was gone. Two men or one taking several trips?

After ten minutes, Jax phoned Tilda and left a message. Another five minutes and she was itching with tension, pacing the grass, irritated and impatient. Zoe whined about the heat and hunger. Jax wanted to kick in the front door and see what was left of her possessions. She needed something to do to stop her fingers twisting themselves into knots. There were dandelions growing in a patch of grass by the driveway, little yellow flowers blooming in the summer heat.

'Hey, Zoe, why don't you make a daisy chain? You can show Aunty Tilda when she gets home.'

While Zoe hummed and laced flowers, Jax pulled the notebook from her bag and updated the lists, adding what she'd learned from Kate Walsh, thinking about Kate's version of the man who'd sat in Jax's car. Nothing like the bad guy Jax had assumed was waving a gun in her face. More like the sad, sorry, distraught man she'd tried to hold on to at the edge of the motorway. Brendan *had* loved his family, it wasn't something his mind had invented. And his family loved him back. He was injured by war and he'd tried to get well; he'd wanted to make amends for the disruption to Kate and Scotty's lives. He hadn't been violent and aggressive by nature. Whatever had happened inside his head last weekend had made him think carjacking was his only resort. A good man who believed he'd been driven to desperate measures.

Which left the question: had Brendan imagined people were after him, or had they just been inside Jax's house?

Two uniformed officers arrived twenty-one minutes after Jax spoke to Aiden - longer than it took him to find her in the building site. Her adrenaline peak had sunk by then and her array of minor injuries and sore muscles felt like one throbbing mass.

'I don't have my keys but the sliding door downstairs is wide open,' she told a tall, thin young woman with pupils that darted everywhere. It wasn't clear if the eye action was trepidation or surveillance but it made Jax wonder what Aiden had told them.

The woman disappeared around the side of the house ahead of a beefy, chummy thirty-something cop, who opened the front door a few minutes later and beckoned Jax and Zoe inside. He told them the intruder was gone, that entry and exit appeared to be through the down-stairs slider, and directed Jax to the alarm pad in the foyer. 'Was it armed when you left this morning?'

'I don't know. I wasn't the last to leave.' She filled him in on the living arrangements, said she'd have to check with her aunt, told him her daughter needed a drink of water.

'A detective is organising for fingerprinting, so try to touch as little as possible. Then I need you to take a look around and start a list of what's gone. It's usually sellable items: electrical equipment, cameras, jewellery, cash if there was any around.'

Was that it? A simple robbery? Not two men searching her house after they'd failed to find her the night before?

She stood at the bottom of the stairs, her eyes scanning the sitting room. It wasn't vandalised or plundered. It looked like it had been picked up and dropped. Sofa cushions were on the floor, the table was at an odd angle, one chair was toppled, the rest higgledy-piggledy. Removalists' boxes were open, a couple were on their sides; kitchen appliances had been shunted along the bench; Zoe's box of toys lay on its side, dolls scat-tered like they'd been thrown from a horse and cart. It was the kind of disarray that happened when you tipped a table or lifted cushions to see what was underneath.

Did house thieves do that? Or had the man - or burglar and accom-plice - been searching for something?

Zoe sat quietly in a corner with a glass of water and a handful of crackers while Jax walked the room eyeing the furniture, her arms folded, touching nothing - not to protect evidence, but because the room seemed dirty, contaminated, covered by something ugly and ominous that had swept through her home.

Her DVD player was gone, too. So was her iPad but its dock was still there, and the TV had been left like the one upstairs - even though both were relatively new, Tilda's a large and expensive model.

Zoe's room was the first door off the hallway. The only sign of disturbance was the mattress sitting skewed on its base, the sheets hanging loose as though someone had lifted the whole thing up to take a look under.

Jax paused in the doorway of her own bedroom, took in the mess with a single sweep of her eyes, and her gut tightened. He - they - had been through everything. The mattress was upturned, the bedside table toppled, packing cartons ripped open, clothes scattered. The big laptop from her desk was gone, along with its charger and carry bag. But it wasn't the mess or the theft or the mounting alarm that pushed the cry from her throat. It was the files. Nick's files. Dumped on the floor, crumpled and trampled by shoes that had left dirty, disrespectful marks.

She wanted to rush in, scoop them up, protect them like she hadn't been able to protect Nick.

'Jax?' Aiden, at the other end of the hallway.

She swung her head towards him, felt the cool damp of tears on her cheeks.

There was caution and concern in his face as he took long strides to her side. He didn't touch her, just propped in the doorway as though he'd expected a body, blood. 'What is it?'

She didn't know how to explain. It was just paper. She had copies saved to both of her laptops, and the mini one was still safe in her shoulder bag; there were back-ups on USB sticks and in web storage files - she was fanatical about it. But *these* were the copies she took to bed at night. She'd made notes on them, spilt coffee, dropped crumbs, slept with them when she couldn't sleep with her husband. They were her hope for an answer. Her connection to Nick.

God, Nick. Gasping, lunging forward, she got only a step before Aiden caught her around the waist, his arm a lasso, hauling her back until his body was against her spine.

'There are good, clear footprints on the pages,' he told her urgently, apologetically. 'We need to keep them intact.' It was a directive but whispered into her hair like a secret, his breath warm on her cheek.

She wanted to take comfort from the gentleness of him, let his muscles hold her up, absorb the heat and smell of him, and for half a second she did, clutching at his arm, dropping her head to his chest. But her husband was in the room with them, what was left of him was battered and abused on the floor at her feet. She lifted Aiden's hand away, sank to her knees at the edge of the spread of files, pressed fingers to her lips and sobbed.

'Where's my mummy?' Zoe's voice came from the hallway.

Jax sucked in a breath, wiped at her face.

Maybe Aiden sensed her need to keep the tears from Zoe, maybe he would have done it anyway, but he stepped into the doorway. 'Hey, Zoe. Do you remember me from yesterday? Detective Hawke.'

There was a beat of silence.

'Your mum's in here.' Aiden used his body to block Zoe's view. 'There's a bit of a mess so you can't walk all the way in, okay?'

'Why?' Zoe said.

'Because the police have to take photos.'

'Why?'

'So they can work out what happened.'

'Why?'

'Because -'

'I'll explain it later, Zoe,' Jax said, glancing up at him, smiling her thanks. 'You can come in just a little bit.' She shuffled back against the wall, cradled her daughter between her knees as Aiden squatted beside the files, his eyes moving over them.

'What are they?' he asked.

Jax tipped her head, trying to find a way to explain. Zoe did it for her. 'They're Daddy's files.'

Jax nodded agreement. Aiden used the tip of a pen to slide a page around. Jax couldn't read it from where she was, but knew the shape of the words on the page. It was a statement from a resident of the suburb where Nick died.

'What was he working on?' Aiden asked.

'They're Mummy's files *about* Daddy,' Zoe said. 'I'm not allowed to look at them until I'm a grown-up.' She whispered to Jax, 'I can see them but I'm not looking at the words.'

'Good girl,' Jax said - it wouldn't have mattered, Zoe couldn't read well enough yet. 'It's just stuff I've been collecting,' Jax told Aiden. 'It's only important to me.'

Aiden lifted his eyes from the page he'd been reading. 'Did Anita Lyneham give you these?'

'Anita Lyneham wouldn't give me anything.'

'Where did you get it?'

'I wrote it.'

'I mean the information.'

'I knocked on doors and asked.'

His focus drifted sideways to the mound of paper, came back to Jax. A small crease had tightened between his brows. 'It's not just statements here.'

'No.'

Another pause as he chewed on it. 'Where were you this morning?'

She wondered where his thoughts had taken him, not sure where they'd lead if she told him. But there was no point dodging it, not after someone had broken into the house. 'With Kate Walsh.'

For half a second, his gaze stayed on her, then his face swung away, a hand pushed through his dark hair. When he looked back, there was something new in his eyes. Something less restrained, more direct, a little forceful.

'We need to talk. Outside. Now, Jax.'

31

'I'm going to make a sandwich for Zoe first,' Jax said, waving a hand at the fridge door. 'What can I touch?'

'Here.' Aiden pulled a latex glove from his trouser pocket. He produced another one, slipped it over his right hand, reached for the kettle. 'I'll make coffee.'

'God, no. I'm already on caffeine overload.'

'I wasn't thinking of you.'

'You need a caffeine hit to talk to me?'

He flicked the switch, folded his arms. 'I've driven to Sydney and back since my last coffee.'

'So you're not about to interrogate me?'

'I haven't decided yet.'

She wasn't sure if it was an act.

He waited until she'd cut two slices of bread into Vegemite fingers. 'Does Lyneham know what you've got in your files?'

Jax noted he'd ditched the Homicide cop's first name, wondered if it was shop talk or if he was siding with Jax. 'About four months ago, she heard I'd been knocking on doors. She asked me into the station, made me wait an hour, then told me to cease and desist.' Jax slid Zoe's bread fingers and a tub of yogurt onto a plate. 'Zoe, honey, come and get your lunch.' Jax watched her skip across the room, relieved the break-in hadn't left her daughter quiet and frightened. It was just Jax who felt like her lungs had forgotten how to breathe.

'Did you?' Aiden asked.

'What?'

'Cease and desist.'

She gave him a look: *You think?*

He huffed a brief laugh. 'Is that the problem between you and her?'

'No. It started long before that. From the first day, I asked too many questions. She didn't like them and it went downhill from there.' The kettle reached boiling point and clicked off. Jax passed him a jar of coffee grounds and pointed at the plunger on the bench. Then watched, impressed as he filled it. Okay, so the guy knew his way around fresh coffee. He nodded at a table-and-chair set in the courtyard, out of the sun in the shadow of the house: his 'outside' meant all the way outside. She followed him through the door with mugs.

It was just past midday and the air was humid and hot but an early afternoon breeze was keeping it moving, bringing a briny tang and the distant rumble of surf up the hill. Aiden sat and waited until Jax was opposite him, two filled mugs between them. 'Is it because you don't trust Lyneham to do her job?'

Was that why they were here? He wanted another chance to explain he ran a different kind of investigation, to say, *Trust me and stay out of it.* Well, she could make use of an opportunity too. 'I can't make a judgement on that. She won't tell me anything.'

A fleeting frown. 'She won't share the details of a police investigation, so you run your own?'

'It's not like that.'

'Then what are the files about?'

She'd been here before, was tempted to tell Aiden it was none of his damn business, but he was her only link to the investigation into Brendan Walsh - and she wasn't ready to give that up. Not yet.

She took a breath, willed herself to keep it together. 'My husband was an investigative reporter. He worked on complicated stories that other people gave up on. He didn't do it because it was a job. He did it because people needed justice and closure. And because once he'd started, he couldn't stop. He had a compulsion to understand, to unravel the details, to uncover the truth. If someone brought the Nick Westing story to him, he'd pull it apart until he found out what had happened. If it was me, if I was the one who'd been run down, he wouldn't let it go. Not ever.' She jerked a thumb in the direction of her bedroom. 'Those files in there are for him. Because *he'd* want to know. Because he'd want me to know and because he'd want his daughter to have something more than the easy, throwaway explanation for why she has no father.'

Tears were blurring her vision by the time she finished. She lifted her coffee mug to her mouth to hide the tremble in her lips, looked away from Aiden towards the huge expanse of ocean. She'd given the same speech to worried friends. Russell and Deanne listened to her theories without adding to them. A few days ago, Tilda had fingered through the box of files with concern in her eyes. Across the table, Detective Senior Sergeant Aiden Hawke leaned on his forearms, his eyes pinned to Jax's face. If he thought he was going to convince her to give it away, he needed to revisit his Psychology studies.

'My first case as a detective involved a twelve-year- old girl,' he said. 'She got up one morning and found her mother almost beaten to death in the kitchen. I held that girl's hand for three hours. Her name is Bethany and she's nineteen next week. Her mother has brain damage and is in a wheelchair. The perpetrators haven't been found. Once a month, I go back through the files, then I ring her and we talk. She tells me what she's been doing, I tell her what's new. I want to find out what happened. For her. So she can move on with her life.'

Jax sensed the solidarity of a quest. She hadn't expected that. Not with a cop. Not with the cop who'd told her to keep out of it. She wanted to ask him why - and tell him not to lose hope. But he took a breath and she let him speak.

'Are you trying to honour Brendan Walsh?'

She frowned: at the switch in subject, at the assumption underneath it that she couldn't grasp.

'He held a gun to your head, Jax. I saw it.'

'I know. I was there.'

'You don't owe him anything.'

'I'm not paying him back.'

'Are you sure?'

She leaned forward, hands gripping the edge of the table. 'Brendan Walsh was in *my* car. He almost killed *me*. I thought people were after me - I believed him. I tried to hold on to him but he slipped through my fingers and I watched him run into the traffic and die. I want to know *why* that happened.'

Aiden waited a beat. 'Is that all?'

Not even close, but if his need or duty or whatever it was that made him ring a young girl every month didn't give him a clue, Jax wasn't going to tell him the rest of it. And she didn't think it was what he meant. Last night, he'd accused her of omitting details, told her it would be bad for her when he figured it out. 'Is this why we're out here having coffee in the shade? So I'll tell you everything?'

'I'm giving you the chance to do it now, Jax. There might not be another one.'

Did that mean he was close to working it out? If he thought she knew something that would make a difference, he was way off. But he'd passed her the baton - it was time to run. 'All right, I'll talk to you. I'll tell you what I know, but only if you're straight with me.'

'As straight as I can be.'

'You'll answer my questions?'

'Where I can.'

She huffed. 'You think that's going to do it?'

'How about this, then? I'll answer your questions if you answer mine.'

She'd been answering his all along. 'Fine. But I get to ask the first one.'

He held up his hands. 'Go for it, Miranda.'

She smiled to herself. He'd called her Miranda: surrender with a reminder of who was the cop. 'What do *you* think is going on?'

It made him hesitate. She understood why. If he told her what he thought, she could tailor her answer to suit - but she needed him to say it before she laid it all out.

'Okay,' he started, as though he'd decided to uphold his end of the bargain, 'I think Walsh got in your head. I think you deliberately omitted details from your statement and that you know more than you claim about Brendan Walsh's situation. And I think you're involved somehow in whatever he had going on.' It wasn't complimentary, but he'd tried to give her a way out.

'All right,' she said, 'that's the obvious conclusion - I won't hold it against you. How do you think I'm involved?'

'Nuh-uh. My turn to ask a question.'

'We didn't agree on tit for tat.'

'Give me a break here, Jax. I'm making all the concessions.'

A smile turned up one side of her mouth. She liked him better this way - a little pushy, an edge of humour, his energy not locked up in his professional suit of armour. 'Fair enough.'

'Walsh's car was found burnt out in Sydney last night,' he said. 'I went down to look at it this morning. An accelerant was used, there's not a lot left. It's in Hornsby, one suburb from Wahroonga, walking distance to the motorway on-ramp. Did he contact you? Did he tell you to meet him there?'

'That's two questions.'

'Are you dodging?'

'No. And no, he didn't, but . . .' She frowned, trying to work out the connections Aiden had made. She'd told him she didn't know Brendan before he got in her car but Aiden had read a little of the files on her bedroom floor; she'd given him an impassioned speech about why she was investigating Nick's accident; she'd told him she was with Kate Walsh again this morning.

'You're putting the wrong pieces together. I didn't lie to you about knowing Brendan and it's not about Nick's accident or my files. If it was, they wouldn't still be on my floor. Whoever was here would've taken them with my laptop. But I think Nick's got something to do with what's happened since.'

'So your husband knew Walsh?'

'No. You're on the wrong track. But it's the same track I think others are on. That's the point.'

'What track?'

'Okay.' She moved the coffee mugs aside, shuffled her chair closer, still sorting the ideas in her head. 'If I'm a former reporter and my husband was an investigative reporter, the assumption is that we were a team. Both of us involved in the investigating and reporting. At the very least, I was the sounding board for his ideas. I'm certainly capable of asking questions and writing about the answers, and possibly with the same insistence as my famous husband.' She raised her eyebrows.

'Okay.' It meant *go on*, not agreement.

'What if Brendan Walsh actually had information of some variety? He was reported as leaving Sydney in a car driven by Nicholas Westing's wife, so the first guess would be that the transport arrangements weren't random. The second might be that his intention was to pass on said information. The third, that I planned to do something with it.'

Aiden's eyes narrowed. 'So you're saying Walsh gave you information?'

'No. It's conjecture.'

A flash lit his eyes for an instant. 'Come on, Jax, you think conjecture's going to do it?'

'I'm trying to tell you -'

'Listen to me. I'm crossing a line by giving you this opportunity. Tell me or I go.'

She rubbed a hand across her face. 'Look, four days ago my name was in every newspaper and on every news bulletin. But not just *my* name. I'm Miranda Jack, wife of Nicholas Westing. Nick is the adjective the media uses to describe me. Not single mother, not 35-year-old woman, not former journalist. I'm Nick Westing's wife. He was an investigative reporter, he was famous for it and he's famously dead. You're not the first person to wonder if all of this had something to do with him. And I have, too. I mean, what are the chances of someone hijacking a driver and ending up with an investigative reporter's wife. It's a big coincidence, right?'

'Yes. It's a big coincidence.'

'The thing is that it *is* a coincidence. Brendan chose my car at random. He didn't know who I was until I told him and I haven't omitted anything from my statement. But what if someone else is making the same assumptions as you - that we were in communication, that the pick-up was arranged, that Brendan was rational when he got in my car? I've just been robbed but the TVs are still here and so is some cash I left on the fridge. Two computers, digital DVD players and an iPad are gone. Items that store digital files. Video and voice recordings. My phone does too and it'd be a reasonable assumption that it was in my car on Monday and in my bag yesterday when I was chased.' She paused, let the details settle. 'What if someone is worried about how much Brendan said when he was in my car? And how well I listened?'

32

It was a full minute before Aiden said anything. He filled the time watching the sludgy remains of his coffee, scratching his head, dropping his elbows to his knees and staring at the view. Jax left him to it, knowing his brain was picking at her theory. He'd been convinced she'd done something unlawful, he'd tried to help her out of it. Maybe he was shifting ideas and evidence about to make her theory fit. Maybe he thought he was being conned and was deciding he'd given her enough chances.

He finally folded his arms on the table, cop-look in place as he took a breath. 'If your original statement is accurate -'

'It is.'

'- then Walsh didn't mention having the kind of information you're talking about.'

'He said a lot of things that I didn't understand. He wanted to get to his wife and son. If he didn't make it, he wanted me to tell her something. He thought people were after him, he said he was a target and that someone had called him "Already Dead".'

'He had PTSD. His doctor says it was a psychotic episode.'

'That doesn't mean what he said isn't true.'

'Jax -'

'No, wait. PTSD doesn't explain it all away. I did some reading and yeah, it was a Google search and that doesn't make me an expert, but I didn't find anything that claimed PTSD sufferers were prone to inventing whole new lives. Their issues are about real things, things that happened to them, memories that won't find a place to lie down. They have bad dreams, they get hyper-vigilant, they can feel numb. All things Kate Walsh told me Brendan suffered at various times. She said he'd had flashbacks, too. Recently. A couple of months ago when he caught up with some mates from the army.'

'And you think he was having a flashback in your car?'

'No, if he had a flashback, it happened before he got in my car. The thing is, flashbacks are memories thrown up from the depths of your mind that are so intense it feels like they're happening. They can occur out of the blue or be triggered by a sound, a smell, anything.' She motioned with a hand, palm up, as though trying to show him. 'Maybe he remembered something. Maybe it was about Afghanistan. And maybe someone knew he remembered.'

Aiden sat back in his chair. 'If he did have a flashback - which can't be proved - it might've been something that happened ten years ago. His wife might know all about it. He might've told her twenty times already. Every time he had a flashback.'

'Except that two guys chased me yesterday, someone broke into my house today and the house I sold in Sydney was vandalised.'

A frown creased his forehead. 'Today?'

'No. The night of the carjacking. Apparently there was damage along the street, cars scratched, a brick thrown through someone's window. My house was the only one broken into.' She pulled in a breath as she remembered the details. 'The new owners had computer equipment smashed and boxes sliced open. A door was kicked in and there were a couple of holes in the walls, too, so either vandals or someone trying to make it look that way.'

'When did you hear about this?'

'The morning after.'

'There's no report in the system.'

She couldn't tell if he doubted her or the efficiency of his colleagues in Sydney. 'My name won't be on a report. The sale went through the day before I left. I wasn't the owner. It was the agent who told me.'

Aiden got to his feet in one fast movement, as though the information had driven him from his chair. He stalked to the edge of the small rectangle of grass, stood at the view over the neighbour's roof, his back to her.

'There's more,' Jax said. 'Wait there.' She took the mugs inside, suggested Zoe play on the grass, grabbed the notebook from her bag. Aiden was where she'd left him when she returned, fingering the screen of his mobile phone. 'I made some notes,' she told him, taking them to the table and flipping through to her original lists.

Aiden kept his phone in one hand as he stood at her shoulder. 'A lot of notes,' he said.

'Once I got started . . .' She lifted her shoulders and let them drop.

He took her arm, turned her to face him. 'I told you I'll keep you informed. You don't need to do this.'

He was close enough for her to count the fine, dark stripes in the pale blue-grey of his irises. 'Yeah, I do.'

'Did you call the victim support group?'

'I don't need support. I need to work this out.'

'It's not the best way to get closure.'

'Have you been a victim?'

'No.'

'Then don't tell me how to get closure.'

His fingers softened on her arm. 'I've seen it before, Jax. Victims, people hurt by circumstances out of their control. They think if they can understand it, they'll be okay. But understanding can be worse. You need to let it go.'

She nodded. 'And let the police handle it?'

'I know that's not what you want to hear, but yeah.'

Lifting her chin, she let sarcasm swim into her words. 'And you'll tell me all about it when you've figured it out.'

'It's my job to protect people. I'm trying to protect you.'

She took a step back, folded her arms. 'What would you do if you were in my position? If you'd had a gun to your head, if you'd been chased, if someone had trampled through your home. If you'd had to run with your child in your arms.'

'I'm a detective. Of course I'd want to do something.'

'Well, guess what? That just makes you human. You don't get the right to feel that way because you've got a badge and you've done the training. My father taught me to ask questions and find answers. That's what I'm doing. So are you going to look at what I've got or leave?'

A long, tense silence hung in the air between them. She didn't have the patience for it. He looked like he could do it all day. What was with him? He jumped into action when a gun was involved, but needed to cross every mental 'T' to piece a concept together. Did he tick off a check-list before he got laid?

Their silence was interrupted by Zoe pushing a plastic wheelbarrow full of dolls through the door, giving instructions for them to hold on as they bumped over the step.

Jax picked up the notebook, held it in front of Aiden. 'I wanted to work out how much of what Brendan said was real. This is the Real side. Two pages of it.' She ran a finger down the list, flipped over to where it continued.

Aiden glanced at Zoe tipping her dolls onto the lawn, at the uniformed cop walking through the house, at his phone, maybe deciding how much time he had.

'This is the Not Real side.' Jax pointed to the blank column. Aiden finally looked at it. She saw a frown grow between his brows, felt a tick of victory. 'I've got a list of potentials for the Not Real side but so far every-thing I've tried to confirm has ended up on the Real list.'

He lifted the page, took a look at the one underneath.

She gave him a second to read then flipped to another. 'I broke down everything Brendan said to points that could be proved or disproved. I mean there are a couple here that could probably go straight to Not Real. Nano spiders, for example, but I want ...' Jax stopped to stare at Zoe.

She was surrounded by dolls, using her hands to knock her head from side-to-side, going cross-eyed and grinning as she sang: *'Nano spiders in my head. Nano spiders in my head."*

The sight of it made the nerve endings on Jax's skull prickle as though something had crept across her scalp. She knelt in front of her daughter. 'I've never heard you sing that before. Did you learn it at school?'

'No. That boy taught it to me.'

'What boy?'

'That boy from this morning. At the sad house.'

Jax remembered the kids had been in the sandpit, waving their arms and laughing. Zoe blinked at Aiden as he stepped closer.

'He sang a song about spiders?' Jax asked.

'*Nano* spiders.'

'What are nano spiders?'

Zoe shrugged. 'It's his daddy's song. He sings it when he gets a sore head from thinking too much. Look, Mummy, Barbie's got nano spiders in her hair.' She held up a doll with a head that looked like it'd been attacked with gardening shears - Zoe's attempt to 'fix' its hairstyle.

'It suits her,' Jax said, her mind rolling back to her conversation with Kate. She'd listened to Jax's account of the carjacking without comment, then she'd talked about Brendan's past and his PTSD. Jax had asked questions but she hadn't thought to ask about nano spiders - she'd assumed they were a new symptom, something that had helped tip Brendan over the edge.

Aiden cocked his head towards the notebook on the table - or perhaps to somewhere out of Zoe's earshot.

Following him across the lawn, Jax said, 'Brendan talked about nano spiders in his head. He kept bashing at his skull, saying they lay their eggs in your brain, that they breed inside your skull, that once they're there, you can't get them out.'

'He might have had a headache.'

'I'm sure he did but maybe it was more than that. Information is in your head. Once it's there you can't get it out. And it can breed, grow big and strong. Maybe make his PTSD come back with force.'

'It's conjecture, Jax.'

'It's not much on its own, I know, but the Real side is seriously outweighing the Not Real.'

In the sitting room, the uniformed cop greeted two men. One was carrying a fat case. Fingerprinting, Jax guessed. Aiden watched them as they surveyed the room like painters getting ready to pull out the rollers.

'Okay,' Aiden said, 'show me what you've got.'

He pulled the notebook towards him as he sat. Jax flattened a hand on the pages. 'Just to be clear: this is still under our rules of engagement.'

'Sure.' He said it too fast.

'Tit for tat. I'll tell you what I've got, if you tell me what you've got.'

He hesitated. Maybe trying to work out what she'd accept. Maybe just taking his damn time to annoy her. 'I can't promise that. It's a police investigation.'

'And I'm contributing information.'

'You're personally involved.'

'Yes, I am. Do you want to see what I've got?'

He folded his arms, looked like he wasn't fussed either way. 'You know I could get a warrant for your notebook.'

She'd worked in a newsroom, she'd seen it threatened before. 'Uh-huh. How long would that take?'

He sucked in a long breath, lips tightening to a hard line. But the anger was an act and it lasted about two seconds before he shook his head. 'You're a pain in the butt, Miranda.'

'Thank you, Detective Senior Sergeant. I try hard. What's it going to be?'

He smoothed his tie. 'Same as before. I'll answer your questions if you answer mine. That's the best I can do.'

It wasn't an invitation to the police station to look over evidence - it wasn't bad, though. But she pretended to think it through, making him wait, enjoying his eyes - the uncertainty in them, their cool steadiness, the hint of brain matter working hard behind them. 'Okay.'

She found the page where she'd started the lists and talked him through her process. Speaking fast, volume rising, she used her hands to explain, gestured with her arms, touched Aiden's sleeve to make a point, glad to be saying it out loud at last. There was an energy to it, familiar from days on the job when big stories were breaking and she'd gathered details, going through them with editors, colleagues, people on the end of phones.

As she spoke, Aiden's focus moved between her and her notes, listening and observing. Maybe he thought it was amusing to see a civilian get overexcited about evidence. Maybe he thought she was losing it. She hoped she wasn't because it felt damn good.

'This morning at Kate's, I confirmed more,' she told him. 'Scotty looks just like Brendan and he could read before he started school. Kate's a teacher and she had trouble getting work because they moved around. She told me how Brendan used to tell people she was the best thing that ever happened to him. You took my statement. He used the same words, remember?'

Aiden kept his gaze on her notes.

'Brendan said Kate was smart, tough and soft,' she said. 'You've met her, Aiden. That's exactly what she is. I would use the same words to describe her.'

He lifted his face. She could see reservation in it.

'Look.' She laid fingers on his forearm, the skin warm under the fabric of his shirt. 'I know none of Kate's information confirms anything Brendan said about people being after him, but the Real side of the ledger keeps growing.'

Aiden glanced at her hand, made no attempt to shift it. 'It's good investigating, Jax. Your methodology is clear and you've gathered some compelling material.'

'And?'

A small tilt of his head. 'It's not evidence. There's nothing here to prove or disprove Walsh's claims.'

Jax winced a little, feeling suddenly, ridiculously amateurish. 'They were more than "claims" when he had a gun to my head.'

'You're too close to it.'

'Have I convinced you I'm not involved?'

'There's more than one way to be involved. Nothing comes off the table yet.'

She frowned at him.

'It's a process.' Explanation, not apology.

'How about the concept that people were after him?'

'The break-in and the incident at the beach last night opened that up as a possibility.'

'Only a possibility?'

'There's always more than one. It's good investigating, Jax,' he said again. There was reassurance in his tone - it still felt patronising.

'Sarge?' The uniformed cop was at the door. 'Forensics wants a word.'

Aiden flicked his eyes to the activity inside the house - fingerprint powder being dusted on her dining chairs - then back at Jax. 'No more questions?'

She hesitated, unsure, a little embarrassed. She'd heard his meaning: she'd given him nothing momentous, no nice mystery-solving piece to the Brendan Walsh puzzle, so it was time to move on. It was his job, she got that. And she *was* an amateur. Aa stay-at-home mother with a fixation problem. Aiden was right. She was too close, her perspective had been skewed - and she clearly couldn't investigate her way out of a cardboard box.

He stood, lifted a chin to the cop at the door.

'Actually . . .' She rose to her feet. He'd promised free rein on questions - and she had an obsession that needed a damn break. 'I've got more questions and we've got a deal.'

33

A iden told her that deal or no deal, forensics got first priority. He didn't sit when he came out again, just stood with his feet apart, arms folded and mobile in hand - body language for let's-get-it-done.

He told her he'd have to stick to their bargain: answer her questions, not provide a running commentary on his investigation. His phone pinged several times with incoming texts and she wondered if he'd had it switched to silent before or whether he was suddenly in demand. Jax managed to hold him in place long enough to recount his discoveries of Brendan's whereabouts in the days before the carjacking.

Brendan Walsh spent the Friday and Saturday on a Secure Force assignment: a property protection detail driving from Sydney to Melbourne to pick up a woman's jewellery collection, then returning with it ahead of a removalist's van. Nothing suspicious about the job, no papers or documents in the inventory, all delivered well within the estimated time, customer satisfied. And why not, Jax thought. She'd transported her own meagre collection of jewellery in a toiletries bag.

Kate Walsh spoke to her husband for the last time via the landline in his flat late on Saturday afternoon. He told her there was an extra shift going; she accused him of wanting to stay away. Kate found several missed calls from his mobile on Sunday and Monday but nothing in the message bank, and she was unable to make contact with him. So far,

Brendan's mobile hadn't turned up. Aiden was having forensics check the burnt-out car for any indications the phone was inside.

According to Secure Force, Brendan didn't have an extra shift over the weekend and didn't turn up to the one he'd volunteered for on the Monday. He'd been assigned as one of three bodyguards to protect an American actor during a whistle-stop tour of Sydney and there'd been a scramble finding a replacement for him. Brendan's boss had tried repeatedly to contact him without success. Brendan's flatmate hadn't seen him since the Friday morning, when he left for the Melbourne job.

'So that's two days he was out of contact,' Jax said. 'In the car, he said he'd been holding it off for two days. I thought he meant he'd been trying not to kill himself.' Aiden didn't comment. Well, it wasn't a question.

She pressed on. 'The men who were waiting for me at my car last night - maybe they turned up at Brendan's flat or he saw them somewhere and he spent the time trying not to be found. Holding "it" off could have meant holding *them* off, couldn't it?'

'We know one chased you. We don't know they were after Walsh.'

She dragged her teeth across her bottom lip. 'Meaning they could have been *with* him before he got in my car?'

'Meaning I'm not jumping to any conclusions.'

'It's got to be connected, though, don't you think?'

'I agree that's a possibility and I'd like to know where he was in those two days, but we can't assume he was being pursued by them.' Aiden's phone signalled another message. He checked its screen before continuing. 'There could be other explanations. He could have been acting with them. He could have committed a crime and was evading police. Or Kate Walsh might have been right that he wanted to stay away - he could've been having an affair and was off on a dirty weekend.'

Jax straightened with surprise. 'You think an affair's a possibility? That he spent the weekend with a woman then lost touch with reality.'

Aiden's phone pinged again. He didn't look at it, just spread his hands in apology. 'Jax, I've got to go.'

She thought of his capable-looking colleague, Suzanne May, and felt a beat of self-consciousness. Was the detective constable texting so he could make excuses and escape? 'Aren't you going to read it?'

'I know what it says,' he said over his shoulder as he headed for the door.

'Stop wasting your time?' She made it sound like a joke.

He looked back at her. No guilt at being caught out. Not laughing, either. 'We'll unravel it, Jax, trust me. But I've got to get to another crime scene.'

'Oh, right.' She'd been prolonging someone else's drama.

Inside, the uniformed cop was gone and the forensics officers had their heads down dusting the living room. Outside, the courtyard was empty except for Zoe and her dolls. She was six, old enough to play on her own, but there were cops here - not to protect her but to collect evidence of someone uninvited. 'Zoe, baby, come inside while I walk the detective to the door.'

Holding Zoe's hand, following Aiden through the living room, Jax told herself to be grateful he'd stayed as long as he had. She eyed the well-sprung effortlessness of his legs as he climbed the stairs, figured if Brendan had remembered something about Afghanistan, it would take time to track the answer down.

'I've got more questions, you know,' she told Aiden as he opened the front door.

'I'd be surprised if you didn't.'

Sweet talker. 'When do I get to ask them?'

A chuckle rumbled in his throat as he stepped off the threshold. 'Give me a call, buy me a drink and bring a list.'

'It might need two drinks.'

He slipped black sunglasses on. 'Then you're buying both.'

She grinned at his departing back for about two seconds before the amusement fell from her face. Was that flirting? What the hell was she thinking? She was holding her daughter's hand and he was a cop whose interest was now reduced to getting her victim support. Still ... she'd thought her sense of male-female interface had died with Nick.

Taking Zoe upstairs, away from the fingerprint powder and the array of questions it would generate, Jax remembered Aiden's, *We'll unravel it*, and wondered if the 'we' included her or just his team of real investigators. Ignoring the boundaries she'd wanted to establish, she helped herself to Tilda's fridge, throwing together a cheese sandwich and sitting with Zoe on the deck in the breeze, thinking about where she'd gone wrong with her research.

She didn't have access to the kind of information a cop might gather - at least, not in the three days since the carjacking. She'd approached it all like a feature article, as though her time with Brendan was one long interview and her job was to verify everything he'd said. Her speciality had been human interest, she looked for the truth in people, tried to give a sense of who they were while she wrote their story. She'd hoped to discover *who* Brendan was, hoped it might explain his intentions.

Aiden, on the other hand, was a cop. He wasn't interested in who but *what* Brendan had done in a timeframe that was relevant to a coroner's investigation. Information that proved or disproved, not ideas that suggested what he'd been thinking and feeling. Aiden assumed an affair or a crime or bad company as easily as he might assume Brendan ate toast for breakfast.

Maybe Aiden had seen too much. Maybe Jax was naive and idealistic.

'Hello?' a voice called.

Jax met one of the forensics guys halfway down Tilda's stairs.

'I was told there was electrical equipment missing from up here.'

Jax pointed him to the TV unit and the walnut desk and watched with Zoe while he worked, fielding her daughter's questions and telling herself that Aiden wasn't shutting her out - he'd promised to answer her questions so long as she was buying.

Except he was considering culpability and collecting facts for an inquest. He wasn't interested in the level of desperation that made a person get in a car and point a pistol at a stranger.

The forensics guy packed up his kit and stood. 'I think you've got a budding scientific officer there,' he said, nodding at Zoe.

'I think she's aiming for interrogator.' Jax smiled.

'We're finished downstairs. You can go back in there now.'

Jax made a start, straightening chairs, wiping off fingerprint dust and thinking. Of Kate Walsh.

Brendan's wife was stuck inside Jax now, like a splinter that was deep and sore in the palm of her hand. She wanted to figure out Brendan's message and give it to Kate so at least one of them could move on.

Jax checked her watch. 'Come on, Zoe. We're going out again.'

'Where to?'

'A cafe.' To see a man who might have some of the information she needed to put it all together.

'Can I bring my dolls?'

Jax glanced at the mound of them in Zoe's wheelbarrow. 'You can bring two.'

'Three?'

Zoe had been brilliant all day. A long, sensitive, fraught day. 'Okay, three dolls.' Jax pointed to her cheek, leaned down for Zoe to kiss it, bundled her into a quick, tight hug in return.

She phoned for a cab, locked the house, made another call while they waited for it on the driveway and was told her car was ready to be picked up from a police compound in the city. She wanted it back; after the break in, she wanted to know she could leave in a hurry. But two men had found her Mazda on the street yesterday, so she figured it could stay where it was for another few hours and she'd pick it up when she was ready to drive home again.

She dialled another number as the cabbie headed down the hill towards the beachfront.

'Russell, it's Jax,' she said.

'Hi, Uncle Russell,' Zoe called from the other side of the back seat.

Jax turned the phone as he called back. 'Hey, Zoe-bear!'

'We had some police at our place today,' Zoe said, as though she'd been dying to tell someone.

Jax returned the phone to her ear. 'She's a blabbermouth. I wasn't going to tell you.'

'Everyone okay?'

Her eyes drifted to the long, gentle curve of beach that stretched ahead of them. Sand the colour of egg yolk, an ocean fringed with the crisp white of breaking surf, all baking under a deep blue sky. 'We're fine. We had a break-in. Some electrical stuff was taken. And my big laptop.' He was already worried about her - he didn't need to know she'd almost chased a guy.

'Geez, Jax. Did you run over a black cat recently?'

'Yeah, I hit a pack of them the day I left Sydney.' Could it just be bad luck? A random carjacking, a couple of over-zealous guys looking for YouTube fame last night, a simple neighbourhood robbery today ...

'Daddy's files were all messed up,' Zoe called.

'Shhh.' Jax pointed a warning at her.

'You got Nick's files back?' Russell asked.

'No. *My* files on Nick. They were dumped on the floor when someone went through the bedroom. It wasn't about the files, though.'

'So the cops think it's just a robbery?'

The cab pulled up at traffic lights and Jax eyed the occupants of the car beside her. Young surfers - not anything like the men who'd chased her. 'I don't know but I've got a theory, though. I talked to the detective about it at the house but came off sounding like Agatha Christie.'

'Hercule Poirot or Miss Marple?'

'Either is relatively humiliating.'

He laughed. 'So what's this theory?'

Jax rolled her lips together, not sure if he'd be concerned or a good sounding board. Either way, he had access to sources she didn't have. Keeping it simple, trying not to say anything that might prick Zoe's ears, Jax talked him through the possibility that if Brendan had sensitive information, a ride up the motorway with the wife of Nick Westing might make a third party concerned.

The cab negotiated a corner before Russell responded. 'What are the cops saying?' The reservation in his voice made her wonder if she was still sounding like Agatha.

'About the break-in, not much. But Brendan Walsh was out of contact for almost two days before he got in my car. He had an argument with his wife on Saturday, didn't turn up for work on Monday and his flatmate didn't see him.'

'You dug all that up?'

No, he didn't think she was Agatha. He was worried she was starting a new box of files. 'No, the investigating detective told me.'

'What, he just offered it up?'

'Yeah, right. No, I made a deal. I gave him what I had in return for some information on Brendan.'

'What *do* you have?' It wasn't reporter's eagerness. He sounded reluctant, as though the thought of her answer was making him wince.

She tried to tone down her attitude. 'Just some notes I threw together. I talked to Brendan's wife, thought it might put things into perspective. You know, for her. For both of us.' When Russell didn't say anything, she added, 'I made my material sound better than it is. I definitely got the better end of the bargain.'

'Jax, what are you doing?' Reproach and concern.

'It's not what you think. I'm not starting more files. I'm thinking about writing a story,' she lied. 'You've been telling me I should start writing again so I'm, you know, pulling ideas together, thinking about where I might go with it, and the detective had information I thought I could use.'

Another pause. Maybe he was deciding whether to believe her. 'Are you sure you want to start with this one? It's pretty close to home.'

The cab slowed and she saw the cafe up ahead in the next block.

'It won't be a firsthand account of the carjacking,' she said. 'Kate

Walsh told me about Brendan's PTSD. I thought I might use that as the angle, unless something else crops up in the research.'

'Well, you know I'd be happy to sort through a few angles with you. I haven't run a Miranda Jack by-line in years.'

Now she felt bad. 'Thanks. Actually, you might be able to help. Have any of your guys spoken to Brendan's employer? It might be useful to know what he actually did at Secure Force and some of the clients he worked for.'

Russell's answer was slow in coming - either writing himself a note or wondering what he should give her. 'I'll ask around and get back to you.'

34

J ax had been to the cafe with Tilda on the visit to Newcastle before she sold the house. The barista knew her aunt by name and made a great cappuccino and the aroma from the muffin baking had made Jax want to move in there. It was on a busy corner with huge windows that looked out to both streets and, back then, it'd seemed sunny, busy and trendy. Now, after being chased by two men, possibly the same men who'd broken into Tilda's house, it felt more like a fishbowl. Taking a table in the rear, glancing uneasily at the expanse of glass, Jax wished she'd known the name of a smaller, more private cafe when she'd talked to Hugh Talbotson this morning.

They were fifteen minutes early - enough time for Jax to cool down, settle Zoe and her dolls, and work up some anxiety. Hugh hadn't called her, which she hoped was because he planned to meet her, not some passive-aggressive payback to inconvenience her. Brendan had been Hugh's friend and Jax was with him at the end; she'd been left with a gun and Hugh with a distraught Kate Walsh. This conversation could go any number of ways and not all of them good.

She watched Zoe talking to her dolls, impressed and grateful for her daughter's capacity to entertain herself this week. It'd been a big five days in six-year-old terms - new house, new food, new people, late nights. The excitement had probably helped to sustain Zoe this far but it was hot and humid and she was tired. Probably tired of being dragged around today. Maybe bringing her here wasn't a great idea. Maybe Hugh wouldn't want to talk. Maybe Russell had a point: what the hell *was* she doing?

'Miranda?'

'Hugh.' She got to her feet, held out her hand. 'Thanks for coming.'

He was tall, muscular and clean-cut. It would be difficult to mistake him for anything but military. She'd seen him earlier under a harsh midday sun and in a dim hallway. He'd looked robust, hard. Here in the gentler light of the cafe, she saw a shadow of fatigue under his lower eyelashes, a hint of grey in his pallor, and thought the tiredness made him seem more human, a little vulnerable. Someone better for Kate to lean on.

They busied themselves with the small talk of ordering, Jax gabbling a little, thrown by his stern composure. She ordered and paid at the counter, found Zoe setting up doll school on the table when she got back, Hugh watching in arm-folded silence.

'How about you use a chair for the classroom, baby?' Jax pulled a seat from another table and set it next to Zoe.

'But they're already at their desks.' Something slightly whiny had arrived in Zoe's voice.

'We need the table for the drinks.'

'But, *Mu-um*, my dollies need to go to school.' Foreboding fluttered in Jax's gut. Zoe was too old for a terrible twos-style, hit-the-floor-and-scream tantrum, but she was six and she could whine and interrupt and lose her temper and cause a fuss, and like any mother with a tired child, Jax knew she was on borrowed time.

Willing Zoe not to lose it yet, she tried to inject a hang-in-there vibe into her tone. 'Well, table-school is closed for the holidays but if the students transfer to chair-school, the teacher gets a smoothie. And look, here it is.' She took the glass from the waitress and held it out of Zoe's reach. 'Better get those guys to class.'

While Zoe rearranged the dolls, Jax turned to Hugh, worried he might be having second thoughts. 'Sorry about this.'

'It's fine.'

'Have you got kids?'

'No, but I'm Uncle Hugh to about twenty of them.' He took a mock surreptitious glance around. 'If you've got another one lurking, you might need a school principal.'

She laughed a little - relieved and surprised at his joke. She thought he was shaping up as a hard arse. 'No, it's just Zoe.'

'Ready,' Zoe called.

Jax handed her the glass, turned back to Hugh, wanting to get started while Zoe was occupied, cautious of jumping right in with intimate questions about dead friends. 'How's Kate?'

'Her neighbour gave her some herbal thing to help her sleep. She took it at one-thirty and was asleep when I left. Scotty is playing next door for two hours.'

An official report - this process could be difficult for more reasons than she thought. 'They seem like good neighbours.'

'Yes, but I'm biased. Jock was a navy man. Not army but a close enough relative.'

Nodding as though she had some clue about military camaraderie, she said, 'Is that how it was with Brendan? He was family?'

'Something like that.'

As his long black and her peppermint tea were settled on the table, Jax glanced at Zoe, decided the direct approach might suit them all. 'Can you tell me what Brendan was like?'

He didn't right away. He tore the top off a sachet of sugar, let the contents slide into his cup and stirred. Jax wanted to reach across the table, grab him by the shirt front and shout, *Talk, goddamn it!* But she poured her tea, telling herself that just because he was here didn't mean it would be easy - or that he wouldn't change his mind.

Finally, he laid the spoon on the saucer, folded his arms on the table and lifted his eyes. He seemed different now, as though the muscles in his face had been rearranged, softening the mouth, relaxing the stern angles. There was resolution, too: reluctant, sad, possibly dutiful, but no misgiving about discussing Brendan.

'He was a likeable bloke,' he said. 'Popular with the guys, a lot of fun sometimes. But ...' His head dipped to one side, as though he was disappointed to have to say the rest. 'He could be a bit loose around the edges.'

Jax sipped tea with no clue what that meant. 'How so?'

Another tip of his head. 'Brendan wasn't the steadiest of blokes. He was a good soldier, but he could be up and down. Loose, you know. Unpredictable.'

She'd seen unpredictable, didn't think Hugh was referring to a tendency for carjackings. 'What kind of unpredictable?'

'He was moody. Sometimes his decisions were questionable. He didn't always make good choices about who he got friendly with.' A checklist: attitude, decision-making, associates.

'Do you mean when he was in the army or recently?'

'Both.'

Jax liked Kate's version of Brendan better. 'It was generous of you to help him find work.'

'I've made some useful civilian contacts over the years. Sometimes they come to me for personnel, sometimes it's ex-ADF looking for jobs. I've been able to help out a few.'

'Which way was it with Brendan?'

'He came to a reunion, told a few of the blokes he was trying to get work, and one of them suggested he talk to me.'

'Did you know about his PTSD?'

'Yeah. He said he was over it and I wanted to help him get his shit together.'

Kate had said the PTSD made Brendan feel less of a man. It couldn't have been easy for him to ask this tough guy for help.

'Mummy?'

Jax turned, found Zoe standing beside her. 'Yes, baby?'

'How long are we going to be here?' Her voice was more plaintive than grisly - Jax figured she could hold out a while longer.

'Just for a little bit. I brought some of your books. Why don't you get one out?' While Zoe peered into her bag, Jax turned back to Hugh. 'You weren't worried about Brendan being unpredictable in a job you put him in?'

He held up a hand. 'Don't get me wrong, he was a solid soldier. So long as he had clear boundaries to work within, he was fine. I figured he'd be okay with the kind of soft jobs he'd get.'

She frowned. 'Brendan was doing private security work, right? Being a bodyguard, transporting money, debt collection. It can't be that soft.'

'It's Australia, not Afghanistan.'

Right. Movie stars and jewellery, not insurgents and bombs. 'But he *did* have problems with it?'

'No, he did the job fine, like I expected him to.'

'Except for the PTSD.'

He made a doubtful, downward turn of his lips. 'There have always been soldiers with PTSD. If you want the job, you better have a cup of cement and harden up.'

She fought to keep the distaste from her face, and the urge to debate his macho attitude. 'Is that your advice?'

'Plenty of them learn to live with it. A few nightmares don't stop them doing their jobs.'

It was the other side of the military mental health coin. Jax had read about the warrior culture that taught soldiers they were weak if they talked about their feelings, and encouraged them to put up with the symptoms. 'Is that what you do? Live with it?'

One side of his mouth turned up. 'I don't have PTSD.' He didn't have a lot of compassion, either. 'But Brendan did.'

'Yeah, I saw it.'

35

'**M**ummy, can I play with your phone?'

'Sure.' Jax pulled it from her bag, passed it to Zoe with barely a glance. 'How was his PTSD showing?'

Hugh rubbed a hand across his short-cropped hair, changed the subject. 'After he moved to Sydney, we kept in touch a bit. I came up here for a weekend once. Kate asked me to keep an eye on him. It was said in front of Brendan, kind of a wife joke - but afterwards he told me not to tell her anything.'

'About what?'

'How he was, what he was doing.'

'What didn't he want her to know?'

The reluctant tilt of the head again. 'He said he wasn't sleeping. I could see for myself he was wound up, knew he'd been drinking a fair bit. I figured he didn't want her nagging him, which was fair enough. And the other stuff, well, it wasn't the kind of thing you want a wife to know.'

'What stuff?'

'He was making friends and picking up.'

Picking up drugs? Something illegal? Something that might make people chase him? 'What was he picking up?'

Hugh paused a beat. 'Women. One-night stands. Some of them he paid for.'

Oh, right. She made a face. So Brendan *was* a bad guy. Another kind of bad guy. Maybe Aiden had been right about an affair.

'Mummy?'

'Yes, baby.'

'What else can I do?'

'Here.' Jax pulled the canister of sugar sachets closer. 'Build a house with these. Did Kate follow up? Ask you how he was doing?'

Hugh watched the sugar-house construction as he answered. 'Yeah, she called a couple of times but I wasn't going to tell her. Not after he asked me not to.'

'What did you say?'

'I lied. I said he was doing great.' There was a regretful twist of his lips. 'I like Kate, she was still holding out for him. Not all the spouses do that. So I felt ... accountable. I tried to talk Brendan around. Told him to get his arse home more regularly. But like I said, he didn't always make good choices.'

Yeah, like cheating on Kate. 'Who was he making friends with?'

'Some guys at a gym.'

'What was your issue with them?'

'They're civilian.' His smile was more scoff than humour.

'Not part of the family?'

'Something like that.'

'Is it possible Brendan got involved in something with them? Something that might make him frightened of them.'

'I think it's more likely they did his head in.'

Had they wanted to know about Afghanistan? Maybe they'd made him remember what it was like. 'In what way?'

A quick upward flick of Hugh's eyebrows. 'I read in the paper he held a gun to your head. That should tell you something.'

Her body stiffened at the memory of cold metal against her temple. Did Hugh think that was what civilians did? Irresponsible use of weapons as opposed to the organised use of weapons. 'Brendan thought people were after him. Do you think it's possible it could've been those guys?'

'He was always a bit of a conspiracy theorist. A lot of soldiers were after the green-on-blue incidents started. Do I think there were people after him?' A skeptical shake of his head. 'I doubt it.'

'Mummy, I'm bored.'

'I know, baby. I'm sorry. Just a little longer.' *Please.* Jax dug around in the bottom of her bag, found a pen, pulled out her notebook and turned to a fresh page. 'How about practising your name some more?'

Zoe heaved a protest sigh but took the pen, her tongue poking from the side of her mouth as she started. When Jax looked back at Hugh, he reached across the table, the tips of his fingers stopping just short of where hers resting around the saucer of her teacup. 'Look, what happened is sad,' he said, 'really sad, but it's not a complete surprise. He had PTSD. Have you seen the suicide rates?'

She'd searched but there weren't any clear statistics. PTSD among current and former military personnel was significantly higher than in the general population, and suicidal behaviour in serving ranks was more than double that in the community, but the number of veterans who took their own life - PTSD sufferers or not - was apparently hard to determine. She understood what Hugh was getting at, though. He thought PTSD and suicide went hand-in-hand.

Jax eyed the powerful forearm stretched across the table, wondered if Hugh's 'cup of cement' had already rationalised Brendan's death as a statistic. 'Kate didn't see it coming,' she said.

'No, she wouldn't have. She thought he was doing okay.'

'What have you told her now?'

He paused, a kinder tone in his voice when he spoke again. 'That Brendan loved her, that he talked about her all the time, that he was working in Sydney because he wanted to look after her and Scotty. I don't think she needs to know the rest. Do you?'

After all the 'harden-up' chitchat, Jax was surprised by his sudden compassion. She'd expected him to suggest Kate grow some balls and get over it. But his message was the same one Jax had wanted to deliver in that first visit with Kate - and considering the rest, his question had merit. Kate was already struggling with difficult memories, did she need to add to them?

Jax had posed the same question to herself. Before Nick's death, she'd assumed she would have known if something was up with him - they lived and worked together, their daily life was interwoven. But he was mown down forty minutes from home and she had no idea why he'd crossed the Harbour Bridge in late peak hour, driven to a residential neighbourhood, parked in a side street and went for a run in a suburb with no park, no track, not even a footpath. She'd thought plenty about the half-dialled number on his mobile, questioned whether the person he'd tried to call in his last moments was a woman. Someone he loved - someone he loved more than Jax - whose voice he wanted in his ear as he died.

If it was, did she want to know? If Nick was cheating or concealing something? If he was losing his mind? If he was a serial killer and leaving a trail of dead bodies?

If it explained why he was dead - yes, yes, yes and yes. She wanted the truth. She wanted it to be noble or just dumb luck, but even if it was ugly and humiliating, she wanted it. Because the truth was better than never really knowing.

But that was her choice. 'I wouldn't want to make that decision for Kate.'

Hugh smiled a little, edged his fingers forward, stroked the back of her hand with a knuckle. It seemed like reassurance that she was doing the right thing, but the intimacy of it suddenly made the proceedings feel less Q&A and more the kind of meeting she wasn't ready for.

Tucking her fingers away, fumbling for her teapot, she told herself that men and women met this way sometimes, sharing empathy. She had a friend who'd married a man she met at a funeral. But Jax wasn't ready. Not even close. And she didn't know how to play this game. What was the appropriate way to say, *Thanks, but I need to finish asking my questions and about six months to evaluate my life?*

She spoke quickly, wanting to cover her discomfort. 'Brendan was trying to get to Kate and Scotty when he ran in front of that bus.' Across the table, Hugh straightened, his smile dropping. 'I'm sorry,' Jax added. 'Maybe *you* didn't want to know that.'

'No, it's fine.' His jaw tightened as he ran a hand across his stubble - it looked like both strain and fortification. Taking a moment to sip on the cement, she thought.

'Can you write something, Mummy?'

Jax took the pen from Zoe, wrote *Mummy, Daddy, Aunty Tilda*, knowing there was no chance she could be interested in a man who thought being hard was a positive character trait.

When she'd handed the notebook back to Zoe, Hugh said, 'So Brendan thought someone was after him because he hadn't gone home for a while?'

Could it have happened like that? Could Brendan have got it into his head that Kate and Scotty weren't safe because he hadn't been home?

Across the table, Hugh read her silence as confirmation. 'Jesus, did I do that? I told him I'd come after him if he didn't do the right thing by Kate.'

'Not unless you threatened him with guns and missiles.'

'That's what he thought?'

She nodded. 'He wouldn't let me pull over because he thought we'd be ...' she curled fingers in the air '... picked off.'

He watched her a moment, his eyelids tightening as it sank in. 'Tough day for you.'

'Yeah.' She laughed a little at his gruff sympathy, taking some comfort that it came from someone who knew worse kinds of tough days. 'By the end, I thought there really was someone after us.'

'Us? He thought they were after you too?'

'Only because we were in the same car. And that was only because Brendan got in mine and pointed the gun at me.'

'How did you respond to that?'

Did he think she'd employed a tactical manoeuvre? 'Well, I froze, then I did what I was told and tried to ignore the yelling and the gun in my face.'

'Sounds like you handled yourself well.'

'For a civilian?'

He cocked his head. 'You ended up with the gun. You must have done something useful.'

It hadn't felt like that. 'I talked to him. It seemed to calm him down.'

'Did he talk back?'

'Eventually. Most of what he said didn't make sense. It was just disconnected thoughts - crazy, emotional stuff.' She stopped, assuming Hugh wouldn't want to hear about the ramblings of an ex-soldier who hadn't been 'hard' enough. But he watched her as though waiting for the rest. 'He said he'd been lied to,' she went on. 'He thought he had something breeding in his head, he freaked out when he saw my phone. Told me the people who were after him were trained and wouldn't stop, that they had guns and knives and missiles.'

As she talked, Hugh's face morphed back to the flat sternness he'd arrived with, making Jax wonder if it was his default expression. Perhaps he was naturally walled off and had to dig for compassion. Or had he trained himself to keep a mask over his emotions, choosing the moments he was prepared to reveal what was underneath? What she wanted now,

though, was his reaction to her description of what had happened in
the car.

What she got made her wonder about her own hold on reality.

36

When her story was done, Hugh turned his face away from her until all she could see was the firm set to his mouth and the beat at the hinge of his jaw as his teeth clenched and unclenched.

He knew something, she thought. Now he had the details, he *knew*. Maybe he knew all of it. She held her breath, hope making her spine straighter, her pulse quicken, while she waited for him to come back with a resolute, dutiful explanation.

But he didn't. He just started with a slow swing of his head, left to right and back again. 'Poor bastard,' he finally pushed out. 'What a way to leave the world.'

Jax's brows slid upwards, inwards. Surprise, confusion. The silence hadn't been speechless comprehension? He'd been sucking on concrete?

It was good news, she tried to tell herself. He hadn't conceded to the idea that Brendan's claims might be based in truth. She should be pleased. Massively relieved, even. But what she felt was disappointment. In Brendan, in herself. This new version of him - and that she'd been so wrong about Hugh's reaction.

Did she want it to be real?

Or did she just want more questions to keep her obsession afloat?

'*Mummy!*'

Jax jumped, realised Zoe was beside her, a finger tapping her shoulder. 'Sorry, baby. What is it?'

'When are we going *home*?'

'Soon. Really soon.'

Zoe rattled her legs about, pulled her saddest face. 'Oh, *Mu-um*, that's what you said before.'

Yes, she had. And Zoe was a picture of boredom and fed-up-ness - a lethal combination. Jax glanced at Hugh. There was more she wanted to ask: what state was Brendan in when he'd last seen him, who were the civilians from the gym, what had happened in Afghanistan? But Zoe needed her attention and Tilda would be home soon, needing an explanation about the break-in. 'Okay, Zoe, changed my mind. Let's go.'

As Zoe packed up her dolls, Hugh stood, cupped a hand to Jax's elbow and drew her around to face him. 'I don't know what you wanted to get out of this, Miranda, but I hope I've helped.' It was his soft expression.

'Thanks, you have, I think.' Maybe it would feel that way when she'd had a chance to mull it over. She picked up her notebook from the table, held it a moment before pushing it into her bag. 'It's just ... there are things that don't make sense.'

'What things?'

'My house was broken into this morning while I was at Kate's house. And I was harassed by a couple of blokes last night.'

'You should've told me.'

'Would it have made a difference?'

'No, but you must be shaken up. Was much taken?' His hand slid upwards along her bare skin, curled gently around her upper arm.

It was probably meant to be comfort, but she wanted to shake her arm free and take a deep breath of personal space. 'A few electricals,' she told him, taking a step back out of his reach.

'Did you call the police?'

She nodded. 'Fingerprinting has been and gone.'

'Kate said you've just moved in. Classic time to get robbed.'

'I suppose.' She tried to focus on what she wanted to know. 'There was a lot of truth mixed in with Brendan's rambling. He was so adamant ... and I'm having trouble believing that it wasn't all real.'

'Ready,' Zoe said, doll bag strapped across her chest. Hugh signalled for them to go ahead of him, making no attempt to respond to Jax's statement. Heat rushed up at them from the footpath as they stepped from the air-conditioning. As Jax lifted a hand to her forehead to block the glare, Hugh put his sizeable body between her and the sun. 'Everything Brendan said *was* true.'

His words made Jax pull Zoe a little closer.

'In some shape or form,' he clarified. 'He *was* chased by trained people with guns and knives and missiles. In Afghanistan. He *was* lied to - by the military, by our allies. Everyone gets lied to. *I* lied to him. I told him I'd come after him if he didn't play nice with his wife. I don't know what was in his head. Not spiders, obviously, but there's probably an explanation. Maybe he had a headache.'

It was what Aiden had said.

'You all right now?' Hugh asked it as though she'd come to him for reassurance instead of information.

'Yeah, sure.'

'You've got my number. Call if you want to talk again. Or if someone else tries to break into your house. I can be a big, scary body if you need one.'

She smiled a little. 'I imagine you can.'

'Where's your car?'

'We came in a cab.'

'Can I give you a lift somewhere?'

'The police kept my car for fingerprinting last night and I was planning to pick it up now. Thanks, but it's out of your way.'

He checked his watch. 'Scotty is next door for a while longer and I'm sure Kate would appreciate the downtime.' Jax glanced along the street. It was a small strip of shops - no cab rank, no cab in sight, and Zoe was tired. 'Okay, thank you.'

Jax gave him an address and directions as they walked around the corner. His car was a big, dark four-wheel drive, maybe as close to army transport as he could get. She had to lift Zoe into the back seat, haul herself into the front.

'Did the police get any useful prints from your car?' Hugh asked as he pulled away from the kerb.

'I don't know. I haven't heard yet.'

'What about the break-in? Do they think it had something to do with Brendan?'

'Maybe. I don't know.'

'What about you?' he asked. 'What do you think?'

She squinted out the window. Her head hurt from thinking about it.

'I want to know what happened to Brendan. If it's got something to do with that, I guess I'll find out.'

'Why do you want to know?'

A cynical laugh heaved its way from her throat. 'Because I get stuck on things like that. Because sometimes the only thing I can do is ask questions. Because I can't stand a mystery. Because I'm a civilian and it's all I'm trained for. You want me to go on?'

'You're a journalist, you're trained to write newspaper articles.'

She turned to face him, not sure from his tone if he was encouraging or correcting her. Or telling her to grow balls.

'Is that what you're planning?' he asked.

She'd told Russell she was writing a story. It'd been a lie but writing had saved her sanity once before - maybe her subconscious was telling her something. 'Maybe. My life at this point is largely unplanned. I'll decide when I figure Brendan out.'

Hugh came to a stop at an intersection, sat a moment. More than a moment. Five, ten seconds. Jax leaned forward, checked the cross street. Nothing coming. Had he forgotten her instructions?

'Straight through *then* a right,' she said.

A beat passed. His head swung towards her, eyes obscured by sunglasses, the rest of his face still and unreadable.

What? she wanted to ask. But something about him - the movement, the posture, the watching - reminded her of Brendan. Of the suspended, unpredictable moments that had made her skin bead with sweat as she waited for his next move. She clenched her teeth, breath frozen in her chest, waiting for Brendan to start yelling.

'Mummy, I need a pee.' Zoe's voice was like glass breaking in Jax's head.

She had a sudden urge to leap into the back seat and shield her with her body. But she couldn't move, just held on to her seatbelt with a locked fist. Hugh wasn't Brendan, she told herself. This wasn't the motorway. It wasn't the precursor to another bloody nightmare.

Across the car, Hugh looked back then front. Just like Brendan. 'We better get going then. Straight ahead then right.'

Jax's mouth was still dry by the time they made the turn. Her heart still hammering when Hugh let them off at the police compound. She thanked him, waved goodbye, thought, *What is wrong with me?* Maybe she was the one with the mental health issues. She'd flipped out because he'd looked at her sideways. She'd wanted Hugh to tell her Brendan *wasn't* crazy, that there *was* someone after him. She was holding on to her questions as though they were keeping her breathing.

Driving home through a blur of tears, Jax listened to Zoe's prattle with clenched teeth, trying to push down the tide of emotion that was filling her chest. She'd thought Brendan was a nice guy under pressure and now it seemed he was a cheating, nasty, crazy arsehole. How wrong could she be?

Cresting the hill, seeing the stunning coastline stretched out in front of her, she wanted to pull into the car park, soak up the heat and the view and the energy of the ocean; pry loose Brendan Walsh's hold on her. But two men had found her at the beach yesterday. She had Zoe with her today. She couldn't stop until she'd locked the car in the garage.

She couldn't stop. That was the problem.

'Are you crying, Mummy?'

Jax knuckled away a tear. 'Just a bit, baby.'

'Are you sad again?'

'No, I'm not sad.' She forced a smile through trembling lips - probably not as reassuring as she'd intended. 'I'm just ... worked up.'

'Why?'

'Because.'

'Because why?'

'Not now, Zoe. Please.'

TILDA WAS at home when they came in from the garage, standing at the top of the stairs with a glass in hand and an anxious frown between her brows. 'There you are. I was starting to worry where you'd got to.'

'Tilda, I'm so sorry about the break-in,' Jax called up.

Her aunt waved a hand, part dismissive, part come-on-up. 'No, it's my fault. I didn't set the alarm this morning. I often don't bother but I'll have to be more conscientious now that you two are here. You'd think after the last few days I would've ...' she cut the thought off as Zoe hit the top of the stairs, gave her niece's ponytail a quick tug as she scooted past. 'Anyway, I'm cross I didn't remember and you've lost your things.'

'You've lost some too,' Jax said, kissing Tilda's cheek. 'And I don't think they broke in because you forgot the alarm, although I think we should make an effort to remember now. What are you drinking?'

'Gin and tonic. Just so long as you're both all right.'

'Scared shitless for about fifteen minutes. Can I have one?'

'Of course. Long or short?'

Long might put her in a coma. 'Short, thanks.' She followed Tilda to the kitchen, leaned wearily on the counter as her aunt poured. How much did Tilda need to know about the break-in? That it might be about Brendan Walsh - both the robbery and the chase?

'Olives?' Tilda asked as she slid the drink across the counter.

'Mmm, please.' No, Jax couldn't bear to go through it again - not after she'd promised her aunt to let it go. 'Can I ask you something?'

'Of course.' Tilda perched on the stool beside her and fluffed at her chic white hair as though the conversation might be taped for television.

'I had coffee with Brendan Walsh's friend Hugh Talbotson this afternoon.'

Tilda blinked, didn't comment.

'When we were talking, he made a point, left his hand on the table, then brushed the back of mine, like this.' She made the same slow, gentle stroke on her aunt's hand. 'He's this big, gruff, tough guy. He's done four tours of Afghanistan and he didn't really want to meet with me. Then that. It seemed weirdly intimate. It threw me. I didn't know what to make of it.'

'It's flattering, Jax.'

'So you think it was ... *that*?'

'What do you think?'

Jax pushed out a gust of breath. 'I don't know. I don't know what to think about anything.'

'Are you attracted to him?'

Jax gulped at her gin and tonic. She was talking to her seniors-card-holding aunt about men again. 'I don't know. A bit, maybe. Only in an he's-attracted-to-me-and-I-remember-that's-quite-nice kind of way.'

Tilda patted Jax's leg. 'Well, that's a start.'

'I'm not ready for a start. I don't want ... I'm worried about -'

'The sex.'

'What? No.'

'It's only natural. The worrying and the sex.'

A chuckle bubbled in Jax's throat.

Tilda pulled a face that was halfway between you-may-laugh and let-me-tell-you. 'Eventually you stop worrying or the sex is good enough to make you forget.'

'God, Tilda, I haven't thought that far.' Jax picked up an olive, glanced across the room to where Zoe was laying out playing cards, lowered her voice so her daughter wouldn't hear. 'I know Nick's dead. I know he's not coming back. I've accepted that. But he still takes up space inside me. I don't want to lose that.'

Tilda's hand closed around Jax's. 'You won't. It'll never leave you. It won't always be right in the centre of you, but you'll always be able to find it.'

Tears filled Jax's eyes with a suddenness that made her gasp. 'Shit. I was meant to be pulling myself together up here.' A faint ping sounded from inside her handbag.

'You can't do it with dry eyes,' Tilda said.

Jax wiped hers with one hand, reached for her phone with the other. A text message: *Finished work. Need a drink. You buying tonight?*

'Aiden Hawke,' Jax explained. 'He wants to have a drink tonight.'

'And just when we're done with the sex education.'

'A *drink*, Tilda. I offered to buy. I didn't expect it to be tonight.'

'You should go. It'll do you good. And if you're going to worry about sex, it may as well be while you're with a handsome man.'

Jax rolled her eyes. 'Zoe's had a long day and I haven't done anything about dinner yet.'

'Well, I never cook on my art class day.' Tilda waved her glass at the kitchen as though it was a masterpiece. 'I stopped on the way home and bought a quiche. Does she like quiche?'

Jax pushed a hand through limp hair. She'd been in and out of the heat all day, panicking and crying. She needed a shower, a hairdresser, a quiet night. And she wanted to hear what Aiden had to say. 'If you tell her it's egg-and-bacon pie, she does. Are you sure you don't mind?'

Tilda took the remaining gin and tonic from Jax's hand. 'You can have another one with Detective Hawke.'

Jax texted: *And questions?*

And questions. Same place?

Give me half an hour.

37

Jax managed the shower and a quick spray of perfume; the best she could do with her hair at short notice was a ponytail. Aiden was waiting for her on the deck of The Beach House - same clothes as earlier plus his black-framed sunnies. FBI G-man. Something rather nice rippled through her stomach.

Making a show of looking him over, she said, 'So your other crime scene didn't involve wading thigh-deep through mud?'

'Not this one.'

'So you've done that?'

One eyebrow rose above the frame of his sunglasses. 'Have we started already?'

'Started?'

'With the questions.'

She grinned. 'You want to wait until the drink is in your hand?'

He made a face, like she had a point. 'Have I waded through mud? Absolutely. Mud, stormwater drains, garbage. Sewage once. Whatever it takes.'

She watched him leaning against the railing, surf at his back, and remembered his words from the other night in his car. *I'm good at my job, Jax. I will work it out.* More often than not, she imagined. 'In or out?' She hooked a thumb at the door to the bar.

'Out. I need the fresh air. Not all houses are as clean as yours.' He nodded to somewhere behind her. 'There's a table down there.'

She saw the spot, set off on a winding path through the throng of late-week patrons. The press of other drinkers kept him close at her back, his hand brushing her hip as they walked, breath fluttering on her neck when she stopped. 'What are you having?' she asked.

There was space behind him but he didn't step back. 'A beer, thanks.'

Waiting in the queue at the bar, glancing around the busy hotel, Jax felt the apprehension slide back into the pit of her stomach. There were no familiar faces but after the media coverage this week, it wouldn't be difficult to find her in a crowd - if someone decided breaking into her home wasn't enough. Her gaze caught on Aiden at the table, his attention moving from group to group around the deck. Not the quick flick around she'd done. It was slow and casual, as though he was marking time. Except she saw there was more to it: roaming, pausing, focusing, restarting. Cop habit, she wondered, or was he watching for someone too? His eyes found her as she returned through the doors. Stayed there until she sat opposite.

That wasn't cop habit. That was something else.

She tapped her gin and tonic against his beer. 'Cheers.'

He watched her some more over the rim of his glass as he took a sip. 'How are you, Jax?'

Was the long, lingering thing concern? 'Well, I'm over the heat.'

'You've had a rough few days.'

She waved a dismissive hand. 'You call that rough?'

'I wanted to make sure you were all right after the break-in.'

'I'm fine. Thanks.'

'You okay with everything we discussed?'

She should be grateful, considering the other cops she'd dealt with, but really? 'I have more questions, obviously. Hence your drink. Don't gulp it down, I've got a few.'

He smiled a little. 'I wouldn't normally encourage someone who's been through what you just have to focus on the details, but when I saw your files today, I realised you were going to anyway. I wanted to make sure it hadn't upset you.'

She pushed irritation away, smiled as she held her arms wide. 'Do I look upset?'

'No, you look great.'

Okay, she hadn't expected that.

'You didn't seem upset at uni, either. Not in public.'

Or that. Anger put spice in her tone. 'That's right. I was your stakeout.'

'Yes.'

'So you figure you know something about who I am fifteen years later?'

'I know that fifteen years ago, when you weren't being the cool party girl, you were grieving alone.'

'And what, you think I'm being all chatty with you, then taking myself off to cry?'

'Are you?'

She swung her face to the window, tears threatening to return. 'It's none of your damn business.'

He didn't speak for a moment, which she was more than happy about. She blinked hard, sipped at her drink. She'd come here for answers, not psychoanalysis. Was she going to have to do the tell-me-what's-going-on dance all over again?

'Jax?'

She turned, steeled herself for whatever misplaced, psychologist-cop piece of advice he was about to give her. But he didn't offer any, just settled his gaze on hers. There didn't seem to be a message in it, only a tight focus.

'I still have questions,' she said.

'The girl I told you about,' he said. 'Bethany, the one whose mother was assaulted. She thought that knowing everything would make it better, that somehow seeing it for what it was would ease what she was feeling.' He reached across the table, turned her palm up and, with an index finger, drew a line across her wrist. 'She has scars here from trying to understand why a person would do that to someone she loved.'

Jax tried to tug her hand away, horrified at what a young girl had done, at the feel of it on her skin. But he kept hold of her fingers, her wrist exposed, his eyes on hers, the message in them now unmistakable. This wasn't about Jax, it was about him. He wasn't doubting she could handle the information - he was making sure she could.

Was that what he'd been worried about all along? Why he'd told her to keep away from Kate, to not get involved?

'Fifteen years ago I was learning to live again,' she said. 'I'm not that person now. I *have* lived. I've been happy. I have a daughter.'

He released her hand. 'I don't want to be sorry we talked.'

Did he feel responsible for what Bethany had done? Did they discuss her case before she'd hurt herself? Jax had thought of him as a cop - law enforcer, investigator, gun-toting action guy. Not someone who could be hurt by his own investigations, who felt responsible for someone else's victim. Jax wanted answers - she didn't want Aiden waking in the night, wondering if she'd found a knife or pills or a cliff to jump from.

Searching for a way to tell him he wasn't responsible for her, she realised it wasn't words he needed. So she lifted her chin, kept still under his scrutiny and tried to fill her eyes with determination, hoping he didn't see the fear and anxiety her questions were keeping at bay.

Finally, he raised his glass to his lips and took a long draught of beer. 'Shall we make a start, then?'

For half a second, Jax wondered if there was anything else he'd seen in her eyes, decided there were other things she wanted to know first. She fired questions as they came to mind, not bothering to put them into any kind of order. Aiden answered with the facts.

CCTV had placed Brendan's car at various points around Sydney in the time he was unaccounted for. Most pictures didn't confirm he was the driver, although cameras on the Harbour Bridge showed him behind the wheel on four crossings - once on Saturday evening heading south towards the city, and three times on Sunday: going north around 2 am, presumably on a return trip, then south early Sunday afternoon and back again two hours later. Which meant his vehicle was set alight sometime after that.

'Any indication yet of whether there was a phone in his car?' Jax asked.

'It'll be a couple of days, at least, before I hear back on that.'

'Can you tell from the CCTV footage if he was being followed?'

'There's nothing obvious.'

'Are you looking?'

'It's a coroner's investigation, Jax. I need to work out the chain of events that led to Brendan Walsh's death. He wasn't speeding or driving erratically and there's no indication from the CCTV vision that what he was doing in his car on Sunday led to him getting in yours on Monday.'

'Except he thought he was being followed. He talked about trying to hold something off for two days.'

Aiden drained his beer. 'At this point, the information provided by his doctor explains that better than the footage.'

She rolled her lips together, pointed at his empty glass. 'Another?'

'You said two.'

She stood at the bar again, glad to have a moment to think without Aiden's eyes on her. Food was being served at the other end of the counter. Pub grub that smelt great and reminded her of how little she'd eaten today. She bought beer and a mineral water, ordered a serve of potato wedges and thought about Hugh Talbotson while she waited.

He'd wanted to know everything, had offered up plenty about Brendan in return - more tit-for-tat than anything Aiden had given. The senior sergeant was sticking to his policy and answering only what was asked. It was like trying to prise open a vault with her fingernails and the challenge was ... making her brain buzz with energy.

'I was hungry,' she said when she got back to the table, off-loading the drinks and food. 'I thought we could share.'

'We could have had dinner.'

'I didn't think you could handle that many questions.'

'Well, yes, we would've had to find something else to talk about.'

She chewed on a potato wedge and thought about dinner and conversation. 'You do that kind of thing sometimes? Eat and talk?'

'Sometimes. How about you?'

'Not in a long time. I might have forgotten how.'

'It's easy. You go somewhere, eat some food, talk a bit, pay.'

'You think that's how it works?'

He huffed a laugh. Lifted his full glass between them. 'You've got this much time for more questions.'

It was a smooth change of subject, back to where she felt comfortable. 'I talked to Brendan's friend Hugh Talbotson today,' she started.

Aiden frowned. 'You know him?'

'I met him at Kate Walsh's house this morning, asked if he wouldn't mind talking to me about Brendan.'

'You didn't think I was going to answer your questions?'

'I had different ones for him.'

'What did you want to know?'

'How Brendan was when he was in Sydney, what happened in Afghanistan.'

A pause. 'Go on.'

'Hugh said Brendan didn't always make good choices about who he got friendly with. Said he'd been spending time with some guys in a gym and suggested they weren't a good choice.'

Aiden didn't respond.

Back to prising open the vault. 'Is it possible Brendan was involved in something with them?' she asked.

'Like what?'

Was Aiden checking what she knew before disclosing information. 'I don't know. Have you spoken to Hugh?'

'He's one of a number of Walsh's associates that are scheduled for interview.'

Was that yes or no? 'Are some of the associates inappropriate choices for Brendan to be spending time with?'

'I'm not in a position to make a judgement about people Brendan Walsh should have spent time with.'

A slow smile curled her lips. 'Nice answers, Detective Senior Sergeant. You must do well in court.'

He cocked an eyebrow, took a sip of beer.

'Okay, how about this? Should I be worried about his poor choices chasing me and breaking into my house?'

'Jax, I don't know what choices Talbotson was referring to. As far as I've confirmed, Walsh was going to work, spending time at a gym, making contact with a handful of former military colleagues, seeing his psychologist and not much else. And there's no evidence he was being followed.'

She frowned. 'Hugh suggested Brendan was involved in more than that.'

'Okay.'

It wasn't a request for details. What wasn't she asking? 'He suggested Brendan had been ... socialising regularly.'

'Okay.'

Man, she was over his evasions. 'Have you got a problem with Hugh's information?'

There was the briefest hesitation before he answered. 'No. I have a problem with you talking to him.'

'You agreed to answer some questions. That doesn't mean you get to be my sole source of information.'

'This is a police investigation.'

'I'm not tampering with evidence.'

'A reporter on the prowl makes people nervous.'

'I'm not a reporter and I'm not prowling.'

'You're visiting Walsh's wife, talking to his mate and asking people to dig through newspaper archives for you. If you're right and someone thinks you had a relationship with Walsh and the relationship was because you're a reporter, your behaviour could make people nervous.'

It was a twist on her own theory. She'd thought the chase and the break-in were an attempt to find out what she knew, not as a result of what she'd done since the carjacking. She took a second to consider Aiden's version. Who would know she'd asked Russell to pull an old story? Had he told someone at the office she'd asked him to dig out the old story? 'Someone would have to be watching me to know I'd visited Kate Walsh. Or watching Kate.'

'Yes.'

She straightened, eyes flicking to the group of drinkers at the next table. 'You think that's a possibility?'

'I haven't ruled anything out.'

Apprehension snagged across her shoulders, made her scan the deck.

'No-one's watching you here,' Aiden said, 'other than me.'

'How do you know?'

'I've checked. Look, Jax, it's possible there are less complicated reasons for the break-in and the chase. You need to keep that in mind. But it's also possible Brendan Walsh dragged you into something. You don't have to investigate it yourself, though. I don't settle for throwaways. I'm on it. I want you to believe that.'

'Except you want to know what happened. I want to know why.'

'Sometimes the "what" explains the rest. Give it a while, Jax.'

'A couple of days?'

'Let me do my job then decide if you need more answers.' He raised his glass, downed the dregs of his beer. 'Okay, we're done. I survived, where do I get the T-shirt?'

She smiled a little.

He stood. 'Come on, I'll walk you to your car.'

38

It felt like deja vu outside: just past dusk, hot and humid, Jax's car on the same street and her mood jittery and wary. A lot had happened since the last time they'd walked this path - not much had changed.

'How are your feet?' he asked.

'Not too bad.' If she walked carefully. Right now, she was ready for a distraction. 'At uni, did you ever try to talk to me?'

'No, I had a girlfriend.'

'You weren't allowed to talk to other girls?'

'She thought I had a crush on you.'

'Well, you were stalking me.'

'And I had a crush on you.'

She turned to look at him.

'You were cool and secretive and sad. An irresistible combination for a serious Psych student.'

'Oh, so not because I was hot.'

'Okay, that too.'

'Yeah, right.' Hot was not a description she'd ever applied to herself - and back then? She still remembered what it was like to be that girl. Reckless, spontaneous, a little wild. Cool only in the sense that she'd kept her distance, wanting to find herself before she let anyone close. But she'd joined in, had a ball, laughed a lot. And yes, she'd kept her sadness in a box, only lifting the lid and allowing it to breathe when she thought she was alone. 'I'm not her anymore.'

'No-one's the same after fifteen years.'

'So you don't stalk sad girls anymore?'

'Not for a while.'

'You ever been married?'

He laughed quietly. 'More questions?'

'You know more about me than you should. The information ledger needs balancing up.'

'Fair enough. Married once. No kids. Divorced.'

'When?'

'It lasted three and a bit years. The divorce went through six months ago.'

'Is that why you moved up here?'

'No, we were separated for two years before it was signed off.'

Married for only eighteen months. She wanted to ask - for no other reason than she was nosy. She didn't, though, just looked at him, wondered if he'd take the prompt.

'I didn't cheat, if that's what you're assuming. Neither did she, at least not that I know of. She told me she would've had more attention if she'd been laid out on a morgue slab.'

'Ouch.'

'Yeah. Probably not far from the truth. It's hard to go home for romantic dinners when you've spent the day picking up bloodied bodies and telling families you'll find the arsehole who did it. It wouldn't have been easy to live with.'

She had some idea. Nick had been driven, although not by bloodied bodies.

'Sorry,' he said, 'I could've phrased that a little less gruesomely.'

'No, your phrasing was excellent. Gruesome yet perfectly clear.'

He chuckled as they stopped at her car. 'You got it back okay?'

'Yes, this afternoon.' She found her keys, leaned against the door. 'Did you get fingerprints off it?'

'Some. I'm still waiting for the results.'

They were alone in the quiet, narrow street, a few blocks from the beach, in a patch of post-war Newcastle suburbia that was holding out against the steady tide of new and spectacular contemporary homes. Small single-fronted cottages were just metres from the footpath, separated by low brick walls and tiny gardens that were spilling the scent of jasmine and passionfruit. Grey flickering from a TV danced silently in the front window of the closest house. Beside the car, Aiden was just beyond the bright glow of a streetlight, his face in soft shadow.

'Why did you come to Newcastle?' Jax asked.

'It was a promotion. I got my senior sergeant's stripes.'

'Bit different to Serious Crime in Sydney.'

A tilt of his head. 'Yeah.'

'Not so many bloodied bodies?'

He turned his face away. 'Or crying loved ones.'

It wasn't a jaded cop phrase. It sounded weary, burned, a burden. He'd lost a marriage because of victims and their loved ones. He'd seen people on very bad days. More than one bad day for the girl who'd cut her wrists. He'd been there on Jax's bad day, too, but she didn't want to be his burden. Didn't want him thinking of her like that.

She found something light in her voice. 'Just women pointing guns at you.'

A smile tipped one side of his mouth as he looked back at her. 'Only one so far.'

'You expecting more?'

'Are there any more like you?'

'I'm not sure how to take that.'

He didn't explain, just watched her with his unwavering gaze, pale irises filled with amusement and exasperation. Empathy and intelligence and . . .

A pulse tapped in her throat. Something inside her let go. She took a step towards him. Within arm's reach. He didn't move. She could see he wasn't going to. His eyes were on her mouth now, but he was level-headed, well meaning, insightful - and he was waiting for her to decide.

She should think about it in a clearer moment, she told herself. When the air wasn't perfumed and the humidity didn't make her skin feel naked. But he'd reminded her of the girl she was at uni, made her yearn for some of that reckless freedom.

She took another step. Close enough to feel the heat coming off his body, to smell the hint of aftershave on his throat. She curled fingers around his tie, pulled his face down to meet her. Felt the start of a smile on her lips as they found his.

She'd expected something like it used to be. Heady but detached. She was an idiot. It wasn't even close. His mouth was warm and tender and the sensation was like a gust of hot air on a freezing day - the promise of heat and relief, the thawing of everything that was frozen inside her. She broke away, stunned, heart thudding, a forgotten awareness rousing deep within her.

Aiden watched for a moment as though he could see it all, then cupped her face with his hands and kissed her again. Not a cautious step but a bold pace forward. His lips moved across hers as if they'd been set free. Exploring, confident, hungry. His thumbs traced the line of her jaw, the nape of her neck, before his arms closed around her. The lean, fit hardness of him pressed against her breasts, her stomach, her thighs. She opened her mouth to him, felt the pressure of his tongue, and awareness flared into need, a desire that lit a fire in the pit of her belly.

His lips left hers, worked their way to her throat, drawing a moan as she released a long, deep breath that seemed to have been held in her lungs for ... for ...

She opened her eyes, saw the street in lamp light, the flickering grey of the TV, and her hands tightened into fists. 'Please, stop.'

He lifted his head, eyes moving fast over her face.

'I'm sorry.' She took a step away, her skin suddenly cold. 'I shouldn't have done that.'

'Started or stopped?'

'Started. I'm sorry, I didn't ... it wasn't ... what I expected.'

His intake of breath was sharp. 'What did you expect?'

'I don't know. I didn't expect ...' What? To want him? To want anyone but Nick? 'To enjoy it.'

He licked his lips, slowly. 'You didn't want to enjoy it or you thought it'd be bad?'

'No. Neither.' Bloody hell, she was making it worse. She swung away from him, braced her hands on the roof of the car, needing something solid to hold on to - and for the desire steaming inside her to settle the hell down. 'I didn't think. I'm not ... I haven't done this,' she waved a hand between them, 'in a long, long time.' A million years since she'd kissed anyone but Nick. Since the day she'd met him, she'd never wanted to kiss anyone else. Until now.

Aiden moved alongside her, pressing his back to the chassis, ducking his face so she could see him. 'Jax.' There was comprehension in it - and something that said it was okay, he had patience, they could take it slowly.

She let her mind go there. His hands on her, his mouth, his body. Loosening the hold on herself, opening up, breathing hard and heavy until the flame he'd lit had been consumed. She wanted that with a need she hadn't known was there. Wanted to press her lips to his and start over. But there was more in his face, etched into the pale, undaunted gaze of his eyes. It wasn't just sex he was offering to take slowly. It was intimacy, a connection. A beginning, not a single experience. She didn't want a one-night stand and a quick, sweaty release - she clearly wasn't *that* girl anymore. But the alternative scared the hell out of her.

'I'm not ready.' She didn't want to be, not yet. 'I'm sorry.'

For a second, maybe two, he stayed where he was. Then he nodded, eased off the car, smoothed a hand down his tie - and the Aiden who'd kissed her, the one who'd talked about crying loved ones, disappeared behind a shutter, replaced by Detective Senior Sergeant Hawke. Sensible, professional, finished for the night.

'Okay.' He pushed hands into his trouser pockets, took a step back.

'Aiden

'It's okay, Jax.' No anger, no resignation. Nothing but a flat full stop.

She unlocked the car, pulled the door. 'Thanks for answering my questions.'

A cursory upward lift of his chin. ''Night.'

Fuck. When she was in, he pushed her door closed, moved back from the kerb, watched as she started up, flicked on lights, steered into the street. At the corner, she checked his reflection in the rear-view. He was in the same spot but not watching wistfully. Not watching at all. He had his phone out, face lit by the screen as he tapped on its surface.

39

Her mobile rang three minutes later as she wound her way up the hill in the dark. If it was Aiden, it wasn't the first call he was making after kissing her - if that's what he'd been doing. She hit the answer button on the steering wheel, spoke cautiously anyway. 'Hello?'

'Hey, Jax. I heard about the break-in.' The sound of honey and vice.

'Oh hell, Deanne. I've just made a bloody fool of myself.'

'I'm sure you haven't. What happened?' The beauty of friends who could start a conversation in the middle.

'I just kissed someone.'

'*You* kissed *him*? Was it a him?'

'It was the detective investigating the carjacking!'

A pause. 'The one on the TV pointing a gun at you?'

'Yeah. Him.'

'Oh. Well. He seems ... nice.' Deanne's phone-sex chuckle rumbled through the car.

Jax rolled her eyes and, despite the mortification, a laugh gathered in her throat. *Oh, what the hell.* She let it out, sharing a stupid girlie cackle, feeling not so ridiculous for a couple of seconds.

'Are you okay?' Deanne finally asked, perhaps hearing some desperate in Jax's cackling.

'No, I don't think I am. I messed it all up.'

'The kiss can't have been that bad. I mean, it's not like you don't know how.'

Jax wanted to close her eyes and bang her head on the steering wheel but she just clenched her teeth, blinking at the tears that were heating behind her eyes. 'God, the kiss. It wasn't rusty. It was ...' She rolled her lips together, still feeling Aiden on them. And the guilt. 'I didn't even think of Nick.'

'Oh, Jax.'

'I told Aiden I wasn't ready. And he was done, like *that*.' She snapped her fingers. 'He stepped away, said goodnight and pulled out his phone. And now I've screwed up everything.'

'Jax, come on. It was your first kiss since Nick. It was always going to be difficult.'

'It wasn't difficult. It was intense, spectacular. And it freaked me out.'

'Oh. Well ...'

'But he was finally including me. He came to the house after the break-in, saw the files scattered all over the bedroom. I convinced him to look at what I'd pulled together about Brendan. He thought I was a complete bloody amateur but he was answering my questions. We met for a drink to talk about it. And then I kissed him and now he's taken a giant step back and I'll get *nothing*. It'll be Anita Lyneham all over again and I did it to myself. *I* screwed it up.'

'Jax, slow down. Where are you?'

The sudden concern in Deanne's voice made Jax search the view in her mirror. She was at the top of the hill, turning off the main road towards Tilda's, the city lights behind and a four-wheel drive that kept going. 'I'm in the car. Almost home.'

'Can you pull over?'

She flicked eyes at the mirror again. 'What for? Where are you?'

'At home. You sound upset.'

Like she couldn't drive responsibly? She felt wired and ticked off, and she'd wanted an opinion on the mess she'd made, not driving instructions. But she slowed anyway, concentrating on negotiating the darker neighbourhood streets. 'I'm okay. I don't want to stop, not after those guys chased me last night.'

'Why don't I come up tomorrow?'

'Here? No. You do voice-overs on Fridays.'

'You sound like you could do with some company.' She must sound like she was out of her mind if Deanne was going to cancel work for her. 'No, really, I'm okay. I was exaggerating before. Just feeling like an idiot.'

'I could help with the unpacking, we could take Zoe to the beach, check out the Newcastle cafe culture. I've heard it's good up there.'

And Jax heard the subtext: get her mind off Brendan Walsh and Nick's files and the men who'd chased her. She steered into Tilda's street, remembering other times Deanne had kept her company. The empathetic head nods, the show of interest, followed by suggestions to let the police handle it, to try to get back to normality, to learn to live again. Jax didn't want to hear it. She wanted answers.

'No, look, you guys are coming up next week. And didn't you have something you were doing this weekend? That posh political dinner with David Escott and his A-lister mates? You were booked in to have your hair done on Saturday morning. Don't come up. I'm fine. Both of us. All of us.'

Deanne's silence sounded like are-you-sure?

'Anyway,' Jax said, 'why did you call?'

'Oh, right. Russell said he sent you an email.'

'He didn't want to tell me himself?'

'He thought you could do with a phone call.'

'I'm fine.' Jax bumped onto the driveway, hit the button for the automatic door. 'I'll talk to you soon. Got to go.'

JAX SET the motion sensor on the house alarm as she walked through the entry level. Zoe and Tilda were playing cards around the coffee table, some game that involved code words and catching each other out.

'How was the date?' Tilda asked as Jax perched on the arm of the lounge with leftover quiche.

'Mummy, did you go on a date?' Zoe's nose was a little pink from being out in the sun and a new dusting of freckles looked like someone had sprinkled cinnamon over her cheeks.

'No, baby, it wasn't a date. Aunty Tilda is teasing me. And it was ... fine.'

Tilda looked at her over the top of her half-moon reading glasses. 'Fine?'

'We had a couple of drinks and a chat. *Fine.*' Jax wasn't going to tell the rest of it with Zoe there. Perhaps she wouldn't tell Tilda at all - she didn't need any more of her aunt's theories.

Tilda added a card to her hand. 'Well, I hope Brendan Walsh wasn't the only topic of conversation.'

'Not more than eighty-five per cent.'

Tilda cast her a *tut-tut* glance and dropped a Jack of Hearts on the table.

Jax watched the game through two more hands, exhaustion coming on fast after the food, flattening her mood, making her more despondent than agitated, glum rather than angry. When Zoe started yawning, Jax announced bedtime. She listened to her daughter chatter through teeth cleaning, face washing, pyjama dressing and finally book selection. Jax rejected the first two on the grounds they were too long and read a short one they both knew by heart. Then she kissed Zoe goodnight, went to the sitting room, plugged in her laptop - the mini one that had escaped the break-in - and opened her email account.

Requests for interviews were still coming in. She ignored them, found Russell's name in the inbox and clicked. There were two attachments to a brief note: *Something came up in the conference this afternoon. Attached pic was taken last Saturday night by social pages. Looks like your guy, thought you could confirm or deny. Will be here till late if you get this today. R*

Jax clicked on the first attachment, waited for the high-resolution photo to load and wondered who was 'her guy': Brendan, Aiden ... Nick?

Then she saw the image and recognition made her gasp. Nina Torrence, high-profile solicitor and Jax's former courtroom source. She was in a group of guests arranged for the photo, everyone else diminished by Nina's trademark radiant confidence. And the next day, she'd been found stabbed and thrown from a cliff. Why the hell had Russell sent that? Jax didn't need another reminder of the shitty world she was inhabiting.

She tried the second attachment. It was an article on PTSD. An in-depth piece, something for her non-existent research. She didn't bother to save it.

Clicking back, she read Russell's note again. The 'conference' he mentioned was a twice-daily meeting of desk editors. Nina's murder was almost a week old but it would still be an item for discussion. They were probably planning a feature - for years, Nina had appeared in both social pages and news stories, ones involving high-profile crimes and court hearings. But Russell had written 'your guy'. Had he sent the wrong picture? Or ... Jax clicked on the photo again.

Glowing in a long slip of a gown, Nina was tanned and toned, hair blonde and glossy, smiling like a cat who'd feasted on the cream. Back when Jax knew her, Nina's breasts weren't so large or her lips so full - she'd obviously bought some enhancement with her status salary.

Jax eyed the others in the shot: an older woman with a large, dark rock at her throat, two younger ones, early twenties, looking impossibly thin and expensively dressed. *Why, Russell? Where is the 'guy'?*

Sitting back, taking a wider look at the group arrangement, Jax saw part of a statue on the left, possibly an ice sculpture. On the other side and facing away, a slightly out-of-focus couple smiled for another snapper. A man and a woman. Jax focused on the man: shorter than his companion, bald, filling his suit like a potato with legs. Not anyone Jax knew. A few heads could be seen in the spaces behind the central figures. Three of them. Maybe guests waiting their turn for a chance in the social pages, maybe just drinking and chatting.

Jax slid the image around, zoomed in on a man and woman standing close enough to kiss. No-one she recognised. Slid and zoomed some more, squinted. Saw why Russell had sent it and sucked in a sharp, fast breath.

40

Between Nina and one of the younger women, side-on to the camera, was a man in a jacket, tie and white shirt. Dark-haired, unsmiling. The image was out of focus and pixelated, not much more than an outline and contours, but the high cheekbones were there, and the shape of his mouth. It was the chin that sold her, though. Held slightly high, a little forward. In her mind, Jax saw it swinging front to back, back to front.

It was Brendan Walsh.

He'd been a guest at the party?

Sydney had a large and active party scene and the newspaper's social pages followed the A-listers. According to Hugh, Brendan had been making friends at a gym and paying for sex - not the usual entree to glamorous events. But he was also a bodyguard. Jax ran her eyes over the serious expression on his face. He was standing behind Nina - had she bought protection, too?

Jax understood how it might have come up in the news conference. A photographer or desk editor sorting through pictures of Nina, taking a closer look at the most recent ones. Maybe the same person - someone who looked at photos for a job, who had an eye for faces and detail - had also sorted through the ones of Brendan and made the connection. And the photo had gone to the meeting and they'd discussed the implications, deciding the first thing was to confirm the identity.

What were the implications? That Brendan was a bodyguard for Nina on the weekend she was murdered. Jax's gaze slid from the screen, unfocused and drifting as words she'd written in her notebook found new places in her mind.

Brendan was unaccounted for after Saturday afternoon, except for CCTV footage of him driving back and forth over the Harbour Bridge. His car was set alight sometime after that. He didn't go nuts in Jax's car - he was already off the rails when he opened the door with a gun in his hand. It hadn't started there, it had started sometime between Saturday evening after he argued with Kate and Monday afternoon.

Saturday to Monday.

Nina Torrence's body was found on Sunday, after the night Brendan was snapped in a photo with her.

I've been holding it off for two days.

Jax closed her eyes and saw Brendan again. Yelling, rambling, his paranoid, panicked phrases coming back-to-back as though they'd been cut out of the whole and edited together: holding it off, nano spiders, Scotty, Kate, trained people who won't stop. The phone, the radio, knives and missiles, cops.

Jax shook her head, stood up, walked to the window and stared into the courtyard. The glow from Tilda's rooms above spilled into the darkness, casting pale light around the edges of the garden. The view of the ocean beyond was prettier but Jax wasn't looking.

She was trying to pull everything apart and put it back together in a different context.

Brendan had PTSD but he was getting better. He'd gone off his medication, he was working - then something unravelled him.

Brendan's version was that people were after him. He knew he was going to die and he wanted to get to his family first. To protect them. He had a gun. He'd tried to hold something off for two days. He couldn't get rid of what was in his head. He'd shouted: *You don't want to know anything I know.* When they'd played Zoe's what-if game, he'd said, *Gun or knife?* Then he'd cried like a child, repeating words like a mantra: *I didn't know. I didn't know. I swear I didn't.*

Jax rested her forehead on the cool glass. She'd thought it was about Afghanistan, something he'd seen or done that came back to haunt him. She'd wanted Brendan to be a good man. He'd loved his wife and child and she wanted that to be enough. The proof of his goodness.

She watched the reflection of her eyes and asked herself what she'd really wanted from all the questions she was asking now. Was it about Brendan or Nick? Had she wanted to believe in Nick, and Brendan was her proof? That no matter what had taken Nick to that road, he would've been thinking of her and Zoe in his final moments. That he would have tried to protect them despite the outcome. Like Brendan.

Or was it about her? Her need to be clever and whole again, not the wife obsessed with an unsolvable case, or the idiot taken in by someone else's paranoia.

Pushing away from the window, she thought about Hugh Talbotson's story. The one in which Brendan wasn't so good. Where he made bad choices and mixed with the wrong people and slept around like he didn't give a shit about his wife and child. Maybe his love was just deathbed regret.

And maybe Brendan Walsh *was* a bad guy. A very bad guy. Maybe he spent two days evading people who were after him, got a gun, set his car alight to destroy all the evidence and made it as far as the motorway on-ramp.

Maybe he did something that made people want to hunt him down.

Maybe he murdered Nina Torrence.

JAX PACED THE ROOM, edgy, restless. It was more conjecture. Trying to make the pieces fit a picture that possibly didn't exist. That she'd invented because she was a Miss Marple wannabe heading for a breakdown.

Tiptoeing fast across the tiles, she went back to her laptop and started a search for Nina Torrence. Jax had watched the TV news reports of the murder on Sunday night, sitting alone in her old house, drinking red wine and feeling miserable after leaving Zoe with Tilda. She'd been aware of radio reports the next day, too busy packing and cleaning and locking memories in her heart to listen to the detail. Then she was carjacked - and she'd read about herself without the stomach or the concentration to think about anything else that might have made head-lines. Now, as she scanned the stories on the internet, she saw she'd missed a lot.

Nina Torrence had topped the TV news on Sunday night and the print headlines on Monday, slipped on Tuesday in the wake of the carjacking, then shared the lead for the rest of the week with other stories, including the Brendan Walsh/Miranda Jack drama. The media coverage began late morning on Sunday, as a series of breaking news items and continued on the following days with angles on the police investigation, calls for information, and background details on the life of a woman who'd mixed in both social and criminal circles - a tale just waiting for a dirty, sexy TV series.

Jax tried to skim the information, having no desire to think about what had been done to someone she'd known, especially after her own brush with violence. But she was drawn in, horrified and fascinated, perhaps more so because of Nina's connection to Brendan. Whether or not he'd killed her, within two days of each other Jax and Nina had both been in his company - and the company of serious, headline-making aggression.

Nina's body was found around sunrise on Sunday morning by a fisherman clambering around the base of a cliff on Sydney's South Head. Media was there by the time a recovery operation winched her up to the park above, photos showing a covered body on a swinging stretcher. Within hours, there were unconfirmed reports she'd been stabbed. That night, police detailed a single stab wound that punctured the diaphragm on the way to her heart, announcing they were now conducting a homicide investigation.

Later stories discussed the unfolding case, talking about defensive wounds to Nina's hands, arms, face and neck - scratches and bruising that suggested she'd put up a fight. Witnesses at the party on Saturday night said she'd arrived with a driver, told friends she was meeting someone later and that she liked to make an entrance but preferred to leave unseen - to 'let people think she was still holding court long after she'd gone'. It might've been good for her reputation, but police were unable to establish exactly when and how she'd left the party. Conflicting statements ranged from Nina being seen walking to a car by herself, getting into a vehicle with one man, with two men and a woman, and driving herself away, alone at the wheel.

There was also speculation about what had actually happened at the top of the cliff. Forensics determined the murder took place in an area that was more suburban bushland than park - no grass, no seating, just a dense patch of native growth: cliff-top path on one side, a road on the other, and a hundred metres from a parking zone at a nearby viewing platform. Questions centred on whether Nina went there herself or was taken there. Was it a random attack as she contemplated the view or was she waiting for the mystery 'someone'? Was the original plan to throw her to her death and make it look like suicide? Had her struggle forced the killer to end it quicker - and perhaps quieter? Had he - 'he' for the strength required to lift her over the chest-high railing - expected the tide to wash Nina and her tell-tale stab wound away?

Still more stories suggested a link to the upcoming trial of a notorious gang member, others that the fatal injury was the kind inflicted by someone who knew how to kill with a knife, someone who might be employed by the sort of people Nina had defended - and socialised with, if the gossip was right. Jax had heard more crudely phrased rumours from journalists over the years, using nouns like 'affair' and 'mistress' and 'fuck money'. Not the kind of stuff anyone wanted in their obituary.

It took time to find the information Jax was after, but she eventually tracked it down among the thousands of words already written on Nina. Police were quoted as saying her death occurred in the early hours of Sunday, sometime in a five- to six-hour period from when she was thought to have left the party around eleven-thirty and when she was found shortly after 5 am.

Jax pushed away from the keyboard, scrubbed at her eyes, got up and walked. At the sink, she picked up a sponge and started wiping benches. Hard, forceful strokes. Brendan had been at the party and the chances were slim he was there as an off-duty bodyguard who happened to get caught in a photo with Nina. He'd crossed the Harbour Bridge heading north at 2 am on Sunday morning - the direction he'd drive if he was going from South Head to his flat in Hornsby. He'd crossed the Bridge twice later in the day, south then north again. Then, almost twenty-four hours later, he'd got in Jax's car wearing crumpled clothes, smelling of old sweat, panicked and paranoid, and using a gun to get the hell out of Sydney.

She threw the sponge at the sink, angry, appalled, nauseated. Why would he do it? There were any number of reasons but she didn't want to think about them. She'd wanted Brendan to be the one who was wronged because ... because of Kate and Scotty, because there was something stuck in his head, because Nick was ...

She caught sight of the laptop on the dining table, checked her watch. Ten-thirty. Russell was at the office until late. She grabbed her phone, hit speed dial.

'Did you get my email?' He sounded stressed.

'Yeah, I've seen the photo.'

'What do you think? Is it him?'

She opened her mouth, ready to blurt out everything that was careering around in her mind, and hesitated. In front of her were the sofas, Zoe's toy box, the packing cartons, tidier than they were this after-noon - but reminding her someone had been there, someone who possibly was worried about a reporter writing a story.

'It's *like* him, yeah, but it's not a clear image by any means. I wouldn't want to call it. Sorry. I wondered about a bodyguard, though. The guy looks kind of serious. Was Nina Torrence a client of the company Brendan worked for?'

'No.'

'They confirmed that?'

'They're not saying who their clients are. No surprises there. But our guy got talking to one of their guys. He wouldn't give names but said Nina Torrence was definitely not on their books.'

'Is anyone saying she needed a bodyguard?'

'It's been mentioned she used one occasionally. There's a suggestion it was PR, to make her look dirty or clean, depending on the angle.'

'Dirty because there are criminals who are pissed off with her?'

'Or clean because there are criminals who are pissed off with her.'

And it was possible she'd needed to be protected from her body-guard. 'Have the police seen the photo?'

'They've got it - I don't know whether they've seen it. They asked for everything we shot at the party the day. We did the usual, "If the murderer is in one of ours, we want the exclusive," and handed over all seventy-eight shots. But you've seen the photo, it's easy to miss the guy in the back. It only came to our attention when the photographer was going over the stuff from early in the night. We've been using the later ones for our "last shots of Nina Torrence".'

Easy to miss if they weren't looking for Brendan Walsh. Possibly easy to miss unless you'd been in a car watching him swing his head from front to back. 'Will you point him out to the police?'

'A decision hasn't been made on that yet. There's no reason to if it's not Walsh.'

'Yeah, okay.' Jax rubbed the back of her neck. Should she confirm it? To the media? It was Russell, but it was also out of her hands once he knew and she wouldn't be able to stop it becoming a story. It wouldn't have her by-line but her name would be on it by inference: Nina Torrence, Brendan Walsh and Miranda Jack, linked by death and circumstance.

'You sound exhausted,' Russell said.

'I am.'

'It's not too late for Deanne to cancel work and head up. She could take Zoe for a while. And you could take advantage of my wife's predilection for drinkies and have a few later. Relax, forget all this.'

'Not you too?'

'Yeah, me too.'

'Exhausted is no state to be having guests.'

'Okay. You gotta give me points for trying, though.'

She smiled a little. 'You get one.' He hadn't mentioned the kiss. She hoped that meant Deanne hadn't told him. She could do without discussing it with Nick's best friend, regardless of where he stood on the issue.

Hanging up, she took a restless, agitated tour of the room, a thought repeating in her head: *Nina Torrence, Brendan Walsh and Miranda Jack, linked in death and circumstance.*

Jax was the only one of them still alive.

41

S he needed to sleep but she couldn't sit still, let alone lie down and drift off. Tilda must have gone to bed - the courtyard was black and the clusters of lights from ships off the coast floated in a mass of darkness. Jax checked the locks and the alarm, peered in at Zoe and took her mini laptop to bed. She'd told Russell she wasn't opening new files, but he didn't have to know. No-one did - unless she came up with more than conjecture.

She started with Brendan, collecting everything she had on him. Newspaper articles, the story from the airbase, the photo Russell had sent. Then she typed in the lists from her notebook, updating, adding, making notes in the margins.

Then she started a file covering her own account of the carjacking. It didn't take long to write: she just closed her eyes, saw it in her mind and hammered on the keyboard. No emotion or narration this time, just each chronological step of Brendan's unravelling, simplified to bullet points:

- Order to drive
- Lashing out at the radio
- Confused by the phone
- Surveillance, head back and forth

On and on until she got to:

• Runs into traffic

Starting more files, Jax included newspaper articles and web links for Nina Torrence, as well as information she'd gleaned from her conversations with Kate and Hugh. While she was at it, she Googled Hugh, finding little more than references to genealogy sites listing Hugh Talbot, son of various old-English ancestors.

It was 1.27 am when she shut down the last file. If nothing else, the process had taken the edge off her agitation. Stretching, yawning, she slid under the sheet, propped an elbow on the pillow and pulled the laptop closer for one last search.

Two weeks after Nick's death, when the channels of communication with the Homicide unit showed signs of trauma, Jax began documenting meetings, conversations and phone calls. She also searched the internet for references to Anita Lyneham, finding articles on investigations, court appearances, police media releases, and her Facebook page. At first, it was to understand who Jax was dealing with, an attempt to find some common ground. Eventually she used it as a weapon when she wanted the cop to appreciate Jax wasn't sitting on her hands waiting for a detective to tell her when to breathe.

For the same reasons, and a few others, Jax now typed: *Aiden Hawke.*

He wasn't the only Aiden Hawke - real or simulated - but the one she was interested in had no social media pages. Which meant nothing except that he hadn't been updating his status on his phone as she left him tonight.

There were plenty of photos and stories mentioning him and the dramatic, gun-wielding end to the carjacking. Jax skipped past them, looking for anything pre-Brendan Walsh.

Ten search pages in and she found Detective Aiden Hawke, of Serious Crime, Sydney, quoted in a four-month-old story about a series of stabbings. A year earlier, he was talking about an arrest in a long-running and particularly nasty arson case. Before that, a vicious assault on a train. He was also mentioned twice in stories around an investigation into the disappearance of a three-year-old girl that made headlines for its outpouring of neighbourhood emotion. And again two years later after the little girl's body was found in bushland and her stepfather charged.

Snippets of conversations with Aiden came back as Jax read. Crying loved ones and bloodied bodies; how unproductive cases were frustrating for everyone; Bethany, the young girl who'd tried to kill herself. Jax wondered whether the end of an investigation ever felt like a victory.

Thinking again about Bethany, Jax started a new search for a report on that attack. What she found was a story about an assault - not the one she'd been aiming for, but two names within a single paragraph jumped out at her. It was a court report: Detective Sergeant Aiden Hawke was a prosecution witness; the solicitor for the defendant was Nina Torrence.

Aiden knew her too?

Jax rolled onto her back, pressed the heels of her hands into her eye sockets, her head thumping. Was it weird that Aiden knew Nina?

Or was it understandable, predictable even? Aiden had arrested people for serious crimes, would have interviewed them in the presence of a solicitor, following them all the way to court. Nina was a criminal lawyer, and Jax knew from her days as a reporter that both sides of the courtroom could share a drink. Some ate together; sometimes they slept together. She'd known a cop whose public prosecutor wife had become a better-paid criminal defender.

It was 2.13. She should sleep, she told herself. She should. She tried one more search: *Aiden Hawke + Nina Torrence*. Three court cases. The last one concluded two weeks ago, something about a fraud and a restaurateur. Jax couldn't hold on to the details, couldn't get her fingers to hit the right keys, too exhausted to do anything but let it all float in her brain.

Nina Torrence, Brendan Walsh, Aiden Hawke and Miranda Jack - connections, crossed paths, violence. Jax had no idea what it meant. Maybe it didn't mean anything. But it was definitely weird.

SLEEP, when it came, felt like something she'd experienced once after a strong dose of hay fever medication mixed with a stiff drink. Heavy and black, restless and confused. She thought she was being chased, running for her life over broken glass, slowed by the weight of her own exhaustion. Then she was driving and shouting into the airstream that was pouring through the open window, bellowing until her throat was dry.

In the moment before she woke, Aiden held a gun on her while Brendan smashed a fist into the car radio, trying to stab the newsreader. When Jax opened her eyes, her mouth was parched, her face ached as though she'd been frowning for hours and a deep, hollow sense of dread filled her chest. Either the Brendan of her dreams had reinfected her with a new level of paranoia or her nightmares had woven themselves into her late-night research - but she now had more questions *about* Aiden than *for* him.

She sat up, woke her laptop, opened the file she'd started on Aiden and wrote some more. Not theories, not even conjecture. Just ideas that she'd taken at face value and that now, from a different angle - one that involved connections with Nina and Brendan - might mean something else.

Brendan had thought people were after him. It wasn't a vague concept. He thought they were going to find him on the motorway. Aiden *did*.

Aiden told Jax he'd started following her after she'd swerved into another lane. She'd assumed it was diligence and was grateful. But was he already searching the motorway?

She remembered her indecisive fear when she'd seen him that first time in the car park. And later, when his gun was pointed at her, and when she'd sat in the back of his car watching the massive police operation fall into place. *Overkill for bad driving.*

Since then, Aiden had taken every opportunity to dissuade her from asking questions. Had only begun answering after seeing the mountain of information she'd collected on Nick and it was clear she wasn't easily put off. Last night, he'd suggested it was to protect her from the horror of the details, his finger sliding across her wrist in a demonstration of where it could lead. She'd liked him better for it, thought it made him a better cop, perhaps a better person. But was it all an act? Like when he'd held a gun on her?

What else was an act? The unwavering gazes. The long silences. Had Aiden been trying to read her or just deciding how much she knew?

The stuff about watching her at uni - was that invented too? She took her hands from the keyboard, closed them into fists. No, that had to be for real. If he was involved - *if* - those details, her partying and sadness, weren't on any record. But he could have added some spin, right? Murder Week, the crush, the *irresistible combination*. If he thought it might make her trust him, convince her to let him do the investigating. Maybe he figured kissing her would seal it. She'd been embarrassed, upset - and he'd been on his phone before she was out of the street.

And then there were his accusations that she was researching a story and leaving details out of her statement. He'd said her behaviour could make people nervous. Was it Aiden who was nervous?

About what?

Aiden knew Nina. Nina knew bad people. Nina was dead. And ...?

Jax tried it from another angle. Brendan was with Nina just hours before she was murdered. Brendan thought someone was looking for him. Aiden found him on the motorway. And ...?

She shook her head. Brendan got in her car while she was waiting at traffic lights. She spent time alone with Brendan before he died. And ... Aiden was managing her. He'd thought Brendan got in her car by prior arrangement.

Was *he* worried about what was said - or did he know someone who was?

She leaned against the pillows, pushed hands through her hair. Was this nuts? Aiden had come to her rescue when she'd been chased under the house. His well-sprung readiness going into action. Or was it? It took only minutes for him to find her. Maybe he'd already been looking. Maybe someone had told him she'd run - Guy Number Two, the one who'd disappeared when the chasing started.

Across the hall, the toilet flushed. Three seconds later, a tap ran in the bathroom. Zoe was awake.

Jax closed her laptop, asked herself if she was a complete idiot. She'd trusted Aiden when she knew about cops. She'd thought he was different. And maybe he *was* - in a way that was a whole lot worse than shutting her out of an investigation.

42

'Morning, Mummy,' Zoe sang as she flung herself at the bed. Jax winced as the mattress bounced. Two days after running four hundred metres and second-day muscle soreness made her feel like an old toy that needed its joints oiled. 'Morning, baby.'

'Are we going to the beach today?'

If she could find an ounce of Zoe's morning energy. 'We'll see.' Jax bit back a groan as the grazes on her feet touched the floor. She held out a hand to her daughter. 'Do me a favour and pull me up.'

Zoe dragged on her arms as though her mother was a dead weight. Maybe she was. Maybe she'd researched and written through most of the night because she was paranoid. Because she was embarrassed she'd kissed a man. Because she was stuck in a hole and needed professional help to get out.

In the kitchen, she fixed two bowls of cereal then sat at the table in the courtyard with Zoe, in pyjamas and sunglasses, squinting into the morning glare like she was in the throes of a hangover.

'Fifteen boats,' Zoe said, pointing at the horizon.

'Ships.'

'Can you swim to them?'

'I don't think anyone would bother.'

'What if they did?'

Jax watched her daughter for a moment. Spoon in her hand, chewing as she bounced, freckles and sleep-messy hair and soft brown eyes sparkling with curiosity. Were the questions a habit she'd learned from Jax or was it in her DNA? Did they both have it fixed into their double helix? And were the questions Jax woke with going in the same pointless circles?

'They'd probably get eaten by a shark before they got there,' Jax told her.

'Do sharks have breakfast?'

The ringing of Jax's mobile drifted from the kitchen. 'Will Zoe stop asking questions long enough to eat her breakfast?' Jax stood slowly, her feet smarting. 'You finish your cereal while I answer the phone.'

The name on the screen made her stomach lurch: *Kate Walsh.*

Since talking to her, Jax had discovered ugly things about Kate's husband, thought it was possible he'd stabbed a woman and heaved her body over a cliff. Yesterday she'd wanted to tell Kate that Brendan loved her. Now she had other information she didn't want to be responsible for hiding or providing. Jax held the phone in her palm, tempted to let it ring out, worried her voice would reveal the disgust and suspicion that had burrowed inside her.

Only tempted, though. If Jax had new details, maybe Kate did too. 'Hello?'

'Miranda, it's Kate. Kate Walsh. I hope you don't mind me ringing early again.'

There was no urgency or tears in her voice this morning. But it was hesitant, strained.

'No. I was already up.'

'I was wondering if you'd have a coffee with me.'

Well, that was unexpected. When she last left the Walsh house, Kate looked as though she never wanted to see Miranda Jack again. Jax rubbed at the ache of tiredness in the centre of her forehead. Did she want to? She wasn't sure she had the energy to tiptoe around Kate's emotions. Did she want another chance to ask a few more questions? 'When would you like me to come around?'

'I don't. Can we meet somewhere?'

Wariness crept across Jax's mind. Nina, Brendan, Aiden - and Kate? 'You don't want me at your house?'

'Sorry, it's not that. I've got to get out and ... pick up a few things and

...' Her voice trailed off, the silence filled with the hiss of a long sigh. 'Actually, I just need to get out of the house, you know?'

Jax closed her eyes, reminded herself that Kate had just lost her husband - she hadn't chased Jax down a street or broken into Tilda's house. And that grief could be suffocating. 'Yes, I do know. Where would you like to go?'

'There's a little cafe on the beachfront at Merewether. The coffee's good and the view is - well, it's a lot better than my four walls.'

Jax had bought a bottle of water there two days ago before she was chased down the street. She was in no hurry to revisit that particular spot, but Kate could walk there from her house. Maybe she needed the exercise as well as new scenery. 'Sure. I know where it is. What time?'

'In an hour?'

'See you then.'

She held on to the phone after disconnecting, wondering if she was a cold-hearted bitch for wanting to ply Kate with more questions.

IT WASN'T a cafe in the normal sense of the word, just a kitchen tucked into the underside of an old surf club and a stainless steel counter that opened on to the path above the beach wall. The tables were all in the open, battered from sitting in the weather and scattered haphazardly like remnants from a garage sale. This was Newcastle, a city that loved its surfing lifestyle, and the ambience was appreciated. Half the customers were wet and sandy; there were walkers and cyclists, yoga students from a nearby studio, and collections of mums with kids enjoying the cool of the morning. Not trendy or visible enough for school kids to hang out, even in the holidays. No men in business shirts and ties.

The sky was a clear, high, pale blue - the forerunner to another scorcher but still kind enough this early that Jax didn't automatically search the shade beside the building for Kate.

She saw Scotty first. He was on his knees, pushing a dismembered toy truck across the bumpy sandstone top of the beach wall. Kate was sitting at a table behind him, its umbrella teased by a sweet offshore breeze. Her chair was angled towards the vastness of the Pacific Ocean but her face was turned away, her attention focused on something further along the path. It made Jax slow as she neared, pulling Zoe closer, checking over her shoulder to where she'd left her car.

How much did Kate know? Maybe Zoe should have stayed with Tilda.

Jax stopped beside Brendan's wife, a hint of reproach in her tone. 'Kate?'

As she swung around, a single fast-moving tear ran from under one lens of her sunglasses.

Kate wasn't watching for bad guys, she was out of the house and crying. Her swift, unselfconscious swipe at the droplet reminded Jax of herself, of when tears had been a daily event. Not an outpouring but simply toppling from her lashes in silent, unabashed sadness whenever and wherever the moment struck. They'd blurred her vision as she'd sat at the lights in the seconds before Brendan opened her car door.

Kate shuffled her chair back, stood, made a move towards Jax then stopped, as though she wasn't sure of the appropriate greeting. Jax wondered the same - handshake, hug? There was no protocol for widows with their connections. Kate eventually flapped a hand at the view. 'I needed this.'

'Better here than a supermarket.'

Kate's smile was tired and fragile but there was a hint of the metal that had got her this far today. She lowered her eyes to Zoe. 'Hey there. I told Scotty you might come. He was looking forward to seeing you again. I hope you like playing with trucks. He brought some extras for you.' Zoe shrugged, a six-year-old's *whatever*, and sauntered over to where he was playing.

'I'm glad you brought her,' Kate said. 'Most of Scott's friends are away for the school holidays.'

'Zoe doesn't know anyone else in Newcastle. They're doing each other a favour. Have you ordered?'

'Not yet. And I'll get this.'

'You don't need to ...'

Kate put a hand on Jax's arm, stopping her from pulling the wallet from her bag. 'Please, Miranda. You didn't have to come. What will the two of you have?'

Jax sensed it was more than generosity, intrigue and uneasiness prickling at her scalp, but she understood this protocol. Kate had her purse out already - it wasn't good form to make a fuss when someone else was resolved to pay. 'Thanks. A skinny cap and an orange juice then. And please, call me Jax. Friends call me Jax.'

A small smile. 'Jax, okay.'

Jax sat with her back to the ocean where she could see her car and the path in both directions. Behind her, the tide was out and the wide strip of soft sand still wore the tracks of the early morning graders. She watched Kate in the queue at the service counter taking a swipe at another tear on her cheek - and felt anger spark for everything Brendan may or may not have done.

'Thanks for coming,' Kate said, returning to the table to wait for the order. 'I know it's a little weird, the two of us meeting like this. After everything.'

'I can handle a little weirdness. How are you?'

Kate was brave about it for maybe three seconds before her lips trembled. 'Not great. Shit, I told myself I was going to hold it together.'

'It takes time.' And it got worse before it started to get better.

'I want to be strong for Scotty,' Kate said. 'I thought it would be harder to lose it out in public but now I'm here, I feel like I can barely keep it in.'

'There's no rule that says you have to. I brought tissues, if it helps.'

Kate did a small laugh-cry, pulled a wad of white from the top of her bag. 'Me, too.' She wiped under her sunglasses, scrunched the tissue in the palm of her hand. 'My best friend here went to Wales with her husband for Christmas. I've spoken to her on the phone but ... I know other people, of course, and they've been kind, but they didn't really know Brendan. You seem to want to talk about him and you're new here and I thought we could ...' She broke off, folded her arms, battling tears again. 'I'm sorry, it was a stupid idea. You probably don't want to deal with me like this after everything you've gone through. It's just, I thought ... oh fuck, I don't know what I thought.' She glanced at the kids. 'Sorry for swearing.'

'Oh fuck, don't mind me.' Jax said it gently, wishing there was something she could say to get Kate past it, knowing it wasn't words that would get her there.

'*Kate!*' A voice called from the counter. Their order was ready.

'And about fucking time.' Jax grinned as she stood. 'I'll grab a tray, you stay here with the kids.'

She headed to the counter, trapped between a desire to help Kate and a pressing need to find out more about Brendan. Kate wanted to talk about him; she'd offered the same for Jax - their own little support group. And yeah, Jax wanted that, perhaps needed it, but maybe Kate should have someone who'd listen without motive. Who wouldn't possibly turn out to be her husband's accuser.

'Hey, kids. Orange juice is up,' she called.

'Your phone went off while you were over there,' Kate told her.

Jax off-loaded the drinks and checked her mobile. A text from Aiden: *Sorry about last night. Can we talk?*

Wariness made her glance around. Conjecture, assumptions, unfounded leaps of logic, she told herself - and yet suspicion felt like a lump in her throat.

'Everything okay?' Kate asked.

'Yes.' Jax killed the screen, left Aiden's text unanswered. 'And it's not a stupid idea for us to be here. I'm glad you rang.' She didn't want to tell Kate to find someone else to have coffee with. She wanted to know what the hell was going on - for both their sakes.

43

'Before I lose it again,' Kate said, 'I want to apologise for how things ended up yesterday. I knew as soon as you'd left I'd got it wrong and I felt bad because I'd asked you to come and it can't have been easy for you. Hugh said he passed on my apology when you met up but I wanted to do it myself. So,' she smiled a little, 'sorry.'

Hugh must have told Kate about their conversation, at least the bits he was happy to tell. He hadn't passed on anything from Kate - but there were other issues he'd wanted to make clear. 'He thought you'd be upset if you saw me again.'

'Yes, he suggested I didn't.' Kate gave a little lopsided smile. 'I'm not good at following other people's advice.'

Now Jax liked her more - and that made her want to be honest. 'Actually, you were right to be suspicious of my questions yesterday but not for the reason you thought. I'm not planning legal action, I want to know what happened on the motorway. Why, how. For myself. To make sense of it. Because I can't make sense of other things in my life. Selfish reasons.'

Kate stilled, her fingers firming around the handle of her cup.

'I understand your need to talk,' Jax went on, 'and for a whole lot of reasons, I'd like to be the one you talk to. But Hugh could be right. The things I want to talk about might upset you more than you already are.'

Shifting her gaze to the beach, Kate watched as a wave surged, crested then pounded the shore before responding. 'I want to talk about Brendan. He's not the one making me cry. It's walking around knowing he's not here anymore. That there's no more time to get our lives back on track. I want to know why that happened, too.'

Jax wanted to cheer her kindred spirit but just nodded. 'Brendan said a lot of things that didn't make sense. I've been trying to work out how much was real and how much was in his head - and I guess how much I was sucked into it.' She paused, decided to jump right in. 'I think a lot of it was real. I think something happened to him last weekend. Something that wasn't just his PTSD.'

It was a second or two before Kate did anything but grip her coffee in both hands. 'What?' she finally asked.

'I don't know yet, and I'm not sure that what happened won't be awful or that it won't be Brendan's fault. I was chased by two men a couple of days ago and someone broke into my house yesterday. I think it's got something to do with it.'

Kate winced like she was in pain.

'Look, I could be completely off the mark,' Jax tried to reassure her. 'I could be seeing bad guys everywhere. I've got questions you might be able to answer, that might help piece some of it together. I won't tell you what I find if you don't want to know, but I will keep looking.'

Jax watched as Kate sat in tight-lipped silence for a long time. Was it anger? At Jax or Brendan - or something else? Eventually, lifting her chin, Kate said, 'What do you want to ask me?'

Digging the notebook from her handbag, Jax placed it and a pen on the table and found a smile, hoping it conveyed empathy more than eagerness. 'Did Brendan know anyone who'd run over a pedestrian?'

Kate blinked, frowned, maybe wondering if she'd agreed to answer questions from an idiot.

'Wait. I'm sorry.' Jax held up a hand. 'I'm trying to fill in gaps and the questions might seem pointless. It's possible they are, but please, bear with me.'

A lip chewed: doubt and thought. 'When we lived in Darwin, one of our neighbours hit a guy outside a pub. It happened before we knew him but he told us about it. He didn't like to drive and he asked for lifts sometimes.'

'Brendan said the sound of it had kept his friend awake for months.'

'Something like that.'

Jax made a tick in her notebook. 'Did Brendan ever talk about wanting to meet with a reporter?'

'No.'

'Did he ever think he was being followed, or that people were after him?'

'No.'

'Did he have friends in Sydney?'

'A couple of his army mates live not far from his flat. Marty and Simon. He met them for a drink a few times and he went to Simon's for dinner once. The wife is English. God, I can't think of her name now. Anyway, they've got four kids and she cooked a huge roast with Yorkshire pudding and sent him home with leftovers.' Kate smiled a little, as though remembering the conversation with Brendan afterwards. At least the answers were achieving something.

'Did you ever meet them?'

Kate nodded. 'I haven't seen either of them since Brendan left the army but they both phoned this week. They're organising a group to come up for the funeral.'

'People Brendan was spending time with in Sydney?'

'No, his old unit.'

'Did Marty or Simon see Brendan last week?'

'The three of them had a drink the week before. Brendan talked to me on the phone while he was with them at the pub.' She looked away. 'They're both really shocked about what happened. They thought he was doing great.'

Her voice had grown slower, sadder, and Jax felt as though she was on borrowed time, like she had with Zoe in the cafe. There was no tantrum brewing, of course, but Jax's compulsion to get through her questions was racing Kate's capacity to continue.

'Hey, Mum!' Scotty called. He and Zoe were standing at the top of the beach stairs, hopeful expressions on their faces. 'Can we go down to the sand?'

Kate looked a question at Jax.

'Hard to say no when it's so close,' Jax said.

'More suncream first,' Kate told them.

'Can we have a swim?' Zoe asked.

Jax did a quick scan of the shoreline. 'The flags are way down the beach today. And we don't have swimmers or a towel. Let's stick to sand-castles.'

Five minutes later, Jax followed the children down the steps, the hot, dry sand oozing between her toes like liquid. Standing beside Kate while Zoe and Scotty started their dig, she sensed the other woman's relief at the wind in her hair and the interruption.

'Are you okay?' Jax asked. 'Do you need a break?'

'No. It's bringing back some good memories.'

'Okay.' She touched Kate's arm briefly for encouragement. 'Brendan told me he tried to warn you but,' she checked her notes on his words, 'he said you didn't know what he was telling you.' She looked up again. 'Detective Hawke said you had some missed calls from Brendan last weekend. Was there anything about them you might have considered a warning?'

Kate's eyes drifted up and away. 'There were two missed calls from him when Scotty and I got home from the beach on Sunday morning. Brendan rang again that night. Twice, but he didn't get through. The phone was beside the bed, it only took a couple of seconds to get to it but he was already gone. I thought it was bad reception and when he's working, he can't always take calls, so I sent him a text but he didn't try again. On Monday, it was early. I was still asleep and by the time I got my eyes open, it'd stopped ringing. I had to pee before I could call back and it went again while I was in the bathroom.'

'Same thing, two attempts?'

'Yes. I phoned back and sent a text but got no answer.'

'Did he get through to your message bank?'

'No.'

'So they were all hang-ups?'

'Or bad reception.'

Brendan was on CCTV on the Harbour Bridge on Sunday and he got in Jax's car in Wahroonga, in the northern reaches of Sydney, on Monday afternoon. Sydney had its dodgy reception points but it wasn't hard to find a better place to phone. 'Did you ever talk about using hang-ups to send messages to each other?'

'When we only had one car, we had a signal. If one of us was out and needed a lift home, we'd call then hang up after three rings. It saved on phone credit.'

'Three rings? Not two?'

'You think it might've been a message?'

Three rings to be picked up, two hang-ups for ... what? Stay away?

Stay put? Get the hell out? Don't forget to buy milk? 'There's a pattern, so ... maybe.' Jax lifted a shoulder and let it drop. 'I really don't know.'

Beside her, Kate folded her arms around her waist, stared at the surf. If she was feeling bad about missing a message, the next question wasn't going to help. But they'd come this far.

'Your argument with Brendan over the phone on Saturday,' Jax said, 'it was about taking an extra shift, right?'

The hands at Kate's waist curled into fists. 'Yes.'

'Did he end up working on Saturday night?'

'I don't know. I never talked to him again.' She swallowed hard, her voice thick as she spoke again. 'He was waiting on a call when I spoke to him. He thought there might be a shift going.'

'What was the job?'

Her shrug was taut with remorse. 'I was ticked off he was even considering it. He hadn't been home for two weeks, we'd barely seen him since New Year and he'd just driven to Melbourne and back. He was tired, he needed a break and we wanted to see him. I wasn't interested in the details. I just said my piece and told him the decision was his.'

Jax remembered arguments like that. She'd supported Nick's work but when it took over their lives, she'd had to take a stand - and sometimes not showing an interest was the only way to make a point. Brendan had either missed Kate's point or chosen to ignore it because it looked like he'd worked for Nina Torrence later that evening.

The indistinct photo of him at the party flashed in Jax's mind as she composed the next question. 'Did he ever mention working for the solicitor Nina Torrence?'

'Oh yeah,' Kate said, no surprise in it at all. 'It's awful what happened to her.'

44

Jax had conducted interviews in the past armed with information she knew the other person didn't have. It was tricky and the questions depended on the answers she was hoping to get. She'd caught a politician in a big lie once - kudos for her, embarrassing for him. But this wasn't an interview. It was personal, more than likely hurtful. *Don't let Kate know what you're thinking*, she told herself, *or she might tell you nothing.*

Lacing her tone with the oh-wow intrigue of the average newspaper reader, Jax said, 'How well did Brendan know Nina?'

'Not that well. He was her bodyguard at a few Christmas parties last year. It was only two or three shifts, a trial run to see if she liked him.' Kate talked on quickly as though pleased to be discussing something less painful than her final argument with Brendan. 'Nina wasn't like some of the others he worked for. He said she was a bit over it, just wanted him to keep a low profile. Drive her around, hang about, be discreet, that kind of thing.'

'So she wasn't expecting anyone to run at her with a knife or a gun?'

Kate shook her head. 'He thought the job was more chauffeur than bodyguard. Chauffeur with skills, I guess.'

'What was Nina like?'

'A talker, a bit needy, Brendan said.'

'A bit of a princess?'

'Yes, but lonely. He thought she needed a friend more than a body-guard. Reckoned she only talked to him because she knew he couldn't blab. He had to sign a confidentiality agreement, so I guess she thought she was safe. Pretty bad that you can only talk to someone when they've signed a legal document.'

Maybe not safe even then. 'I met her a few times, years ago,' Jax said. 'She was just starting to climb the ladder. Clever and gorgeous and a hoot at a party. I guess the top rungs are lonely, though.'

'Oh, she had company. That's why she couldn't talk to anyone.'

'Because of the people she knew? The clients?'

'Not people. One person. She was having an affair. A long one.' Kate scrunched a toe into the sand. 'I didn't sign anything and I guess it doesn't matter now. It was with a politician's son. That rich one.' She rubbed her head. 'God, I can't remember his name either today.'

'Stan Fairfield?'

'No. A state MP. The one with the family business and the son who was up on fraud charges.'

'David Escott.' Long-serving parliamentarian and government minister several times over. A big fundraiser for various causes, his parties were always listed for the social pages - hence Deanne needing her hair done for tomorrow night.

'Yeah, him. Only Nina was having the affair with another son. The one who runs the business.'

'Dominic Escott.'

'Mmm, well, she told Brendan all about it. She was the guy's lawyer before she started sleeping with him.'

'She still was when she was murdered,' Jax said, remembering the clients mentioned in the media stories she'd read during the night.

'Well, the arrangement must've worked because he put up half the money for that big house in the eastern suburbs. I saw it in a magazine a couple of months ago. Unbelievable.'

Jax had seen the same glossy spread. Lots of glass, lots of expensive things, hints of too-much-for-one-person. She'd read it with a smile, remembering the share house she'd dropped Nina home to years ago. Lawyer and lover, she thought now. Lawyer with benefits or lover who kept professional secrets? 'Did they break up? Was that why she wanted a bodyguard?'

'No. It was Dominic who organised them for her. He had them, too. I think he used some of the same ones. They were cash jobs, which was why Brendan was keen. The money was almost double what he got with Secure Force.'

'So Brendan was a bodyguard for Dominic first?'

'No, only for Nina. Hugh recommended him - Dominic only takes people on recommendation.'

'Hugh works for Dominic Escott, too?' Was Dominic one of the 'useful civilian contacts' he'd mentioned?

'Not as a bodyguard. He's a personal security advisor - I think that's what he calls himself. After Brendan moved to Sydney, Hugh put his name forward. Then he had to have an interview and sign the confidentiality agreement before he was allowed to even meet Nina.'

Jax frowned. 'So Dominic wanted the confidentiality agreement?'

'Yeah. He's a real control freak, apparently. Brendan had to report back to some guy after each shift, even if it was God-knows-what-time in the morning. Tell him where Nina had been, if anyone had joined her, how much she'd had to drink - that kind of thing. And one time, there was this complicated set-up to get her to a rendezvous with Dominic. Brendan had to drive her to some house to get the address of another place, then ring ahead when they were on the way.'

'Wow. The ups and downs of being a kept woman.'

'Brendan said she put up with it because she wanted to be Mrs Escott.'

'Mum?' It was Scotty, standing in front of Kate, his hands covered in sand. 'I need to go.' The way he was dancing from foot to foot said he wasn't talking about home.

'Okay. Brush off the sand and we'll head up.' Kate shot a glance at Jax, signalling for her to follow.

But Jax was still thinking about Nina and Brendan - about orders to report back and complicated arrangements for rendezvous. Did Brendan fail to call in on Saturday night? Or not deliver her? Had something happened after the party and he'd killed her, then panicked realising that someone would know it was him? Did Brendan throw Nina's body over a cliff, hoping the tide or sharks would make her a missing person instead of a murder victim?

'Jax?'

She refocused, saw Brendan's wife and son in front of her, and wanted to be sick. 'Sure. Come on, Zoe.'

As they worked their way back across the sand, squinting under hats in the sun that was now almost overhead, Kate said, 'Nina was drunk one of the nights Brendan took her home. She wanted him to stay for a drink. She was crying and pouring more alcohol down her throat so he hung around and made her tea and toast. He said he felt like a butler then. Anyway, that's when she told him about the affair and pretending for years she wasn't with the guy and being at the same parties as his wife, and how she thought the bodyguards were to protect Dominic, not her. Keep her in line in case she felt like spilling any secrets when she got drunk and resentful. She was still holding out for the ring and the kids, though. She wanted the whole box and dice. Brendan felt really sorry for her.'

Brendan made tea and toast for her? Jax did a mental shake of her head.

Did he feel sorry enough for Nina to sleep with her? Was that what happened after the party last weekend? Or did it happen on one of the earlier jobs? Maybe more than once. And ... what? Nina threatened to tell his rich, powerful, control-freak boss so Brendan killed her.

'Did Brendan put the tea and toast in his report that night?' Jax asked.

'No. He figured it wasn't anyone's business if she needed a shoulder to cry on.'

'He told you, though. Despite the confidentiality agreement.'

They were at the top of the stairs, Scotty dragging on Kate's hand as she talked over her shoulder. 'No-one really expects you not to talk to your wife about stuff, do they? And he needed to tell someone. I was glad he was talking to me about his work.'

Jax sat on the wall with Zoe and watched as Kate walked Scotty to the Men's, as she pushed sunglasses onto her head and waited in the shade by the door for her son to reappear.

Brendan had wanted to protect Kate. If he'd slept with Nina, Kate didn't know. But she knew about the affair with Dominic Escott. Was someone worried Kate might tell? Who could one school teacher-wife tell that would make the world sit up and say, 'Oooh'?

Then Jax's spine stiffened with realisation. Kate had told her - a former reporter, the wife of Nicholas Westing, someone with friends in the media. Was someone worried about what *Kate* might have told her? If someone was watching either one of them, there was plenty of reason to assume information was being passed back and forth.

About an affair? No, that didn't make sense. Wealthy sons of politicians don't chase people and break into houses over an affair. They paid people off or got lawyers in. Lawyers who knew what needed to be kept quiet.

Jax held on to that thought for a moment. Nina was Dominic's lawyer - right up until she was murdered on Sunday morning. Was there more that Nina talked to Brendan about - that he didn't tell Kate? Had Nina been drunk and resentful again on Saturday night, spilling the beans on whatever it was Dominic wanted kept quiet?

'Mummy?'

Or was it the other way around? Had Brendan talked to Nina about something he'd remembered from Afghanistan? Something he thought he needed legal advice for. That someone else wanted to keep in the past.

'Mummy?'

Jax blinked at Zoe. 'Yes, baby.'

'Can Scotty come to play at my new house one day?'

'Sure. Why not sometime soon? Would you like to ask him?'

'Can I?'

The question made Jax wince with guilt. Zoe hadn't had many play dates in the past year. Nick's death, the investigation, Jax's preoccupation - they'd all taken something from Zoe. Jax didn't want to let it happen in Newcastle. She had to get to the end of this. 'I think you should. Here he is now.' She waited until Zoe started her spiel before asking Kate, 'Did you tell the police Brendan had been a bodyguard for Nina?'

'I mentioned it to Detective Hawke. He wanted to know about Brendan's job, so I told him about some of the clients, including Nina.'

'Was he surprised when you mentioned her?'

'It's hard to tell with him - he doesn't give much away. He asked if I remembered when Brendan worked with her. I had to find last year's calendar to check the dates. And that was about it.' Kate cocked her head, reconsidering the conversation. 'It's possible he already knew.'

Jax's eyebrows lifted, her shoulders tensed.

'Oh, Mum!' Scotty's voice was suddenly loud. 'Can I open this now?' His fingers were tugging the edge of a yellow padded postal envelope, the other end of it still in Kate's handbag.

'I forgot about that. Sure, Scotty.' Kate glanced back at Jax. 'The postie left a notification slip a couple of days ago that it was at the post office. It's for Scotty, the other reason I had to get out of the house today.'

'Is it your birthday?' Zoe asked as he tore at the top.

'Nuh-uh.' He pushed his fingers inside. 'Oh, Mum, look. It's a phone!'

He pulled the slim black smartphone from the envelope and, for half a second, Jax wondered how her mobile had found its way there. Then a memory, a voice in her head: *What's this? How the fuck did you get this?*

The phone in Scotty's hand looked like hers. Exactly like hers. Same model, same black rubber cover. The sight of it sent something scuttling up her spine.

Brendan had been confused by her phone. Had demanded how she got it.

Hers was in her bag.

This one had been posted to Brendan's son.

45

'It's Dad's phone!' Scotty's seven-year-old cry was filled with oh-cool.

A frown creased Kate's face.

Jax's heart thumped in her chest. Her first impulse was to grab it off the kid, but she swung her head to Kate for confirmation. It didn't tell her much - Kate just stared at Scotty while he held a finger to the power button, her lips parted as though she wanted to speak but the words were stuck.

'Kate, is it Brendan's phone?' Jax asked.

'It doesn't work,' Scotty said, both he and Zoe looking to Kate, like she'd know what to do.

She took it from him, turned it over, checked the back. Jax stepped closer, eyes flicking across the black rubber. There were no initials scratched into it, no blobs of paint or swipes of nail polish. Just scuff marks. The anonymous kind of scrapes you'd recognise if you'd seen them enough times.

'Is it his?' Jax pressed.

Kate still didn't answer. Just pulled in deep breaths as her thumb slid up and down a wide gouge along one edge of the rubber. Then her fingers tightened and she pressed the phone to her chest. 'Yes,' she whispered. 'It's his. It's Brendan's.'

Jealousy rose and burned in Jax like a hot coal pushing its way into her heart. *She* wanted a phone. Nick's phone. Delivered in the mail with all the answers to her endless, unsatisfied goddamn questions.

'Why did Dad send me his phone, Mum?' Scotty asked, excitement still bubbling.

Kate pulled it from her chest, frowned at it. 'I don't know.' She blinked at Jax. 'Why would he send it to Scotty?' Without waiting for an answer, Kate snatched the padded envelope from the table where Scotty had dropped it. She pulled at the opening, checked inside, stuck her fingers in, shook it upside down.

'Anything?' Jax asked.

'No.'

'What about the address?'

Jax watched at Kate's elbow as she read the front. Neat, old-fashioned handwriting in fine black marker: *Mr Scott Walsh.* The home address below in the same hand.

'Brendan didn't write this,' Kate said.

'Are you sure?'

'Absolutely. He doesn't do cursive.'

'What about the return address?'

Kate flipped the envelope over. No handwriting at all.

'Mum, why did he send it?'

'I don't know, honey. I don't know.' There was exasperation in her voice now.

Jax wasn't sure if it was aimed at Scotty or Brendan, but she felt it too. 'The battery is probably dead,' she said.

'Yeah,' Kate answered, but the concept did nothing to prod her into action.

'Have you got a charger at home?'

'No. I don't have the same phone and he always took his charger with him.'

Jax's fingers itched. 'The police will want to have a look.'

'What will they do with it?'

Keep it for as long as they damn well like. 'Go through the contents, download files, probably. Maybe send it for fingerprinting.'

'They'll give it back, right? I want it back.'

Jax didn't answer straightaway. Not until Kate had met her eyes, needing reassurance. 'Maybe. Eventually. I'm still waiting for Nick's to be returned.'

'How long have they had it?'

'Since the accident, a year ago. It was in his hand when he died.'

A flash of horror swept across Kate's face - at the image and the time-frame, Jax guessed. 'Brendan kept photos on his,' Kate said. 'Of us. The three of us.' She glanced at Scotty, licked her lips. 'Were you allowed to get the photos from your husband's phone?'

'I haven't had access to any of the stuff the police claimed.'

Tears welled in Kate's eyes. She covered them with a hand. Beside her, Scotty wrapped his arms around her hips, rested his head on her belly, as though he sensed her freshening sadness.

'Mummy, what is it?' Zoe whispered from across the table.

'It's okay, baby.'

'Are they sad again?'

'Yes.'

Jax wanted to tell Kate to get a lawyer to make sure the phone was returned in reasonable time. Except she wasn't sure it would work that way - not if the police decided it was key to their inquiries.

She was tempted, too, to suggest Kate keep it to herself. But Jax wanted the phone - or at least the information on it - included in the police investigation as an official record for the inquest.

'I've got a charger in my car that'll fit Brendan's phone,' Jax said. 'We could fire it up, save the pictures somewhere else.'

'No. No, I can't look at them yet.' Kate was still thinking photos when there might be more she'd want.

'Kate, there could be something on there that explains what happened.'

'But he didn't send it. It's not his writing.'

Had someone found it and posted it home? Who kept their home address on their phone? And why to Scotty? That didn't make sense.

Jax picked up the envelope, squinted at the ink stamp in the corner. 'It was mailed on Monday morning. That's only a few hours before Brendan got in my car. He could have given it to someone to post for him. He could've asked someone to write the address. It was posted to Scotty for a reason.'

Kate aimed her eyes at her son.

Jax said, 'Brendan might have left a message on it. For Scotty. Or for you.'

'Oh, God. It might... he might ... blame me.'

As Kate's lips crumpled, Jax clutched her trembling shoulder. 'He loved you, Kate. He was trying to get to you.' Whatever else happened, that much was true.

'I can't. I know I should, but I can't look at it. Not here with Scotty. Not today.'

Jax's heart thumped, her teeth clenched. The phone was part of it, it had to be, it didn't make sense any other way. Maybe it was even the answer to it all. She wanted to see what was on it - more importantly, she knew what would happen if Kate didn't.

'I know how you feel,' Jax told her. 'It's hard but this is your chance. Once the police have the phone, you've lost everything on it. If Brendan left a message, you might want it. It might be all you want.'

She'd hoped to inject some of the metal that got Kate out of the house today, but it tipped her the other way and tears tumbled down her cheeks as her whole body shuddered with her sobs.

Jax opened her mouth, closed it again, obsession pushing and shoving. The phone was evidence; she wasn't sure what the legal ramifications were of accessing the phone of a man whose death was under investigation. Probably not good. And the information on it could be incriminating, ugly, hurtful. But Kate had a right and Jax could ... 'I could do it for you.' Yes, and take a good look through it - for both of them.

Kate wiped her cheeks with the heel of a hand, possibility in the look she directed at Jax.

'I could save the photos for you,' Jax told her. 'And whatever else can be downloaded. It won't be everything but you'll have it, and you can hand the phone over to the police and it won't matter if they don't give it back.'

Kate straightened, tucked hair behind her ear. Maybe finding strength in the thought that she didn't have to deal with it herself. 'Okay. Do it. Please.'

'It won't take long. An hour, maybe two. I'll bring it straight back. Then you give it to the cops, okay?' *Let them deal with it.*

46

The car was hot after being locked up in the sun. With the windows down, the kids in the back and sand on her feet, it felt like a summer holiday road trip, except Jax was only driving three blocks to drop Kate and Scotty off, and neither of the parents was feeling the vibe.

'If you find a message from Brendan,' Kate said as Jax stood by the car to say goodbye, 'warn me before you show me, so I can brace myself.'

Jax felt the beginnings of a friendship in the brief hug they exchanged - one that might be blown apart by the phone in her bag. It made her impatient as she drove off, pulling to the kerb when she got out of sight.

'What are you doing, Mummy?' Zoe leaned forward in the back seat, hoping to catch a look.

'Checking something.' Jax plugged Brendan's phone into her car charger and hit the power button. Waited.

The only action was a flashing light. Which meant there was a battery in there but it'd been in the post since Monday - she'd have to wait.

'Phone, Mummy,' Zoe sang as Jax's mobile sounded an incoming text. She pulled it from her bag, saw Aiden's name, hesitated a moment before swiping the glass.

Jax? Can we talk ?

She glanced at the other phone, the one that had been sent to the son of a dead man, guilt and suspicion doing a dance in her chest. She tossed hers back in her bag.

'Didn't Scotty's mum want the phone?' Zoe asked as Jax pulled onto the road again.

'Yes, baby. She wants it.'

'Then why have you got it?'

Jax answered Zoe's questions on autopilot, her mind turning to Aiden as she headed for home. Did Aiden know Brendan had worked for Nina Torrence before Kate told him? He'd talked to Brendan's boss at Secure Force at some point but Brendan had signed a confidentiality agreement, it was possible his employer didn't know about the extra work. Jax had asked Aiden a hundred questions; he'd answered and offered nothing more. He'd made a point of it. Now she wondered what he hadn't shared - and whether it came from his investigation or some other source.

As she turned at the top of the hill, uncertainty squirmed in the back of her skull. She'd started out assuming Aiden was another cop trying to keep her out of his territory. He'd told her he was different and she'd believed him. More than that. She'd liked him - his company, his perception, the banter, his eyes.

Had she been fooled or was she the fool? Had she subconsciously wanted someone to trust and he'd ticked all the right boxes? Or was she so blinkered by her own cynicism that it was easier to accept another cop was an arsehole.

She'd know soon. As soon as she could get into Brendan's phone. She hoped.

'Is Aunty Deanne here?' Zoe asked as Jax slowed for the driveway. Deanne's black hatchback was parked at the kerb.

'Looks like it,' Jax said, trying to rein in the eagerness and urgency brewing in her chest, both grateful and not that Deanne had turned up. At the very least, her friend's arrival meant a delay in getting to Brendan's phone. More than likely, the mobile would require an explanation - Jax could hardly give her friend a quick peck on the cheek and disappear downstairs with it. Possibly the explanation would extend to what the hell she was doing obsessing over another death on a different road. And there would definitely be a rehash of last night's kiss. She could really do without that.

Zoe ran ahead, calling Deanne's name from the entry foyer, waiting to see if the reply came from upstairs or downstairs.

'Zoe-bear!' Deanne's long dark hair and grinning face appeared at the top of Tilda's stairs.

Jax followed her daughter up, waiting for Deanne and Zoe to finish their standard hugging and giggling. Tilda watched from the sofa, two mugs and an empty plate on the coffee table. Deanne had been there a while.

When she turned her attention to Jax, her eyes widened with concern. 'God, Jax, you look . . .' She wrapped her into a hug, didn't finish.

'Look what?'

'Exhausted. I think you've lost weight.'

'It's been a busy week.'

'That's an understatement.' Deanne made a face that somehow encompassed the carjacking and everything since.

Jax shrugged, not wanting to host a postmortem. 'You didn't need to come all this way.'

'I know. I wanted to.'

And it *was* good to see her, to be reminded Jax hadn't cast off her friends when she left her life in Sydney. 'Thank you.' She hugged Deanne again, the weight of the extra phone like a stone in her bag.

'Can we go to the beach again?' Zoe sang and jumped.

'Again?' Tilda said. 'I wondered where you'd gone.'

'But where are your swimmers?' Deanne asked as if it was a mystery game.

Zoe took Deanne's hand, swinging it as she talked. 'I didn't take them. I had orange juice and played with my new friend Scotty. His daddy died and I'm being nice to him.'

Two sets of concerned eyes settled on Jax. 'We had coffee with Kate Walsh and her son,' she explained.

'I had orange juice,' Zoe chipped in.

Deanne and Tilda exchanged a glance across the room. It wasn't a leap to guess what they'd been discussing in her absence. Her last few phone calls with Deanne must have sent some mixed messages - and now Deanne was here to see for herself how Jax was holding up. No guesses required how Tilda had reported.

'Kate rang me this morning. She wanted to talk.' Jax mentally winced at the it-wasn't-me tone of her voice.

'What did she want to talk about?' Deanne asked.

It was a loaded question, designed to make Jax open the subject of

Brendan Walsh. She aimed instead for lighthearted deflection. 'She thought we could be friends. It was an adult version of, "You wanna play in the sandpit?" There was sand and all but we let the kids do the work.'

In the tentative silence that followed, Zoe chipped in. 'I got to play with Scotty's front-end loader, then we went on the sand and built a big castle, except we didn't get to finish the ... the thing that goes around the outside.'

'The moat,' Jax said.

'Yeah, the moat.' Zoe grinned, waiting for some enthusiasm. Jax waited too, wondering if Deanne's visit was more organised than the spur-of-the-moment idea she'd suggested last night. Whether she and Tilda - possibly Russell, too - had planned a more specific discussion: *We care about you. We think you should see someone.*

'Do you think that's a good idea?' Deanne finally asked.

Jax thought briefly about joking that they didn't really need a moat. Then suddenly, overwhelmingly, she couldn't be bothered with it. Any of it. Their concern, her defensiveness or the explanation. She wanted to know what was on Brendan's phone. She wanted to know who to trust. She wanted the focus and energy that filled her when she was opening files and figuring stuff out.

She wanted to feel like herself. Her old self. The one who knew what she was doing and how to do it.

And she wanted some answers.

'Actually, I don't care if it's not a good idea,' she snapped. 'The woman's husband is dead. She needs more than a police report to understand what happened to him. If I can help her, then at least the past year hasn't been a complete bloody waste of time.'

'But, Jax -' Deanne started.

'No, don't say it. I know you're concerned.' Jax shot a glance at Tilda. 'Both of you. I'm grateful and you're right. I'm not looking after myself and I am obsessing and yes, I probably do need professional help. And I will get it, but not yet. Because I don't *want* to let this go. I *need* some answers. And I need you to understand that.'

No-one spoke for a long, tense moment. At least Tilda and Deanne were smart enough not to share another worried glance. Zoe stopped jiggling and swung her face from adult to adult, sensing something brewing, not knowing what it was about. Deanne met Jax's impatient gaze. They'd been friends a long time, through good times and tough ones. Jobs and differing opinions, death and children (in Deanne's case, her inability to have them). They both knew some things were more important than others - and that some were hard to forgive. Deanne reached for Jax's hand and squeezed it.

Jax nodded. 'I know you came a long way to see me but there's something I have to do.' She turned for the stairs.

'Where are you going?' Deanne asked.

'Downstairs.'

'Can I join you?'

'Only if you don't try to stop me.'

'Can I come too?' Zoe cried.

'Why don't you stay up here with me, honey?' Tilda said. 'You can help me make lunch. Let Mummy and Aunty Deanne catch up.'

Possibly Tilda thought Deanne had a better chance of talking sense into Jax if they were alone. Jax saw no reason to change that notion, just threw her aunt a grateful smile and kept going.

Downstairs, as Deanne flicked her eyes around their new home, Jax plugged her phone charger in and ran the lead to the dining table where she opened the laptop from her bag. As it revved itself into life, she found Brendan's phone and attached it to the power cord.

Deanne pulled up a chair and sat. 'What's going on?'

Jax held a finger on the power button. There might be fewer questions if she just told her. 'This is Brendan Walsh's phone.'

'It's the same as yours.'

'Yeah. I'm going to see what's on it.'

Deanne's eyebrows rose, the significance just dawning. 'The police gave you his phone?'

'The police have been looking for it. It was mailed to his seven-year-old son. Kate Walsh picked it up from the post office this morning.' A brand name appeared on its glass face: the first steps in powering up.

'Jax.' There was something close to accusation in Deanne's tone.

'No, I didn't steal it, if that's what you're thinking. I told Kate what happened to Nick's stuff. Hold on.' There was a keypad on the screen asking for a password. She found Kate's number in her own phone, typed a text: *I need a password. Any ideas?*

Jax glanced at Deanne as she sent it. She was holding to their deal but not enjoying it. Maybe she deserved more. 'Kate said there were photos on the phone but she wasn't ready to look at them. It was sent to Scotty - I thought Brendan might've left a message for them.'

'It's part of an investigation, Jax.'

'Exactly. Kate should get to see it.'

'What are you doing with it?'

'I'm going to set up an internet storage account for Kate, save the photos, look for a message and give the phone back to her.' Her mobile buzzed. 'And you're not going to talk me out of it.'

Deanne didn't try. She sat quietly while Jax tapped in the numbers Kate had sent and pulled in a sharp breath as the screen filled with colour.

'Is that him?' Deanne tucked a long rope of dark hair behind her ear and leaned closer.

'Yes.'

Icons were scattered over the photo but it was clear enough. Brendan, Kate and Scotty, somewhere sunny and green. Not just smiling but happy, as though the picture had captured a moment of sheer joy. Brendan was at the top, his arms encircling his family. Protective, supportive, loving.

'What the hell happened, Brendan?' Jax murmured.

Deanne laid fingers on Jax's forearm. 'This, the phone, Kate Walsh, it's about Nick.'

'You want to make *that* point as I prepare to tamper with evidence?'

Deanne lifted her hand, held it up like surrender. 'I'm not trying to stop you.'

'I get it, Deanne. I see myself in Kate. I see Zoe in her son. Brendan was killed on the road and no-one knows what happened to him. The parallels are flashing at me in neon ... and I still want answers.'

'Why, Jax? I mean, I get it with Nick. But why this guy? It won't change anything.'

Jax rubbed at her forehead, irritated to be explaining herself when the explanation she wanted might be in her hand. 'It will, don't you see? I won't be the person walking away without a scratch. I won't be the fallout or the consequence or the unfortunate side effect.' She stopped, wanting to end it there, but she had Brendan's phone in her hand. 'I couldn't help him. I tried, I held on to his hands but he ripped them away from me. I couldn't help Nick either, or ... or Mum and Dad. But I can do *this*. I can ask questions for him. For all of them. Have something to give to Zoe or to Kate Walsh. To myself. I want to move on, Deanne, but I refuse to go without making some noise.'

47

S omething shimmered in Deanne's eyes - tears and ... hesitation. Maybe she was deciding whether to debate it. Jax didn't wait to find out. She swiped through Brendan's screens, checking the icons for something obvious. There were the standard apps for making calls and sending texts, taking and storing photos, access to email and internet, jotting down notes, and a calendar. Plus a few extras: a torch, a fitness schedule, Skype, weather, rugby league scores. Aside from the sport and running, it looked a lot like her own set of icons.

Jax tapped the one for his texts, ran her eyes down the list of recent senders. Kate's name was at the top. Hugh's was there, too. Also 'Marty' - the Marty he knew from the army? None from Dominic Escott. None from Nina Torrence.

'No unopened messages from Kate,' Jax told Deanne, taking her silence for curiosity, if not support. 'So sometime between Sunday morning and Monday when he - or someone - put the phone in a post bag, Brendan saw Kate's texts.'

'Does that mean something?'

'That he had enough reception and battery power to receive them. That he was accessing his phone. That he wasn't texting Kate back.' Jax shook her head. 'I suppose he could've given the phone to someone else and they were checking his messages. I don't know - except that if I wanted to leave someone a message on my own phone, I'd probably write it and leave it as a draft.'

She touched Kate's name on the screen. A series of texts in speech bubbles came up. The last one first, Kate to Brendan: *Try again. Please. Or txt. Please. Miss u XXX.* Even texting, there was an edge of desperation.

Jax scrolled through, finding a dozen more from Kate before there were any by Brendan. The last time he texted his wife was early on Saturday morning: *Should be home by 5. Talk to u then.* Jax pointed to it. 'He drove up from Melbourne on Saturday - he must have sent this before he left.'

Deanne watched her a second, maybe realising just how much Jax knew. 'No drafts?'

'No. Let's try emails.' Swiping and tapping at the screen, she said, 'He might have sent it to himself if he thought Kate would have access through his phone.' Except all she got was a request for a password. 'I'll text Kate again.' She picked up her own mobile and held Brendan's out to Deanne. 'You try his notes.'

Deanne snatched her hands away. 'I'm not putting my fingerprints on it.'

She had a point. 'Okay.' Jax swapped the phones around. 'You be me and write a text asking for an email password. I'll check his notes.'

As Deanne typed, Jax found Brendan's app for notes, tapped on the first note in the list - and the chill of an ugly memory scuttled through her. 'Whoa,' she whispered.

Deanne hit send, glanced across. 'What the hell?'

The notes application was designed to look like a page from an exercise book. The one Jax had opened was pale blue with fine dark lines. There were about twenty on the screen and each one had the same words written on it: *I didn't know.*

She scrolled the page up - the mantra continued for a few lines more. She swallowed, rolled her lips together. 'He said that in the car. Over and over. Just sobbing and saying he didn't know.'

'He was crying?'

'I thought he was going to shoot himself but he just hung his head and cried.'

'What didn't he know?'

Jax lifted her shoulders and let them drop. 'He thought there was something stuck in his head. When he was crying, I wondered if it was something he knew or saw, maybe something he did that wouldn't stop going around and around.' She thought of Nina Torrence - stabbing a woman and hefting her over a cliff would stick in your head.

'Maybe that's the message for his wife. That he didn't know,' Deanne suggested.

'I hope not because it makes no sense. Not on its own.' Jax found the index for his saved notes, saw they were sorted by time, with the most recent at the top. She brought up the next one. It was the same but different. *I didn't know* was repeated for half a page but the words were messed up: spaces in the wrong places, apostrophes and quote marks, as though he was mis-hitting keys. Twice, the sentence wasn't finished.

'Maybe he was in a hurry when he wrote this one,' Jax said. 'Or panicking and trying to get it down as fast as he could.'

'Or losing touch with reality.'

'He wrote it again without mistakes.'

'You think that makes a difference?'

'Okay, but it started somewhere. It meant something.' Jax tapped on the next note. Lots of repetitions, different words - and they made Jax feel like her stomach was trying to rise up through her throat. *Nina Torrence.* Over and over. Like a nano spider breeding in his head.

'Nina Torrence? What the hell?' Deanne said.

'Brendan did some work for Nina -'

'And what? He heard what happened to her and wrote her name over and over? And you thought he wasn't losing touch.'

'Did Russell tell you about the photo?'

'Yeah. He said you didn't know if it was him.'

'I lied. It *was* Brendan. Which means he was with Nina on Saturday night.'

'Shit, Jax. He might have killed her.'

'Yeah.' Saying it out loud made her mouth go dry. 'Something happened between Saturday evening and Monday afternoon when he got in my car. Something that made him go a little crazy.'

'A *little* crazy. She was stabbed and tossed off a cliff, for God's sake. If he did this, he was more than a little crazy. And you're bloody lucky he didn't just kill you and dump your body by the motorway.'

'He didn't, though. He didn't hurt me at all.'

'Have you heard the latest on Nina?' Deanne's question sounded like a reprimand.

'No, what?'

'I don't know the source and possibly it's not true but I heard she was pregnant.'

Jax's eyebrows lifted as though they were on strings.

Deanne nodded. 'Only ten weeks.'

Which meant if Brendan killed Nina, he'd killed her baby, too. Jax lifted a hand to her mouth. Brendan had been Nina's bodyguard at Christmas parties. Weeks ago. How many weeks? Had he killed his own baby?

'What?' Deanne asked.

'I thought Brendan might have slept with Nina. If the baby was his and someone found out about it, he might have ...' What?

'Killed her and run?'

'Why kill her? Why not just run?'

'You've seen what he wrote. Pretty sure he wasn't thinking logically.'

'Yes, but ...' Jax didn't continue. She opened the next note.

It was a single line: *17 Walker St, Woollahra.*

The next one: *Nina Torrence. 7 pm pick-up. Home address.*

Jax went back to the previous one. 'Is that Nina's address?'

'No. Her house is in Bronte. Been reading about it all week.'

Jax checked the time code on the address. 'This note was created just after 10pm on Saturday. Presumably when Nina was at the party and he was working for her. Being a bodyguard or chauffeur. What does that mean?'

'Someone gave him an address and he wrote it down?'

Jax thought about complicated arrangements for a rendezvous. 'Maybe Nina gave him the address. Can you look it up on the laptop? I'm going to check his phone log.'

Deanne didn't move.

'What?' Jax asked.

'I thought you were just looking for a message to Kate and down-loading photos.'

Jax hesitated, said it anyway. 'Don't you want to know?'

'Well, I do now, no thanks to you. But ...' Deanne twisted her lips - maybe-it's-a-bad-idea.

'I've already opened a dozen files.'

'With Kate's permission.'

'Does that make a difference?'

Deanne shrugged. 'No idea.'

'Will the police know if I've looked at logs?'

'Still no idea.'

Jax checked the time. It was 12.28. She'd told Kate she'd be an hour or two with the phone. It was fifty minutes since she'd dropped her off and the photo download could take a while. 'All right, I'll set up the internet storage and get the photos moving, then I'll check the log and you can leave the room if you want.'

'If you're going to do it, I'm staying to read over your shoulder.'

'Good. In the meantime, you look up that address.' Brendan had several hundred photos in his gallery, but he hadn't taken one for three weeks. The last one was a selfie of him and Scotty, squinting and grinning, their hair wet, both their noses covered in white zinc, the surf behind them on a glorious day. Maybe the last time he was in Newcastle. He didn't look like a man who was having an affair - or who could kill a pregnant woman. Didn't look anything like he had in Jax's car, either.

She scrolled further, looking for pictures of Nina Torrence. If he was having an affair, it didn't mean he was smart enough not to take photos. Jax knew two people who'd found evidence of 'the other woman' on a phone and another who'd been caught out. But no pictures of Nina leapt out as she whizzed through.

Jax set up an internet storage account, using her own email address and assigning a password that she'd give to Kate later - something anxious and uneasy gathering in her chest as she tapped at the keyboard. 'I wish Nick was here to tell me where to look,' she finally said out loud. 'He'd know how to make sense of this. I haven't made sense of anything since ...' Nick was gone. She glanced at Brendan's phone. Maybe it was right there and she didn't know how to find it. Maybe she couldn't without ...

'Nick was hopeless with this kind of thing,' Deanne said.

'What do you mean? It was his job.'

'Nick was good with stats and systems and hard data. He was hopeless about people. Without a trail, he just assumed everyone would make the same decisions he would. This,' she pointed at the mobile, 'is about people and that's what you know.'

'Then I've been out of it too long because Brendan is not what I thought he was.'

'What did you think he was?'

'A good guy.'

'He held a gun to your head.'

'I know. He was desperate, he loved his wife and child and he wanted to protect them. He wanted to protect me, too.'

'He tried to drag you into the traffic.'

She closed her eyes, remembered Brendan hauling on her arms, wrenching her towards the road, the cops careering in behind them. *Come on. We can still make it from here.* 'Not to hurt me. He thought he was saving me.' She hit the key to start the download, walked to the windows and stared into the courtyard.

Was he good and bad?

'The Woollahra address is a townhouse complex,' Deanne said. 'Very nice townhouses, according to Google Earth. Gardens, pool, security gate, looks like underground parking.'

Jax thought about it, turned around. 'Is that where Dominic Escott lives?'

'Escott in a townhouse? Are you kidding? He's got a gobsmacking mansion in Vaucluse.' Deanne frowned. 'Jax, no. If that's where this is going, you've got to stop now. Give the phone to Kate and back away.' Deanne didn't need to explain. The Escotts were big fish - the high-profile politician father, one son the head of a multi-million dollar business with friends of questionable repute, the other recently making headlines when fraud charges were unexpectedly dropped.

Jax chewed her lip. Nina was having an affair with Dominic Escott. Nina was dead. So was Brendan.

She leaned on the window. Brendan was with Nina the night she died. He thought people were after him. Nina's 'people' were the Escotts - or at least Dominic. Were they after him? If Brendan killed Nina, then yes, it was possible one or more of the family might want vengeance.

Brendan made tea and toast for Nina and she told him things. Personal things about being unhappy and wanting to marry her lover. Had she told him other things, about the Escotts? It was likely they all had secrets. Brendan had signed a confidentiality agreement; Nina felt she could talk freely. Except it wasn't only Nina who'd wanted her secrets kept safe. Dominic Escott had insisted on the document.

Kate said Brendan felt sorry for Nina. Brendan died attempting to protect Kate and Scotty. What if Brendan hadn't killed Nina? What if he'd filled a page with her name because ...

'Jax? Did you hear me?'

'Yes.' She pushed herself off the glass. 'I'll give the phone to Kate as soon as the download finishes. I just want to check the call log.'

Deanne huffed a sigh, pursed her lips, didn't say anything until Jax reached for Brendan's mobile on the table. 'That's yours.'

Looking at the twin phones side-by-side, she heard Brendan in her head again. *How the fuck did you get this?* 'I should take the cover off mine so I can tell the difference.' She picked it up, started to push at the rubber, and stopped. Dropped her eyes to the one still on the table.

Brendan's. Sent to Scotty, not Kate. A seven-year-old. Who took toys apart. *He takes everything apart*, Kate had said.

Jax put her phone down, picked up Brendan's, fingers fumbling at the rubber. The covers were meant to be a snug fit so they didn't come off easily - and this one was doing its job, holding on like a claw. She got a thumbnail under a top corner, stretched it up and over, dragged at the other side, peeled it back, looked inside ... and adrenaline tingled in the tips of her fingers.

Stark against the black rubber was a slip of white paper.

48

J ax dragged the phone cover all the way off, saw the paper was a shop receipt, folded in half with the printing on the outside, thin enough for her to see the bleed of blue ink from something written on the inside.

Picking it up with fingertips, Jax opened it out. The receipt was from a post office: long and wide, lots of information she didn't need - time and date, tax, terms and ... It was for a padded bag and postage. Handling it carefully, heart hammering in her throat, Jax turned it over. The other side was covered with the scrawl of tiny handwriting, crammed tight with letters and abbreviations as though the author knew from the start there was a lot to get down in limited space. Jax held it closer, squinted. It wasn't the repetitions on Brendan's phone - and it started with, *I fucked up, Katey ...*

Jax slid her eyes to the bottom right corner. The final words were squashed together as the space ran out: *I love u, B x*

'It's from him.' Jax's voice was hoarse around the lump in her throat.

Deanne was at her shoulder. 'Should we read it?'

'Absolutely.' Jax picked up her phone first, though, wrote a text to Kate: *I found something u should see. I'll b at yr place in 15.* Then she sat at the table with Deanne and squinted at the paper.

I fucked up, Katey. U were right. I was 2 tired 2 work, 2 tired 2 do anything but sleep in my clothes & wish I'd gone home 2 u. Now she's dead coz I was tired. She told me 2 go, told me she was holding all the cards, but I should've stayed. I'd probably be dead 2 if I had. He'll probably kill me anyway. He was there for the drop, said the boss was getting paranoid. I couldn't b stuffed with another fucking covert op 2 get her 2 him so I left & she's dead. I know what it's like 2 want 2 give up, Katey. I never did. Not on u & Scotty. But I thought she had. He said he took her home, I told him it was his fault she went looking for a cliff. Then I heard it on the radio & I knew. I knew, Katey. I KNEW. They tried 2 get me 2 come in, they wanted 2 give me money. The boss had the cash. Enough 2 look after u & Scotty for a long time. I almost did, I almost got there but its like I killed her. Like her blood is all over me. I just drove. I cldn't stop. They kept calling & I kept hearing her. Crying. He said I was already dead. Said if he didn't find me, he'd find u & Scotty. I won't let it happen, Katey. I won't let you down. Trust me. I love u. B X.

JAX'S EYES were filled with tears by the time she finished reading. Anger and sadness, realisation and regret. Brendan's words were disjointed, rambling, and he'd assumed Kate knew who he was talking about. Maybe he'd thought he'd already told her, maybe he'd wanted to, maybe it's what the calls to her were about. Whatever the reason, there was no doubt he was talking about Nina Torrence.

In her mind, Jax saw Brendan in a post office - crumpled shirt, tense and agitated. Not like he was in her car. Not that desperate yet. Together enough to form a plan and make some sense: buy the bag, pay for postage, find someone to write on the envelope, use the receipt for a message to Kate in case he didn't make it to her. He could have left his car by then and had nothing else to write on. Possibly he thought he could risk only one brief stop.

Jax remembered the package was posted hours before he got in her car. Did something happen after that to make him confused and out-of-control? Or did panic and ugly memories eat away at him?

'He didn't kill Nina,' Deanne said. 'You were right. He was the good guy.'

'Yeah.' And there *were* people after him, he *did* have something stuck in his head, he didn't know what was going to happen to Nina when he left her.

There was a very real reason he was desperate enough to get in Jax's car and point a gun at her. The phone, the knives and guns, being called Already Dead - it all made sense. Freaking out over the radio?

'Was Nina's murder still running on radio news last Monday afternoon?'

It was a few months since Deanne had read a bulletin but she listened every hour with a news hound's interest. 'It's January, quietest month of the year. Nina was lead story right up until you were.'

Jax rubbed a hand around the back of her neck as reality started to filter into her thoughts. 'Kate told me Nina was having an affair with Dominic Escott.'

'That's been around the traps.'

'She said it'd been going on for years, that Nina was holding out for the ring, that she wanted to be Mrs Escott.'

'I've met the real Mrs Escott. I imagine she wouldn't go without a fortune.'

'Okay, right. But Nina was his lawyer as well as his lover. She knew stuff - about him, about his business, maybe about his father and brother. So if she was pregnant after all these years ...' Jax paused a moment, waiting to see if Deanne was on the same track. 'Nina told Brendan she was holding all the cards. Maybe she had something more than a baby to hold over Dominic's head. Maybe the baby was her reason to use it. Or threaten to use it if he was hesitating about leaving his wife.'

'I ... don't know.' It sounded like she didn't want to.

'Kate said Dominic hired Nina's bodyguards. Which makes him "the boss". Right?'

Deanne pointed at Brendan's note. 'You have to give this to the police.'

'Brendan doesn't say who "he" is.' She picked up his phone again, lit the screen, tapped until she got his call register. 'He had a lot of calls - Kate, a few from his friend Marty. A bunch from unsaved and blocked numbers.' She found Deanne's eyes. 'Someone, maybe more than one person, being cautious about leaving a trail?'

'Jax -'

'Whoever "he" is, Nina knew him. At least well enough to go with him.'

'She defended some bad people.'

'She knew cops, too.'

Deanne frowned. 'You think a cop is involved?'

'Why not? The Escotts are rich and powerful. Dominic's brother had his fraud charges dropped, there were calls then for an inquiry.' It wasn't the first time the government's Independent Commission Against Corruption had been urged to look at David Escott, the father.

'Can you take it to the cop you kissed?' Deanne asked.

Jax pushed a hand through her hair, not wanting to explain that the cop she kissed might be the cop who'd been after Brendan. She swallowed hard as the next thought took hold ... that possibly Aiden was the man who'd turned up for 'the drop'. Who'd stabbed Nina through the heart and thrown her from a cliff.

Could he have done that? Jax wiped sweat-damp hands on her trousers. He'd played nice with Jax for days, shared drinks, showed concern, kissed her like he meant it. He was a good actor but it would take more than acting to kill Nina then pull that off. He'd have to be a emotionless sociopath. She jumped as her phone buzzed.

'A text from Kate,' Deanne told her.

Jax grabbed it up: *Don't come to the house. Don't want Scotty to be around when I see it. Meet me at Strzelecki Lookout.*

Her jaw tightened. Strzelecki Lookout was on the tip of the headland Jax could see from Tilda's lounge room. It was a long, sheer drop to the ocean below. The view was endless and breathtaking; the breeze on a hot day, one like today, was unbeatable. It was also a launching pad for hang gliders, often crowded during the winter whale-watching season. And popular for people thinking about jumping.

Was Kate? Was the cliff a stand-by option if she didn't like what Jax found? Or did she just need the wind in her hair and a place to breathe when she looked at Brendan's phone again? *Warn me before you show me,* she'd said an hour ago. But Jax was thinking of another time.

She'd had a stand-by option. She wasn't proud of it, but grief, frustration, desperation, the thought she might never have an answer for Nick, had made the idea of suicide cling to the edges of her thoughts. Not for long. A couple of weeks when Anita Lyneham first played hardball. She didn't return Jax's calls, told her detectives not to speak to her, accused Jax of engineering media stories about the case being mishandled. Then Jax decided there were better things to do than plead and cry and think about what happened if the police didn't figure it out. She'd filled her head with questions and details and there wasn't room for anything else.

But she wasn't Kate Walsh. She hadn't spent years watching her husband struggle with horrific memories. Hadn't thought it was almost over, then blamed herself for his violent and exceedingly public death.

'I need to show the note to Kate,' Jax said. It was ugly and sad but Brendan *wasn't* the crazy guy on the motorway with a gun. He was the hero trying to save his family.

'I'll come with you,' Deanne said.

Jax remembered her bad days - a stranger in the midst could make it more difficult. 'No. It'll be better if it's just me. I'm sorry to leave again. I'll try not to be long.'

'But ...' Deanne stood as though she might insist but just watched as Jax moved fast around the room, collecting her bag, the laptop, pulling her hair into a ponytail. 'What will you do with the note?'

'Talk to Kate about it. It's up to her. But I'm taking out insurance first.' She picked up her phone, flicked to the camera, took photos of the note. Both sides, open and folded, close-ups of Brendan's handwriting and the post office receipt. Then she put the paper back in the rubber cover and took another shot of it there. Evidence, if she needed it - automatically saved to her own internet storage account.

Upstairs, Tilda was anxious about Jax leaving again, Zoe hung on her neck, wanting her to stay, and Deanne hovered with indecision, maybe regretting the promise to not stop her. Jax apologised and hugged and left anyway, running down the stairs to the car, more worried about what Kate was thinking. Outside, the heat had cranked up, the air was still and heavy with humidity, the sky a vivid blue - and the view, as she turned onto the downward slope of the hill, was breathtakingly clear and huge. She hoped Kate would be buoyed by it, not shattered.

Passing the surf, she was forced to slow for groups of meandering beach-goers taking their time to cross the road. She tapped her fingers on the steering wheel, registering the buzz of an incoming message, imagining Kate already at the lookout. Out of her car, standing above the cliff, texting desperate last words.

Jax pushed at the accelerator as she wound her way up to the headland, hung a right at the top, craning her neck for Kate's car, unable to see into the parking bay above the street until she was there.

She stopped in its centre. The small space was empty in the hottest part of the day. So were the bench seats beyond it. Would Kate have parked at the bottom and walked up the hill in the heat, while there was an empty car park up here? Jax pulled into a spot and got out, jogged quickly to the strip of grass that marked the lookout. Not a soul, just the stomach-lurching drop to the ocean.

Back in the car, she wound the windows down, let the afternoon breeze in before digging her mobile from her bag. Not Kate texting. Aiden: *We need to talk. Soon. Call me.* Should she? Before she talked to Kate?

There was also a missed call and a voice message from him. He'd rung from somewhere quiet, his voice low and serious, his words more order than suggestion: 'Jax, I've got information. We need to talk. Call me.'

Was he crossing another line, wanting to pass on information he shouldn't? Or had he spoken to Kate, knew about the phone and was trying to stop it before it went any further?

Jax heard a noise, raised her head, searched the scene through her windscreen: bush on her right, house to her left, grassy strip in between, and the empty car park. It was quiet, she was alone and a tingle of nerves up her spine felt like hackles rising. A movement in her rear-view mirror made her lift her chin for a better look. Something large and dark loomed on the passenger side of the car. She swung her head, saw a figure. Then the door was yanked open and her heart stopped.

49

Jax saw Brendan: wild-eyed, panic-stricken, desperate and with a gun in his hand. It was in her mind but she was already backed up against the driver's door when the figure lowered itself into her passenger seat.

'What the hell? You scared the shit out of me!'

Hugh Talbotson smiled. 'Sorry. Thought it'd be cooler in here.'

Her heart pounded against the hand she held to her chest. 'I was carjacked four days ago. That's not an appropriate entrance.'

His smile turned apologetic. 'I figured you saw me.'

Turning away, she swallowed at the dryness in her mouth, held tight to the steering wheel while she waited for her pulse to simmer down. Two cyclists rode bikes across the entrance to the parking area, standing up on the pedals, working hard on the incline, reminding Jax what she'd heard hadn't been a car. He'd walked?

She frowned. 'Where's Kate?'

His smile didn't waver but his hazel irises flattened to hard discs.

'Hugh? Where's Kate?'

'Give me the phone, Miranda.'

Her body stilled as something inside her rolled and pitched like a ball in a bowl. Brendan was in her head again. Not the words from the motorway but ones he'd written to Kate. *I knew. I knew ... I KNEW.*

Four days ago, when Brendan got in her car with a gun, Jax had wasted minutes in stunned incomprehension. Not today. Her flight instinct was primed. She swung around, grabbed for the door handle, was throwing herself sideways when a vice closed around her forearm.

Hugh's hand was large and solid and strong. It yanked her from the door, hauled her body around to face him, squeezing her arm as though he wanted to crush the bones. His voice when he spoke was calm, passive. 'Not yet, Miranda. Give me his phone.'

She watched him on the other side of the arm lock, trying not to wince, panic rising in her lungs. 'Then you'll let me go?'

His lips did a brief downward curl. 'Sure.'

The phone didn't matter, she told herself. Everything important was saved and photographed and in internet storage. And she didn't have a choice. 'It's in my handbag at your feet.'

'Nice try. I saw it in your hand five seconds ago.'

How long had he watched her? And from where? 'That was my phone. Brendan's is in my bag.'

'I'll have yours, too. Pass it over.'

She'd dropped it when the door opened. He kept hold of her forearm as she twisted in her seat to find it, maintained the painful grip as he lifted her bag from the floor and searched it one-handed.

He took a second to eye off the two mobiles. 'Who were you texting?'

'I wasn't.'

His fingers tightened on her arm.

'I was reading a text.'

'Who from?'

If she told him it was a cop, would he still let her go? 'From a friend.'

'What do they want?'

She hesitated, struggling to think fast around her fear. 'Lunch next week.'

Hugh watched her a moment, eyes narrowing. Watched her phone a moment more, maybe deciding whether to turn it off or keep track of her messages. He pushed each mobile into the back pockets of his jeans. 'Okay. Start the car.'

'You said you'd let me go.'

He quirked an amused eyebrow. 'You believed that?' Reaching around his waist, he came back with a handgun - bigger than Brendan's, black all over, with another lethal hole pointed right at her. Hugh laid it on his thigh, index finger resting on the trigger guard. 'I release your arm, you start the car and drive. You attempt to get out and I shoot you.'

Her vision fixed on the gun. Her brain said, *Here?* The two cyclists had propped their bikes and were enjoying the view from the grass. Close enough for hearing damage if there was a gunshot - and she'd be a bleeding body in the driver's seat. His escape would mean getting out of the car and running past them.

Maybe he saw her doubt or maybe he'd just paused for impact, but when he spoke, his voice was ice. 'And then I find your kid and slice up her face. Do you understand me?'

Jax's lungs seized as Zoe's freckles flashed in her mind. Nina Torrence had been stabbed through the heart with a single thrust. Her killer knew what he was doing with a knife. Jax lifted her gaze, looked into Hugh's flat eyes. She'd thought Aiden might have done it, figured he'd need to be an emotionless sociopath to pull off the last few days of earnest conversation and sympathy. She wasn't sure yet what Hugh had done, but he'd smiled at her over coffee, expressed regret and sadness, and now he was holding a gun on her and threatening to hurt her daughter. In this moment, she had no problem imagining him wielding a blade. And he was waiting for an answer.

She clenched her teeth, found voice. 'Yes. I understand.'

'Start the car.'

She turned the key in the ignition.

He moved her other hand to the steering wheel, released his grip. 'Drive.'

This was happening again? Seriously?

Anger flared as she hauled the seatbelt over her shoulder and shoved it into its clasp. Slamming the stick into reverse, she backed across the parking bay and steered to the entry, lips tight as she turned to him for instructions.

He fastened his own belt then held her in his sights for a moment, taking in the attitude, making her wait like it was some kind of power play.

She didn't. 'You want *me* to pick a destination?'

He straightened his gun arm across the space between them, pushed the muzzle into her thigh. 'Turn left.'

She worked the clutch with gunmetal pushed into her flesh as though it was drilling to her bones. It stole her anger, replaced it with stark reality. This wasn't a carjacking. He wasn't stealing her car or making a getaway or hitching a ride. This was something entirely differ-ent. The man beside her wasn't panic-stricken, he hadn't lost touch with

reality. He was cold and planned and trained. He was everything
Brendan Walsh had been terrified of.

And Jax felt his fear all over again.

At the bottom of the hill, Hugh said, 'Straight ahead.'

Passing the beach, more sandy pedestrians slowed her progress. She
watched them through the windscreen, willing one to make eye contact
and see the terror in hers. Turning her head as they passed near the
driver's side, she felt metal press deeper into her thigh.

'Think about it, Miranda,' Hugh said. 'I know where your kid lives.'

Nausea swelled into her throat. She locked her jaw, keeping it down,
holding back a howl.

'Take the road up the hill,' he ordered.

It was the way home. Up the hill, left turn at the top. Was he taking
her to the house? Did he have Zoe in his plan now? She clamped her
hands on the wheel. She wasn't going home. She wasn't letting him near
Zoe. Tilda and Deanne were there too. Screw the gun. She wouldn't do it.

Breathe. Think. She'd done the what-ifs on this. Had pictured it in her
mind. She could hit something. It would have to be close to the road so
she didn't lose pace, slew to the left so the passenger side took the
impact.

Taking the winding path up the hill, she pictured what was at the top.
Past the street on the left was a stretch of bush. No kerb, just tarmac
meeting rubble, then grass, shrubs and a grove of gum trees. She'd need
to floor the accelerator and hope she didn't get stuck in a ditch before she
hit something big enough to stop them. Hope she didn't kill herself. She
had airbags; so did Hugh. Right now, she didn't care who caught the
worst of it or her odds of survival - just so long as Hugh couldn't get out
and find Zoe.

Almost at the top, Jax shifted down a gear to gather speed. The
engine whined. Hugh turned, watched her, said nothing as they
approached the crest. Nothing as Tilda's street came into sight. Nothing
as it sailed past his window.

Not Zoe. Not Tilda and Deanne. Jax let out a gust of breath as though
she'd been punched. Clinging to the wheel as the trees at the summit
flew past, she wondered if she should have done it anyway. Crashed the
car and finished it.

Now? Before the rocketing fear inside her had settled enough for her
brain to make sense of what was going on? Die or be seriously injured
before she'd had a chance to *ask*?

'Where are we going?' It wasn't the top question on her list but the T-intersection for the Pacific Highway was approaching fast. Right was north and they were five minutes from the centre of Newcastle. Left was south and the possibilities were endless.

'Turn left.'

She merged into the outside lane, edged up her speed. Sydney was in this direction - about a two-hour drive. Between here and the motorway, the highway wound its way through the suburban outskirts of Newcastle and the eastern shore of Lake Macquarie. It was also access to long stretches of coastline in one direction; the entire Hunter Valley in the other.

Jax glanced across the car. Hugh had a hand hooked over the handle above the door, watching the traffic with lazy eyes. No hint of stress or decision-making. He wasn't making it up as she drove. They were heading somewhere - she hoped it didn't involve coming back without the driver.

'Where are we going?' she asked again.

'For a drive.' His voice was flat, no agitation, no urgency. Maybe abducting a woman at gunpoint was easy after Afghanistan.

'Will it be far?'

He didn't answer. Didn't respond at all. Just viewed the road and the scenery as though she hadn't spoken.

Jax focused on the driving while they passed through outer suburbs - strip shopping, cinemas, a huge mall. Drive-in takeaway joints, petrol stations, high schools. Patches of bush shielded housing from the noise of four lanes of cars and trucks moving in and out of Newcastle at eighty kilometres an hour.

Beside her, Hugh reached into his back pocket, her familiar ring tone flaring as his hand came back with her mobile. 'It's the cop. Hawke.'

Her gaze flicked to the phone, back to the road. She hadn't called Aiden because she'd trusted the wrong man. She'd seen herself in Kate and Russell in Hugh. Big mistake. 'I can answer it on speaker.'

'No.'

Hugh studied the device like it was sending code. Jax listened with breath frozen in her chest. She wondered if Aiden and Hugh were working together. Two bad guys trying to figure out what Miranda Jack was up to.

When the tone finally stopped, Hugh said, 'What does he want?'

No, not working together. 'I don't know.'

A couple of beeps signalled an incoming message. Hugh checked the screen, read the text. 'What's the password?'

She didn't have a choice but to tell him.

He tapped, tapped again. From the corner of her eye, Jax saw a log of texts, assumed he'd found the ones from Aiden.

'He's been telling you to call all morning.'

'Yes.' And if she'd rung from the lookout? Too late for that what-if.

'Does he know about Walsh's phone?'

'Not from me.' She remembered the urgent tone of Aiden's phone message, wondered again if he'd spoken to Kate. He'd told her two nights ago he would work it out. She hoped he had - and that he didn't wait to cross all his T's before he did anything about it.

'What did you find?' Hugh asked.

Jax frowned.

'You told Kate you found something.'

'A letter.'

He pulled Brendan's phone from his other pocket. 'What's the password?'

She could send him on a scavenger hunt but he was going to find it eventually ... probably better if he wasn't ticked off when he did. 'You don't need it. It's on paper inside the cover.'

He ripped the rubber off, found the receipt, opened it long enough to scan Brendan's handwriting, then tore it in two, wound down the window and tossed it out.

Jax gasped, swinging her head to watch as the pieces were whipped away. It'd been photographed and saved to techno heaven but they were Brendan's last words to his wife. Written by his own hand, lost on the wind. Jax took a second to glare at Hugh before turning her eyes back to the traffic.

He seemed amused by her anger, smiled as he hooked an elbow on the doorframe.

Arsehole. 'Don't you want to know what it said?'

'I saw enough.'

'And you already know what happened, right?'

His gaze stayed on the road.

'So you know it didn't implicate you. You've done that all by yourself.'

Hugh turned then, aimed a flat, hard stare in her direction, didn't bother with an answer. He didn't need to. His cold silence said plenty.

And it scared the hell out of her.

50

They were out of suburban Newcastle and travelling the strip of land that ran between the ocean and Lake Macquarie. Jax caught occasional glimpses of the wide, calm basin of water as they passed boat sales yards, a golf course, pubs, houses. Then Swansea Channel was up ahead: deep green water moving fast as it spilled into the Pacific on an outgoing tide.

Another text beeped. Hugh checked the screen. 'Are you fucking the cop?'

Jax stiffened, the memory of Aiden's mouth making her face warm, the metal grid of Swansea Bridge humming under her tyres before she answered. 'No.'

'You sure about that?'

'Yes.'

A chuckle. 'I thought there was a chance you might've spiced things up for me the other day. Widows are always good. The fresher, the better.'

Jax stopped for a red light, bile churning in her gut as she remembered the slide of his knuckle across the back of her hand. It wasn't a compliment. It was repulsive. Had he been playing two widows - her and Kate?

The hour she'd spent with him in the cafe ran through her memory like a time-lapse film. His face as it morphed in and out of sternness and compassion. She'd wondered then if he put a mask over his emotions, understood now that the sentiment was an act. He'd sized her up, given her grief, regret, concern, in return for what she knew.

And in his car afterwards? Jax remembered her crawling, irrational panic when Hugh stopped at the intersection and watched her across the car - and she wondered if he'd considered doing this then, with Zoe in the back seat. Jax had thought there was something wrong with *her* - she should have trusted her instincts. Thank God Zoe wasn't with her now. That Deanne had arrived, that Tilda had been home, that she'd done this on her own.

Up ahead, the Pacific Highway veered out of the suburbs and became the link road for the motorway. Dual carriageway, high-speed traffic, the stuff of her nightmares. 'Where are we going?' she asked, fear adding a tremor to her words this time.

'Stay on the highway.'

'Not to the motorway. I don't want to get on the motorway. Not with another gun on me.' The lights turned green. She didn't move.

'Miranda.' It was an order.

She crawled forward. It wasn't just the motorway that scared her. Someone had killed Nina Torrence; her body was found before she was discovered missing. There were plenty of places along the M1 - even before they got there - to do a better job of hiding a body.

'Where are we going?' Jax asked again, pitch shifting up an octave.

His eyes moved over her face as though deciding how much she needed to know. 'We're going to Sydney to see a man. You'll give him the phone and he'll explain why you'll forget you ever saw it.'

Sydney? He was delivering her? Like Nina had been delivered to 'the boss' before she was tossed off a cliff. Jax glanced across the car, wondering if Nina ever saw Dominic Escott that night - and if Hugh was lying now. How the hell would she know? 'Not with a gun on me.' She was moving at twenty k's, wasn't sure she could make herself go faster with a lethal weapon jammed into her thigh and the prospect of the motorway in her windscreen.

For three seconds, he didn't move. Then he took the gun away, tucked it into the waistband of his jeans. 'Happy now?'

'Ecstatic, you arsehole.'

He grinned. 'Drive the fucking car.'

She started along the wide ribbon of the link road, easing the car up to a hundred k's, feeling safer at the speed limit than as an obstacle in the slow lane.

She could make it to Sydney if Hugh didn't go nuts or try to kill her between here and there. *Just focus on the road*, she told herself. Block out the gun and the hard, cold man beside her and drive. Work out what to do when they got there. Get hold of a phone, bolt on foot, jump in front of a car. There would be options in Sydney.

The highway wound south through bushland, leaving Lake Macquarie's invisible boundary and entering the Central Coast. Traffic was sparse. Hugh was silent. She let half-formed thoughts grow, meld, take shape. Then her phone rang.

Hugh pulled it from its dashboard recess. 'What's this cop's problem?'

Uncertainty beat a rhythm in her temple. Would Aiden try to find her? Drive to the house and ask Tilda where she was? Head to the lookout and ... find an empty car park? Would it ring alarm bells? Or would he go back to work and try again later?

The ring tone stopped. A text message beeped.

'I need to shut him up,' Hugh said. 'What happened last night?'

She glanced at the screen in his hand, saw the text log again, remembered the exchange of messages last night: *Drink and questions?* And the one this morning: *Sorry about last night. Can we talk?* 'Nothing,' she said.

'Bullshit. Why did he apologise?'

She wasn't going to tell him. 'He stood me up.'

He tapped out a message. It took a while. He hit send and grinned. 'What did you say?'

With a droll lift to one eyebrow as he turned her phone off, he said, 'I suggested he was a fucking loser and asked him nicely to fuck off.'

Jax clenched her teeth. She hadn't questioned the text from Kate telling her to go to the lookout, but it must have been sent by Hugh. Would Aiden believe this one? He knew she wanted answers, that she was obsessing about them. Would he know the words weren't hers or would he welcome them? He'd spent days trying to discourage her questions. Maybe he'd see it as good news, decide it was better not to share whatever information he had.

A phone rang. Hugh reached into his shirt pocket, came back with a third mobile and answered it. 'Yeah.' Listened a moment. 'We're on the road.' Pause. 'I'll send confirmation.' He hung up, returned it, set his gaze on the passing bushland.

Jax steered off the Pacific Highway and joined the motorway. She'd passed this intersection on Monday, travelling in the opposite direction with Brendan. She'd been terrified then. She was now - but the answers to the questions Brendan had launched were close. They were right beside her.

He was there for the drop, Brendan had written, *said the boss was getting paranoid.* Which meant at least two other people knew what happened the night Nina Torrence was murdered. Maybe more than that: *They tried 2 get me 2 come in, they wanted 2 give me money.*

Dominic Escott was Jax's pick for 'the boss'. The 'he' killed Nina. Was it Hugh? Or was Hugh a third person, part of 'they'?

This morning, Kate said Hugh was a personal security advisor. He'd told Jax he had useful civilian contacts, had found jobs for other ex-military colleagues. Maybe one of them murdered Nina and Hugh got called in when Brendan became a loose cannon. Jax didn't have to be sitting in the car with Nina's killer, right?

She wanted to believe that; wanted to believe his job was to deliver her to Sydney to sign her own confidentiality agreement. She wanted to think about other things.

'*You* were chasing Brendan, weren't you?'

Hugh didn't move, didn't speak, didn't react at all.

'You didn't see him get in my car, did you? You just knew he'd head to Newcastle and he knew you were close.'

The thick ropes of muscle in Hugh's neck twisted as he turned and settled his eyes on her. He said nothing. He thought he could frighten her into silence.

'Did you burn his car?' she said. 'Was that a warning? *Look, Brendan, I found you, I'm close.* Maybe to flush him out, make him take a run for Newcastle.'

One side of Hugh's mouth slid slowly upwards. 'Okay, Miranda. Give it your best shot.'

She kept her eyes on the road, her pulse picking up. 'You got stuck in the traffic after the crash that killed Brendan, decided it was pointless trying to get to Newcastle with the cops out in force, headed back to Sydney to check out the reporter who'd given him a ride.' She glanced at him. His expression hadn't changed. 'You couldn't find Brendan for two days and when he turned up, he was with me. I think you were worried he'd been holed up at my place, telling me secrets. I think you broke into my old house and made it look like vandals. I think you wanted to know if he'd left a trail, if something needed to be done to shut the reporter up, too.'

Still no response but the pieces were coming together and it was easier now she knew whose eyes to look through. A part of her brain suggested it might have been wise to stop there, but now she'd started, she had to see it to the end. Obsession was like that.

'And well, damn, you discovered the stuff at the reporter's house wasn't hers. She'd moved out and hadn't left a forwarding address. What the hell did that mean? Did she go into hiding with Brendan's information, planning to stay out of sight until she'd finished her tell-all? Or was she under witness protection?' A glance in Hugh's direction. 'The cops didn't lay charges the next day, though, which meant she either didn't have enough on you or she hadn't told them. But where was she? The media said she'd left the scene with police. You didn't know where she went after that.' Jax flicked her eyes at him again. 'I think you watched Kate's house to see what *she* did and bingo, I turned up. The questions then were: What was the reporter talking to Kate about? And how much did they both know?'

Jax gave a grim, satisfaction and relief at finding a clear path through it all.

Beside her, Hugh tipped his head, doubtful. 'You got me in a lot of places, Miranda.'

'Yeah, I do, don't I?'

It had to be more than Hugh and 'the boss' cleaning up. It would take more than one person to vandalise a street and break into her old house without being spotted - and it was on the south side of the Harbour Bridge, a long drive from the M1. It wasn't Hugh who chased her, either. Two other men had drawn police attention. Maybe it was why Hugh arrived the next day to play Uncle Nice-Guy. Or maybe he'd needed to put some distance between himself and the detectives in Sydney investigating Nina's murder. Whatever the reason, it wasn't him who'd broken into Tilda's place. He'd been with Jax while she invited him for coffee.

What of that meeting in the cafe? Hugh told her Brendan was a weak, cheating, irresponsible suicide risk. He'd also covered his own arse, claiming remorse for telling Brendan he'd come after him if he didn't do the right thing by Kate. 'Was everything you told me about Brendan a lie?' Another glance across the car got her an exaggerated shrug.

'You're telling this story,' he said.

Okay. Then what? 'You turned up at Kate's house this morning and she told you Brendan's phone had turned up. That she couldn't bear to deal with it and had given it to me to go through. Maybe she told you I'd found something, or maybe you went through her messages, but you sent me the text from her mobile and waited for me at the lookout.' Why wasn't Hugh worried about Kate telling the police this part? She swung her face around. 'Where's Kate?'

He tipped his head to one side, making a show of thinking about it. 'I left her at home.'

Safe? *Alive*? If he was trying to cover tracks, Brendan Walsh's wife murdered in her own home wasn't going to do it. Unless ... Yesterday, over coffee, he'd said Kate had taken something to sleep. Had he given her more? A lot more?

'What did you do?'

His answer was a chuckle as he turned his face away - and ice worked cold fingers up Jax's spine.

She drove on in silence, arms aching from the tense grip on the wheel, back stiff from leaning forward, body instinctively braced and ready to flee. She had nowhere to run yet but she had answers. Not all of them and Hugh hadn't confirmed her theories, but she was willing to take his silence to mean she was close. Now, in the silence, she remembered the scratch she'd noticed behind his ear the day she met him and the reports about Nina's defensive wounds; thought about his threat to slice Zoe's face and the gun jammed so quickly and casually into her thigh. *Gun or knife*, Brendan had said.

'You killed Nina Torrence, didn't you?'

There was a new expression on Hugh's face when it came around. It wasn't surprise or fear at being found out. Not admission or denial or anger. None of the sentiments she'd thought her question might generate. It said: *And there it is.* Confirmation. Validation. 'Take the next exit.'

The outskirts of Sydney were an hour away. She shook her head. 'You said Sydney.'

'We're making a stop.'

'Out here? Where?'

He lifted the gun from his waistband, aimed it at her chest. 'Take the exit, Miranda.'

51

Jax followed a curving stretch of bitumen that took them under the south- and north-bound sections of the motorway and quickly became a narrower byroad - one lane in each direction, bordered by bush and distant mountains. There were small communities out this way, with names she knew from signs on the M1 and trips as a kid: Wisemans Ferry, Peats Ridge, Mooney Mooney. There were also state forests that were densely wooded and isolated.

She wanted to believe they were just making a stop. People had holiday homes out here and huge cruisers moored on the Hawkesbury River.

'Take this right,' Hugh said, nodding at an approaching junction.

The Hawkesbury was straight ahead. Fear lifted her foot from the accelerator. In one swift move, he wedged the gun under her arm, shoved the muzzle hard up against a rib. Her lungs froze. She found the pedal, made the turn.

The bush was thicker here, native scrub filling the spaces between stands of gums that came right to the edge of the road. She licked her lips, cleared her throat. 'Where are we going?'

He didn't answer, just took the gun from her side and laid it on the seat beside him, hand still firmly around the grip.

Okay, be calm. He just wanted her to follow his orders. She eyed the potholed road and the canopy of towering ghost gums on either side,

told herself it wasn't inconceivable for drugs to be grown or manufac-
tured out here. Hugh was delivering Jax - maybe there was another
package that needed to be picked up and delivered.

She tried again. 'What are we stopping for?'

Eyes forward, just a passenger in a car.

He'd told her he'd let her go if she gave him the phone and he hadn't.
He told her they were going to Sydney and they were here. Her chest
tightened, fingers tingled. *Don't panic. Think.* What if she just stopped the
car? Slammed on the brake and made a run for it? He had a gun. He
could shoot her before she had the door open. Okay, what about
demanding answers? Yeah and he was a liar with a gun. No reason to tell
her anything.

Talk to him, Jax. Just ... talk.

'If the man in Sydney is worried I'll tell someone or write something,
he doesn't have to be. I don't need to be told to forget. It's already forgotten. Done.'

His expression this time made dread ooze into her bones. She'd
hoped for assessment, second thoughts, something she could make an
appeal to. But he watched her with intrigue, as though her attempt at
persuasion was an interesting development.

She wanted to scream, kick the dash. She understood now why
Brendan had done it. But she held it inside, figured Hugh might just find
it entertaining. Figured it wouldn't change his mind. His brief phone
conversation had ended with, *I'll send confirmation.* It was his job, like
Brendan had told her. Probably like it had been with Nina. But Hugh was
human - he could reason, make a judgement, change his mind, couldn't
he?

And she was still driving. It wasn't over yet. Zoe needed her to drive
all the way home.

'I was never going to write a story,' Jax said. 'It was never about that. I
just wanted to know why. Now I know, so that's it. No more questions.'

Across the car, Hugh finally acknowledged her words with a slow,
reproachful tilt of his head. 'But you had to keep asking, didn't you?'

'It won't go any further.'

'No, it won't.'

'Hugh, please. I -'

'You fucked it up for yourself, Miranda. You're just like Nina. You
wanted too much.' He turned back to the windscreen, the side of his
mouth turning up just a tad. When he spoke again it wasn't to her. His

voice was low, amused, the punchline to a private joke. 'Not exactly like her. No cliffs out here.'

Jax turned her face to the windscreen, no need for conjecture or what-ifs. She had the answer she needed.

There were no tears to blur her vision as she focused on the road ahead. She was glad of that. Easier to see the bend approaching fast and the three wide-bodied gums standing like barrier posts in its elbow. The speedo was at eighty k's. She had no idea if that was enough, just tightened her fists around the wheel and braced her arms.

Time slowed. Her heart thumped. Gravel sprayed the chassis like applause. The rear tyres snaked sideways. The front end thumped the dirt, flung her forward. She kept her foot on the accelerator and floored it.

Jax had seen crash test dummies in slow-mo. Airbags exploding in faces, heads snapped back, bodies thrust forwards and upwards, limbs flailing like rag dolls. It must have been what happened but it didn't feel like that.

There was a stunning, deafening screech. A sharp suck of breath in her chest as her seatbelt locked. An explosion in her face as the airbag deployed. And ...

She had no idea how long it took for her throttled brain matter to start receiving messages. The first one she got was light. A glaring, burning red behind her closed eyelids. She registered a high-pitched hum like the whine of a jet engine filling her body, vibrating in her bones, shuddering in her head. Then the nerves that had been reeling in shock shook it off, took a look around and found pain.

Jax gulped at the air, coughed, moaned. It hurt her chest to breathe. Her face and neck burned. A shoulder felt ... dislodged. She tried to open her eyes. There was something wrong with one of them. Blinking, leaving the right one shut, she saw the wide girth of a ghost gum beyond her shattered windscreen. It was a little left of centre, surrounded by the crumpled green metal of her bonnet.

Awareness grasped for focus. White airbag hung limp from her steering wheel. Hot engine smell. Heart thumping. Then she had her first real thought: she needed a phone. Her phone.

It took long seconds for her left eye to trawl across the dashboard and down to the recess where it was kept. Except it wasn't there. It must have fallen. When ....

Oh, God, Hugh.

She wanted to swing her face to the passenger seat, wasn't sure she could move. Straining to listen, she heard nothing more than her own shallow breaths. No engine rumbling, no flames crackling, no groaning. Had he gone? Was he sitting beside her with the gun and a smile, waiting for her to turn? She inched her face to the left.

He was upright, his head tilted back, wedged between the headrest and the passenger window. Eyes closed, mouth slack and open, a thick smear of blood down the front of his shirt from a wound she couldn't see. Was he dead? Had she killed him? She tried to sit forward but dizziness made her vision swim. Reaching out a hand, wincing as she leaned, she pressed fingers to his throat.

A pulse tapped back.

Come on, Jax. Move. He could wake up.

She unclipped her seatbelt, raised a hand to the door, pulled the handle and gasped at the pain that sliced through her shoulder. A metallic screech then hot, humid, engine-smelling air wafted in. She kicked, tumbled out and was on the ground, coughing, dry-retching, curling into a ball.

The phone. Get the phone.

On hands and knees, she crawled back across gravel to the car, searched the driver's foot well, found her phone under the seat. She wanted to take it and get the hell away but Hugh had a gun. She was dazed, possibly concussed - not enough to leave him with a weapon.

Clambering in, trying not to touch him, she hunted around his legs, his seat, his body, hoping he didn't grab her by the throat. She checked the rear seats and floor. Nothing. Maybe it fell the other way, was lodged between him and the door.

She kept a hand on the car as she worked her way around the outside, one eye closed, dizziness making her stumble and weave. The passenger side of the chassis was crumpled all the way to the rear panel. She hauled on the handle at the front, the door didn't budge. She looked inside, saw Hugh's face. A neat, straight gash on his cheek - clean skin above it, the streaks of a red waterfall below.

She reared back, caught sight of herself in the window, and a hand flew to her face. It was slippery with blood spreading from her hairline; thick and clotting in the misshapen swelling of her eye, wet on her cheek, chin, throat. She held her palm in front of her face, breath growing short and sharp, head going fuzzy.

Don't look. Just go.

Stumbling back, staggering to the road, she pulled the phone from her pocket, trembling so hard she had to hold it with both hands. She found the On button, squatted on the tarmac as she waited for it to power up, legs unable to hold her. Head ringing, copper on her lips, in her mouth. She left a smear of blood as she swiped the screen. A bunch of missed calls: Tilda, Deanne, Kate. Two from Aiden. He hadn't given up. It took three goes to start his number dialling.

He answered before it rang. 'Jax, where are you?' It was urgent, measured, sounded like he was in a car.

'I ... I ...' Jax sank to her butt on the hot road, woozy, sucking at the air so hard she could barely speak. 'I drove my car into a tree.'

There was a pause, something tight in his voice. 'Where are you?'

'I wasn't trying to kill myself. I ... I planned it.'

'Do you know where you are?'

She looked at the car, at the trajectory, the shattered rear window, and started to cry. 'It's Hugh Talbotson.'

'I've been looking for you. Where are you?'

'He's in the car but I couldn't find the gun. There's blood and my eye won't work.' She couldn't find the right answers and the sobbing hurt her chest.

'Listen to me, Jax.' It wasn't nice and soothing. Aiden's voice was hard, a directive. 'I'll find you but you have to help. What can you see?'

She looked back along the road, alarm firing like needles. Nothing but trees. No, wait, that's not what he meant. He thought she was in shock. Maybe she was. Her thoughts were flapping about like fish out of water. She licked her lips, tasted blood, dirt, sweat. 'I took the Peats Ridge exit.'

A pause. 'You were on the motorway?'

'He said we were going to Sydney but it was a ... he was going to ... he was ...'

'Jax, hold on.'

She listened to muffled words, giddiness filling her head like a fog. She sat on the tarmac, ignored the heat burning through her trousers, kept her eyes on the car where the rear window used to be. Hugh's skull was a silhouette between the headrest and the door.

'Do you know where you are now, Jax?'

'I went under the motorway lanes then turned right. I'm in the bush. There's a road with no lines in the centre.'

She heard sirens start up, glanced along the road - realised they were on his end of the phone. He was coming. She was crying again. Sobbing and hitching and gasping at the pain in her chest.

'Jax, you're doing great. Really great. I'm going to find you, okay? Keep talking to me. Can you do that?'

She pressed her lips together, forced it down. 'Yes.'

'Are you in the car, Jax?'

'No. I got out.' She looked back. 'Hugh's still there. He's unconscious.'

'Are you shot?'

Had the gun gone off? She patted herself down. Blood was wet on her shirt, dripping on the road. 'No. My head's bleeding.'

'Can you walk?'

'Yes. My legs are good.'

'Yeah, Jax, your legs are great. You need to use them, okay?'

'Okay.'

'I've got a chopper in the air. Can you see open ground?'

'Wait.' She pushed to her feet, turned a slow circle, eyes searching the dark shade through the trees, ears only now registering the wall of noise from cicadas. 'I think . . .' There were bright pinpricks of light off to the right. 'Hold on.' She checked the car for Hugh's silhouette, started towards the bend, saw a break in the line of bush further down the road. 'There's something up ahead. A field, maybe.'

'Can you get there?'

She touched her hairline, felt the soft, ragged edge of an open wound, the tender mountain of swelling around her eye, the dizziness in her head, the sharp pain in her ribs. 'It's a long way.' Six hundred metres, maybe more. A long, long way just now. She tipped her face to the canopy of gums overhead: the helicopter wouldn't see her here. 'I can try.'

'Good. Start now, Jax.'

She did, walking as she spoke. 'Tell them to hurry.' A sound made her stop, turn, gasp.

'Jax? What is it?'

It was Hugh Talbotson. Out of the car, bent at the middle, holding on to the driver's door with one hand. The gun in the other.

52

The blood from the gash in Hugh's face looked like it'd been painted in one long stroke of a wide brush, cheek to thigh. He was unsteady and swaying, his head moving one way then the other. Not lolling uncontrollably but searching the road, the bush. Searching for Jax. It was his job. Brendan had said he wouldn't give up.

'Oh shit.' *Move, Jax.* She willed her legs to work, pushed them to a lurching gait.

'What's going on?' The panic in Aiden's voice matched her own.

She swung a glance over her shoulder, fear rocketing through her. Hugh was standing, braced against the car, gun arm raised, the pistol pointed at her.

The roar of a shot echoed into the bush. Jax screamed, stumbled, almost fell, kept going. Phone to her face, she yelled, 'Find me, Aiden. I don't want to die out here.' She didn't wait for an answer. Just shoved the mobile in her pocket and ran.

Her vision swam, she couldn't keep to a straight line and there was something really wrong in her chest. A knife lodged in her ribs when she tried to fill her lungs.

Half breaths, she told herself. *Or you'll pass out. And then you're dead, Jax.*

She pulled in through her nose, out through her mouth, two foot-beats per breath. She felt the oxygen reach her brain, clear some of the fog. Come on, her legs were fine - it was everything above them that hurt.

Chancing another glimpse over a shoulder, swaying as she did, she saw Hugh on the road. He was concussed: staggering, lurching, but moving towards her down the bitumen, the gun in a fist at his side. He'd missed the first time. How long before his aim improved?

Forget the pain, Miranda. It's the four-hundred, pain comes with the territory. Her first coach had told her that, the one at school who'd said she didn't have the puff for the fifteen-hundred. She didn't have to run that far today. Six- hundred, maybe a little more. She could do it. She had to.

For Zoe.

And the chopper.

Another glance behind. Hugh was moving better. A loping, limping pace, the hand without the gun clutched to his ribs. Injured but on top of it. He was a soldier - maybe he'd been there before.

She set her eyes on the clearing ahead, the bright sunlight, the promise of green pasture, the tunnel of mottled shade she had to travel to get there. She thought of Nick in his last moments, running, sweating, breathing hard. Was he running from someone too? She didn't want to die the same way.

Work it, Jax, Nick would tell her now. *Find your rhythm.* A different rhythm, she coached herself. Short breaths, short stride. She heard his voice in her head. *We're not doing the four-hundred this morning, babe. Take it easy. Relax.* He had a point. She shook out her hands, loosened her shoulders.

A roar filled the bush like a pulse of energy.

She screamed, ducked. Was Hugh shooting because he couldn't go on, or was she an easy target in the centre of the road? She cut right to the gravel, hoping the dense bush at her side might make her more difficult to pick out.

A swift look at Hugh. The gap between them had opened up when he stopped to fire. Now he was moving again and it looked like hard work. A hundred metres ahead of him, Jax was sucking at the air like she was suffocating, dripping blood on the road, but adrenaline had kicked in and her legs were working from memory. She just had to hold on.

The phone was ringing in her pocket. *Not now, Aiden.* The clearing was close, the sunshine beyond the trees blazing gold and green. She searched the bush to her right, saw patches of light stretching way back into the scrub as it climbed gently upwards. A pasture, maybe. Cattle or sheep and a farmhouse. *Please.*

Another shot rang out as she neared the break in the trees. She didn't scream this time, didn't have the air in her lungs for it. The bullet missed but she hurt anyway. Chest, throat, head, shoulder. She wanted to stop and gasp, fall to the ground and hold the stitch that was splitting her open.

Kiss Zoe for me, Nick said in her head. It's what he'd always said in those late-night phone calls when he was away. Jax had kissed their daughter for him every night for the past year.

Why don't you kiss her yourself, Nick? Why aren't you at home looking after her while someone tries to kill me? Why the fuck didn't you call me?

She clenched her teeth. Nick went to his grave with the answers to those questions. Jax wasn't going to die without them.

And she wasn't dying with Kate's answers locked in her head. She might be the only one who had them. No point having goddamn answers if she didn't tell anyone.

Run, Jax. Just run.

Up ahead, in the sunlight, she could make out uneven, grassy terrain. Not as wide as the distance she'd run, more dense bush on its other side, a dirt trail leading in off the bitumen. Then she was out of the shadows and under a searing sun, standing at the bottom corner of a rectangular paddock. No crops or cattle, no farmhouse, either. Just a rutted track that led to a barn.

The scene looked like something a photographer might shoot for an outback calendar. High blue sky, deep green forest, a rusting tin roof and weathered, wooden planks nestled into the long grass of a dry summer field. Its picturesque quality didn't impress her. The farm shed did. It wasn't an abandoned relic; it was the kind used to store tools and machinery - something a cop in a chopper could identify.

And up a goddamn hill.

If she stopped, she might not be able to start again, so she didn't even pause. Just slowed her pace for the incline, keeping close to the scrub as she forced herself forward. The barn was about twenty metres up, another ten in from the tree line, a rutted track approaching it from the other side. The slope felt like Everest.

Lungs heaving, pain slicing her ribs, she dropped to a walk as she drew parallel with the building, remembering Hugh's excuse of making a stop. He'd lied about letting her go, about going to Sydney, probably about the stop, too, but she wasn't taking any chances. If someone *was* waiting, she didn't want to be caught out.

There were no windows or doors on the sides she could see, no car at the rear. She checked down the hill. Hugh hadn't reached the paddock yet. Maybe his injuries had pulled him up. Maybe he'd ducked into the trees and was approaching out of sight.

She eyed the bush for a moment, took a couple of deep, painful breaths, and ran for the corner of the barn.

The sun was in the west, casting a solid block of dark shadow on the barn's high side, and it was cooler there after the full force of the after-noon blaze. Smooth greying timber ran in long horizontal lines, the earth at its base more rubble than grass, as though the spot was used as a parking pad. She pulled the phone from her pocket.

'Jax, talk to me.' Aiden's words were hard-edged but she heard the relief in them, glad he didn't waste time with it.

Eyes searching the trees, she spoke quickly, quietly between gasps for air. 'I'm in a paddock. Cuts into the bush. Road runs right past. There's a shed. I'm behind it.'

'Hold on.' Her legs trembled as she listened to muffled words, a muffled siren. 'Okay. The chopper's almost there. Stay where you are.'

'Can't promise that. Hugh was behind me. I can't see him now.'

'Then stay out of sight. I'll find you.'

Her head snapped to the right. Something moved in the bush. 'Don't take too long.'

She hung up, stuffed the phone away, moved along the side of the shed, keeping her eyes on the bush. The barn cut her view of the down-ward slope but she wanted the doorway. She needed a weapon.

One almost tripped her up before she got to the front. It wasn't a rifle and a box of bullets, nothing as helpful as that. A shovel lay on the ground as though it had been propped against the wall and toppled over, maybe forgotten as someone packed up and left. It must have happened a while ago because the metal blade was crusty with the start of rust, the timber handle rough and splintering. She picked it up, weighed it in bloodied hands. She could swing it, it would hurt. She'd killed a snake with something similar once. She didn't want to get that close to Hugh, but it'd do if she found nothing else.

She rounded the corner, stepping into the sun on the rutted track, squinting towards the single barn door. It was wide, hinged to one side and locked in place with a large steel padlock and hasp. She looked longingly at the barn, considered her injuries and exhaustion and the old shovel in her hand, and knew it was a waste of time to try to break in.

So what now? Wait for the chopper and hope Hugh was unconscious on the road?

A quiet scatter of small stones made her scalp tingle ... told her Hugh was moving and close.

53

J ax listened. Where had it come from: the gravel on the parking
pad? She hadn't seen the other side of the shed up close - maybe
there was gravel there, too.

She took three fast steps to the door, aware of the scuffle of
dirt under her own shoes, pressed her back to the timber, glanced both
ways - saw her shadow. Black on the ground and stretching towards the
shaded side of the barn. If she went that way, he'd see it before she got to
the corner. If she went for the other side and he was waiting, he could
shoot before she could swing the shovel. Where was the damn chopper?

Then she heard the sound again. Shaded side. Small stones shuffling.
He was limping before, maybe it was worse. Treading carefully, she
moved away, across the front of the shed, around the corner, pausing,
straining to hear. Then it wasn't a limp she heard. It was the distant
rumble of a helicopter.

The chopper was coming. So was Hugh.

The grass was thicker this side of the barn, the western sun blinding,
scorching. She moved along the timber, stopped at the far corner, ducked
her head around before making the turn. She assumed Hugh was doing
the same - hiding and walking around. Now what? Round and round
until the chopper arrived? Make a run for the bush?

She gripped the shovel in both hands and made a lunging start for
the trees.

Five steps. The shot came from behind, close enough for her to hear the *fzzzt* as the bullet passed her ear. She turned and bolted back to the western side of the shed. Hit the wall with a thud, more concerned about not getting shot than letting him know where she was.

The rumble from the chopper engine was louder now. She looked up, saw it small and high above the bush on the opposite side of the paddock, guessed it was still minutes away. Hugh was closer. He had a gun, she had a spade. She wiped at blood under her nose, licked dry lips, cleared her throat.

'Hey, Talbotson. It's the police,' she shouted, louder than she thought she could, the sound carrying into the open field.

There was no answer.

'They know we're here. I told them where to go.'

Silence.

'There'll be cars here, too. We'll hear the sirens soon.' She glanced both ways, checked she was still alone. She could hear the beat of rotor blades over the engine rumble now. 'I'm not going to die out here, Talbotson. Not for a phone.'

The chopper was beyond the clearing further down the slope, dropping, turning, its front window looking back at the barn. Would they see her against mottled lines of timber? From that angle, they wouldn't have a view of Hugh on the other side. She wanted to run out, wave her arms, knew it might get her shot. From that angle, Hugh could do it unseen, slip back into the bush and disappear.

'That's them, Talbotson,' she yelled. 'They've found us. You're not going to shoot me in front of the cops. This is over. I'm walking out to them.'

But she turned the other way, headed down the length of the barn and along it's short, rear end.

With a quick out and back with her head, she saw the block of shade that marked the parking pad. Hugh was where she'd hoped - at the far corner, not watching helplessly while the chopper found a place to land, not preparing to make a run for it. He had the gun gripped in both hands, held high and ready to aim.

They won't stop, Brendan had shouted. *They're trained for it, it's their job.*

Hugh stabbed Nina and tossed her body off a cliff. He hounded and threatened Brendan to his death, then played nice with Kate and Scotty.

He'd spun lies for Jax with a smile on his face. Forced her here at gunpoint without a hint of remorse about killing her.

It was more than a job now, though. She'd put the pieces together - him and Nina and Brendan. He wasn't just cleaning up for 'the boss', he was making sure Jax couldn't tell anyone. Possibly it was even more personal than that. She was a civilian and she'd driven him into a tree, made him come after her - it had to piss him off. How long would he wait for her to appear? How long before he realised she'd gone the other way?

Not long, was her guess.

A wind had picked up from the force of the rotors, the engine noise too loud for anything but raised voices. Not that she wanted to talk anymore. She wanted to live - and she was dead if she stayed where she was. She had to move fast, act without hesitation.

Gripping the shovel like a baseball bat, she ran at Hugh. Was still paces away when he heard her, started to turn, gun coming with him.

She lunged, swinging hard, pain rocketing through her chest. The shovel blade caught him across the side of his face as he dodged. His head hit the timber with a sickening thump. His body followed and dropped to the gravel.

For a second, Jax was held to the spot by panic and shock. Horror at the blood streaming from his nose, at what she'd done. The gun was still in his hand. She stepped forward, kicked it so hard she almost lost balance. The weapon skittered into the sunlight.

Then he was swearing, spitting gobs of blood, rolling onto his back. Not dead. Not even unconscious.

She stumbled more than ran for the pistol. Slid as she reached for it, landed on her arse as she closed her fist around its grip. Hugh was standing when she lifted her eyes. His face and shirt were streaked with blood, one hand on the shed for support - and he was smiling.

'You're something else, Miranda,' he called. 'Who the fuck would've picked it?'

It was her turn to keep quiet. She just sat in the dirt and pointed the gun.

'What are you going to do now?' He left the barn and the shade, took a few faltering steps towards her. 'Shoot me?'

She straightened her arms. 'If I have to.'

He spat blood, chuckled. 'It's not like the movies. You don't just point and shoot and the bad guy dies.'

She'd fired rifles and her dad's shotgun. She'd aimed first. There was recoil and noise. And the information bank in her head told her the target needed to be close for a pistol to hit its marks. Ten metres might be okay. Five would be better. She tightened her trembling hands. 'Thanks for the advice.'

He lifted a hand to his brow, shielding the glare, checking for the chopper. Jax had her back to it, could hear it was still in the air. Not so loud now. Was it leaving?

'We could come to an arrangement,' he called. 'You give me the gun now and I won't shoot you.'

'You can't shoot me if I keep it.'

'You won't keep it. You'll miss and I'll take it from you and if it happens like that, I'll shoot you in the head and spread your brains around this fucking paddock. So what do you say?' He smiled, like he had in the car. Amused, entertained.

'Fuck you.'

'You've been interesting, Miranda. It'll be a shame to kill you.'

Her heart pounded like a gong, blood thumped in her ears. She took her eyes off his grin as he limped forward, fixed them on his torso. Powerful, broad, muscular - a bigger target than his head.

'Don't wait to shoot,' he called. 'You'll need a few goes.'

But she did. Until he was almost on her. 'Stop!'

He laughed.

She pulled the trigger. Recoil hammered through her arms, swinging them upwards. He pitched sideways, rocked back, kept coming. She fired again. He went down this time. Howling, grabbing at his thigh, bright blood running through his fingers. Another blast. And another - her hands shaking too hard to hit anything but clean air.

Then, scrambling in the dirt, clambering to her feet, she staggered, stumbled. Getting away, tripping, gasping, on the ground again. Swung her head. Hugh was on his side, writhing, pulling at his leg.

Get up, Jax. He's not dead. Move! She got to her haunches, searched the sky. The chopper was skirting away over the trees, its back to her like it'd seen enough. Behind her, Hugh rolled to his side, hoisted himself up. No. No.

She was on the rutted track, sobbing now, bent over to stop the rushing dizziness. If she fell and didn't get up, if he got to her ... She stopped, swayed, hurled the weapon high and wide, out into the field.

The momentum unbalanced her. The bare earth hit her shoulder hard. Rattled in her head.

Something gave in her chest. Small sips of air were all she could manage. Her vision swam, blurred. There was hissing in her ears.

No, not like this. Not with the answers locked in her head.

Rushing, thudding foot-beats.

Movement beside her. She wanted to flinch. Nothing happened.

A word hissed - hard, urgent. 'Jax!'

Hot fingers jammed hard under her jaw, cutting off her breath.

Same voice, shouting, 'I've got a pulse.' A hand covered her forehead - a lighter touch, a little shaky. 'Jax, hold on.'

She forced an eye open, saw Aiden above her. He was breathing hard, a sheen of sweat on his face, and something in his eyes she'd never seen before. Fear. It made panic tighten to a fist in her chest. She gasped, wanted to run.

A palm on her shoulder held her in place. 'Don't move.'

'Where is he?'

He didn't throw himself in front of her. He patted her down, searching for injuries.

'I shot him,' she said.

'It's okay. He's down.' But Aiden's eyes were still frantic.

'What? What is it?'

'Keep still, Jax. The ambulance is two minutes away.'

Her chest hurt. Her shoulder, her head. 'Is it bad? Am I ...?'

'No, Jax. No, it's okay. You're okay. I got here. I found you. You're going to be ...' He didn't finish, just swung his face away, a muscle flexing in the side of his jaw.

It wasn't Hugh, it was Aiden. He'd thought he was too late. She stretched fingers towards him, caught his sleeve. 'I found the field. I got here.'

Something softer was in his gaze when he looked back. 'You did great, Jax.'

'The chopper left.'

'It couldn't land in the field. It's down on the road.'

She swallowed. 'I didn't miss him.'

'Yeah, you made a real mess of him.'

'Is he dead?'

'No, but he's not going anywhere.'

'Good. He killed Nina Torrence.'

The muscle in Aiden's jaw flexed again. 'I know that now. I'm sorry I didn't know sooner.'

She should've trusted him. She should've called him back. 'Kate? Is Kate okay?'

'She thought Talbotson was collecting the mobile from you. I assumed he was planning to come back without you or the phone.'

'He didn't hurt her?'

'No.'

Jax licked her lips, swallowed at the dryness in her throat. 'Brendan wrote a note. I found it.'

'Your friend told me.'

Deanne. He'd been to the house. 'It's gone. Hugh tore it up, threw it away, but I took a photo. I saved it.' On her phone, to the internet, with passwords only she knew. 'It's on my phone. In my pocket. You need to see it.' She tried to reach around, winced at the pain.

He cupped a hand to her cheek. 'Shhh, it's okay.'

'No, it's not. Kate has to see it.' Jax tugged on his wrist. 'It's in my pocket.'

His head lifted as footsteps approached.

'Please, Aiden.'

He watched her as two ambulance officers walked into her view. 'We've got this now,' one said.

'Two seconds,' Aiden told them. He reached around Jax, found her pocket and pulled the phone.

'Brendan knew,' Jax said. 'He left Nina with Hugh. He thought it was his fault.' Her voice was little more than air. 'It's what was in his head. It makes sense now. I have to tell you ...' She followed Aiden with her eyes as he moved to one side.

'You're going to be okay, Jax. You can tell me later.'

'No, I need to tell you now. No more questions, just the answers.'

An ambulance officer felt for her pulse. Her head wound was inspected, equipment was retrieved from somewhere, Aiden was shoved out of the way. She couldn't see him.

'Are you still there?'

His voice was in her ear. 'Right here.'

She tried to look at him. Someone stopped her with a hand to her cheek. 'You need to hold your head still, Miranda.'

She needed to say it, all of it, before concussion or drugs wiped it from her memory. 'Aiden, it was real.' She held out a hand. 'I have to tell you. For Kate. Don't go. You have to make sure she knows.'

A hand closed around hers. 'I'm not going anywhere, Jax. I just found you.'

54

J ax stood at the railing, looking out at the beach and took a deep breath of the humid, salt-laced breeze, enjoying a moment away from the noise in the bar.

She thought Brendan Walsh would be okay with the glasses being raised at The Beach House in his memory. He'd wanted his family to be proud of him - and today, his wife and son were here with his friends, remembering the man he was, not the one Jax met on the motorway.

Brendan had been ready to use a gun so Jax figured he'd be okay with the two bullet holes she'd put in Hugh Talbotson. Possibly more okay if she'd killed him, considering the threats to Kate and Scotty, but then she'd have to live with that.

'Miranda?'

She turned to the voice at the door, smiled. Brendan's army friend Marty had organised the wake. With Brendan's last photo in mind - he and Scotty at the beach - Jax had suggested The Beach House with its deck overlooking the surf.

'I'm heading off now,' Marty said. 'Just wanted to say it was good to meet you. Brendan picked the right car to get into.'

Jax made a face as she touched the tender skin in her hairline. 'I might debate that point.'

'You did a good thing.' Marty kissed her cheek. 'I'll email you those names for your article. And don't hide the bruises, they make you look tough. I'd think twice before I took you on.'

'Thanks, I think.'

He grinned, turned to leave, then paused. 'By the way, your cop friend just arrived. He was looking for you.'

She nodded and watched through the windows as Aiden and Detective Constable Suzanne May made their way through the group to Kate. It was nice they managed to get here.

Jax hadn't seen Aiden since leaving hospital a week ago. It wasn't avoidance on her part - after two brushes with death, a couple of days with head-reeling concussion, cracked ribs, five stitches in her hairline, a face like a bruised balloon and a dozen minor scrapes, she was more than ready to stay out of sight for a while. And Aiden had plenty of work to keep him going. It was why he didn't make it to the funeral.

Zoe had needed her mother at home, too. Jax had succeeded at keeping the gritty details of the incident with Brendan from her daughter, but it was a different story when Hugh was behind the gun. When Aiden realised Jax was missing, he sent uniformed police to the house in case they were needed, and there'd been frantic phone calls and frightened tears from Tilda and Deanne, both of them blaming themselves for letting Jax leave. She'd ended up in hospital looking like Frankenstein's monster - and Zoe didn't want to let her out of her sight.

Inside The Beach House, Kate pointed Jax out to Aiden, then held up a hand and made him wait while she walked to the door. 'You okay out here, Jax?'

The connection Jax had felt for Kate wasn't just about dead husbands and unexplained deaths. Brendan's wife had her answers now and Jax still liked her. Kate had been to the house twice - once with Scotty, who'd taken one of Zoe's dolls apart. The kids had milkshakes and played; Jax and Kate shared coffee, tears and a few laughs, and it felt like the friendship Jax had sensed developing a week and a half before. Today was the funeral and wake for Kate's husband and they were looking out for each other. 'Just enjoying the breeze,' Jax told her.

'Aiden has news for us.'

'Tell him to bring a drink, I might have questions.'

He carried three onto the deck, passed one to Kate, held the other out to Jax and waited for her eyes to meet his before he released his hold.

'I like the haircut,' he said.

Jax ran a hand over her new, short crop. She'd been overdue for a trim before but the stitches in her hairline had forced a makeover. 'It was the only way to disguise the bald patch in my fringe. I'm still getting used to it.'

'I think it's a keeper. How are the ribs?'

'Getting there, like my face.'

He didn't comment, just let his gaze slide across the jagged pink line where the stitches had been and the bruising that coloured her eye socket. Then the clear green of her untouched eye. The crease in her cheek from a small smile, her mouth. Reading, seeing, the way he always did. She wondered what he saw there this time: the healing or the horror that came before it.

A victim or a survivor - or the peace that had arrived since she'd found some answers.

'So, ah ...' Kate glanced back and forth between them as though she wasn't sure if she should interrupt. 'What's your news, Aiden?'

He took another second to refocus. 'I was at the hearing this morning. Hugh Talbotson was remanded in custody. His lawyer didn't enter a plea.'

A day and a half after Jax shot him and while he was hooked to drips and oxygen, Hugh was officially charged with a string of offences in relation to the abduction and attempted murder of Miranda Jack. Other charges were being considered, involving the destruction of evidence and conspiracy to murder, but the police were holding off on that for the moment.

'Bastard,' Kate said.

'Was he in court?' Jax asked.

'Yeah, he was there,' Aiden said. 'In a wheelchair and looking like he'd been dragged from a coffin, but the judge deemed him well enough to be transferred to the prison hospital.'

Jax's first bullet shattered Hugh's collarbone, the second nicked an artery in his thigh. He would've bled to death in the paddock if Aiden and a convoy of police hadn't been two minutes down the road. Not bad considering she'd been aiming for Hugh's torso, hadn't fired a gun in years and had just driven into a tree. It helped that she'd waited until he was almost on top of her. Any further away and the bullets would've gone high or wide - and she'd be dead.

'I hope he rots in there,' Kate said.

Jax gave Kate's shoulder a brief rub.

'That's not all.' Aiden aimed a look in Jax's direction. 'And this is off the record. It's just for the two of you.'

Jax mimed a zipper across her lips. 'Done.'

'I was informed today that a task force is being set up to investigate a connection between the Nina Torrence murder and Dominic Escott.'

It seemed obvious to Jax that Escott was involved. Brendan had written *the boss was getting paranoid* and *the boss had the cash.* Her guess was that Nina never saw him after the party, that the decision to have her killed was already made when Brendan left her with Hugh. It had to be why Hugh was there for 'the drop'. Jax's photos of Brendan's letter could be used as evidence - but Brendan hadn't named him and conjecture didn't hold up in court. A task force was good news.

'Was it Nina's sister's claims?' Jax asked.

Alison Meyers went public with Nina's affair a week after the murder. She confirmed that Nina and Escott had been in a relationship for ten years, that he and Nina stayed with Alison and her family at their holiday home on numerous occasions, and he was the father of Nina's ten-week foetus. None of which implicated Escott as a killer or conspirator. Except Alison also claimed that when she talked to her sister the morning before the murder, Nina told her she was meeting Escott later in the day to announce her pregnancy, and that this time he 'wouldn't dare' not leave his wife. It wasn't proof of Escott's involvement but it raised questions about motive and what Nina had over him.

'Not just Alison,' Aiden said. 'A certain state government MP allegedly made a couple of quiet calls to police headquarters suggesting his son was the victim of a vendetta and it might prove embarrassing for the police if it was taken seriously.' He raised one eyebrow, smiled a little. 'Cops don't like being told what not to investigate.'

David Escott might have difficulty keeping anything quiet, Jax thought, if the rumours were right about an Independent Commission Against Corruption inquiry finally getting off the ground.

Meanwhile, Hugh's involvement in Nina's murder was still being investigated. He was being as noncommittal with the cops as he'd been with Jax, but the police were building a case, some of which included Jax's statement about her encounter with him and the photos of Brendan's note. It might be a while before charges were laid but Hugh wasn't going anywhere.

Maybe a conviction for that murder would help to quell some of Kate's anger - it was the reason Brendan was dead.

For Jax, there were pieces of the Brendan puzzle that would only ever be conjecture: the missiles and helicopter he'd worried about, the phone hang-ups to Kate, how he got the gun, why he was the last-minute choice of bodyguard for Nina that night. But just knowing the rest had been enough to calm the loud, compulsive circuit of questions in her head. Even the ones about Nick. The psychologist she was seeing suggested the obsessiveness was more about Jax than her husband, the theory being that her search for answers was a search for herself - the person she was without Nick. And not getting anywhere made her feel like a failure without him.

Okay, the theory had merit - but Jax still had questions. She was Miranda Jack: what was the point without them?

There were more people on the deck now and Kate was kissing cheeks and calling Jax over. Aiden caught her elbow as she started to move.

'Are you staying long?' he asked.

'No. I promised Zoe I'd be home to say goodnight. Are you going back to work?'

'I'm done for the day. Thought I could walk you to your car. I parked behind you.'

'Think I might get lost?'

'Can't trust you walking the streets on your own.'

The last time he'd walked her to her car, it had been ... complicated, messy. According to Tilda, it could be like that with handsome men. 'I won't leave without saying goodbye.'

She met more of Brendan's army mates. Kate introduced her to Anna, the best friend who'd been in Wales, telling them she wanted to have them both over for lunch sometime soon. Suzanne May cornered Jax at the bar, wanting to know what her senior colleague was like in his uni days. Jax still didn't remember Aiden back then - either testament to his surveillance skills or evidence of his minimal partying - but she spun a yarn about smart girls lining up for the only hot guy on campus who could discuss Freud. Aiden could untangle that one.

Half an hour later, she found him on the deck watching the surf. Joining him at the railing, she followed a crest of foam as it made its way to the shore. As soon as her ribs could handle it, she was taking a plunge out there - she wanted to, for herself and Zoe. 'Time for that walk?'

'Ready when you are.' He smiled but there was something serious in his eyes.

It felt the same as it had both times before - hot, humid, Aiden at her side. Except she wasn't frightened or neurotic this time. Maybe it would lead to better choices, or a smoother handling of the aftermath.

'Would you have a problem being included in a story about Brendan Walsh?' she asked.

'I thought your article was about PTSD.'

'It is. I'm not talking about that. I got a call from a publisher yesterday - she asked if I was interested in writing a book.'

'Are you?'

'Yes, I am.'

It was no surprise the publisher had been able to track her down. The media had gone nuts with rumour and theories on what had actually happened to put Jax in a car with two different gunmen in less than a week. The only upside was that she'd lost her previous title and was now referred to as 'motorway carjack victim, Miranda Jack'.

She'd made a start on the feature story she'd pitched to Russell - a long piece about soldiers and the invisible injuries many bring home, and the far-reaching cost of their pain. It felt like the right thing to do for Brendan: information instead of another replay. The idea of a book, though, had lit a flame she thought was extinguished. A desire to write, really write; to bury herself in words and meaning, to bring some depth and truth to Brendan.

'Can I quote you?' she asked Aiden as she stopped beside her car.

He made like he was thinking about it. 'Only the good stuff.'

'That'll limit me to a couple of lines.'

'Gee, thanks.' He shucked her on the shoulder.

It felt nice, fun, relaxed. She needed more of that. 'About the last time we did this beside my car ...'

'Hmm?'

'Who did you call as I was leaving?'

He thought for a second. 'Suzanne May.'

'You told your detective constable you kissed me?'

'No, I told her to run Hugh Talbotson's name through the computer.'

'Oh. Good call.' He'd told her the rest while he was sitting beside her hospital bed late on the night she was admitted - and how assumptions and separate investigations had kept the connections hidden between Brendan and Nina and Hugh.

Aiden hadn't known about Brendan's job as Nina's bodyguard until Kate told him and he'd called the Homicide unit in Sydney with the information. There was a discussion about the dates of parties he'd attended with her and the more recent timeframes and crime scenes. There'd been nothing to link Brendan's event to Nina's murder: she was killed in the early hours of Sunday and the carjacking was a day and a half later on the other side of the city. And Kate said Brendan had only done a few shifts for Nina Torrence. A doctor claimed he suffered a psychotic break and Brendan never mentioned the names Nina or Hugh. There'd been no reason to assume his 'guns and missiles' and people wanting to pick him off had anything to do with the death of a socialite solicitor.

Other pieces of the puzzle also misled detectives on both cases. The extra shift Brendan mentioned to Kate was presumed to be with Secure Force, which had been trying to crack down on assignment-swapping between staff. The Homicide unit looked in other directions for the man who drove Nina to the party. The indistinct image of Brendan taken that night hadn't been singled out by police or shown to Aiden, who might have recognised him.

Hugh Talbotson on a list Aiden had slated for interview as part of the coroner's inquiry into Brendan's death. When Hugh was initially unavailable, there was no urgency to chase him down. It was Jax's account of meeting him at the Walsh house and their discussion over coffee that piqued Aiden's curiosity. Suzanne May's computer check led to a connection with the Nina Torrence investigation, but Hugh was listed as 'personal security advisor' for Dominic Escott. He'd never been a bodyguard or driver for either Nina or Escott.

A hit on the fingerprinting from Jax's car and Tilda's house raised questions - one set was at both scenes and was ex-military. It didn't directly connect Hugh, but Aiden wondered about Jax's Afghanistan theory. His first phone calls to her that Friday morning were to warn her off talking to Hugh.

Then a link: Talbotson, Brendan and the man with the fingerprints had fought in the desert together. Aiden didn't know what that meant, but when he couldn't reach Jax, he thought she might've figured it out and asked the wrong person the right questions.

It was Kate who told him about Brendan's phone. She'd been anxious and upset thinking about what Jax might have found; Hugh had persuaded her it would be better if he collected it and screened it first. That piece of information made Aiden hit the alarm. It wasn't until Deanne explained what they'd found inside the mobile cover that he started to put it together. Too late to stop Hugh getting in Jax's car - not too late to realise what was happening.

'So, about the last time we were here,' Jax said.

Aiden smiled. 'Hmm?'

'I didn't explain it properly.'

'You didn't have to.'

Her fingers inched towards him, found the warmth of his palm. 'I was thinking we could try again.'

His hand closed around hers but he didn't take the cue. Instead, his eyes moved over her face and seemed to stall: undecided, maybe unconvinced.

Jax wasn't that girl from uni and she wasn't the one from two weeks ago. She was somewhere in between, still learning where exactly, only knowing she wanted to move forward, not stand in one spot. So she closed the gap between them and pressed her mouth to his.

For half a second, he didn't move, then his arm slid around her waist, his mouth softened, deepened, kissed her back. But there was hesitance in it - and in his eyes when she stepped back.

'See, I didn't fall apart,' she tried.

He took a breath, held it as though he didn't know how to say it.

She did it for him. 'It's okay. I understand. I'll just -'

'No.' His grip tightened on her hand when she tried to pull away. 'I want this. I wanted it fifteen years ago. But ...' He ran his teeth over his bottom lip. 'I've got something for you. You should see it before . . .' He cocked his head at the car parked behind hers.

What would make her say, *Whoa, buddy, that cancelled you out.* 'You got a body in there?'

'No, it's ...' He kept hold of her hand as he took her to the back of his car and lifted the lid. Three document boxes, side-by-side, unlabelled.

A pulse pumped in her throat. 'What are they?' Not waiting for the go-ahead, she lifted the top on the closest one. It was full of files, stacked upright, front to back. 'What are they?' she asked again, her voice tight, fingers already tugging at the first folder.

'Your husband's documents. Everything of Nick Westing's that Homicide kept. His phone and computer have to stay in evidence but whatever was downloaded is there. You can't have the originals or notes from the investigation but I thought you could do something with this.'

She couldn't answer, couldn't take her eyes off the boxes, but she reached out and squeezed Aiden's hand, hoped he understood it was heart-tearing gratitude. Tears filled her eyes as she threw the lids off the other boxes, running her palms over hundreds of pages as though she might sense Nick in them. Aiden waited silently while she perched on the edge of the boot, pulled random folders, flipped through their contents. Stories and research, photocopies of Nick's diary and hand-written notes. She swatted at free-flowing tears so they didn't drop and smudge the words - and for the moment, she had no questions. Just a hunger to read it all.

'You okay?' Aiden finally asked.

Jax pushed a folder back into its box, stood and hugged him. Five minutes ago, she'd kissed him, had allowed herself to think about where it might lead. Now Nick was here with them. She stepped away. 'Thank you.' She wiped her eyes. 'I ... I'm ...' She shook her head. 'It's Nick.'

'That's why I wanted you to see this first.'

She nodded, grateful for much more than just the documents. He understood her need to find out - maybe he had boxes like this of his own. And he knew it would be like this, that she'd need to back away, and he did it anyway. 'Thank you.'

'Give me a call when you've got some questions.'

'About Nick?'

'About anything.'

She smiled. 'Drinks and questions?'

'We could mix it up, make it food and conversation sometimes. When you're ready.'

'There's a lot to read. It might be a while.'

'Try not to make it fifteen years.'

'It's like police work, you'll need patience. But you're good at that. Give it a while.'

ACKNOWLEDGMENTS

Many thanks to the team at my Australian publisher, Penguin Random House, and especially my publisher Bev Cousins for listening to my garbled, half-formed ideas on this one and trusting that I'd find a way to the end.

Thanks also to my agent Clare Forster, and to Kate Cooper and Rebecca Ritchie at CBLO, for championing my words.

For research, thanks goes to Sam Findley once again who provided much appreciated research assistance, time and discussion. Thanks also to Michele Oshan and Wendy James for reading drafts, helping me shift through ideas and sharing experiences – and for the coffee and wine that went with it. And to Cath Every-Burns for reading and discussing - it made all the difference.

To my writing family: Christine Stinson, Isolde Martyn, Elizabeth Lhuede, Melinda Seed, Kandy Shepherd, Carla Molino, Simone Camilleri and Carol Casey; also Louise Reynolds and Dayley Black. Also to Fiona McArthur, Cathryn Hein, Monique McDonell and Trish Morey for their Indie advice and support. It would be so much harder without you all.

And to my family: Mark and Claire, who have moved far away but are always with me, and Paul, who has to live with all my imaginary friends – I couldn't do it without you.

In writing Already Dead, I looked at Post Traumatic Stress Disorder (PTSD) as an injury of war but it can affect anyone. I found many online resources, from information about symptoms to online discussions and where to find help. If you think you or someone you care about is suffering PTSD, there is support – don't wait to find it.

ABOUT THE AUTHOR

Jaye Ford is the author of five chilling suspense novels, *Beyond Fear*, *Scared Yet?*, *Blood Secret*, *Already Dead* and *Darkest Place*. *Beyond Fear* won Best Debut and Reader's Choice at the 2012 Sisters in Crime Davitt Awards. Under the name Janette Paul, she is also the author of two best-selling romantic comedies, *Just Breathe* (ebook only) and *Amber and Alice*.

Jaye is a former news and sport journalist, was the first female presenter of a live national sport show in Australia. She also worked in public relations before turning to crime fiction. She in Newcastle, New South Wales, Australia.

DON'T MISS THE PREQUEL ...

ALREADY GONE
A Miranda Jack novella
Prequel to crime thriller Already Dead

Two months has passed since Miranda Jack's husband Nick was killed in a hit-and-run and she is no closer to understanding why. The police have stopped taking her calls so Jax has gone back to the street where Nick was found in search of her own answers.

Eighty-five year old Irene Newton has been haunted by the death of a man on the road beyond her fence two months ago. The appearance of his wife at her door reawakens painful memories of the daughter she lost and the questions she was told to forget.

Jax is horrified Irene has waited forty years for answers and frightened she could face the same fate. But when the questions surrounding Nick's murder won't let her rest, Jax reaches for Irene's mystery – because finding any answers is better than finding none.

Until the questions become dangerous.

DARKEST PLACE

Carly Townsend is starting over after a decade of tragedy and pain. In a new town and a new apartment she'd determined to leave the memories and failures of her past behind.

However, that dream is shattered in the dead of night when she is woken by the shadow of a man next to her bed, silently watching her. And it happens week after week.

Yet there is no way an intruder could have entered the apartment. It's on the fourth floor, the doors are locked and there is no evidence that anyone has been inside.

With the police doubting her story and her psychologist suggesting it's all just a dream, Carly is on her own. And being alone isn't so appealing when you're scared to go to sleep ...

BLOOD SECRET

Nothing ever happens in Haven Bay, which is why Rennie Carter – a woman who has been on the run for most of her life – stayed there longer than she should.

But the illusion of security is broken one night when Max Tully, the man she loves and the reason she stayed, vanishes without a trace.

Rennie, however, is the only person who believes Max is in danger. The police are looking in the wrong places, and Max's friends and his business partner keep hinting at another, darker side to him.

Rennie Carter, though, understands about double lives – after all, that's not even her real name ...

And she has a secret too – a big, relentless and violent one that she's terrified has found her again ... and the man she loves.

SCARED YET?

When Livia Prescott rights off a terrifying assault in a deserted car park, the media hails her bravery. After a difficult year – watching her father fade away, her business struggle and her marriage fall apart – it feels good to strike back for once.

But as the police widen their search for her attacker, menacing notes start arriving – and brave is not what she feels any longer.

Someone has decided to rip her life apart, then kick her when she's down. But is it a stranger or someone much closer to home? In fact, is there anyone she can trust now?

When her family and friends are drawn into the stalker's focus – with horrifying consequences – the choice becomes simple. Fight back or lose the people she loves most ...

'The menace dogging Liv's every move creeps into your bones ... Scared Yet is a thriller that's all too terrifyingly believable.' *The Australian Women's Weekly*

BEYOND FEAR

From the award-winning author of five bestselling Australian psychological thrillers.

At seventeen, Jodie Cramer survived a terrifying assault at the hands of three strangers. Now thirty-five, she is a teacher and mother, her memories of that past horror are buried deep – so when she sets out for a weekend in the country with friends, all she has in mind are a few laughs and a break from routine.

Unknown to the four women, their secluded cabin was once the focus of a police investigation and, like Jodie, it nurtures a dark secret.

As her friends relax, the isolation reawakens Jodie's terrifying memories. When she finds evidence of trespassers, she is convinced they are in danger. But the other women don't believe her and suffering flashbacks that threaten to ruin the weekend for everyone, Jodie begins to doubt herself.

Until two men knock at their door ...

Winner of two Davitt Awards and described by Australia's Sisters in Crime as 'so deliciously scary, it's hard to believe this psychological thriller is a debut novel.'